Praise for *The Mysterious Case of the Alperton Angels*

'Hallett is the queen of the narrative twist. She takes the conventions of the modern mystery novel and upends them as Christie did'
S. J. Bennett, author of *The Windsor Knot*

'It's not enough to say that this book is fascinating, gripping and clever. It's an astonishing piece of work. Janice Hallett is playing a different ball game to the rest of us'
Ian Moore, author of *Death and Croissants*

'Hooked me in completely . . . It's travelled with me to work, to the dentist's and even up a couple of mountains! A real treasure trove of a read'
J. M. Hall, author of *A Spoonful of Murder*

'I loved *The Mysterious Case of the Alperton Angels*. It's fresh, whip-smart, dark and intriguing with a brilliant, compelling heroine. Janice Hallett is surely the queen of the brain-twisting, just-one-more-page mystery novel'
Gilly MacMillan, author of *The Nanny*

'Janice Hallett has done it again. Engrossing from the very first page, it's deviously clever and as charming as it is chilling'
Tom Hindle, author of *A Fatal Crossing*

'Constantly surprising, witty and fresh. I really enjoyed it!'
Emma Curtis, author of *One Little Mistake*

'Fantastic. Keeps the "found footage" narrative structure that Hallett does so well and injects some real darkness into it'
Tariq Ashkanani, author of *Welcome to Cooper*

'Compulsive, dark, twisty and unputdownable. A work of true genius, masterfully plotted, funny and unique'
Sarah J. Harris, author of *The Colour of Bee Larkham's Murder*

'I genuinely don't know how Janice Hallett does it. The detail, the plot twists, the humour, even in dark places. She creates a brilliant puzzle for the reader to solve. I loved it'
Victoria Scott, author of *Patience*

'A masterclass. It's exactly what you've come to expect: compelling written and utterly addictive. It's funny, dark, and the puzzle comes together brilliantly at the end'
Chris McDonald, author of *A Wash of Black*

'Brilliantly clever, ingenious in structure and thoroughly compelling. Full of wonderful characters and extremely funny!'
Sarah Bonner, author of *Her Perfect Twin*

'I slowed down because I didn't want it to end. Heavenly and creepy combined with twisted genius. Outstanding'
Joy Kluver, author of *Broken Girls*

'What an absolute treat. Twisty and dark, packed full of angels and demons and monsters, with a thrilling mystery that keeps you guessing till the end'
Lynsey James, author of *The Single Dad's Handbook*

'It's so good. Gripping but my favourite thing is the humour – actual laugh out loud moments despite the shocking tale. Genius'
Heather Darwent, author of *The Things We Do to Our Friends*

'Another absolutely brilliant mystery by one of my favourite crime writers. Take the role of investigator and let yourself be immersed in this fantastic novel. Five stars!'
Louise Mullins, author of *One Night Only*

The Mysterious Case of the ALPERTON ANGELS

Janice Hallett studied English at University College London and spent several years as a magazine editor, winning two awards for journalism. She then worked in government communications for the Cabinet Office, Home Office and Department for International Development. After gaining an MA in screenwriting at Royal Holloway, she co-wrote the feature film *Retreat* and went on to write the Shakespearean stage comedy *NetherBard*, as well as a number of other plays for London's new-writing theatres. Her debut novel, *The Appeal*, was a *Sunday Times* bestseller, a Waterstones Thriller of the Month and *Sunday Times* Crime Book of the Month. Her second novel, *The Twyford Code*, was published in 2022 and was an instant bestseller. Her fourth novel, *The Examiner*, will be published by Viper in 2024. When not indulging her passion for global travel, she is based in West London.

Also from Janice Hallett and Viper

The Appeal

The Twyford Code

The Examiner (2024)

'Is anyone telling stories quite like Janice Hallett? It feels interactive, with readers invited to solve the mystery alongside the brilliantly tenacious protagonist. Intricate, funny and a total page-turner'
Amanda Block, author of *The Lost Storyteller*

'Hallett is a wording wizard. Her storytelling ability is enviable. Characters whom I loved very quickly and intrigue are the beating heart of this book'
J. M. Hewitt, author of *The Other Son*

'Agatha Christie has found her heir. A genius premise. A perfect puzzle. Crime fiction fans will not want to miss this one!'
Victoria Selman, author of *Truly, Darkly, Deeply*

'What a switchback ride it is! The big twist made me drop my book but there are *so many* smaller shocks along the way. I enjoyed it hugely!'
Hope Adams, author of *Dangerous Women*

'Janice Hallett dials her brilliance up yet another notch, exploiting the compulsive readability and inherent slipperiness of her chosen form to dazzling effect'
Leonora Nattrass, author of *Black Drop*

'I absolutely loved it. It is the funniest, cleverest and most innovative novel I've read for years'
Sarah Stovell, author of *The Home*

'Very clever, twisty, shocking, and yet another reinvention of the crime novel by Janice Hallett. Brilliant, unique and compelling!'
Guy Morpuss, author of *Five Minds*

'Wickedly clever and immersive. I just can't get enough of Janice Hallett's writing'
Sophie Flynn, author of *Keep Them Close*

'I genuinely don't know how Janice Hallett does it. The detail, the plot twists, the humour, even in dark places. She creates a brilliant puzzle for the reader to solve. I loved it'
Victoria Scott, author of *Patience*

'A masterclass. It's exactly what you've come to expect: compelling written and utterly addictive. It's funny, dark, and the puzzle comes together brilliantly at the end'
Chris McDonald, author of *A Wash of Black*

'Brilliantly clever, ingenious in structure and thoroughly compelling. Full of wonderful characters and extremely funny!'
Sarah Bonner, author of *Her Perfect Twin*

'I slowed down because I didn't want it to end. Heavenly and creepy combined with twisted genius. Outstanding'
Joy Kluver, author of *Broken Girls*

'What an absolute treat. Twisty and dark, packed full of angels and demons and monsters, with a thrilling mystery that keeps you guessing till the end'
Lynsey James, author of *The Single Dad's Handbook*

'It's so good. Gripping but my favourite thing is the humour – actual laugh out loud moments despite the shocking tale. Genius'
Heather Darwent, author of *The Things We Do to Our Friends*

'Another absolutely brilliant mystery by one of my favourite crime writers. Take the role of investigator and let yourself be immersed in this fantastic novel. Five stars!'
Louise Mullins, author of *One Night Only*

The
Myster
Cas
of the
ALPER
ANG

Janice Hallett studied English at Univ
several years as a magazine editor, win
She then worked in government co
Office, Home Office and Department
After gaining an MA in screenwriting
the feature film *Retreat* and went on t
comedy *NetherBard*, as well as a num
new-writing theatres. Her debut novel,
bestseller, a Waterstones Thriller of the
Book of the Month. Her second novel,
in 2022 and was an instant bestseller. H
will be published by Viper in 2024. Wh
global travel, she is based in West Londo

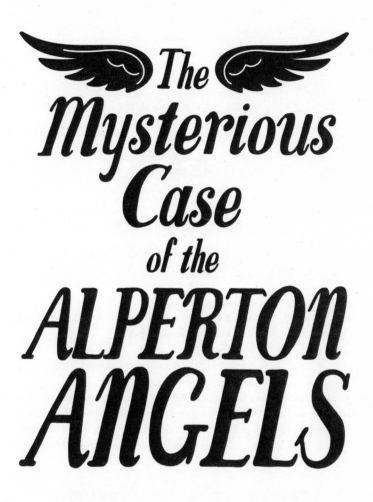

The Mysterious Case of the ALPERTON ANGELS

of the

Janice Hallett

VIPER

First published in Great Britain in 2023 by
VIPER, part of Serpent's Tail,
an imprint of Profile Books Ltd
29 Cloth Fair
London
EC1A 7JQ
www.serpentstail.com

Text design by Crow Books

1 3 5 7 9 10 8 6 4 2

Printed and bound in Great Britain by
Clays Ltd, Elcograf S.p.A.

A CIP catalogue record for this book is available from the British Library.

ISBN 978 1 80081 0433
eISBN 978 1 78283 9811

For Jill, Michelle and Lyra

YOU HAVE A KEY THAT OPENS A SAFE DEPOSIT BOX.

INSIDE IS A BUNDLE OF DOCUMENTS, ARCHIVED RESEARCH MATERIAL FOR A BOOK THAT HAS JUST BEEN PUBLISHED.

YOU MUST READ IT ALL AND MAKE A DECISION.

EITHER:

REPLACE THE DOCUMENTS AND THE BOX, THEN THROW THE KEY WHERE IT WILL NEVER BE FOUND...

OR:

TAKE EVERYTHING TO THE POLICE.

1

Correspondence, Background Reading and General Prep

> **Amanda Bailey**
> The murder cases I've covered so far are all the same. Dead blonde, media frenzy, police fumblings, lucky psychopath.

Nita Cawley
It's our bread and butter.

> **Amanda Bailey**
> Already chewed over and spat out by every newspaper and crime reporter in the land. Same old, same mould.

Nita Cawley
I hear you. What do you have in mind?

> **Amanda Bailey**
> Something else. Different. New. Oh, I don't know ... a novel?

Nita Cawley
Shit! Didn't realise things were *that* bad 😂 Look, on my way to lunch with Pippa at Kronos. If certain rumours are true, I might have something interesting for you later today.

Email from my agent Nita Cawley, 26 May 2021:

TO: Amanda Bailey
DATE: 26 May 2021
SUBJECT: Your next book
FROM: Nita Cawley

OK. Why novels? Flowery language describing every wrinkle in the carpet ... What you do is miles better. You're a master of real life, Amanda. You connect with the common reader. People want mainstream, accessible books that explore violent crime in a safe space, and that's what you give them. Which leads me smoothly to Pippa at Kronos.

She's planning a new series of true crime books called Eclipse. Each will put a fresh, dark spin on a well-known crime (like when the moon passes across the sun during an eclipse). Could be a new angle, a new theory, a new link to popular culture; anything that breathes life into an old story.

Nothing too fancy. She wants a holiday page-turner for connoisseurs of the genre. Core reader is likely familiar with the cases already, and happy to revisit 'old friends' if they think something new will get them intrigued all over again.

She rattled off a few classics. Basically, cases you think have no mystery left and nothing to uncover. The usual suspects: Jack the Ripper (yes, really), Fred and Rose West, Harold Shipman, Moors Murders ... So nothing to get us excited until she mentioned the Alperton Angels.

Remember it? Early noughties. A chilling story ripe with possibility. Inspired so many tacky horror things it's stayed in the public eye – so still has legs. But that's not why she mentioned it.

A *lot* couldn't be reported at the time (several of the bods were underage) and that brings me to why they've flagged it: the baby is due to turn eighteen this year. She said they want to look at the case from the grown-up kid's POV. Never been done before. Now, Amanda, this is exactly what you're looking for. A story you can *own*, am I right?

Also, *you* are exactly what Pippa is looking for. She has no budget for a private investigator to find the baby. She needs your lovely contacts in social services, and your endless creativity when convincing reluctant bods to talk. If you can find the baby, I can negotiate something else, listen to this ...

Pippa's gf has a TV production company and went to school with Naga Munchetty. Once you've found the baby, she wants to nail them to an exclusive deal, so they talk only to *you* – and eventually Naga – with TV timed for when the title is on the shelf. I've already suggested they interview you prominently in that documentary. Not that I've confirmed you'll do it, of course.

Don't want to hurry you on the decision, but like she said we're not the only ones with the baby's birthday in our diaries, so the sooner we can start to mine those connections the better ...

There are no tragic blondes. Just a wacky cult, four dead, mutilated men and a mystery no one's had the chance to uncover properly yet. You'll be the first. Imagine that. N x

Amanda Bailey

Sorry to do this by WhatsApp, but you're away and I've got a new job about to start so here goes ... You're the best, most thoughtful guy I've ever known, yet still I'm happier single 🙍
Looks like I'm not cut out for this, or any, relationship. You've taught me that, so thanks.

Amanda Bailey

And sorry 🙈

Email from my editor Pippa Deacon, 10 June 2021:

TO: Amanda Bailey
DATE: 10 June 2021
SUBJECT: Welcome!
FROM: Pippa Deacon

Dear Amanda,

First of all, may I say how delighted we are that you're on board for the Eclipse series. It's an important launch for us with so many exciting people involved. Craig Turner, who I think you know, is presenting Dennis Nilsen's killing spree as a harbinger of the AIDS crisis during the 1980s. He's spoken to all the gay celebrities and has brought the whole case into the twenty-first century. Lovely Minnie Davis has identified the most shocking coincidences in the lives of Myra Hindley and Rose West – she's pulled it out of the bag with this one. Even taken photographs that show visual similarities in their childhood homes and schools, really chilling stuff! The Alperton Angels is such a dark, emotive tale, and with the youngest child about to turn eighteen, the case is totally ready for a reboot.

I hear you have an 'in' with social services in the area and can trace where the baby was sent. You'll understand we have a teeny tiny budget that doesn't stretch to private detectives, so any short cuts you can make ... We know how doggedly determined you are when there's a story to be had and trust you implicitly to seize the heart of this case, rip it out and throw it at the page.

You only have to google to see how much is in the public domain already so it won't take you long to get up to speed. Call as soon as you locate the baby. I'll get wheels turning with the TV people.

Thanks, Amanda; I look forward to working with you.

Pippa

INTERVIEW WISH LIST

The Angels
The Baby
Holly*
Jonah*
Gabriel Angelis, currently residing at Tynefield Prison
*not their real names

Contacts (amended over the weeks)

Police and legal
Don Makepeace, retired detective chief superintendent
Jonathan Childs, police officer who found Singh's body
Grace Childs, his wife
Aileen Forsyth, police officer
Mike Dean, police officer
Neil Rose, police officer
Fareed Khan, police officer
Nikki Sayle, retired police sergeant
Farrah Parekh, police sergeant

Health and social care
Sonia Brown, senior social worker
Julian Nowak, social worker
Ruth Charalambos, former social worker
Sabrina Emanuel, retired social worker
Maggie Keenan, former duty manager at Willesden Children's Centre
Penny Latke, A&E nurse
Caroline Brooks, criminal psychologist
Jideofor Sani, retired paramedic

Media, etc.
Phil Priest, TV producer
Debbie Condon, TV producer

Louisa Sinclair, former reporter for *Wembley Informer* (now editor of WembleyOnline)
Corin Dallah, former press officer at the Ministry of Justice
Gray Graham, retired reporter
Clive Badham, writer of unproduced screenplay *Divine*
Jess Adesina, author of the *My Angel Diary* series
Mark Dunning, author of *White Wings*
Judy Teller-Dunning, writer, wife of Mark Dunning
Duncan Seyfried, Neville, Reed & Partners, Mark Dunning's agent

Amateur contributors
David Polneath, amateur detective
Cathy-June Lloyd, chair of the Cold & Unsolved Murder Club
Rob Jolley, member of the above
Dave 'Itchy' Kilmore, host of the *Fresh Ghost* podcast
Galen Fletcher, school counsellor whose brother knew Harpinder Singh

Miscellaneous
Reverend Edmund Barden-Hythe, parish rector, St Barnabas Church, Sudbury
Jayden Hoyle, London Fire Service, public relations
Ross Tate, former prison associate of Gabriel Angelis

Miscellaneous items printed from online news sites or torn from newspapers and held together with a paperclip. All date from a three-week period in December 2003:

THE STARS ALIGN

Tonight, five planets in our solar system align in a rare astral occurrence that should be visible from dawn tomorrow, 10 December. Mercury, Venus, Mars, Jupiter and Saturn align in the sky every 20 years, but on this occasion, they will be at their closest distance apart since 16 July 1623, a phenomenon known as a Great Conjunction.

BREAKING NEWS

Police have cordoned off a derelict warehouse in Alperton, north-west London, amid unconfirmed reports multiple bodies have been discovered inside.

BREAKING NEWS

A police source suggests the incident in Alperton is a 'mass suicide'. Four bodies remain at the scene.

BODY LINKED TO 'BLOODBATH'

Police believe a body discovered in an empty flat on Tuesday (9 December) may be linked to the three men who died in an apparent suicide pact at a nearby warehouse the following day. Police were called to a flat in Middlesex House on Ealing Road, Alperton, when residents reported suspicious noises. Police constable Jonathan Childs, who was first on the scene, described the body as male and 'in a state of decomposition'. He urged members of the public to come forward with any information.

'ANGELS' LINK TO LOCAL CHURCH

Members of the so-called 'Alperton Angels' cult were familiar figures at St Barnabas Church in Sudbury. Three men and two teenagers, who believed they were angels in human form, occasionally attended Sunday service, raising questions over whether the church failed to exercise safeguarding responsibilities.

BODY IN FLAT NAMED

Police have named the man found dead in Middlesex House last week as Harpinder Singh, 22, a waiter at the Punjab Junction restaurant in Southall. He was temporarily housed at Middlesex House but was not found in the flat he had been allocated, police say. They have linked his death to the Alperton Angels but cannot be more specific for fear of jeopardising that ongoing case. They urge anyone with information to contact Crimestoppers.

---

1. Formal email template, sent out from 10 June 2021 onwards:

Dear X,

Let me introduce myself. I am Amanda Bailey, the best-selling true crime author of *The Doorstep*, *Common Ground* and *Kipper Tied*. I am currently working on a book about the Alperton Angels for Kronos Books. I understand you were XX at the time. In order to avoid misrepresenting your organisation/role/department, I would like to set up an interview either in person or over the phone, at your earliest convenience.

I have a long track record in crime reporting and human-interest journalism. I understand the case is still sensitive, even after eighteen years, so if you are happier chatting off the record, that's fine too. Your participation in this project will help ensure such a shocking failure of safeguarding measures never happens again.

I look forward to hearing from you.
Yours sincerely,

2. Informal email template sent out from 10 June 2021 onwards:

Hi there!

How are you? It's been so long since X. How is/was baby/wedding/retirement/new job, etc.? Honestly, time flies.

Do you remember the case of the Alperton Angels? I'm writing something about it. It was soooo long ago and I must get up to speed really fast. Do you have records going back to 2003? Can I use you for ambient info about that time period in social services/police/media? I'll be eternally grateful!

Happy to meet for twilight drinks or daylight coffee.

Best,

WhatsApp messages between true crime author Minnie Davis and me, 11 June 2021:

Minnie Davis
Hello, gorgeous girl! Haven't seen or heard from you for AGES.
Then Pippa said you're working on something for her. Snap!
How are you?

> **Amanda Bailey**
> The Alperton Angels. So much redacted at the time due to underage victims and no one has come forward to tell their stories since. Not the teenagers (now in their 30s) and not the baby (nearly 18). It's still a mystery. What's your memory of the case?

Minnie Davis
I mean how are YOU, not work. Angels and devils, wasn't it?

> **Amanda Bailey**
> They were a small cult of men, who all died, plus a teenage couple and their baby, who survived. A grisly mass suicide – with no true crime coverage. Found a few novels 📷

Minnie Davis
There were at least two TV dramas.

> **Amanda Bailey**
> Must be strange for the real people.

Minnie Davis
Does the baby know they were the baby in the Alperton Angels case?

12

Amanda Bailey

Soon will.

Minnie Davis

They could've watched and read stuff oblivious it's about them.

Amanda Bailey

You've given me an idea. The bods who fictionalised the case early on might be useful. Mark Dunning wrote a novel called White Wings. He thanks 'everyone involved in the Alperton Angels case' who 'helped' him – the book came out eighteen months later. He must've been chasing the hearse.

Amanda Bailey

Hearses.

Minnie Davis

I've struck gold with my commission. Most people connected to the Moors Murders are dead and relatives of the Wests stopped speaking to media years ago. No interviews, thank God.

Amanda Bailey

Lucky you 😂

Minnie Davis

And that's not the best thing. Met a girl who wrote a feminist thesis on female murderers. Sent me her piece on Rose and Myra – drop dead brilliant – photographs that will chill the flesh from your bones, Mand. She said use whatever you want, just credit me in the acknowledgements. I've based the entire premise on it.

Amanda Bailey

She's OK with that?

Minnie Davis

Absolutely. She's really into women helping women.

Amanda Bailey

I dunno. Wary of using amateurs.

Minnie Davis

Me too. Till I met this girl.

> **Amanda Bailey**
>
> They get clingy, demanding, resentful, then vengeful

Minnie Davis

BUT they throw themselves into it and work their butts off for a mention in a book about their favourite murder. Also, they get through to people naturally suspicious of journalists. This girl is smart and so easy-going. Anyway, you, me and Craig should get together for drinks.

> **Amanda Bailey**
>
> So much to do on this. Been reading all night, sending the first phase of emails. Now have to send targeted messages, arrange interviews, reach out to the fiction people. Argh! Need, need, need to find the baby!

Waterstones order, 11 June 2021, books for research (receipt filed for self-assessment):

Cultish by Amanda Montell [pre-order as released 22 July]
My Angel Diary, Books 1–4 by Jess Adesina
Cults That Kill by Wendy Joan Biddlecombe Agsar
Cults Uncovered Emily G. Thompson
White Wings by Mark Dunning
Terror, Love and Brainwashing by Alexandra Stein

Email to social worker Sonia Brown, 11 June 2021:

TO: Sonia Brown
DATE: 11 June 2021
SUBJECT: Favour
FROM: Amanda Bailey

Hey Sonia,

I'm writing about the Alperton Angels case. Need to contact the teenagers

Holly and Jonah, but in particular the baby they rescued. Where did it go? And where is it now? If it was born in 2003 then it's eighteen this year so you should be able to find out where its last care placement was, especially if it was adopted.

I'm reading news reports from the time and they give nothing away about the young people. Names, images, birthplaces – all obscured 'for legal reasons'. If Holly was capable of looking after her baby, I assume they would have been supported in a unit? Or it could have been placed separately. Either way, I'm looking to trace the baby first and foremost, then the teenagers.

Amanda

Text messages between Sonia Brown and me, 11 June 2021:

Sonia Brown
They've shut down access to archives.

> **Amanda Bailey**
> There must be weak spots in the system.

Sonia Brown
We have to apply for permission, wait for approval, then write
a report on how what we found is relevant to an active case.
I can't link it to my current workload. Sorry but it's just not
possible this time.

> **Amanda Bailey**
> Is there another way I can get that information? Any people
> who might remember, or have access to records? Any external
> agencies? Anything?

Text messages between me and retired social worker Sabrina Emanuel, 11 June 2021:

> **Amanda Bailey**
> Hi Sabrina 😊 miss you!

Sabrina Emanuel

Hello darling how you?

> **Amanda Bailey**
>
> Quick question. Were you around for the Alperton Angels case?
> Remember it?

Sabrina Emanuel

Oh yes. Yes I remember.

> **Amanda Bailey**
>
> It's been so long since we spoke. Let's arrange a catch-up asap!
> When are you around?

Sabrina Emanuel

October.

> **Amanda Bailey**
>
> I was thinking next week.

Sabrina Emanuel

😄 I've just landed at Faro. The Algarve, baby! I'll call when I'm
settled in the villa.

Reply to my initial email from Louisa Sinclair, a local journalist I started out
with at the *Wembley Informer* years ago. Currently editor of WembleyOnline:

TO: Amanda Bailey
DATE: 12 June 2021
SUBJECT: Re: The Alperton Angels
FROM: Louisa Sinclair

Hi Mandy,

I remember this case well. Just googled and a couple of our headlines
popped up. Those were different times, we'd never get away with that
now. We certainly milked the more salacious aspects for all they were
worth. Well, if I recall, there weren't that many facts we could report, so
what do they expect?

In the cold light of day it was a shitshow of safeguarding failures. If you
want a 'lessons learned' approach, then we should've seen through the
smokescreen and asked questions of the system. Don't quote me on that.

Give me a while, I'll dig out my old files. Might have something that helps. Yeah, we'll meet up soon.

Best,

Louisa Sinclair

Editor, WembleyOnline

Email from the Reverend Edmund Barden-Hythe, Rector of St Barnabas Church, Sudbury, 12 June 2021:

TO: Amanda Bailey
DATE: 12 June 2021
SUBJECT: Re: The Alperton Angels
FROM: Edmund Barden-Hythe

Dear Ms Bailey,

Thank you for your email. I've been vicar of St Barnabas in Sudbury for twenty-two years, so yes I was here when the Alperton Angels were in the news. The teenagers mentioned us in their statements, there was a flurry of media interest and as a result we are eternally associated with the case.

I can meet if you think I'll be of help. Tuesdays and Wednesdays are my best days.

Yours sincerely,

Revd Edmund Barden-Hythe

WhatsApp messages between my editor Pippa Deacon and me, 12 June 2021:

Pippa Deacon

Hi Mand 🙈 Quick question: have you found the baby yet?

> **Amanda Bailey**
>
> Hi Pips. It's only been two days.

Pippa Deacon

Are you close?

Amanda Bailey

I've put feelers out with my two main contacts in social services, so 🤞

Pippa Deacon

How long will it take? Rough estimate?

Amanda Bailey

The case is 18 years old, so

Pippa Deacon

It's just the OH is giving me grief about timings. You know TV people. Very competitive. Please try everything. The faster we bag that baby, the better.

Amanda Bailey

Well, there are a few writers who covered the story pretty much as it happened. They may remember names etc.

Pippa Deacon

Good idea! Keep me updated.

Twitter messages between me and YA author Jess Adesina, 12 June 2021:

Amanda Bailey

Hey Jess, hope you don't mind me DMing you on Twitter. I've read My Angel Diary and OMG what a FABULOUS book. It absolutely deserves every award it won. I understand the story is inspired by the Alperton Angels. I'm researching a true crime book on the case and plan to write a foreword looking at the fictional works that draw from elements of it. Of course, yours will be mentioned very positively therein. Can I ask, did you speak to anyone involved in the case while you were writing it?

Jess Adesina

No.

Amanda Bailey

Only you gave an interview to Grazia back in 2011 and in it you strongly imply you spoke to a key participant. Presumably it was Holly? She's obviously who you base the character of Tilly on.

Jess Adesina

[THIS ACCOUNT BLOCKED YOU]

Email exchange between me and Neville, Reed & Partners, US agents of the author Mark Dunning, 12 June 2021:

TO: info@nevillereed.com
DATE: 12 June 2021
SUBJECT: Mark Dunning
FROM: Amanda Bailey

Dear Neville, Reed & Partners,

I understand you represent the author Mark Dunning who wrote the novel *White Wings* and wonder if you'd be so kind as to pass this message on to him.

Dear Mark Dunning,

I've just read *White Wings* and was gripped from start to finish. What a compelling story and one I understand is inspired by events that happened here in the UK – now known as the Alperton Angels. I'm at the preparation stage of a true crime book about the case and wonder if we could chat over Zoom or FaceTime? I'm interested in hearing about your research – you touch upon it in the acknowledgements. Considering when the book was published you must have spoken to key players within weeks of the events known as 'The Assembly'. You'll understand that so long has passed since then, it's much harder to find reliable sources now. I would love to hear about conversations you had at the time with anyone who could boast first-hand contact with the people involved.

I look forward to hearing from you at your earliest convenience.
Amanda Bailey

Dear Ms Bailey,

I'm sorry, but our author Mark Dunning died last night. We are reeling right now and can't provide any more details.

Duncan Seyfried

Neville, Reed & Partners

Dear Duncan,

I've just heard the news. It seems he had the accident at almost exactly the same time I sent my email. How tragic. You have my deepest condolences.

I notice from the obits he was married to Judy Teller. Out of interest, I wonder if, once the initial shock is over, you could pass my message on to her? She's also a writer and I'm sure will understand.

Best,

Amanda

Emails from me to two producers who each worked on separate TV series inspired by the Alperton Angels, ten years ago, 13 June 2021:

Hi Phil, hope you can help me. I'm writing a book about the Alperton Angels and have just binge-watched *Assembly*, your brilliant 2011 TV series inspired by the case. I remember there were two series based on the same incidents, screened just a few weeks apart, but in my opinion, yours was by far the superior of the two. A coven of evil, twisted men were responsible for what happened, so it's a no-brainer to focus on that side of the story.

Can I ask if you, or anyone else involved in the production, spoke to the victims as part of your research?

Best,

Amanda Bailey

Hi Debbie, I hope you can help me. I'm writing a book about the Alperton Angels and have just binge-watched *Dereliction*, your brilliant 2011 TV series inspired by the case. I remember there were two series based on the same incidents, screened just a few weeks apart, but in my opinion, yours was by far the superior of the two. The under-funding of social services by an uncaring government and the failings of key professionals were responsible for what happened, so it's a no-brainer to focus on that side of the story.

Can I ask if you, or anyone else involved in the production, spoke to the victims as part of your research?

Best,

Amanda Bailey

Email exchange between me and Clive Badham, aspiring screenwriter, 13 June 2021:

Dear Clive,

I'm an author researching my next book and wonder if you could help. I see online you won an award in 2005 for a film based on the Alperton Angels. I'd like to watch it as part of my broader research into the enduring legacy of this case, only I can't find it anywhere. Is it available on a particular streaming platform or DVD? Also, did you speak to anyone connected to the case as part of your research?

Cheers,

Amanda Bailey

Hi Amanda,

Your name was really familiar, then I realised: I've read *Common Ground*, your book on Rachel Nickell. And now you're writing to me! I really want to help with your research.

Yep, my supernatural action-adventure script, *Divine*, was inspired by the Alperton Angels. It won Best Unproduced Screenplay in the London Film Academy Awards 2005. Didn't speak to anyone as I'd read everything at the time. Also, the occult is my hobby, so I had a bedrock of knowledge to draw from. In any case, I wasn't so interested in what *actually* happened as much as the idea that demons walk the earth in human form. That's pretty cool, right? That's what inspired me.

You can't watch *Divine* anywhere – yet. Funding wasn't available so it was never actually made. But I sent the script to every producer whose email I could get my hands on and *loads* said how great it is. One got back to me just last month to say she's on a big project for the next two years, but once that's in the can she'll read it! Fingers crossed. Perhaps your book will renew interest in the case.

Are you looking for a screenwriter to adapt your books? I'm only working part-time in a call centre and teaching a writers' class at community college. I can easily fit in a script around that. I don't have an agent, so let me know direct if you're interested.
Clive Badham

Text messages between me and Clive Badham, 13 June 2021:

Amanda Bailey
Thanks, Clive, could I read your DIVINE script anyway? It fascinates me how much fictional material this case inspired. Even though your film was never made, it's still an example of contemporary fiction based on it. I can name-check you if I mention it in the book 😊

Clive Badham

Tricky. See, I'm not comfortable with that. As a writer yourself, you'll understand. Literally anyone could change the name on the title page and claim it as theirs. But if you want a script written, let me know.

An email sent to the contact page of my website, amandabailey.co.uk, 13 June 2021:

TO: Amanda Bailey
DATE: 13 June 2021
SUBJECT: A small favour
FROM: Cathy-June Lloyd

Dear Amanda Bailey,

I am chair of a small murder club here in Guildford called Cold & Unsolved. It's a monthly meet-up where we discuss cold cases and unsolved killings – just for fun, but I'm sure we hit on some interesting theories at least once in a while!

We've been investigating the case of Jill Dando and a few of us read your book *The Doorstep*. It's a real page-turner and we all feel it gets the reader right to the core of that case. I wonder, do you know if the police ever fully discounted all the neighbours? They were on the scene very quickly and the fact any one of them could keep watch over the street, fire the gun and nip back into their house made them our key suspects. We even have their motive: they wanted to buy her house at an 'atrocity discount'. This theory would explain why there are no reliable sightings of the killer running away. A couple of us wondered if, by calling your book *The Doorstep*, you were subtly hinting at a theory you couldn't expound for legal reasons.

Do you ever give talks at small clubs like ours? We're an enthusiastic bunch of amateur sleuths and we'd be delighted and honoured to welcome you. We don't have a huge budget, but if you could make it here, I will personally ensure you walk away with £40 in Amazon vouchers and a bunch of flowers.

Even if you are too busy to come and see us, we can't wait for your next book!

Cathy-June Lloyd

An email from Dave 'Itchy' Kilmore at *Fresh Ghost* podcast, 14 June 2021:

TO: Amanda Bailey
DATE: 14 June 2021
SUBJECT: Fresh Ghost returns!
FROM: David Kilmore

Hey Mandy!

New series klaxon! Yes, the *Fresh Ghost* podcast is back for a twelfth series and I'm lining up guest speakers in good time for once. Can I pencil you in again? You went down a storm last time. Happy to chat about the subject of your choice and include plugs for your books: past, present and future (what are you working on?) as well as chat around our chosen theme. Subjects I've pencilled in include:

Faking Suicide: the murderer's holy grail
Assassination: why doesn't it happen more?
Psychopaths who <u>don't</u> kill: why the heck not?

Open to other ideas. Let me know ...

Dave 'Itchy' Kilmore

WhatsApp messages between retired detective chief superintendent Don Makepeace and me, 14 June 2021:

Don Makepeace
Dear Amanda. Thank you for your email. I remember those events well. Happy to meet for a chat over lunch. Do you realise there's someone else writing a book on the same case? Oliver Menzies. Called a while ago. He's looking at it from the baby's point of view. I can make any day. Don.

> **Amanda Bailey**
> Oliver Menzies? NO WAY. Don, what did he say? Has he met the baby?

Don Makepeace
I can't remember. We had lunch at Quaglino's. Very tasty bread and organic butter. Don.

WhatsApp messages between me and my editor Pippa Deacon, 14 June 2021:

> **Amanda Bailey**
> Hi Pippa, I've thought of a great title for my Alperton Angels book: DIVINE. What do you think? I should tell you something I've only just discovered myself: Oliver Menzies is writing about the same case and from what I hear, he's also focusing on the baby. Is this as much a problem for you as it is for me? Should I rethink the angle before I go any further?

Pippa Deacon
Who is he? Do you know him? Title brilliant btw.

> **Amanda Bailey**
> I do. From another life. We both started on a local newspaper training scheme in the late 90s. I left before the course ended, he left just after.

Pippa Deacon
I see he's co-written a police memoir and ghost-written for a soldier accused of war crimes. Is he any good?

> **Amanda Bailey**
> We lost touch. I heard he went to a radio station, then a building trade magazine and the last I heard he had a swanky job in corporate PR. He must've gone freelance.

Pippa Deacon
Well, we knew it wouldn't be long before someone else started sniffing about. But he won't have your contacts so we're always going to have the edge. So long as we get to the baby first and seal the deal. How close are you?

Text messages between me and social worker Sonia Brown, 14 June 2021:

> **Amanda Bailey**
> About tracing the baby from the Alperton Angels case. All I
> need is a few names, dates and addresses. I'll do the rest. Or
> full-access log-in details so I can find the info myself.

Sonia Brown
Like I said, the system is completely different now. It's
impenetrable.

> **Amanda Bailey**
> Sonia, please think of a way. It's the least you can do after I
> kept the Three Beeches leak secret.

Sonia Brown
Leak? I was helping YOU. Look, I'll be no use if I lose my job, will I?

> **Amanda Bailey**
> You won't just lose your job. You acted alone. Outside of your
> role. After what happened there would most certainly be
> criminal charges.

Sonia Brown
FFS Mandy, after all the help I've given you?

**WhatsApp messages between me and my former colleague Oliver Menzies,
14 June 2021:**

> **Amanda Bailey**
> Whaaaa! So that six-figure stint at The Gherkin was too much
> like hard work? You didn't even stay there a year, you fucking
> job-hopper. That's some record even for you! What did you do,
> rob petty cash? Get your dick out at a press launch? 🍆

Oliver Menzies
My dad died. I wasn't in the best place to give the role my all.
Left by mutual agreement.

Amanda Bailey

Oh. Sorry to hear that.

Oliver Menzies

It is what it is.

Amanda Bailey

Heard you're working on the Alperton Angels. Who for?

Oliver Menzies

Right. It's you. I KNEW there was someone approaching my contacts. Still using email templates like it's 2001?

Amanda Bailey

It's fast and efficient.

Oliver Menzies

The personal touch is king. Quality over quantity at all times. My book is for Green Street and assume yours is for Pippa Deacon's new series.

Amanda Bailey

Is true crime your sort of thing? The Oliver Menzies I remember would consider commercial publishing beneath him 🫤

Oliver Menzies

I'm looking at it from the baby's point of view.

Amanda Bailey

So am I. That's my exact brief. Do Green Street know?

Oliver Menzies

You're late to the party, Mand. I've been on it for weeks.

Amanda Bailey

Have you spoken to the baby?

Oliver Menzies

There's a hundred other angles you can take.

Amanda Bailey

Have you spoken to the baby?

Oliver Menzies

Not exactly. But I'm getting warmer. Have you?

> **Amanda Bailey**
>
> Yes. They're on board and have just signed an exclusive with us, so best you don't waste any more time. But you'll be fine. There's a hundred other angles you can take.

My scripts for phishing phone calls, 14 June 2021:

'Hi, I'm Sergeant Jones from the Metropolitan Police's Child Protection unit. I'm investigating a tricky historical case. I wonder if you could access records that would confirm exactly when three children passed through your care?'

'You can't? Oh. Well, that's disappointing as all I need is confirmation of dates. It could make all the difference to some very brave people. You know how difficult these historical cases are. The victims are courageous enough to come forward, some of them after many years of trauma, then for the sake of a tiny piece of info, the case falls apart. Just one little corroboration – like the time three children passed through your care – would make ALL the difference.'

'That's fabulous, thank you. It was 2003 and I'm talking about the minors in the Alperton Angels case. Two seventeen-year-olds and a baby, a few months old at the time. It's pertinent to a totally separate case I'm working on.'

FOUND IT!
Willesden Children's Service Centre
Neasden Road, NW10

WhatsApp messages between me and my former assistant Ellie Cooper, 14 June 2021:

> **Amanda Bailey**
> Hi Els. Are you still able to turn around transcriptions? Two-speaker interviews as usual, same rates? Starting this Thursday. I'm working on a 'holiday page-turner' for Kronos.

Ellie Cooper
EC ready and waiting!

Meeting with retired detective chief superintendent Don Makepeace at Bluebird, Fulham, 17 June 2021. Transcribed by Ellie Cooper.

AB: Thanks for meeting me, Don.

DM: Pleasure. You look well, Mandy. How is your lovely assistant? [*She's blushing and hating herself for valuing the approval of a man. EC*]

AB: Not my assistant any more. She's moved on. Studying for a PhD. [*I ignored all the boring small talk and cut to the chase. EC*] Don, you were chief inspector at Wembley Central in 2003 when the Alperton Angels case broke. What do you remember about it?

DM: I remember him very well.

AB: Gabriel.

DM: [*He laughs. EC*] Yes. Well, that's what he called himself eventually. Before he discovered God he was plain old Peter Duffy. I remember we put him away for fraud not long after I joined up. This was years before all the Alperton business. He had no qualms breaking the eighth commandment back then! [*Thou shalt not steal. EC*]

AB: What was he like?

DM: You know coppers, Mandy. We watch people all the time. When they're guilty, when they're not. Guilty of something, but not what you think. Hiding a secret or wanting to reveal it. They're all the same. But him ...

AB: What was it about him?

DM: I watched all his interviews. Many times, some of them. And I couldn't tell.

AB: If he was guilty?

DM: If he was telling the truth.

AB: Sure, when someone believes their own lies, your copper's sixth sense is redundant.

DM: Something like that. Will you speak to him?

AB: I'll apply to the governor. Not counting on it, though.

DM: I haven't known him to give an interview. Claims he remembers nothing about what happened that night or the preceding months. Yet maintains his innocence. Well, if he can't remember, how can he be so sure? [*He chuckles. EC*] Classic.

AB: How about the teenagers? Holly and Jonah.

DM: Not their real names either.

AB: Can you remember their real names?

DM: No.

AB: What were they like?

DM: Chalk and cheese. She was bright; he was shy, easily led. Maturity quite different. Still— [*Didn't catch the rest. EC*]

AB: Did you ever find out who the baby's father was, Gabriel or Jonah?

DM: That was social services' domain. We focused on the murder charge.

AB: Harpinder Singh. I've read everything I can get hold of on the case and I don't know ...

DM: What?

AB: The evidence that put Gabriel behind bars seems flimsy at best.

DM: Does that mean he didn't do it?

AB: No.

DM: His fingerprints were found in the derelict flat alongside the body, I think?

AB: A partial fingerprint, on a leaflet on the floor.

DM: Yes. He was forensically aware enough to avoid leaving prints but plucked the leaflet from the letterbox at some point. Probably an automatic reflex on the way out, when the adrenalin was fading.

AB: Singh was a penniless waiter. He worked fourteen-hour days. There's no evidence he'd joined the cult even if he'd had time to. Why would they kill him?

DM: Why do people like that do anything?

AB: Was his murder ritualistic? [*He doesn't seem to answer. Your lunch arrives here. I ignored bits where you talk to the waiter and discuss the food. Blackened cod. Sounds overdone. EC*]

DM: ...We weren't involved much beyond that.

AB: So, Gabriel is convicted of Singh's murder and the post-mortem mutilation of the other three angels. Holly and Jonah give evidence about how he ensnared them in the cult and he's sentenced to a whole-life tariff. But the teenagers were never held accountable.

DM: Given what they'd been through there was no appetite to charge them with anything. Rightly or wrongly. Are seventeen-year-olds responsible for their actions? Given their extreme vulnerability? We focused on him. He was the only adult angel left alive.

AB: But they could've been ...

DM: It was a tricky one. They were both victims, drawn into a cult and used by it. But they'd extricated themselves and saved a baby. The CPS weren't comfortable blaming them. Certainly not while Gabriel was alive and kicking.

AB: And they were minors, after all.

DM: Uh-huh. Although seventeen ... above the age of consent, so ... If adults want to create their own fantasy world and live in it ... [*He doesn't finish this sentence. EC*] Theirs was out there, it wasn't illegal.

AB: But when a cult leads its members to kill themselves—

DM: You've seen the coroner's reports? The angels died from single knife wounds to the throat. Self-inflicted. [*Silence while you – and now me – contemplate this grisly thought. EC*]

AB: A whole-life tariff is unusual for someone found guilty of just one murder. I wonder if the judge suspected Gabriel of killing the others, too?

DM: Indeed, look at the circumstances, Amanda. Gabriel may not have wielded the knife, but he convinced those men to kill themselves then eviscerated their bodies post-mortem, and posed them in a satanic circle. He's insane and yes, we could indeed say he's responsible for the other deaths, so ...

AB: Strange case.

DM: Mmmm. Nutcase.

AB: Where does Harpinder Singh fit in?

DM: [*His mouth is full, ew. I can't hear the first part of his sentence. EC*] ... it's heroic.

AB: Not for Harpinder Singh.

DM: Of course, I mean the baddies died or were caught and the baby survived.

AB: Poetic, maybe. Do you know a police officer called Jonathan Childs?

DM: No, I don't think so.

AB: His name was in a news-bite published online at the time. He found Singh's body in the empty flat. Can't seem to locate him.

DM: I can ask around.

AB: I don't usually draw a blank with police officers, Don. You all seem to know each other.

DM: [*He laughs. EC*] It's the M40 corridor.

AB: The what?

DM: The M40 motorway means areas west of London out to the Thames Valley have a fast link, so officers living and working in the whole area move stations within it a lot during their careers. I'll ask around. Someone will know him.

AB: Cheers, Don. [*Chewing and clinking of glasses. EC*]

DM: Constantly surprised to see what that case went on to inspire. There was an episode of something on telly not long ago.

AB: *Inside No. 9.* I saw it. Brilliant. [*Totally freaked me out. EC*]

DM: That's it. Terrifying! Creepy. It wasn't like that at the time. Just another case of predators taking advantage of the vulnerable, exploiting weakness in the system. Take away talk of angels and demons and you're left with a very depressing but nonetheless run-of-the-mill story.

AB: What happened to the baby?

DM: Ah! That reminds me. I have a favour to ask. Connor is considering journalism as a career. I promised I'd find a friendly hack to give him some advice. Could he speak to you about it?

AB: Sure.

DM: Thank you. Are you free for dinner Sunday?

AB: I'd love that. [*A pause while you both chew and swallow. EC*] What happened to the baby rescued from the Alperton Angels cult?

DM: No idea. [*Slight hesitation, rise in tone. Does he know? EC*]

AB: Was it reunited with Holly or taken into care?

DM: [*Mumbles something. EC*]

AB: Off the record? [*A long pause. EC*]

DM: Off the record, something funny happened. You'll have to get the full story from social services, but I remember someone popped up, made a familial claim. Grandparents, an aunt or someone. Presumably they applied for custody.

AB: If it was adopted by family, then Holly could be involved in its upbringing. That's a happy ending.

DM: [*Mumbles something. Then something that sounds like ... EC*] Funny, the closer you get, the further away you are.

AB: What's funny about that?

DM: Nothing.

AB: You said something funny happened.

DM: [*Sounds like he's chewing. Playing for time? EC*] See, I think like a copper, Mandy. My first thought is, if they couldn't take care of Holly, why would they be given custody of her baby? Not funny, just, social workers see the world one way, police another. [*Some talk here about a mutual friend, Oliver Mingis. You ask DM to find out 'how far he's got' and let you know. Relevant to the interview? EC*]

AB: Is there anyone from that time who might be willing to chat?

DM: By 'willing to chat' you mean ...?

AB: Willing to expose anything they saw as wrong.

DM: I'll think about it, but, Mandy, I will say one thing.

AB: OK.

DM: Off the record. Look after yourself.
      [*Just tedious small-talk from here on. EC*]

Amanda Bailey

The baby was taken in by a family member of the teenage girl.

Sonia Brown

Who told you that?

Amanda Bailey

Someone there at the time. In the first instance they were taken to Willesden Children's Service Centre.

Sonia Brown

I'll ask around.

Meeting with Revd Edmund Barden-Hythe at St Barnabas Church, Sudbury, 18 June 2021. Transcribed by Ellie Cooper.

AB: Thanks [*Echoey! Creeping me out. EC*]

EBH: Let's sit in the front pews. We can see the stained-glass window. It's been dated at 1290. Until the Alperton Angels it was our claim to fame.

AB: Beautiful. Vivid colours. Could I get a little closer, just to see the detail? I have reduced vision in this eye.

EBH: Of course, go right up to it. You'll see, it's all original lead.

AB: Wow. Does it tell a story?

EBH: The siege of Samaria. An episode from the Book of Kings. Ben-Hadid, the figure there, has stopped food supplies to the city. The king, see him on the wall? He walks among his starving people, here. This woman stops him and says, 'Your highness, give us your son, so we may eat him. Then tomorrow, we'll eat *my* son.' So, the king allows his son to be killed and eaten. The next day, the people are starving again. The king goes to the woman, only to find she has hidden her son. There she is, refusing to make the sacrifice she insisted he make, and there's nothing he can do about it. [*That's dark. EC*]

AB: Now we're closer I can see it's not as beautiful as, er, is that …?

EBH: The boiled head of the prince, yes. The story is sometimes interpreted as a pact between two mothers, rather than a king and his subject. Either way, it's a sobering tale about faith and trust in one's fellow human. Not to mention the things people will do and say to survive. In the version with the king, there's also a lesson about the sacrifice and responsibility of leadership. Tea?

AB: Please. [*Some clanging and pouring here, plus some dull chat about the mugs. EC*]

AB: You're the first person I've spoken to who actually met the angels. [*He laughs at that, but doesn't sound cheerful. EC*] When did you first notice them?

EBH: I saw Holly, the girl, first because it's unusual for people that age to be in church without their parents. I asked one of our ladies to speak to her, check she was OK. Holly told her she was an angel and lived with other angels. She was matter-of-fact about it, utterly brainwashed. My parishioner was suspicious and invited them all the following Sunday.

AB: And they came?

EBH: The leader, Gabriel, another younger man I'd later understand was Jonah, and Holly again. I spoke to Gabriel. He described himself as a lay Christian from a small community nearby. Their ethos was that all humans are angels born on earth. He contributed thirty pounds to the collection box.

AB: And that sounded plausible? Your suspicions were allayed?

EBH: I'm not here to judge. It wasn't what he said, but how he said it. People who draw others into a fantasy world are plausible people. There is no one more convincing than the convinced.

AB: Did you see them again?

EBH: No. When the events were on the news, we were all shocked. The police took statements. We had reporters here. Their tone … They blamed us for not alerting the police sooner and perhaps preventing the—

AB: Triple murder?

EBH: What almost happened to the baby. We blamed ourselves. [*He sounds gutted. EC*] But how were we to know?

AB: How does it feel now, to think people who warped Christian doctrine to the extent they almost committed a human sacrifice attended this church, *your* church?

EBH: Christianity is meant to be inspiring. It's inevitable that sooner or later it will inspire bad people. Or good people but in the wrong way. Personally, now, I think the religious elements were given rather too much prominence in what was essentially a small, isolated cult of vulnerable individuals.

AB: Was that it? Did they all believe they were heavenly beings? When you spoke to Gabriel, was he ...

EBH: I think ... this is going to sound ...

AB: Go on. In your opinion did Gabriel believe he was an angel?

EBH: I don't ... I don't know. But in those moments I spoke to him ... *I believed he was. That's the frightening thing.*
[*I cut out your goodbyes. He sounds sad. EC*]

WhatsApp messages between Oliver Menzies and me, 19 June 2021:

Oliver Menzies
Met Don yesterday. You had lunch with him Thursday.

Oliver Menzies
Did you get that?

> **Amanda Bailey**
> I got the message. It was a statement of fact that didn't beg an answer.

Oliver Menzies
Whatever. What did you talk about?

> **Amanda Bailey**
> This and that. Me and Don go back a long way.

Oliver Menzies

FFS it's 'Don and I'. Back to The Informer days, right? Same. He knows Frank the friendly bobby.

> **Amanda Bailey**
>
> Don knows everyone.

Oliver Menzies

That's the old school tie, the regimental blood-bond, special forces brotherhood and a career oiling his way round the Met.

> **Amanda Bailey**
>
> Didn't realise he was ex special forces.

Oliver Menzies

Get some Scotch in him and he'll hint at being the Ant Middleton of his day. Won't talk about any operations, though. So either he's got PTSD or he did FA. But he recommended me for the mad squaddie job, so he's still got connections.

> **Amanda Bailey**
>
> He's good at keeping in touch.

Oliver Menzies

Or put another way, he'll guzzle a free lunch at the drop of a hat. In fact, by the time you've picked up the hat to drop it, he's already at the table.

> **Amanda Bailey**
>
> You haven't found the baby then.

Oliver Menzies

No. And a little bird tells me that neither have you.

> **Amanda Bailey**
>
> The Alperton Angels isn't just about the baby. It's about the teenage girl and boy, the men who controlled them, the system that failed. Go on. Focus on something else.

Oliver Menzies

The men were opportunists, the system full of bleeding-heart do-gooders. And the youngsters? Seventeen is young, but it's old enough to know better.

> **Amanda Bailey**
> Do you remember being seventeen?

Oliver Menzies

Yes and kids that age are the sharpest tools in the box. These ones must've been pig-shit thick to fall for that ridiculous line. OR they were fully on board with the whole ethos of the cult. So no, I'm not interested in THEM. I'm interested in the BABY because they are the only innocent party in all this.

Oliver Menzies

Did you get that?

Oliver Menzies

Are you ignoring me now?

Oliver Menzies

It may sound harsh, but I wonder how the baby reconciles it all. Now they're grown up. How do you live with the fact that you were labelled 'evil' and narrowly escaped being ritually sacrificed by a crazy cult? That is some shit to live with. And it's the most interesting thing to me.

Oliver Menzies

Am I messaging into thin air here?

WhatsApp messages between retired detective chief superintendent Don Makepeace and me, 19 June 2021:

Don Makepeace

Confirming lunch tomorrow, Amanda. Any time after one. In the meantime, here's a few people who might remember the angels:

Aileen Forsyth, Mike Dean, Neil Rose, Fareed Khan, Julian Nowak.

Amanda Bailey
You're a star, Don. Thanks. See you tomorrow.

A conversation with Connor Makepeace in his bedroom, 20 June 2021. Transcribed by Ellie Cooper.

[*Did you mean to record this? Transcribed anyway ... EC*]

CM: So, I start at the LSE in September ...

AB: Swear down! The London School of Economics. That is *so* cool. [*Amanda Bailey, are you altering your speech and accent here to sound more street? EC*]

CM: But I'm thinking beyond education. It's a means to an end, right?

AB: Uh-huh.

CM: I thought journalism is a direction I could go. I mean, I want to enjoy what I do. Current affairs are alright, but I don't really fancy long hours and early mornings writing about traffic on the M25, you know what I mean? I was thinking maybe music journalism, if that's still a viable career ... Amanda?

AB: Who's that on the poster?

CM: Jeff Walker from Carcass. [*You must look blank here. EC*] It's a band.

AB: Is it heavy metal?

CM: Carcass are more grindcore. The posters on this side: *classic* death metal.

AB: Obituary. Dismember. Morbid Angel.

CM: You're a fan?

AB: No, bit too satanic for me. It's just something I'm researching at the moment. Angels. Devils. Beliefs.

CM: Here: the Sabbath, Led Zepp, Deep Purple they were the pioneers. These built on the foundations. The history is—

AB: Do you believe in evil?

CM: Er ... no, I just like the music. [*Heavy metal isn't anti-religious so*

39

much as darkly rebellious in its imagery. EC] and I play guitar, as you can see—

AB: Connor, years ago a group of people who believed themselves to be angels plotted to kill a baby because they thought it would grow up to destroy humanity—

CM: That is soaked!

AB: It's soaked, yeah right, but two teenagers, just a bit younger than you, were drawn in and convinced of it. I'm trying to understand how and why that might've happened. This guy here—

CM: Robert Plant—

AB: What would make you believe he was the devil?

CM: He'd have to prove it. Not just tell me he is. I'd want to see, like, water turned to blood or something – and be sure it wasn't just a cool special effect.

AB: What if these others believed him to be the devil? This guy ...

CM: Nick Menza from Megadeth.

AB: Yep, what if he were to walk through the door and tell you that, beyond any doubt, Robert Plant is the devil?

CM: Menza died in 2016, so he'd know by now, right? [*He laughs, you don't. EC*] I'd need to see proof.

AB: Proof. That's the key. You'd need to prove it. [*I'm cringing at the awkward silence. EC*]

CM: So how did you get into journalism? Which A levels? What degree?

AB: Neither.

CM: Seriously?

AB: I wrote a piece about the care system for a council newsletter. That got me a place on an apprenticeship scheme at a local paper.

CM: Cool.

AB: I suppose it was ... cool.

CM: How long was the apprenticeship and where d'you go from there?

AB: A year, but I didn't finish it. It's a long and boring story. Moved to Brighton for a few years and worked on a local paper there.

But it's all different now. News is online, there are fewer traditional news-gathering roles. As for music journalism ... [*You must switch off the recording as it ends abruptly here. EC*]

Email from my editor Pippa Deacon, 21 June 2021:

TO: Amanda Bailey
DATE: 21 June 2021
SUBJECT: Oliver Menzies
FROM: Pippa Deacon

Thanks for your call, Mandy. Lovely to speak with you and chat through your concerns. I'm sorry you've had this trouble with your old friend, but SO relieved you've nearly found the baby. Phew! Let me speak to Jo at Green Street. I'll explain the situation and suggest they tell this Oliver to back off – I can be quite the diplomat when required. Seeing as we all but have the baby in the bag, they can't not change their angle. You won't have him looming over you much longer and can concentrate on the book.

Meeting with Police Constable Neil Rose at Costa Coffee, Westway Cross, Greenford, 21 June 2021. Transcribed by Ellie Cooper.

AB: Thanks for meeting me [*etc., etc. I cut out the dull stuff. EC*]

NR: I was at Sudbury nick when the Alperton Angels ... Mike Dean was in charge. I can only tell you what I saw – and what I've heard since – for what that's worth.

AB: What was your first encounter with the cult?

NR: A 999 call. Young woman said she had a baby. But it wasn't clear what her emergency was, so they filed it under mental health crisis, possible vulnerable infant. Called us and an ambulance to a warehouse in Alperton. It was a derelict shell by the canal. Total darkness. I wondered if it was a hoax but then a light flashed in a second-floor window. So we went up the old fire escape on the outside of the building.

AB: What was the building?

NR: Abandoned factory or warehouse. It's flats now. We reach the
      second floor and there's no door, so straight in and torches full
      on. [*Hmmm, suspicious pause here. Is it a difficult memory or is
      he trying to remember a lie? EC*] The girl was sat in the middle
      of an open-plan floor with some plastic bags round her. She was
      covered in dried blood. Like a Halloween costume.

AB: It must've been—

NR: My first thought was a stabbing, so we go straight in to see
      where the blood's coming from. But there was no obvious
      wound. We couldn't rule out self-harm, so called to check where
      the ambulance was.

AB: What was she like? Did she say much?

NR: Nothing. She was calm, probably shock. Didn't speak. We
      remembered the mention of a baby and looked around for it.
      This is what we had to answer questions about later. You see,
      there was no baby. She didn't seem to have just given birth there
      and then, she was fully dressed, and the original call had put
      mental health crisis in our minds. Plus it was dark. Anyway, we
      call to find out where the paramedics are and they're nowhere
      near so we cancel the ambulance and say we'll run her to
      hospital ourselves. We reassure the girl and have a look round
      the place. [*Another pause. EC*] I swear to you here and now,
      this happened like I'm about to tell you. There were markings
      on the floor. The paint was dry, but new. Symbols. Nothing I
      recognised. No pentagrams, crucifixes or eyes of Horus. I've
      seen all the horror films. My mum's a Christian. My dad's family
      are Jewish. My colleague was Muslim. Between us we knew our
      religious symbols, right? My colleague mentioned Freemasons,
      and later I looked up their symbols. Nothing like the marks on
      that floor. Likewise, Buddhist, Hindu and Jain.

AB: Did you take photographs?

NR: Didn't have a camera on my phone back then. Didn't cross our
      minds they had anything to do with the girl. We took her to the
      squad car and put her in the back with her bags. It was a fifteen-
      minute journey to A&E.

AB: And when you arrived?

NR: We didn't. Got a code blue, so dropped her off at the entrance. That's when a police officer is in trouble. We drop everything and go to their aid. I shout this at the girl as we're leaving, can't say for sure if she heard or understood, but a colleague was down so ... off we went.

AB: But it wasn't the last you heard of it.

NR: Not by a long way, but we only realised later how significant the case was. The girl went into A&E. Turned out she had ... she had a baby in one of her plastic bags. Jesus Christ. It had been in the car with us, she'd had it with her the whole time. How we didn't know it was there ... [*He exhales. EC*] The hospital reported our failure to spot the baby – thanks very much – and the PCC had to investigate. Months later I'm hauled in to answer questions about the call. Picking over every step we took, every detail we might or might not have seen, and wanting times down to the last second. Two people are never going to remember things exactly the same, are they?

AB: What was the point of their questions? The angle?

NR: Those symbols. They went over and over it. Made us each draw them out, pinpoint exactly where they were on the floor. I tried. But at the end of the day it was all in torchlight. It was only because I found them interesting I remembered them at all.

AB: Strange they should focus on the symbols ...

NR: When the girl got to hospital she must've told them about the angels, The Assembly as they called it. After we'd left, the bodies were found in the basement of that building and all hell broke loose.

AB: Did you get into trouble for not finding the bodies?

NR: No, no. We hadn't known to go down there. They were getting us on the baby. Neither of us were popular with the bosses. Finally, they bring out photographs of where we'd found the girl, taken in daylight the day after. The only mark on that floor was a large circle in blue paint. The symbols had gone. Mystery to me.

AB: Did your colleague remember the symbols?

NR: At first, yeah. But then he changed his story, I don't know why. We were under a lot of pressure. But still. It didn't make me look good, did it?

AB: Can you draw those symbols for me now?

NR: Got any paper?

Meeting with Police Sergeant Fareed Khan at Costa Coffee, South Harrow, 22 June 2021. Transcribed by Ellie Cooper.

FK: It was a long time ago. But I know you've spoken to Neil. I want to get my side across because [*Awkward pause. EC*] you know how things are.

AB: OK, well, can you tell me what you found when you were called to the Alperton warehouse?

FK: Yeah, the girl, Holly, was there, drugged or shocked. We saw it wasn't an emergency so cancelled the ambulance and drove her to A&E ourselves. Where we got into trouble was, we didn't see the baby. It was in a bag. You expect a baby to be in a carrier or someone's arms, right? When we didn't see it, we assumed the call was wrong. You get crazy shit in 999 calls.

AB: Who made the call?

FK: She did. And yeah, she mentioned the baby, but we just didn't see it. We were more concerned about her. She had blood on her. You do what you think is best, then get pilloried for it.

AB: Was the baby OK?

FK: Yeah, but it was silent. What baby that age is totally still and silent for that long?

AB: Neil said you both looked around the second floor of the building.

FK: We checked the place out, briefly. Looked for anything of interest, stolen items, drug paraphernalia. All good intel.

AB: Did you find occult symbols painted on the floor?

FK: [*He tuts or something. EC*] See, this is where it gets ... Neil says
       he saw weird symbols, right? That's what he still says, yeah? But
       they showed me the photo. It was just a circle painted on the
       floor.

AB: Did your story change?

FK: It was dark. We only had torches. Neil said he'd seen them and
       [*Falters a bit here. EC*] I thought we had, so I backed him up.
       When I saw the photo, obviously we can't have seen anything.
       Trick of the light. We both got disciplined for the baby thing,
       they moved us and we haven't worked together since.

AB: Why do you think he still says that? About the symbols?

FK: Look, I dunno. People look at the same thing but see it
       differently. I wanted to make sure you had both sides of the
       story. [*Scraping chair, sounds like he's off. EC*]

AB: Thanks.

**WhatsApp messages between my editor Pippa Deacon and me,
22 June 2021:**

Pippa Deacon

Lunch with Jo at Green Street. Just back. Macs have a double
happy hour and don't know how many cocktails we tried. Have
you been there? It's CRAZY. Did WE have a chat about your
friend Oliver!

Pippa Deacon

I know you'll want all the gossip! Well, he was only
commissioned because their managing editor is an old school
friend and felt sorry for him. Lost his job and dad just died
etc. He's on the phone to them every day with problems and
excuses.

Amanda Bailey
Great. Will they take him off it?

Pippa Deacon

If they do, they'll only get someone hotter to take over. No, I was pissed but I could still th

Pippa Deacon

Sorry, think. It's all fine. Jo and I worked something out together. Here goes. We said YOU focus on the events of 2003 and the baby's perspective on them now. He'll concentrate on their childhood and teens. All sorted.

Pippa Deacon

Did I get that right the way round? You 2003, him since.

> **Amanda Bailey**
>
> I thought you'd suggest he write a totally different book or at least take him away from the baby so we don't clash.

Pippa Deacon

I know, but Jo and I had a long chat about it. Two books on the same subject is not a problem. They rekindle interest in the case. Look at it this way, they have the bigger promo budget. Our book will be alongside theirs in-store and offered as a package online. Win win. Meanwhile, you're the bigger name, so they benefit too. You just make sure they cover different aspects of the baby's life. Then and now. Fans of the case will buy both.

Pippa Deacon

She says this Oliver talks as if he's A. A. Gill but has only ever ghost-written for lucky lowlife. Never conducted proper research before. Reading between the lines, he's struggling and she hopes your influence will help get him through.

> **Amanda Bailey**
>
> So, I have to give him the baby's details.

Pippa Deacon

See this is another thing we discussed. It might be best if you interview the baby together, given its age. Just a thought. Also, some other key interviewees. Perhaps hold his hand? Remember their promo budget will only serve us well in the end.

Amanda Bailey

What happens with the exclusive TV thing?

Pippa Deacon

All fine. I've squared it with the other half. They still have exclusive TV rights. Quicker all round if you and him work things out between you.

Pippa Deacon

All we're waiting for now is the baby.

Pippa Deacon

Amanda, is that all OK?

Amanda Bailey

Has Oliver agreed?

Pippa Deacon

Don't mention it till Jo's had a chance to tell him. She's lovely. He'll be fine.

WhatsApp messages between Oliver Menzies and me, 22 June 2021:

Oliver Menzies

FFS! What the fuck have you been plotting and scheming behind my back?

Amanda Bailey

Nothing.

Oliver Menzies

You get to chew over the exciting stuff everyone wants to read about. I get to list the foster homes the kids were in.

Amanda Bailey

Pippa was worried both books would be too similar so she spoke to Jo and they decided we should spread the story between us. Work together.

Oliver Menzies

For pity's sake! What a nightmare.

Amanda Bailey

You wanted access to the baby, didn't you? Anyway, if you're interested in labels and how they play out, you've got the best angle for you.

Oliver Menzies

Listen. It's all fine. I can work with it. I've got an interview you'll never get, so.

Amanda Bailey

Who? Gabriel?

Oliver Menzies

I'd say 'you'll soon see' but you won't – because you don't know this person exists.

HM PRISON TYNEFIELD

APPLICATION FOR A VISITING ORDER

PRISONER NAME: *Gabriel Angelis.*

DATE: *22 June 2021*

YOUR NAME: *Amanda Bailey.*

REASON FOR VISIT:

I have sent a letter directly to the governor explaining the purpose of my visit. In short, I'm writing a book about the Alperton Angels cult and would like to interview you. I have applied for a visiting order and would very much appreciate if, in consultation with your governor, this could be approved.

Email I sent to the governor of HM Prison Tynefield, 22 June 2021:

Attn: The Governor
HMP Tynefield

Dear Sir,

I am a true crime author with a long track record in crime reporting and human-interest journalism. I've been commissioned by Kronos to write a book about the Alperton Angels and would like to interview Gabriel Angelis.

I believe it is very much in the public interest to explore the confluence of events that led to the formation of the Alperton Angels cult. Not least to understand the life path that led Mr Angelis and his followers to conduct the terrible crimes they committed and ensure such a tragedy never happens again.

I understand he has not, in the past, agreed to media interviews. However, the youngest victim of the cult, Holly and Jonah's baby, is about to turn eighteen and there will be a flurry of coverage. I believe it is only fair he is offered the opportunity to get his side of the story across. Yours faithfully,
Amanda Bailey

Text message from Police Sergeant Aileen Forsyth, 22 June 2021:

Aileen Forsyth
Don said you'd be in touch. I was called out to look after the girl and boy immediately after the awful events in the warehouse. It was a strange case. We can FaceTime or Zoom if you like?

WhatsApp messages between me and Oliver Menzies, 23 June 2021:

Amanda Bailey
STOP watching porn and get back to work. Have you read White Wings by Mark Dunning?

Oliver Menzies
It's over 400 pages. And I don't think you've read it for one second.

Amanda Bailey
Supernatural cold war espionage thriller with floaty, ethereal characters you're never quite sure are real or not. Omniscient

baddies who vaporise horribly, yet most of the action is invisible to humans. Despite this, it's a pretty old-school plot – not to mention the way he describes the female characters ...

Oliver Menzies

What do you mean?

> **Amanda Bailey**
>
> Let's just say I don't know how he met his deadlines typing with one hand.

Oliver Menzies

> **Amanda Bailey**
>
> It says in the acknowledgements 'thanks to those who spoke to me about the Alperton Angels case who were so generous with their time and expertise'. Who do you think spoke to him?

Oliver Menzies

If he flew from the US to London to research his book, then I want his life.

> **Amanda Bailey**
>
> He died in a car crash ten days ago. Didn't you read about it?

Oliver Menzies

Shit. No. Anyway, it's just fiction. Meaningless. I'm only interested in facts. Truth.

> **Amanda Bailey**
>
> The FACT this case inspired so many creative people is interesting in itself. Isn't it? The mythology is all part of the truth. Plus, the baby will have possibly read, but almost definitely SEEN, fictional things inspired by their own experiences – possibly without realising. Crazy, right?

Oliver Menzies

'Starz' by Widmore & Schmoozy. Ace choon. Takes me right back to mid-noughties Ibiza. Inspired by the angels.

TO: Amanda Bailey
DATE: 24 June 2021
SUBJECT: Re: Website contact form
FROM: Rhoda Wisdom

Dear Amanda,

You have reached out to me at the perfect time. I am delighted to explore the use of angels in healing and therapy to help with your book.

Angels appear in multiple established religions. As such they play a similar role to the gods in pagan cultures. They each have a personality, a role and even antagonistic relationships with other angels above or below them in a strict hierarchy. However, we, as angel therapists, consider them forces of energy and healing, with spiritual power that can be harnessed here on earth. We work with people to connect them with their guardian angels. Each of us can channel angelic power for strength, healing and wisdom.

Once you open your heart and mind to your angels, you will perceive their attempts to communicate with you. A white feather where you least expect it means your guardian angel is looking over you. Coincidences that stop you in your tracks mean the forces of the universe are at play. Number patterns. 1234. 1111. 444. Sequential and repetitive patterns are messages from the divine.

If you quote me in the book, perhaps you could mention my Angel Therapy practice in London. If your readers google me I should be the first practitioner they find.

White light and blessings,

Rhoda Wisdom

Angel Therapist (fully accredited)

WhatsApp messages between me and Oliver Menzies, 24 June 2021:

Amanda Bailey
WTF? I've just had an angel woman email me. This is YOU, isn't it?

Oliver Menzies

> **Amanda Bailey**
> Thanks very much.

Oliver Menzies

She advertises on Facebook. I knew you'd want to hear from her.

> **Amanda Bailey**
> How can someone's connection to the spiritual sphere be accredited?

Oliver Menzies

> **Amanda Bailey**
> Laugh away. I'll get you back.

Interview with Police Chief Inspector Mike Dean at Pret A Manger, Harrow, on 24 June 2021. Transcribed by Ellie Cooper.

AB: Thanks, Mike. Neil mentioned your name.

MD: Has to be off the record.

AB: Of course, you said.

MD: We got a lot of flack at the time and I don't want to fan old flames.

AB: No, no. I know it's sensitive.

MD: What did Neil and Fareed say?

AB: Well, I'd rather hear your side first, as their superior officer. Don't want to invoke the power of suggestion.

MD: OK then. [*He sounds weary. EC*] Well, they answered an emergency call to a girl who sounded disturbed and said she had a baby. Neil and Fareed arrived, cancelled the ambulance. Then took their time driving her to hospital. When she arrived, staff there saw she had a baby. The officers hadn't found it. They were called out to a girl with a baby, the baby was in a plastic carrier bag and they didn't see it. Luckily the bag had holes and the kid was warmly dressed, so it was fine. But it might not've been. What if it

52

needed resus? Those few minutes could've meant life or death.

AB: That's not quite what they told me. Neil says they were distracted by strange symbols on the floor. Fareed now says he saw only a circle. What was going on?

MD: A very bad attempt to cover up what they were really doing.

AB: Which was?

MD: Smoking, chatting and looking out over the canal. They got to the call-out, didn't evaluate the crime scene or properly examine the victim, and while they had a few moments to themselves, wandered off for a tab. Smoking in patrol cars had just been banned.

AB: How do you know that's what they did?

MD: Because the girl told us, and I believe her. [*He sighs long and hard. EC*] The two officers weren't our most conscientious. Probably shouldn't have been rostered together. Off the record, both have been disciplined since, on unconnected cases. If you ask me, they realised they were in the shit for negligence, and made up a story about occult signs to detract. All they saw was blasts of spray paint in a sort-of circle, probably a graffiti vandal testing his can. Fareed couldn't keep up the deceit, so he eventually climbed down. Neil has stuck to his account for so long now he can't admit it was all a smokescreen.

AB: And they didn't see the angels' bodies?

MD: They were discovered later, in the basement.

AB: Who found them?

MD: I believe we got another 999 call. Or maybe it was something the girl said to hospital staff? Don't remember now.

AB: Was that the first time you heard of the Alperton Angels? Only, they attended the local church and I wonder if they were well-known faces.

MD: [*Pause. Does he shake his head here? EC*] A while earlier than that, when I was new on the force and to the area.

AB: OK.

MD: A girl came in and said the archangel Gabriel wanted her to steal a credit card.

AB: That must've been entertaining. What did you say?

MD: Told her to get the ... away from him and go back to her mum and dad. She'd refused to do what this bloke wanted so no crime had been committed. Nothing came of it.

AB: What was her name?

MD: Holly.

[*I cut out your goodbyes. He's interesting. Holly tried to report Gabriel much earlier and didn't get anywhere. She must've gone back to the cult. EC*]

WhatsApp messages between true crime author Minnie Davis and me, 24 June 2021:

Minnie Davis

Hello, gorgeous girl! How goes it?

> **Amanda Bailey**
>
> Middle of interviews. Shaking the tree. Seeing what falls out. You?

Minnie Davis

Sitting in the garden trying to read. SO BORED by this book.

> **Amanda Bailey**
>
> Read another one?

Minnie Davis

It's the one I'm supposed to be writing. Or adapting from this feminist tract. At least these are the final edits. Tell me something juicy and exciting. Cheer me up. Intrigue me.

> **Amanda Bailey**
>
> Well, I'm working with someone I started out with back in the day. It's a bit weird.

Minnie Davis

Anyone I know?

> **Amanda Bailey**
>
> Oliver Menzies. We both did a journalism apprenticeship – the kind no one runs any more. Long story short I have to work with him on this Alperton Angels case. Sour ashes of the past

are rekindled with every WhatsApp. Sigh.

Minnie Davis

Rekindled? Do I sense sexual tension?

> **Amanda Bailey**
>
> Absolutely not. Jealousy, resentment, insecurity,
> Schadenfreude? Absolutely.

Minnie Davis

Planning my outfit for the wedding right now.

> **Amanda Bailey**
>
> I can't trace the key contact they all assume I can click my
> fingers and dig up. Bods on the fiction side are paranoid,
> defensive or dead. Plus, no budget for research or paying
> experts. At this rate I'll have to fabricate the whole book.

Minnie Davis

Who do you think you are, me? 😂

> **Amanda Bailey**
>
> Yes, actually. Seriously considering contacting a few amateurs
> in the hope they, in their innocence, might dredge up a lead or
> two I could 'borrow'.

Minnie Davis

Go for it. They'll love being part of the case.

FaceTime interview with Police Sergeant Aileen Forsyth on 24 June 2021. Transcribed by Ellie Cooper.

AB: Thanks for this, Aileen. I appreciate this was all a long time ago. [*I cut out some dull talk here. EC*] So you said you met the teenagers directly after the warehouse events?

AF: Yes. I picked up Holly and the baby from Ealing Hospital. Drove them back to Alperton to collect the boy. He'd been found in the basement with the bodies.

AB: So that was Jonah. Was he injured?

55

AF: Not physically, but traumatised.

AB: Holly still had the baby with her at that point?

AF: Yes. They'd checked it over and it was fine, so ... I think social services made a decision about the infant later, but you try to keep a baby with its mother.

AB: Of course. What did you think had gone on?

AF: They said she'd been found sleeping rough with the baby and that the baby's father was with police at a crime scene. Minimal details, as usual. They asked me to reunite them, so the family could be taken to social services as one unit. All pretty ordinary at first.

AB: When did it occur to you it was out of the ordinary?

AF: Holly was on the back seat with the child. I didn't even know if it was a boy or a girl. Asked its name. She said: 'It doesn't need one.'

AB: How old was it? Had it just been born ...?

AF: It looked one to two months at most.

AB: How did you react when she said it didn't have a name?

AF: It wasn't my place to judge. She had obviously been through a trauma but I knew social services were involved anyway. Didn't have to escalate my concerns at that point. So, I acted normal. When we stopped at traffic lights, I looked over my shoulder, said what a sweet little thing it was, and 'look at the peaceful expression on its face'. [*A pause here, either she's having trouble remembering or the memory is a difficult one. EC*] I can see that look in her eyes now, all this time later. 'It isn't peaceful,' she said, 'it's evil. It'll destroy the world, and no one can stop it.' [*Bet this cop needed a coffee and doughnut after that. EC*]

AB: Well ...

AF: Yeah, exactly. I hadn't had kids myself then, but I knew there was a type of post-natal depression where new mothers believe their baby's evil. So, radar pinged.

AB: Post-partum psychosis?

AF: That's it ... So I wasn't going to leave her alone till she was with a social worker and responsibility for the kid was in someone else's hands. It sounds harsh, but you get to thinking like that. Despite what she said, Holly was behaving in an instinctive, maternal way – holding the baby, rocking it, settling it. That reassured me.

AB: What happened when you got to the warehouse?

AF: I was one-up that day, so couldn't leave Holly in the car—

AB: One-up?

AF: On my own in the patrol car. We would usually be rostered in pairs, but there were too many off. I would've preferred Holly to stay in the car, but like I said, I wasn't about to leave her alone with the baby. I asked her to come into the warehouse with me to 'meet up with the baby's dad'. That's all the information I had at that point. I opened the door, offered to hold it while she got out. She wouldn't budge. 'It's still the alignment,' she said. 'They'll take it.' I reassured her no one was going to touch that baby while I was there. But she was adamant.

AB: The alignment.

AF: An alignment of stars or something. The cult were going to sacrifice a baby at a particular alignment of planets. That's my understanding.

AB: Do you think they were really going to kill it, or was it all part of the ... [*You grapple for words. EC*] world they created for Holly and Jonah?

AF: I think they were really going to kill it. I do. Well, most of them killed themselves when they failed. That's how brainwashed they were.

AB: How did you resolve the impasse with Holly?

AF: I spotted a female officer and asked her to watch the girl while I collected Jonah.

AB: What was her name, can you remember?

AF: It was pretty. French. Something like Marie-Claire.

AB: She's not on my list. No one has mentioned a Marie-Claire as a serving officer at the time.

AF: I didn't know her then and haven't met her since, so ... Anyway, I called her over to explain, but Holly started screaming, saying Marie-Claire had to stay away. That she was 'one of them'. I said, 'One of who?' and Holly said, 'A dark angel.'

AB: What did Marie-Claire say to that?

AF: Well, I should say Marie-Claire was a woman of colour and they get quite enough stick in this job, so I snapped at Holly to shut up, and apologised to Marie-Claire. She raised her eyebrows and whispered she'd keep an eye on Holly and the baby from a distance that Holly felt comfortable with.

AB: Do you remember a surname for Marie-Claire?

AF: No, sorry. I left her watching the car. Holly had shut herself in. She didn't realise the door couldn't be locked from her side, so if Marie-Claire had to intervene, she could. Meanwhile, I went into the warehouse. [*Another pause. EC*] You know in *Jaws*, when Brodie is on the beach, everyone's told him the water's safe, but he's on edge? Just as he starts to relax, he hears someone yell 'shark'. There's this moment, you can see it on his face, but the camera rushes towards him and the focus changes.

AB: I love that scene. [*I do too. EC*]

AF: It completely recreates that change in perception. When you're on sudden high alert. That was me when I stepped into the basement. Where they were.

AB: The bodies?

AF: Hmmm. It was a mess and I was … well, I didn't have to look closely so I didn't. All stabbed. Horribly mutilated. Bodies laid out around a pentagram or something, painted on the floor. We eventually found out it was a mass ritual suicide. One angel arranged the bodies then fled the scene.

AB: That would be the cult leader. Gabriel.

AF: I don't remember the details.

AB: So you walk into the room and …

AF: The smell. Blood. Hideous. But do you know something? I've seen so many bodies, it wasn't those that got to me. It was the boy. He was clinging to one of them. Wouldn't let go. Police tried. Paramedics tried. They'd had to disturb the crime scene to get to him. I had a chat with the SIO and we discussed Holly being brought down to speak with him. I cautioned against that as Holly was so traumatised herself, she didn't need to see all this. So I had a word with him myself.

AB: Which body was he clinging to?

AF: I don't know. Their faces weren't ... I said, 'Come on now, Holly and the little one need you', etc., etc. All he did was tighten his grip on the body. He was covered in blood, I might add. No response. I asked who is the dead man, is he Jonah's dad? He shook his head. I said, 'You've done all you can for him, we'll take over now and find out what's happened. You'll have a chance to see him again and say a proper goodbye.' That's when he looks me in the eye and says, 'I'm not saying goodbye. He won't die. He's divine.'

AB: They believed they were all angels in human bodies.

AF: Yeah. He thought he could bring the dead man back to life just by wishing. I was prepared to carry on, try to encourage Jonah to come away in his own time, but it was taken out of my hands. A paramedic crept up behind Jonah – with the consent of the SIO – and administered an injection of sedative.

AB: Is that ethical?

AF: Yes. In this instance it was deemed a mental health crisis and safeguarding issue. The team were all in agreement, they'd got permission from the relevants, so ...

AB: Did the jab work?

AF: It did. He quickly became compliant. The paramedics checked him over and said he'd be best in the hands of specialist officers, social workers. Being with his girlfriend and baby would also help, they said. Just make sure he's not alone.

AB: Meanwhile, Holly was still outside with Marie-Claire?

AF: Yes. More about that in a second. The paramedics cleaned Jonah up. He was ready in about twenty minutes and I took him back to my car. [*She pauses here, as if she's thinking about how to explain the next thing. EC*] I've never said this to anyone else before, but ... there was something strange about it.

AB: That you realise now, or that you noticed then?

AF: Bit of both. I'd left Marie-Claire watching Holly and the baby. Holly was in the patrol car, Marie-Claire outside. But when I arrived back, Marie-Claire was sat in the back seat of the car and Holly was pacing outside, trying to calm the baby. I was so concerned with getting Jonah settled and getting those kids – all three of them – to social services, I didn't think about it at the time.

AB: Strange. Did Marie-Claire explain why she'd got into the patrol car and allowed Holly out?

AF: No. No, she didn't.

AB: Was she panicked? Was she trying to get out when you arrived?

AF: No. Both acted as if nothing was out of the ordinary. I was preoccupied with getting Jonah in the car and … I wanted to ask Marie-Claire if she'd come with me, or at least follow us in her car, just as back-up in case either of the teenagers made a run for it. But once I'd settled them on the back seat, I turned to look for her and she wasn't there.

AB: She'd already gone back inside?

AF: She must have. So I drove them to a children's centre with emergency accommodation.

AB: What were they like with each other? Affectionate?

AF: Absolutely not. They sat as far apart as they could get. You know what kids in care are like. [*A heavy pause here. EC*]

AB: What are they like?

AF: Troubled. Insecure. Suspicious of others – especially adults …

AB: What happened when you got to the children's centre?

AF: The duty manager was waiting for us. I exchanged a few formalities with her and was about to make my way back to the car, when I looked up to see Jonah with a knife in his hand. He must've taken it from the scene.

AB: Who was he threatening with it?

AF: He was staring at Holly, but I … in those split seconds I thought his intent was to hurt the baby. So the training kicks in, I grab his wrist, knock the knife away, get the handcuffs out. I haul him to the car to cool off. I'd confiscated the blade, but still had to make a decision. Do I take him in and at least threaten him with a charge of possession, or do I release him, on the basis the kid's been through a lot?

AB: What decision did you make?

AF: I should have taken him in and charged him. For his own safety, at least.

AB: Sounds reasonable to me.

AF: But instead I opened the car door, unlocked the handcuffs and ushered him back to the unit. [*Long pause here. EC*] I drove off on my own and radioed that I was free for the next call.

AB: Why?

AF: Even now, I don't know.
       [*I ignored the muted pleasantries from here on. EC*]

Article printed out from *The Bookseller* dated 25 June 2021:

Kronos bag Bailey for Eclipse

The Doorstep author Amanda Bailey is the latest high-profile signing to Kronos Books' *Eclipse*. The new true crime imprint launches this autumn with titles by Minnie Davis and Craig Turner. Bailey will focus on an as yet untitled book about the Alperton Angels for publication in Q1 of 2023.

Email from amateur detective David Polneath. Sent to the contact page of my website, amandabailey.co.uk, 25 June 2021:

TO: Amanda Bailey
DATE: 25 June 2021
SUBJECT: The Alperton Angels
FROM: David Polneath

Dear Amanda,

I see you're working on a book about the Alperton Angels. I am a keen amateur sleuth and have been investigating this particular case for years. I have various theories and opinions and would like to offer my services as an assistant or a researcher, or whatever you need.

For instance, I believe Gabriel Angelis did not kill Harpinder Singh – he was convicted on a single piece of evidence that could easily have been planted. There was a cover-up which started that night and continues to this day. If you doubt what I'm saying, read all the news reports you can find online from that week. Read them, and *then* tell me how many bodies were found in that warehouse.

You won't have to pay me. I'm retired and this is my hobby.
David Polneath

FaceTime interview with Maggie Keenan, manager on overnight duty
at Willesden Children's Centre on 10 December 2003, 25 June 2021.
Transcribed by Ellie Cooper.

AB: Thank you for agreeing to be interviewed. I understand you no
longer work in social services.

MK: No, left years ago. Not for me. Too much aggro. Not enough
money or support. [*I left out a long speech complaining about
bureaucracy, accountability and middle management. EC*]

AB: As I said on the phone, I'm writing about the Alperton Angels
and understand you were on duty in Willesden when the
teenagers and their baby escaped. What happened?

MK: Uh-huh. Well, I was on the overnight shift at the unit. We were
almost full and my colleague had rung in sick. I got the call there
were two seventeen-year-olds and a baby in need of emergency
overnight accommodation. I said we only had one room. It was
then sold to me they were a couple and it was their baby, so I
said, OK, we'll work something out just for the night. What was
left of it, as it was gone one by then. So they arrive. A woman
police officer with these two kids—

AB: Holly and Jonah. What were they like?

MK: Well, for a start those weren't their real names. The Angels
renamed them. That's what cults do. They erase the old you,
along with your friends, family, possessions, life. You're reborn
with the cult as your family. Anyway, I had these two filthy kids
on the doorstep with a baby. They didn't have food, nappies,
nothing. I was pretty sure we were completely out of *all* baby
things – babies usually go straight to emergency foster families.
So that was my initial headache. What am I gonna do with these
three until morning? The teenagers had clearly been through
some shit, though they were fine physically. I recall asking
the officer where their things were, but they didn't have any.

Nothing. We kept a supply of donated clothes, so I was running that through my head. Get them cleaned up, pyjamas, fresh clothes for the morning and into bed.

AB: What was the police officer like?

MK: Nice girl. On her own, though, and shaken from what she'd seen. She left the car engine running, dumped the trio on me, then couldn't get away fast enough. [*Strange, that's not how the police officer remembers it. EC*]

AB: When did Jonah pull the knife out?

MK: Er ... he didn't. Not that I saw.

AB: Really? Didn't Jonah have a concealed blade and threaten the baby?

MK: No! I'd have remembered that.

AB: Well, Aileen recalls an incident with Jonah as she was leaving. She had to wrestle the blade off him.

MK: Who's Aileen?

AB: Sergeant Aileen Forsyth. The police officer.

MK: She had a French name, double-barrelled. Marie-Claude or something.

AB: So, she was a woman of colour?

MK: No. White as me!

AB: I spoke to Aileen yesterday. She explained how she collected Holly from the hospital and Jonah from the crime scene and drove them to you in Willesden.

MK: Only one officer came into the unit with the three kids. Maybe this Aileen was in the police car? Don't know, sorry. But I'd remember if Jonah had done that. [*She seems to have a moment of realisation. EC*] I bet it happened earlier that evening. They knew I wouldn't let a violent kid anywhere near the unit, but they wanted him off their hands ... After so long they forgot the lies they told. It was a toxic culture at that time. [*More bitching about the system. Sister, it was years ago, let it lie. EC*]

AB: Did the youngsters settle overnight?

MK: No chance. It weren't ten minutes between Marie-Claude leaving and police arriving to take the baby.

AB: Police?

MK: Man and a woman. He was white, she was black, if you're asking.

Flashed warrants. The real deal. Asked where the baby was. Marched in, closed the door in my face. Seconds later, walked out with the little 'un. Didn't say a word. [*A sad silence. EC*]

AB: How did Holly and Jonah react?

MK: Didn't sleep a wink. Spent the night staring at each other across the room. They were collected separately the following morning. I never saw either kid again. [*You start to wind up the interview, but she interrupts you. EC*]

MK: The system was in chaos, so I don't know if this is relevant. But the social worker who collected Holly the next day was expecting to collect the baby, too. It was news to them it had already been taken away. [*Bit strange? EC*]

HM PRISON TYNEFIELD

APPLICATION FOR A VISITING ORDER

PRISONER NAME: Gabriel Angelis.
DATE: 25 June 2021
YOUR NAME: Amanda Bailey.
APPLICATION STATUS: Refused by prisoner.

WhatsApp messages between me and Oliver Menzies, 25 June 2021:

> **Amanda Bailey**
> The archangel Gabriel refused to appear before me.

Oliver Menzies
I've not been refused.

> **Amanda Bailey**
> You're approved?

Oliver Menzies
Yep.

> **Amanda Bailey**
> And the governor agreed?

Oliver Menzies

Oh yes.

> **Amanda Bailey**
>
> You're winding me up.

Oliver Menzies

Nope. And he's not the interviewee I was talking about.

Oliver Menzies

Dog-tired. Phone rang at quarter to five this morning. No one there. Had to call Mum's home to see if it was them. It wasn't. By then I was awake.

> **Amanda Bailey**
>
> I can't fucking believe it.

Oliver Menzies

Let it go. I've only got a ten-minute visit. Means he can also have a personal visitor that session. He won't say anything interesting. I'll bet my career on it.

> **Amanda Bailey**
>
> Why you and not me?

Oliver Menzies

Some of us just got it.

Text messages between Corin Dallah, former press officer at the Ministry of Justice, now an artisan foodie, and me, 25 June 2021:

Corin Dallah

My friend says the governor is an old mate of Menzies' father.

> **Amanda Bailey**
>
> WTF? His mother got him a place at The Informer. Did his parents know EVERYONE?

Corin Dallah

She said they don't usually approve media visits. Don't want that cult leader getting any more attention than he has anyway.

Can you believe flocks of women write to him? 🤢 But they saw Menzies' request as an opportunity. Will Angelis finally admit to killing that man? They want to see what he says to a friendly journalist.

> **Amanda Bailey**
> I'm friendly FFS. Argh! So annoyed!

Corin Dallah
Yeah, but he's a family contact, right? Look, they're using your mate for casual intel. I wouldn't worry about it. What's he going to get in ten minutes anyway?

> **Amanda Bailey**
> Thanks, Corin, you're a star. And good luck with your posh cheese. I tried some at a farmers' market a few weeks back. It was the BEST ever.

Corin Dallah
I make bread.

> **Amanda Bailey**
> Sorry, that's what I meant.

WhatsApp messages between me and Oliver Menzies, 25 June 2021:

> **Amanda Bailey**
> 'Some of us just got it' – yeah, well-connected parents. Did you tell your dad's buddy to reject my application?

Oliver Menzies
Paranoid, much? No.

> **Amanda Bailey**
> Say I'm your close friend and colleague, ask if he'll approve my application after all.

Oliver Menzies
Amanda. It's your job to find the baby. Look for the baby 👩🏻

Amanda Bailey

Oliver Menzies

Sorry, can't talk. Preparing for my exclusive interview with Gabriel Angelis 😂

WhatsApp messages between true crime author Craig Turner and me, 26 June 2021:

Craig Turner

Hi babes, how's your weekend?

> **Amanda Bailey**
>
> I got this commission on the basis that I can find the Alperton Angels baby. But my main contact isn't playing ball and the other's retired to Portugal 💀

Craig Turner

Tell Kronos they need to splash out on a PI. Then chill.

> **Amanda Bailey**
>
> Identities masked, key info redacted, contacts melting away. Goalposts changing. Interviewees' stories not adding up and taking me nowhere. One bod died in a car crash before I could speak to him.

Craig Turner

I've never had a contact die on me. Is it something to be proud of? 😂

> **Amanda Bailey**
>
> Worst thing is: old nemesis working on a similar book. Ploy to get him vaporised backfired bigly. Now I'm grovelling to him for access to a prime bod.

Craig Turner

Who's the old nemesis? Spill please.

Amanda Bailey

Oliver Menzies. We worked together twenty years ago. He's competitive, tactless, doesn't appreciate his privilege and, well, let's just say he did something to me once – and I can't forgive him.

Craig Turner

Whoa. Sorry, babes.

Amanda Bailey

NOW HE'S GOT AN INTERVIEW WITH THE ARCHANGEL GABRIEL AND I HAVEN'T. The cult leader, in prison, up north. Grrrr! 😡

Craig Turner

Aw, babes! Hang in there. We must fix a date for a catch-up.

Amanda Bailey

When I'm in a better place with this.

Craig Turner

Will be nice to see Minnie. Heard Myra & Rose is SO good
Pippa's making it Eclipse's flagship title. So pleased for her

Amanda Bailey

Craig Turner

I had a personal relationship with MY serial killer, but fine, make hers the flagship book 🙄

Amanda Bailey

🖤

Craig Turner

I'm over it. So, when are you done writing this one?

Amanda Bailey

Haven't started 😬 Need to get the first chapter down. Then change it as new info comes in. Need to get a grip before HE steals any more of my bods.

Craig Turner

Relax. It's only a book.

> **Amanda Bailey**
>
> He winds me up so much. He can NEVER understand this case. Not the way I do.

Craig Turner

Forget him. Concentrate on that first chapter.

> **Amanda Bailey**
>
> You're right. My boss at The Informer had a mantra: stop sitting, start shitting.

Craig Turner

😄 Perfect! Don't work too hard. You know what you're like. Promise?

> **Amanda Bailey**
>
> Promise.

Divine

by

Amanda Bailey

One

When Metropolitan Police Officer [*find out his ID number*] Jonathan Childs knocked on the door, he had more than a suspicion there would be no answer. The smell.

The flat was on the X floor [*find out the floor and number*] of Middlesex House. A converted office block on the northern bank of the Grand Union Canal. Once inhabited by North Thames Gas, for decades it was the tallest building in this part of London. In 2003 Middlesex House was visible for miles around. Now, it's swamped by colourful, new, privately owned flats that boast luxurious canal-side living.

Neighbours complained about scratching sounds from rodents. A junior council officer was dispatched to investigate. They took one gasp of the putrid air in the corridor outside, and ran straight back down the [*find out the number*] flights of stairs to dial 999 and wait for someone else to do the dirty work, PC Childs thought ruefully. He stood alone in the corridor, keys in hand and a resigned, humourless smirk on his face.

One last knock, an obligatory but vain *open up, police* and he couldn't put it off any longer. *Coming in.*

***

Harpinder Singh had been moved to Middlesex House on a temporary basis just two months earlier. The place he'd been living in had burned down. A notorious residence of multiple occupancy, suspicious eyes fell on the landlord even before the fire brigade arrived. Singh wasn't there at the time. He was working at a restaurant in nearby Southall.

The manager was a distant relation of a distant relation. Singh waited tables, cleaned the kitchen after hours. He caught the 483 bus back to Middlesex House every night.

There was no shortage of people who knew him by sight. One or two mentioned he was looking forward to getting married. Whether that meant he had a bride in mind, or just anticipated a happier time in the future, they didn't seem to know.

He'd failed to turn up for work several days earlier. No one could say exactly when they'd last seen him. Nor could they shed any light on why he would have been in a neighbouring flat. One that was officially unoccupied. Awaiting refurbishment.

All PC Childs knew, as he stood in the doorway that morning in 2003, was that Harpinder Singh had been brutally murdered.

2

Second-Stage Interviews and Interacting with Members of the Public

WhatsApp message to me from true crime author Craig Turner, 27 June 2021:

Craig Turner
Just a thought. You might be able to get in on your buddy's interview. When I visited Denny-boy back in the day, official visitors (media and legal) could bring a PA. Only found out cos I'd just had my carpal tunnel done. Brought along a friend to take notes. He didn't need approval – no one even asked his name. You'd only have to convince matey to take you along 🪦

WhatsApp messages between me and my editor Pippa Deacon, 28 June 2021:

> **Amanda Bailey**
> Hi, Pippa. Gabriel has approved Oliver's visit but not mine. Only a ten-minute visit but still. I know we're focusing on the baby but an interview like that is a coup and it's wasted on him. PLEASE can you get Jo at Green Street to have a word with him and suggest STRONGLY that he takes me along as his PA. Craig says he did that with Dennis Nilsen. Tell her it's because I'm afraid Oliver will fuck it up, but she can tell him whatever.

Pippa Deacon
Can I tell her you're close to finding the baby? Eye for an eye and all that.

> **Amanda Bailey**
> Yes. Yes, absolutely tell her that.

> **Amanda Bailey**
> Surely more 'quid pro quo' than 'eye for an eye'?

WhatsApp messages between me and Oliver Menzies, 28 June 2021:

> **Amanda Bailey**
> Your Gabriel interview. You know you can take an assistant.

Oliver Menzies

I don't need an assistant.

> **Amanda Bailey**
>
> Bear in mind that – in due course – I will share the baby with you. If you take me to see Gabriel, I will do so with joy in my heart and a smile on my face.

Oliver Menzies

I'll think about it. In the meantime, let's visit The Assembly. The Alperton warehouse where shit went down.

> **Amanda Bailey**
>
> It's long gone. Luxury canal-side flats now.

Oliver Menzies

Whatever. We both need to visit, so let's go together. It'll be nice.

> **Amanda Bailey**
>
> You want my local knowledge. That's the only reason you want me there.

Oliver Menzies

Meet you at eleven on Saturday. Outside Alperton tube.

Oliver Menzies

Well? Yes or no.

> **Amanda Bailey**
>
>

WhatsApp messages between retired detective chief superintendent Don Makepeace and me, 28 June 2021:

Don Makepeace

I've tracked down your police officer Jonathan Childs.

> **Amanda Bailey**
>
> Ace! Thanks, Don. Wherever he was, I knew you'd dig him up!

Don Makepeace

He died in May of this year. Bowel cancer.

> **Amanda Bailey**
>
> Oh. Sorry to hear that.

Don Makepeace

He had a wife. Will she be useful to you?

> **Amanda Bailey**
>
> The insight she's likely to have probably won't be worth the
> time it'll take to speak with her. Thanks anyway, Don. Much
> appreciated.

> **Amanda Bailey**
>
> Actually, yes. Please can I have her details?

My email reply to amateur sleuth David Polneath, 28 June 2021:

TO: David Polneath
DATE: 28 June 2021
SUBJECT: Re: The Alperton Angels
FROM: Amanda Bailey

Dear David,

Thank you for getting in touch regarding the Alperton Angels. I'm not
in need of an assistant at this time. However, can I ask what it is about
this case you find so fascinating? I might include some vox pops as part
of the intro. I'll name check you if your quote makes it.

I've read all the news reports as you suggest. It's true there is a change
in the number of bodies reported during that week. Only, I've worked
in newsrooms myself and can assure you that's a very common discrepancy. The police try to keep numbers out of the press, while reporters are
interested almost exclusively in 'how many dead'. It's a whispering game.

However, that's not to say this is an easy case to research. Forthcoming
interviewees are few and far between. Plus, the ring of secrecy around
the baby in particular – and the teenagers, too – makes untangling the
facts all these years later somewhat tricky.

Can I ask: do you have any contacts who worked in police or social services at the time, and who have proven honest, plausible and useful to your own research? If so, then I will be eternally grateful if you could let me have their details – or pass mine on to them. Have no doubt I will mention you in the acknowledgements if they do.

All the best,

Amanda Bailey

Interview with Penny Latke, A&E nurse at Ealing Hospital on the night Holly and the baby were brought in. Takes place at the bus stop outside Ealing Hospital, 28 June 2021. Transcribed by Ellie Cooper.

AB: Thanks, Penny. Really app—

PL: Thank YOU! Really pleased to help.

AB: I'm—

PL: Didn't realise at the time I'd be involved in such a famous case. Been fascinated by it ever since. Read everything I could get hold of. You've seen *Dereliction* and *The Assembly*? I've got both on Blu-ray. Did you see *Inside No. 9*? And now I'm helping you write a book about it. Great, hey?

AB: [*No chance to answer. EC*]

PL: I'll tell you all about what happened from start to finish. Is that what you want?

AB: [*Whether it's what you want or not, it's what you're getting. EC*]

PL: It was an ordinary night shift in emergency. Busy. No hint we were about to go down in history with one of the most notorious mass murder cults of all time. I was on the desk when she came in. This is Holly, the teenage mum. She was covered in blood like Carrie in *Carrie*. What you don't realise when you're watching horror films is that blood *really* smells. I've read that it's primeval, like we can smell blood really clearly. It's part of our hunting and scavenging senses, so when it's animal blood it's basically food. But if we smell *human* blood, there's likely a danger to life, i.e. *our* life, so we're instinctively repelled by that. Food or danger it's all survival. But in a hospital we have disinfectant that neutralises it. Anyway, I'd been working

77

here a few years so I was immune to it all. But this girl. I could smell her as soon as she walked in. People stopped talking and stared. Not only was she RED all over, she had a baby in a carrier bag. Yeah, kid about four, six weeks. When I say she was out of it, I mean she was WELL out of it. First thought was drugs, psychotic episode, severe trauma, all of the above.

AB: Did you—

PL: Yeah, a colleague came straight away and took the baby away for assessment. When you see a child like that. Well, it's what you go into the job for. Turned out it was fine, just stressed and hungry.

AB: Can you remember if it was a boy or girl?

PL: Stupid, but I can't. Not even sure if I ever knew. Like I said, I didn't realise it would be a big case and I was focused on the young mum. All that blood. Later we'd find out it had come from the dead angels. You know the police didn't see it? They picked the girl up, drove her here and dropped her off at the door, but didn't see the baby in the bag. Unbelievable, right? But not if you look at it another way.

AB: It's— [*Let the woman speak, Mand. OMG you're hogging this convo. EC*]

PL: I've heard something really, really interesting. [*She lowers her voice here; this is going to be either interesting or crazy. EC*] I'm not saying I believe it myself, but I know people who do and I'm happy to put it out there. See, people who know a bit about the occult ... they say it's *not* that the police officers were lazy and neglectful and all the other things they were accused of. They didn't see that baby because it was hidden from human sight by a host of dark angels that were protecting it from harm. But you know what? I think there's an even *more* exciting theory. That the baby hid *itself* from their sight. Supernaturally. It doesn't need angels because it has its own protective energy. Anyway, I'm interested in everyone's opinion so I'm open-minded. At the time, other colleagues examined the child and cleaned it up, while we spoke with Holly and ... it's weird. She talks quite calmly but what she says makes no sense. Angels, devils, The Assembly, the alignment. We suspect post-partum psychosis.

Not our department so we prepare a referral – a pathway so she can get a diagnosis and treatment in a psych ward or whatever.

AB: Wh—

PL: About an hour after Holly and the baby arrived, a policewoman turned up asking where the girl and baby were, as she had a call to take them to a specialist centre.

AB: Who—

PL: No idea. But the police who brought the girl in had driven straight off, so it was our best guess they'd radioed for this woman to take over. She was in uniform and seemed to have a plan, so we discharged Holly and the baby into her care.

AB: She had—

PL: Yeah, the policewoman had the letter of referral.

AB: You weren't—

PL: Not at all. She was taking care of the child and seemed bonded to it. That's the strange thing with PP. It's a delusion of the conscious mind, but when a woman gives birth the mothering instinct is so strongly rooted in the subconscious ... they tell you their baby is a demon while changing its nappy and giving it a bottle.

AB: Do you—

PL: No. What happened to them after that was out of our hands. I forgot about it till I saw the murders on the news and realised *that* was the girl who rescued the kid. Real names were kept out of the papers, but eventually they used Holly and the boy's name, Jonah, because they weren't their names anyway. If only I'd known at the time, I'd have asked her more questions.

AB: What—

PL: Oh, I don't think they were actually angels. I just find it fascinating what people believe. If someone you trust tells you something and *they're* convinced of it, do you go with the flow? Or is it that if someone has power over you, you just don't have the confidence or energy or whatever, to challenge them? Because some people have that charisma, don't they? Born leaders. They tell you they have the answers, in such a way you believe they really do. But just because someone is a born leader, doesn't mean you should follow them. [*She pauses here. First time since the interview started. EC*]

79

AB: Is there—
PL: Yes. I think there is.
AB: But you don't know what I was about to ask.
PL: Was it: 'Is there such a thing as evil?'
AB: [*A sharp intake of breath. EC*] Yes.
        [*Just thank-yous and goodbyes from here. Messaging you. EC*]

WhatsApp messages between Ellie Cooper and me, 28 June 2021:

Ellie Cooper
There are some odd discrepancies in what people remember
from that night. Have you noticed?

> **Amanda Bailey**
> I have 😑

Ellie Cooper
Like the disappearing symbols in the warehouse. Whether
Jonah had a knife or not. Whether the baby was taken by police
or social services.

> **Amanda Bailey**
> Police, social services – or someone else.

Ellie Cooper

My email reply to Cathy-June Lloyd, Cold & Unsolved Murder Club chair, 28 June 2021:

TO: Cathy-June Lloyd
DATE: 28 June 2021
SUBJECT: Re: A small favour
FROM: Amanda Bailey

Hi Cathy-June,

Thanks for your letter. I'm delighted you enjoyed *The Doorstep*. Sadly, I will have to turn down the kind offer to speak at your next meeting, as I am currently writing my fourth book. It's about the Alperton Angels. You may remember the story from 2003. By any chance, has your club looked at this case? It's turning into something of a mystery – then and now.

If you have, and can pinpoint any areas of interest, do let me know. Or if you've managed to speak with anyone connected to the case – I'm especially keen to contact the baby, who is now an adult. I will happily credit you in the acknowledgements if you can dig up anything interesting. Best wishes and happy sleuthing!

Amanda Bailey

Text messages between me and Dave 'Itchy' Kilmore at *Fresh Ghost* podcast, 28 June 2021:

> **Amanda Bailey**
> Hey! I loved chatting with you on Fresh Ghost last time, delighted to do it again. I'm writing a book on the Alperton Angels. Can I ask your listeners for information and contacts? Really keen to get grass-roots comment into this one.

Dave 'Itchy' Kilmore
You can ask our listeners anything, Mandy. We love grass-roots comment – it's what Fresh Ghost is all about. Will be in touch with dates and times.

Scribbled notes from my phone call with Sonia Brown, 29 June 2021:

Sonia – Mr Blue – will text

Text messages between Mr Blue and me, 29 June 2021:

Mr Blue
Our mutual friend gave me your number.

> **Amanda Bailey**
> How do we play this?

Mr Blue

What do you need?

> **Amanda Bailey**
>
> The whereabouts of three minors who passed through Brent social services in 2003. I have no budget.

Mr Blue

Their names?

> **Amanda Bailey**
>
> The Alperton Angels teenagers and baby. Names unknown.

WhatsApp messages between me and Oliver Menzies during the course of our visit to the site of The Assembly, 3 July 2021:

> **Amanda Bailey**
>
> If I get to Alperton and you're not there, I'm visiting the site on my own. I mean it.

Oliver Menzies

Chill out! On the train approaching the station now.

> **Amanda Bailey**
>
> Me too. We must be on the same train.

Oliver Menzies

Bet these apartments cost a mint.

> **Amanda Bailey**
>
> Imagine discovering your luxury canal-side flat is built on the site of notorious ritualistic deaths 💀

Oliver Menzies

Wouldn't bother me. Not when I had tube trains roaring past my window every four minutes. We're here.

Later, after we visited the site:

Oliver Menzies
Stop pissing about.

Oliver Menzies
FFS where are you?

> **Amanda Bailey**
> Got something to show you. Quick. Come back past the lifts to the stairs.

Outside an electronic public toilet. After I showed Oliver the symbols and he keeled over:

> **Amanda Bailey**
> Feeling better?

> **Amanda Bailey**
> These Dalek toilets freak me out. Are you stuck? Shall I call 999?

Oliver Menzies
NO! I'm fine. Stop knocking FFS.

> **Amanda Bailey**
> You keeled over! Thought you'd choked on one of my chewy mints. Been looking into where that might leave me, legally.

Oliver Menzies
Thanks for your concern. Didn't keel over! Felt shaky that's all.

> **Amanda Bailey**
> Are you coming out?

Oliver Menzies
No, but there ARE some good-looking guys around 😄 Just sitting here for a bit till shaking stops.

> **Amanda Bailey**
> OK. Well, I'm going back to take more pics of the symbols.

Oliver Menzies

Are you claiming them as occult? Because it's clear to me what
they are: spray-paint graffiti tags the council tried to remove
and almost did.

> **Amanda Bailey**
>
> This area has been razed and rebuilt in the last eighteen years.
> Those symbols were painted recently. There could be people
> who still follow the ethos of the cult and believe themselves to
> be angels.

Oliver Menzies

> **Amanda Bailey**
>
> Let me run something past you. From old photographs and
> what I know about this area, those symbols are painted
> EXACTLY where the Alperton Angels summoned dark powers
> and ritually died. What if you picked up on that negative
> energy and keeled over?

Oliver Menzies

What a pile of bullshit. It felt like one of my coffee-induced
turns. Brain-dead barista must have forgotten I said decaf.
Caffeine doesn't agree with me. That's all.

Oliver Menzies

Didn't keel over.

> **Amanda Bailey**
>
> BTW if it isn't Gabriel, who is this mystery interviewee you've
> got that I'll never know about?

Oliver Menzies

HA HA! I KNEW you wouldn't forget that! I KNEW it! Love
winding you up, Mandy, you're so transparent.

Meeting between Amanda Bailey and Oliver Menzies in a pub, after their visit to Alperton, 3 July 2021. Transcribed by Ellie Cooper.

[*It seems to start in the middle of a conversation. Are you secretly recording him? EC*]

OM: Then towards the end of the process, I saw this other side to him. He suddenly hated the draft. Would call me at all hours. Make threats that weren't threats, but they were. When I tried to escalate my concerns he played the PTSD card. With his military training and all the stuff we had to leave out about him killing civilians, no one wanted to confront his behaviour. They were shit scared! He'd hinted all along he had connections in MI5, MI6 and MI-so-secret-no-one-knows-the-number. Did I mention, that call I got at quarter to five in the morning? Thought it was Mum's care home. Well, not only was it *him*, but he now calls me *every* morning at quarter to five. *Every* morning the phone rings, creepy rasping sounds when I answer.

AB: Switch your phone off. [*He must shake his head here. EC*] Why not?

OM: Landline. I have to answer or it keeps ringing. I could unplug it or get the whole thing taken away, but a legal friend says to log all the calls so there's a decent stack of evidence for future action. I've had to print out digital copies of all my correspondence with him, every email, every message, *and* print out every single one of my WhatsApp convos over two years. Might as well have chopped down a whole tree.

AB: Do you know for sure it's him?

OM: *Yes!* The number's withheld but who else? He's a brainwashed, OCD pedant, with no empathy and a good working knowledge of secret comms. He gets up at three thirty every morning to stand on his head for an hour. He has zero respect for the rules of engagement. Laughed about gouging out the eyes of soldiers they'd captured in Afghanistan. Who else would it be?

AB: He stands on his head then calls you. Every morning?

OM: I'm part of his routine now. Then there's Frank the friendly bobby. He's another story. Mand, I don't want to spend years slaving away just so these brick-headed oafs who left school at fifteen can post on Twitter that their teachers said they'd come to nothing but now they've written a book. I want to do it on my own. I can do it. I thought this would be it. Then suddenly I'm shackled to *you* of all people.

AB: Thanks.

OM: You know what I mean. You're so fucking focused.

AB: Am I?

OM: Yes, it's annoying.

AB: Have another shot. [*He makes a groaning noise, is he drunk? EC*] You OK, Ol?

OM: Yeah, yeah. Since starting this. Not connected to anything, just suddenly, I feel nauseous and ...

AB: Panic attacks? Deadline dread. [*I think he might be a bit pissed, Mand. EC*]

OM: Doesn't feel like panic.

AB: This pub could be a vortex of supernatural activity. You're a sensitive spiritual portal, remember.

OM: Found the baby yet? [*Do you shrug or something? EC*] It's all gone quiet over there.

AB: Takes time to sort out. Lawyers. Back and forth.

OM: Bullshit. You haven't found it. No one's squealing. You're winging it.

AB: Everyone's 'winging it' all the time ... Remember when we were at *The Informer*?

OM: Oh God, *that* shitshow ...

AB: You were like a snail in the headlights.

OM: I was navigating an inadequate training programme. Like we all were.

AB: Inadequate? You know where Louisa is now?

OM: Yeah, she got to be editor right when the paper went online. Talks like she works for CNN – spends all day trawling Twitter for rubberneckers' snaps of police cordons. Doesn't even produce a printed paper any more—

AB: Still, we had training—

OM: [*He bursts out laughing. EC*] They tried to recreate the old apprenticeship schemes. The industry had moved on even then.

Utterly pointless, and I knew it at the time.

AB: That is *not* why you have bad memories. Oh my God, you're gaslighting yourself. *You* couldn't bear to be somewhere everyone else was more talented than you. For the first time in your *life* you had to work. But even when you did, you were *still* running to catch up. And especially with me. I'm not *focused*. I can see the *real* you. That's why I annoy you, even now—

OM: That is such a load of—

AB: Your response was to put me down. Make me look stupid whenever and however you could—

OM: You're talking shit. As ever. That is *not* how it was ...

AB: I was younger than you, I was less educated, *un*-educated in fact, and I was *different*—

OM: Yeah! You smelled of vinegar!

AB: What the fuck?

OM: From the *chip* on your shoulder! [*Mand, you're both hammered. I'm embarrassed listening to it. EC*]

AB: You have no idea ... That scheme was the *best* thing that ever happened to me. It changed my life. [*OMG, Mand, you're getting really upset. It's horrible. EC*]

OM: And I couldn't care less! It was *years* ago – get over it!

AB: You couldn't handle it, so you—

OM: Bollocks—

AB: And that's why you—

UV: [*Unknown voice. EC*] Can you keep it down please? There's people trying to talk at other tables.

AB: Sorry.

OM: Very sorry. [*He whispers. EC*] At least I finished the course. You bottled it.

AB: [*You whisper. EC*] I was *forced* to leave!

OM: Whatever you tell yourself now, you couldn't hack it. Simple.

AB: Are you fucking serious? You genuinely do not remember?

OM: No, I don't. [*Sounds genuine. He really doesn't. EC*]

AB: Nothing plays on your mind from that time? Nothing you might have done?

OM: No.

AB: OK, fine. Fine. You're right. It's in the past. [*Long contemplative silence. EC*]

OM: Look, what's gone is gone. I want us to work together. I don't want to fall out.

AB: Nor do I ... but you ... [*You're both tearful now. Never play this to anyone, Mand. EC*]

AB: I just wish you hadn't ... things could've been different ... we could've been different.

OM: Twenty years ago. Get over it.

AB: I'm over it. Over it. Friends? Ish?

OM: Friends. Ish.
      [*Ends abruptly when you switch off. EC*]

Text messages I should never have sent to Mr Blue when I got home on 3 July 2021:

Amanda Bailey
Where's the baby do you know or not?

Amanda Bailey
Who are you anyway?

Amanda Bailey
Bet you're just Sonia avoiding me? Don't even jucking know, Typical fuking social wprkser.

Amanda Bailey
💩💩💩💩💩💩💩💩

Email from my former colleague Louisa Sinclair, now editor of WembleyOnline:

TO: Amanda Bailey
DATE: 4 July 2021
SUBJECT: Re: The Alperton Angels
FROM: Louisa Sinclair

Hi Mandy,

Remember the days when a junior would cut out and scrapbook news articles so we had a library by subject rather than date? Really useful in future when researching old cases. Well, we'd long since abandoned all that in 2003.

Had to come in on a Sunday anyway, so mined our digital archives and have an envelope of printouts. You'll have found most things online, but these include spiked pieces that never made the paper for one reason or another.

Drop in tomorrow at 1 p.m. and we'll chat about the old days. Only for 15 minutes, mind. There's an editorial meeting at 1.30 p.m. and the queues in Pret are biblical.
Louisa Sinclair
Editor, WembleyOnline

A list of archived news items. No body text, no dates, just headlines:

POLICE: FOUR DEAD, THREE INJURED INCLUDING BABY

POLICE: SCENE IN WAREHOUSE 'GRUESOME'

FOURTH BODY LINKED TO THE ALPERTON ANGELS

CORONER: 'ANGEL' DEATHS SUICIDES

POLICE: ANGEL DEATHS 'RITUALISTIC'

RIDDLE OF THE ALPERTON ANGELS – THE FULL STORY

ALPERTON ANGELS 'ON MISSION TO SAVE MANKIND'

JURY RETIRES IN ALPERTON ANGEL MURDER TRIAL

WAITER'S FAMILY 'RELIEVED' AT GUILTY VERDICT

SURVIVING ALPERTON ANGEL JAILED FOR LIFE

ALPERTON ANGELS 999 COPS 'NEGLIGENT'

SOCIAL WORKERS FACE PANEL IN ALPERTON
ANGELS INQUIRY

WhatsApp messages between me and Oliver Menzies on the morning of 4 July 2021:

Amanda Bailey

DON'T imagine LICKING COLD FRIED EGG YOLK running in GLOBULES down a TRAMP'S CHIN 🤮

Oliver Menzies

So you want to make me feel sick. Nice try. Didn't work.

Amanda Bailey

Can't ever go back to that pub. You OK?

Oliver Menzies

Apart from early-morning wake-up call from mad squaddie.

Amanda Bailey

When are you visiting Gabriel?

Oliver Menzies

Why is everyone so interested in this interview FFS?

Oliver Menzies

Wait. Have you been on to Jo? I BET that's why she keeps telling me to take an assistant! So transparent.

Amanda Bailey

He's allowed a thirty-minute visit per week – either one person or family group, or two separate visits of ten and twenty minutes respectively. We'll have to join a queue of adoring women fans.

Oliver Menzies

Sigh.

Amanda Bailey

I'll record the whole thing, take notes and get the interview transcribed asap afterwards. You concentrate on the chat.

Oliver Menzies

'Get it transcribed'? By a human being?

Amanda Bailey

Yes. Ellie. My one-time protégé. Left Kronos to do a PhD in criminal psychology. She transcribes interviews very quickly and very well. I highly recommend her.

Oliver Menzies

You do, you live in 2001.

Amanda Bailey

Should you take me along, I will pay for her transcription services. Which means the record will be properly punctuated, comprehensive and accurate, with small talk and pleasantries erased so only key, salient points remain. Unlike any software you can run it through. How does that sound?

Oliver Menzies

Spoken to the baby yet?

Amanda Bailey

Nearly there, believe me. Nearly there.

Amanda Bailey

Take me with you. Go on. In front of the archangel Gabriel you'll look like a big shot with your own assistant.

Oliver Menzies

They won't let you in. He REFUSED to see you remember 😄

Amanda Bailey

Not a problem. Say you've had a carpal tunnel op and need someone to take notes. They won't even ask my name.

Oliver Menzies

You expect me to visit the archangel Gabriel with my arm in a fake sling.

Amanda Bailey

Of course not! Just a small bandage.

Another email about the baby from Pippa, 5 July 2021:

TO: Amanda Bailey
DATE: 5 July 2021
SUBJECT: Baby
FROM: Pippa Deacon

Hi Amanda,

The OH is drafting a contract between her TV production company and the Alperton Angels baby. She wants to open up a dialogue with the baby – or if they have people in place, a dialogue with the baby's people – as soon as humanly poss. Now there are two of you working on two books it's particularly important to get the paperwork drawn up, finalised and signed.

Please let me know where we are with the baby.

Pips

My WhatsApp reply, 5 July 2021:

> **Amanda Bailey**
> Can you give me a few more days? Almost there 🥚

Text message to Mr Blue, 5 July 2021:

> **Amanda Bailey**
> Dear Mr Blue, I'm very sorry for the confused messages you received from my phone late Saturday night. It was in my pocket, unlocked, and my rubberised key fob knocked against it. Please be assured I am still very keen to locate the three young people from the Alperton Angels case, but especially, and most urgently, the baby. Any information you can give me to this end will be very gratefully received. Again, many apologies for my phone.

Phone interview with Julian Nowak, a social worker, 5 July 2021. Transcribed by Ellie Cooper.

> [*I'd usually cut out pleasantries and small talk, but there wasn't any. EC*]

JN: Who gave you my name?

AB: I'm in touch with several people across police and social services.

JN: Who mentioned me? Why me in particular?

AB: I can't say, or they'll not trust me again.

JN: [*Silence. He's not happy. EC*] I'm not happy to be associated with this case. I wasn't responsible for the failures just because I spoke out about them.

AB: I know ... What is it about Holly's case that still rankles?

JN: You see something happen. You can choose to escalate it and bring down a ton of bricks on your own head, or you can pretend you never saw it and ...

AB: Nothing happens, sure ...

JN: And the kid fights to stay with their inappropriate boyfriend. So ...

AB: I know, I mean it's ...

JN: All we did was respect Holly's choice. She chose to go off with him and we respected that.

AB: With Jonah?

JN: His name was Gabriel. [*Bit of a pause while you both consider what he's said. EC*]

AB: When did the relationship begin?

JN: I don't know.

AB: The Alperton Angels case was December 2003.

JN: I dealt with Holly not long after I qualified. Early nineties.

AB: It must've been later than that. [*I cut out various frosty pleasantries before he hangs up. EC*] Ellie, I don't think we were talking about the same case. Don must've got social workers mixed up.

> [*I'd already transcribed this, so sending it to you anyway. EC*]

93

TO: Grace Childs
DATE: 5 July 2021
SUBJECT: Jonathan Childs
FROM: Amanda Bailey

Dear Mrs Childs,
Please let me introduce myself. I am a best-selling true crime author with a long track record in crime reporting and human-interest journalism. My current commission is a book about the Alperton Angels. I understand your late husband Jonathan found Harpinder Singh's body – I wonder if he mentioned anything to you about the murder scene, or the victim?

Press at the time took the unusual step of naming Mr Childs. Do you have any idea why they might have done that? Articles say he found the body in an empty flat. Did he happen to mention the number of that flat, or the floor it was on? Also, it would be useful to have his police number.

Anything you recall, however insignificant it might seem, may help me piece together the disparate elements of this case.
Yours sincerely,
Amanda Bailey

TO: Amanda Bailey
DATE: 5 July 2021
SUBJECT: Re: Jonathan Childs
FROM: Grace Childs

Dear Miss Bailey,
Johnny didn't speak much about his work and especially not bodies. But I remember something from around that time. A neighbour showed him his name in the paper, all proud that he knew him. Johnny shrugged it off, as if he was being modest, but later said to me it wasn't him who found that body. He said the timings were all wrong deliberately. I wondered how they got his name, and he said they just wanted to scare him, but that it was nothing and I shouldn't worry.

You probably know that when he was diagnosed with cancer he had been suspended under investigation for alleged offences. They said he was recruited by a gang and had spent years passing information and manipulating evidence. All sorts of rubbish. The stress had an impact on his health. These people are no better than criminals. Once they have something on you, they use it to keep you working for them.

Johnny had a habit of getting pulled into other people's shifty business. His police number was 444.

Grace Childs

Meeting with Louisa Sinclair, editor of WembleyOnline, at Pret A Manger, Wembley, 5 July 2021. Transcribed by Ellie Cooper.

> [*It seems to start abruptly, as if you pressed 'record' as soon as you could without being noticed. EC*]

LS: One minute you know everything there is about a subject, then the article is printed and whoosh, all gone.

AB: I'm the same.

LS: Reading over those old clippings, though ... You'd left by then. Come to think about it, you left before the final assessment. Why was that?

AB: I must've got the job in Hove, so ... You know Oliver Menzies has popped up again.

LS: [*Awkward hesitation. EC*] Yes, actually. Probably shouldn't tell you, but he's asked for info on the Alperton Angels too.

AB: Sounds about right.

LS: You know, I always thought the two of you were similar.

AB: What? Oh my—

LS: Both driven, hungry, competitive and ... Well, you had the talent, but no support or security behind you. He had that grounding, but no talent. [*You both laugh. EC*] Well, not none, but you know what I mean, and he *hated* that.

AB: Believe it or not, we're working together on this case. Saves time and safeguarding issues. I was pissed off at first, but now I'm determined to make it work ... turn it into an opportunity.

LS: [*Gasps so loudly, she almost sucks the oxygen from the room. EC*] Don't tell me you're having a torrid affair!

AB: No!

LS: An opportunity for *what*?

AB: To revisit something in the past that's not been … settled. They say never go back, but if the past comes to find you, there has to be a reason, right? [*You both chew and sip drinks for just under a minute. EC*]

LS: So, you reckon there's something extra shady about Harpinder Singh's murder?

AB: About how it was reported. If police think Singh is killed by an organised crime group and they suspect Childs is involved with them, naming him is an attempt to flush him out. It ties in with what his widow said, about how he reacted to the piece and the fact he was under investigation when he died – but that was recently. Not eighteen years ago.

LS: There's no byline. Let me ask around. [*Oh great. One of you opens a bag of crisps. I expect a medal for transcribing under these circumstances. EC*]

AB: Never mind why I left, why are you still there?

LS: Good question. Still waiting for my moment.

AB: You're already editor.

LS: I mean *that* story. The one where you have it and no one else does. It's yours to break.

AB: Is WembleyOnline the best place?

LS: Good as any. Shit, got to get back. On my own at the news desk. [*Your goodbyes are followed by two whole minutes of thoughtful crunching. EC*]

I sent him an email on 13 June but finally got a reply from Phil Priest, TV producer who worked on a drama inspired by the angels ten years ago:

TO: Amanda Bailey
DATE: 5 July 2021
SUBJECT: Re: The Assembly
FROM: Phil Priest

Hi Amanda,

Good to hear from you. Thanks for watching *The Assembly*. Yes, it was inspired by the Alperton Angels, but we didn't set out to make a realistic dramatisation and took a number of turns away from the real-life story.

All our victims are female, for example, so we could have more explicit scenes. The action takes place in Ireland, where it was cheaper to film. In real life the angels either killed themselves or were jailed. In our series the ground opens up and engulfs them in satanic flame, a finale we are still very proud of.

We kept in touch with Due Process Films who were making *Dereliction* at the same time. Theirs is a much starker, grittier rendering. More realistic, though, dare I say it, boring. Our writer didn't speak to anyone involved in the case so can't see how I'd be of any further help. There was another script knocking around a few years ago. It was pretty good if I remember, but the writer was a beginner and didn't have any traction. It was called *Divine*. Can't remember their name, sorry.

Phil Priest

Executive producer

Longshanks Film & TV

TV producer Debbie Condon also finally replied to my email of 13 June 2021:

TO: Amanda Bailey
DATE: 6 July 2021
SUBJECT: Re: Dereliction
FROM: Debbie Condon

Dear Amanda,

Firstly, apologies for taking so long to reply. I am in pre-production for a new series and can only answer emails one day a week. I enjoyed your Suzy Lamplugh book *Kipper Tied*. It grates with me that most books and screenplays about murdered women are written by men. Happy to help wherever I can.

I'm so pleased you liked our TV series. It's never an easy road when you're bringing authority to account. These people think themselves above reproach. They make poor decisions and cause untold suffering among the most vulnerable in society – then band together to protect each other. *Dereliction* was a labour of love that almost didn't make it to the screen, as an altogether more cartoonish, salacious treatment of the same story was in production simultaneously. We came to a mutual agreement in the end. Collaborated to ensure we each focused on different elements of the story and as a result both series had their moment. I still think ours was the more mature and appropriate. It was hugely satisfying to speak truth to power.

Will you mention the series in your book? You are welcome to use any of the quotes above. I'm not sure how else I can help, but here's my number if you have any questions. 07███████

Best wishes,
Debbie Condon
Executive Producer
Due Process Films

Text messages between me and Debbie Condon, 6 July 2021, with a sensitive phone number redacted:

> **Amanda Bailey**
> Thanks for your reply, Debbie. I'm finding it tough to locate people directly involved in the case.

Debbie Condon
Even if I were as indiscreet as that, the details would be a decade out of date.

CONTACT
Unknown number
'Jonah' 07███████

> **Amanda Bailey**
> I totally understand, Debbie. Thank you. I'll credit you and mention the TV series if I use any of your quotes.

Script for my phone call to 'Jonah', 6 July 2021:

'Hi Jonah, my name is Amanda Bailey. I understand you were one of the teenage victims of the Alperton Angels. Believe me when I say I completely empathise with the circumstances that led you to fall victim to such a predatory cult. I'm writing a book about the case and would like to invite you to tell your side of the story. This way the account will be as truthful and accurate as possible.'

Not his phone any more. Whose? Wouldn't say who she was. Core Abbey, Isle of Wight.

WhatsApp messages between me and Oliver Menzies, 7 July 2021:

> **Amanda Bailey**
> Your mum shares lost dog posts from other countries 😂

Oliver Menzies
I doubt it, she's in a home.

> **Amanda Bailey**
> Confirm you'll take me on your prison visit and you can come with me to interview Jonah on Friday. No one could say fairer than that.

Oliver Menzies
THE Jonah? Seriously? It's all organised?

> **Amanda Bailey**
> You'd be mad to turn this opportunity down.

Oliver Menzies
OK. But only because we should move forward in the spirit of working together and sharing the process.

> **Amanda Bailey**
> Agreed.

Oliver Menzies
OK. Where are we meeting him?

> **Amanda Bailey**
> It'll be a whole day out. An adventure.

Oliver Menzies

So, it's a long drive and I'm at the wheel.

> **Amanda Bailey**
>
> Also, can you book a ferry on your Green Street expenses?

WhatsApp messages between me and retired detective chief superintendent Don Makepeace, 7 July 2021:

> **Amanda Bailey**
>
> Hey, Don. I'm counting on the magic M40 corridor. A police officer called Marie-Claire. Is she still serving?

Don Makepeace

I'd remember that name. Very pretty. Don't know her but will ask around. Don.

WhatsApp messages between WembleyOnline editor Louisa Sinclair and me, 8 July 2021:

Louisa Sinclair

Remember Gray Graham? He was on the ground for that case. Retired now, but says he was given Jonathan Childs's name by a senior officer, with a REQUEST that the name appear in print.

> **Amanda Bailey**
>
> Bingo. My hunch was correct 😊

Louisa Sinclair

Looks like it. The restaurant where Singh worked was raided a few months later.

> **Amanda Bailey**
>
> They wanted to compromise Childs's relationship with the OCG.

Louisa Sinclair

Turn him into an informer. Message Gray yourself if you can bear his war stories from the good old days. Credit where it's due, he

had a sixth sense for a story. No idea how he got half the stuff
he filed. They don't make them like that these days.

Text message from me to retired local news reporter Gray Graham, 8 July 2021:

> ### Amanda Bailey
> Hi Gray, Louisa Sinclair gave me your number. You probably
> won't remember speaking to me at an Informer party years
> ago, but I remember your stories and anecdotes. I'm working
> on a book about the Alperton Angels. You did some initial news
> reporting for the murder of Harpinder Singh. Any ideas why the
> police asked you to name the officer first on the scene?

No reply until 10 July 2021:

Unknown number
This is the Medway NHS Trust. I'm so sorry to inform you Mr Graham
passed away with his phone in his hand. Your message was the last
thing he saw. He'd pressed reply, but sadly suffered a heart attack
before he could type his response. Are you a relative and if not, do
you know if he had any? We are trying to sort out his affairs and
have drawn a blank.

> ### Amanda Bailey
> I am so sorry to hear this sad news. I'm not strictly a relative,
> but we were VERY close. I'm more than happy to pop round to
> his place and help clear out any documents that may be there.

Unknown number
Thank you. I'll pass your details on.

A page torn from the novel *My Angel Diary* by Jess Adesina:

Monday the Pinkish Twelfth of Rainbow Shimmer

I'm Tilly and I'm different. You'll see how. But you won't see why. So, I'm starting this diary. I admit some things you'll read in it might challenge all you believe, but I say wake up, mortal! Smell the rose-scented glitter-puffs. Fact is, I'm an angel trapped on the earthly plane. With parents who think I'm just a human who should accept that not all the girls in my class will like me and absolutely *none* of the boys.

Want to know the most irritating thing about the whole situation? I have a really annoying little brother, who my parents firmly believe *is* an angel. Why else do they let him do what he likes, whenever he likes, with no repercussions? Don't they realise it's *me* who needs to sleep in late, watch TV all weekend and eat cupcakes with heavy sprinkles? They are the only things that restore my angelic power, after all.

My cat Gabriel understands. He knows the truth. That I'm not like anyone else on this planet. I've already told him what I'm telling you now: that if I'm still a double virgin by this time next year I'll have to take drastic measures to restore balance in the universe. It's my gift to humankind.

So, the next 365 days will be my angelic coming out. There'll be no more dreaming over Scott all day. And no more trying to get Daisy's attention by pretending I love swimming and hockey, when everyone knows angels are no good at sport. On the next pinkish twelfth of rainbow shimmer, Scott will be my boyfriend and Daisy will be my girlfriend. Boys, boys, boys. And girls.

A page torn from the novel *White Wings* by Mark Dunning:

Celine lit a pink Ziganov and gazed over the Seine. Its waters were usually muddy at dusk and especially so in winter. Today – a cold, dry Tuesday in January – was no exception. *It's amusing*, she thought, watching life trudge around her, *how utterly normal today seems.*

With one hand plunged deep in the pocket of her Loewe cashmere coat, she gripped her cigarette between Dior-kissed lips and pulled the belt tight around her narrow waist.

Gabriel said he'd be here. Now.

In Celine's experience, and given Gabriel's reputation at the bureau, if he said he'd be somewhere, and wasn't – send a wreath to his mother.

Celine smiled. As if Gabriel ever had anyone who resembled a mother. Her box-fresh Louboutins made satisfying clicks along the sidewalk.

'You're breaking position.' Neither a question nor an admonishment. The voice over her right shoulder had just the right tone, pitch and resonance to cut direct to her heart. That's how he did it.

'I knew you were there,' she whispered, never confident enough in his presence to use her voice at its usual volume.

Gabriel fell into step with Celine. But stayed just enough ahead that she knew who was senior to whom.

A flock of doves lifted into the air before them with a collective thunderclap of wings. Even if it were not part of the plan, Celine would feel it in the air ... what was coming.

Gabriel seized her around the waist. His lips on hers, she melted into his arms, all the time fighting to keep her mind on what he was doing. Quickly, deftly and out of sight.

Passers-by did just that. None saw anything beyond the ordinary. Gabriel's hand as it transferred the package. Celine's eyes as they flicked left and right. The vast white wings that soared into the sky, that made Celine and Gabriel untouchable.

Done. She pulled her coat tighter as they continued walking, hand in hand. She could feel it close to her chest. Wrapped so well, not a drop of blood would escape. It was larger than she imagined, harder. And perfectly still. The excised heart of the Russian ambassador.

Text messages between TV producer Phil Priest and me, 9 July 2021:

Phil Priest

I've just come across that unproduced script for DIVINE. It's pretty good. The writer whose name I couldn't remember is Clive Badham.

Amanda Bailey

Thanks, Phil. Would it be possible for you to send me that script?

Phil Priest

I've only got the first few pages. We didn't request the full manuscript as he was (no doubt still is) an unknown name. Will send what I have.

Divine

An original screenplay by

CLIVE BADHAM

To err is human
to kill is Divine

INT. HOSPITAL A&E RECEPTION — NIGHT

It's busy. A dirty, blood-stained and dishevelled TEENAGE
GIRL (Holly, 17), glazed with shock, walks through the bustle
to a reception desk. The RECEPTIONIST (30s, female) looks
up. Her expression changes … this is no ordinary walk-in.

                    TEENAGE GIRL
         I've had a baby.

The Receptionist picks up the phone.

                    RECEPTIONIST
         When, love?

                    TEENAGE GIRL
         Weeks ago.

The Receptionist raises her eyebrows, professional.

                    RECEPTIONIST
         Where did you have it?

                    TEENAGE GIRL
         The street. I was scared …

The Receptionist nods with warm, knowing compassion.

                    RECEPTIONIST
         (into phone)
         A lady nurse to front, please.
         (to the Teenage Girl)
         Where's the baby now?

The Teenage Girl shakes her head, confused.

                    TEENAGE GIRL
         Here.

She holds up a CARRIER BAG, at the bottom an unmistakable
outline of a very young BABY, apparently lifeless. The
Receptionist's face drops in horror.

PRE-LAP: KNOCK. KNOCK. KNOCK.

INT. FISHEYE OF CORRIDOR — NIGHT — WEEKS AGO

JONAH (17, serious) and Holly appear distorted through a security spyhole. They hold a MOSES BASKET between them.

INT. HALLWAY, FLAT — NIGHT

The front door opens to reveal Jonah and Holly in the corridor, tired and untidy but with an air of achievement. Inside the Moses basket, a young BABY makes small, random NOISES. They grin when they see GABRIEL (late 40s, calm), who greets them with a winning smile. He ushers them inside, warm and fatherly, takes up the Moses basket and kicks the door firmly shut.

INT. LIVING ROOM, FLAT — NIGHT

Gabriel places the Moses basket on the table, steels himself, peers inside it at the wriggling Baby. He's captivated, but his face is unreadable. Holly and Jonah throw off their coats and join him. Finally …

> GABRIEL
>
> You guys OK? Holly — recovered?
> His arm around her shoulder, he pulls her
> in. Holly nods as she and Jonah stare into
> the Moses basket.

> GABRIEL
>
> No one followed you?

Jonah shakes his head. Gabriel searches his eyes for doubt.

> GABRIEL
>
> Are you sure? Really sure? Because now it's
> here, they can circle, close in. Stay alert.

His tone and manner change, his face all warm smiles. He pulls them both to him in an affectionate group hug.

> GABRIEL
>
> Hey! Pizza time!

His arms around them both, and theirs around him, he leads them into the kitchen. Alone on the table, the Moses basket rocks slightly.

INT. LIVING ROOM, FLAT — NIGHT — LATER

The flat is small but clean and tidy. Aside is a stack of baby items: nappies, blankets, formula. Gabriel lounges on the sofa. Holly and Jonah snuggle happily either side. Six legs intertwine, six feet, three plates of pizza crusts. All stare at the TV. On it, a FANTASY TV SHOW ends.

> HOLLY
>
> Gabriel?

Gabriel turns the volume down.

> HOLLY
>
> Can we heal sick people?

He thinks. Holly and Jonah wait patiently.

> GABRIEL
>
> We don't need to. If they're meant to get well, they will.

> HOLLY
>
> But can we send love to them?

> GABRIEL
>
> We can try.

O.S. the Baby CRIES. Holly reluctantly untangles her legs and drags herself to the kitchen.

INT. LIVING ROOM, FLAT — NIGHT — SHORT TIME LATER

Gabriel sits between Holly and Jonah. They watch as he feeds
the Baby from a bottle, inexpert, matter-of-fact.

> HOLLY
>
> Why not just let it starve?

> GABRIEL
>
> It would be born again in another body. It
> has to be done properly, or this'll all be
> for nothing.

They watch the Baby feed.

> JONAH
>
> Is that what we did? Find a mortal body and
> get born in it?

Gabriel nods.

> JONAH
>
> I can't remember.

> GABRIEL
>
> Memories don't cross the divide. But
> you know you're not like everyone else.
> They're mortal souls in mortal bodies.
> Your bodies may be mortal, but your souls
> are divine.

They look at him and nod, sincere, almost unquestioning.

> HOLLY
>
> How do you remember it?

> JONAH
>
> He's from a higher sphere, an archangel.
> We're just angels.

Gabriel smiles as the Baby finishes its feed. He lays it

down on a blanket on the table. It GURGLES angrily. Holly,
Jonah and Gabriel contemplate its tiny hands and feet, its
innocent cherubic face.

                    JONAH
          Is it a mortal soul in a mortal body, or a
          divine soul in a mortal body?

Gabriel's eyes bore into the Baby.

                    GABRIEL
          Neither.

The Baby kicks and MEWLS.

                    GABRIEL
          It's the Antichrist.

To request the full manuscript contact Clive Badham on the
number below.

TO: Amanda Bailey
DATE: 9 July 2021
SUBJECT: Re: The Alperton Angels
FROM: David Polneath

Dear Amanda,

There are several people I could put you in contact with, but I can't risk using email to communicate their details. We must meet in person to exchange such sensitive information.

Why am I so fascinated by this case? Where to begin? Perhaps where I started a couple of years ago. I'd read about the Alperton Angels at the time and something chimed with me. So when I retired I decided to read up about it. The more I read the more engrossed I became and the more I wanted to know.

Everyone is familiar with the story by now: four men, who call themselves Michael, Gabriel, Raphael and Elemiah draw vulnerable teenagers into a cult-like existence by convincing them they are all angels sent to earth with a divine purpose – to kill the newborn Antichrist. Each has a different, but equally important, role to play in this mission.

Holly and Jonah had both absconded from the care system and the cult becomes their family. It brings meaning to their lives that wasn't there before: focus, routine, hope, positivity. It gives them confidence. Much of the behaviour exhibited by Gabriel and the other 'angels' is typical of controlling predators. They isolate the teenagers, keep them occupied with tasks that make them feel as if they are working towards a collective purpose. But these are kids who could easily drift into gangs or drugs, so their involvement in this 'cult' has its upside.

The angels have killed an innocent young waiter in pursuit of their purpose. Just as they are about to sacrifice a perfectly ordinary baby they claim will grow up to destroy humankind, Holly, the baby's mother, comes to her senses and escapes with the child and Jonah, the teenage father. Three of the main perpetrators are ritually sacrificed instead.

And all this takes place in the nondescript suburb of north-west London called Alperton.

You ask what drew me to this case and why I remain interested in those teenagers and what happened to them. It's because I found myself in a comparable situation at a similar age, many years ago. Like them, I looked for a new 'family', but discovered too late they did not have my best interests at heart. I know how those young people felt and how they feel now, as well as how they will feel in ten years' time, twenty, thirty. How they will feel in old age.

When you are forced into a place as dark as that, you spend the rest of your life on the return journey.
David

WhatsApp messages between Oliver Menzies and me, 9 July 2021:

Oliver Menzies
Woke up to the mad squaddie's alarm call and then this email.
Thanks very much. You got me back.

Forwarded email:

TO: Oliver Menzies
DATE: 9 July 2021
SUBJECT: The Alperton Angels
FROM: Paul Cole

Dear Oliver,
Amanda Bailey suggested I contact you. I understand your next book is about the Alperton Angels. I am a former Anglican minister and spiritual counsellor with many years' experience studying human consciousness. I followed the Alperton Angels case and continue to consider it one of the most interesting breaches between our world and the other side. This has occurred as my personal connection with the spiritual realm has expanded, so at the time I did not possess the tools I have now.

In short, I believe anyone entering into a close dialogue with this case should be aware of several elements not commonly known or understood.

From what Gabriel revealed about the angels' philosophy – he had, indeed *has*, access to the other side. He can see it and read it with far greater clarity than is meant to be. Is he an angel sent to rid the world of evil? That I'm a lot less certain about. What I need you both to under-stand is that what he says is not without foundation. There is a dimension to our existence we do not, and should not, understand in this life, much less access.

If you require any background information on this case, please do not hesitate to email me.

Yours sincerely,

Paul Cole

Spiritual Counsellor

WhatsApp messages between Oliver Menzies and me, 9 July 2021:

Oliver Menzies

Nice try, but Mr Cole told me you gave him my email address in the first line. Even if he hadn't, I'd have known it was you. Nil points.

Amanda Bailey

Oliver Menzies

Look, not in the mood. Summoned to Mum's place at midnight. They said she was going into organ failure. It was full-on end-is-nigh. An hour later she's back to her usual self. She'd taken extra tablets by accident. Got to bed at 2.30 a.m. Going into our meeting with Jonah on two hours' rubbish sleep.

Amanda Bailey

Sorry to hear that.

Oliver Menzies

So no more passing each other's details to unhinged conspiracy theorists. Truce?

Amanda Bailey

Truce

Oliver Menzies

See you in an hour.

TO: Paul Cole
Cc: Amanda Bailey
DATE: 9 July 2021
SUBJECT: Re: The Alperton Angels
FROM: Oliver Menzies

Thanks for your email, Mr Cole, but my colleague was playing a practical joke on you. I focus only on the facts.

The Quarr Abbey Files

Amanda Bailey and Oliver Menzies at Quarr Abbey Religious Community (it's pronounced 'core') on the Isle of Wight, and later with interviewee Jonah, 9 July 2021. Transcribed by Ellie Cooper.

AB: Hi, Ellie. You'll see this interview is in a series of files. Now usually I *love* that you cut out the chit-chat and small talk. But this time I need a record of the entire day. Please transcribe these files in chronological order and in their entirety. You will be fully reimbursed. Thank you. [*You got it. I'll call these The Quarr Abbey Files. EC*] And Oliver's surname is pronounced Mingis but spelled Menzies.

File 1

OM: Guess how much this ferry costs.

AB: Two, three million.

OM: I mean the trip. The fare across the Solent. Forty-minute journey. Guess how much. Return.

AB: Fifty.

OM: Nowhere near.

AB: Seventy-five.

OM: Try again.

AB: A hundred.

OM: Still in 2001, Mand, no ... [*dramatic pause. EC*] a hundred and fifty.

AB: Seriously?

OM: The most expensive stretch of water in the world. No wonder they built their reclusive monastery on the other side of it.

AB: Sweet?

OM: Hmmm. Mint?

AB: Yep. [*A pause here while you both eat sweets. Yuck. You asked for everything to be transcribed, remember. EC*]

OM: Good idea we do this together. I'm not as ... whatever, as you are. Digging people up. Winkling them out of their shells. I'm more, wham bam.

AB: My style is more charm and disarm. [*Love it. EC*]

OM: Hmmm.

AB: It wasn't *us* I was thinking of when I suggested we do this together. Some of these interviewees are still vulnerable. We have a duty to protect them as best we can. We're writing about a case that pivots on safeguarding failures, we should at least *try* to observe some protective measures in our own process. Speaking to each of us in turn doubles the number of times a victim has to relive what happened to them. If they only have to endure *one* interview – with both of us – it minimises the number of times that trauma resurfaces.

OM: Yeah, saves time. And we both get to hear their first response. You know how it is when a bod has spoken about something multiple times. They reel it off, don't say anything original, which is bad for us. Worse still for us, they don't let things slip. They're on their guard.

AB: Is that what happened with the squaddie?

OM: He was just a psychopath. *Is* a psychopath. Every morning, quarter to five, phone rings. Stories he told me of the sickest things you've ever imagined run through my head.

AB: Spoken to Don? He may be able to get this guy some help. Special forces must organise counselling or something.

OM: Mentioned it. But how long does that take?

AB: So, turn it round. Get up when he calls. Go for a run. Do some work. Turn a negative into a positive. [*Some background noise here. An announcement. Return to your cars. EC*]

OM: Feel like I'm about to meet a celebrity. Jonah, the Alperton Angel.

AB: Only, that's not his name, it's what the angel cult called him. If we use it, we may trigger anxiety or panic. But at least it will get his attention. Must stop thinking of him as seventeen. He's thirty-four.

OM: How did you get his number? [*You must shake your head to this, EC*] Why not?

AB: Someone risked something to give it to me.

OM: Why did they give *you* his number? Sensitive info that could backfire on them. No one ever gives me leads like that. People suck.

AB: Different reasons. Some believe things need to be exposed. In this case, someone I spoke to trusted me and wanted to help. It's not a perfect science. I've been desperately trying to get information out of someone else for this project. They just aren't playing ball.

OM: Welcome to my world.

AB: It can be luck too. There's a connection with some people. You must find that. We all do.

OM: Never happens to me.

AB: Maybe there's something fundamentally untrustworthy about you.

OM: I don't think so. Anyway, how can someone who barely knows you – or me – make a judgement either way?

AB: The invisible connections between us.

OM: The *what*?

AB: You know, people who study psychology, or who train to be counsellors, that kind of thing. At their first class, the tutor says: 'Everyone walk around the room and find someone else to pair up with.' They do, and the tutor asks them to sit down with that person and each talk about their family life and upbringing. The students find they've – apparently randomly – picked someone whose parents divorced, just like theirs did, whose father died when they were young, whose family life was disrupted by constant moving. Or something as simple as two people who were born in the same place in the order of siblings, or are both only children.

OM: In other words, normal coincidences that mean nothing.

AB: We're drawn to people with similar life experiences. There's an unseen level of communication that draws us to those whose emotional development is similar, or complementary, to our own. [*I've done this and remember telling you about it! EC*]

OM: Can't see it myself ...

AB: We can't see or hear it, much less control it, but it's there and it governs who we are drawn to or repulsed by. Cult leaders

– influential, charismatic people – have an aura that attracts those who are insecure and vulnerable. A perfect psychological storm. [*That's fascinating. EC*]

OM: People join cults because they're weak and stupid. What does that have to do with bods giving you information and not me?

AB: I have more life experience than you, and it means I *connect* with more people than you do.

OM: Doesn't explain why anyone gave you Jonah's number.

AB: They gave me *a* number. I don't know whether you give up your mobile phone when you go into a monastery, but the number Jonah had in 2011 is now with someone else who, when I called it, told me where its original owner is living now. And it's right over there.

OM: Where?

AB: That stone building beyond the trees.

OM: Hey, you can see it from the water?

AB: We're the only passengers still here. Better get back to the car – I'll drive.

OM: I want my hundred and fifty quid's worth of delight out of this plastic chair and sticky carpet.

[*You stop the recording here. Why are you recording all this? EC*]

File 2

[*Crunch, crunch, crunch. Walking on gravel? EC*]

AB: All we know for sure is that he was in foster care. At some point in his mid-teens he joined the Alperton Angels. He was rescued from The Assembly, then disappeared back into the care system.

OM: Not for long, presumably. Being seventeen when it happened.

AB: They didn't have long to break the cycle. The … whatever hold the angels had over him.

OM: He must be mortified.

AB: Why?

OM: If I once believed I was an angel sent from heaven, I'd be embarrassed at the very least.

AB: He may be. We'll find out.

OM: I'd never speak to people like us about it.

AB: Hopefully he won't feel the same way.

OM: What? So you *haven't* spoken to him?

AB: Not directly.

OM: But he *does* know we're coming today.

AB: Not in the strict sense of that phrase.

OM: Then he might send us packing. He may not even be here!

AB: It's a monastery. Monks don't go out. Do they?

OM: Or in prayer or something. [*He's right, Mand. EC*] What are we doing here?

AB: We're here to visit the abbey, look around and if, on the off-chance, Jonah fancies a chat—

OM: How will we know which monk is Jonah? If we get to see any monks at all!

AB: His age. His ... demeanour. We'll pick something up about him. I'll know.

OM: [*Exasperated sighs. You've really pissed him off! EC*] That ferry ticket was a hundred and fifty quid.

AB: You're on expenses.

OM: [*He whispers. EC*] Jesus wept.

AB: Ssh.

File 3

[*I've named the person you speak to here 'Friendly Monk'. EC*]

FM: ... on the site of an old Cistercian monastery from the twelfth century. What you see today was built between 1907 and 1914. These main monastic buildings were added to the original Victorian house, behind you, by an architect who had taken vows with the Benedictine order. [*Dom Paul Bellot. I looked him up. EC*] He favoured Belgian brick. Its particular qualities mean the monastery changes hue throughout the day and the year. Our sanctuary tower is said to remain standing purely through the grace of God and prayer from within. [*Dramatic pause. EC*] Local people at the time had never seen a structure so tall. I assure you it's quite safe.

OM: How many monks are here?

FM: The number changes. We take in guests and interns. Men who are contemplating this life, or simply wish to experience a period of prayer and solitude.

OM: Do you have any younger men in the monastery, say in their thirties?

FM: Yes, men of all ages. From their twenties to their eighties.

OM: If I wanted to speak with one in particular ...

AB: Do you have a press office?

FM: It's best you use our 'info at' email address ... are you media?

OM: Yeah, we—

AB: We're just visiting, but always open-minded about what the wider world may find interesting. The monastery is beautiful and fascinating.

FM: Yes. [*Crunch, crunch ... he's walking away. EC*] Enjoy your visit.

OM: [*Raises his voice. EC*] There's a monk here ... he's thirty-four.

AB: Shush.

FM: [*He sounds further away. EC*] Info at Quarr Abbey dot org. [*Crunch, crunch, crunch. EC*]

AB: Well fucking done.

OM: He was getting on my nerves. He might have all the time in the world to rattle on about architecture and shit, but our return ferry is at six. The monks are all hidden away.

AB: They can't have gone far. Come on. [*Crunch, crunch, crunch. EC*]

File 4

AB: Slowly. Quietly.

OM: Will they charge?

AB: I don't know.

OM: They bite. Definitely bite. And they eat anything. We're food to them.

AB: They're just pigs.

OM: Not friendly ones. Look at him.

AB: Her.

To create a chronological account of what happened next, I tore the following file in two, then inserted printouts of WhatsApp messages between me and Oliver:

File 5

[*This is pretty much all whispered. EC*]

AB: Round this corner is the brewery. Beyond is the vegetable garden. That's the chapel, obvs. I'm banking on the cottage here being their access to a sleeping and dining area.

OM: How do you know all this?

AB: Research, Oliver. Photographs on their website, news interviews, Google Earth. I've built up a mental map of the place. Here, vitamin water – we need to be on our A-game. [*Slurping, followed by silence while you clearly sneak around where visitors aren't allowed. Least of all a woman. EC*]

AB: Ol, if we meet Jonah, let *me* do the talking. [*Clang, clang, clang. Ominous bells. EC*]

OM: Something's happening in the chapel ...

AB: There's a service about to begin.

OM: People are going in.

AB: Follow me. [*Suddenly gets echoey and spooky. Clang! Was that the door closing? EC*] They have a visitors' section. Perfect!

OM: Monks! Monks!

AB: I know. Ssh. [*Whoa! Wailing! That's real shivers-down-the-spine stuff. EC*]

OM: Shit, that's eerie.

AB: Sext. It's twelve o'clock. There's a schedule of devotional services the monks observe throughout the day. If he's here, this is where he'll be. Now. Quick. [*The chanting is louder. Very creepy. EC*]

OM: Who are those guys going into the roped-off area? Can't be monks. That dude's wearing a Tommy Hilfiger hoodie.

AB: Must be the ordinary men here for a spiritual retreat.

OM: They get a ring-side seat. I can barely see the monks from here.

AB: The retreat guys are stepping over the rope. You can follow them. Go on.

OM: It says 'no entry'. They'll know I'm not one of them. I'll get zapped by God.

AB: They won't say anything while prayers are going on. If they do, apologise, say you made a mistake. Get a good look at the monks. See if any could be our man. [*Some of this chanting is in Latin. Sorry, can only transcribe in English. I'll call the next speaker Unknown Monk. EC*]

UM: The wicked have waited for me, to destroy me. But I have understood your sayings. All that seems perfect has its limits. But the perfection of your commands is boundless. [*I looked this up. It's Psalm 118 or 9 depending on which Bible you have. EC*] Glory be to the Father and the Son, and to the Holy Spirit. As it was in the beginning, is now, and ever shall be, world without end. Amen.

When Oliver moved to sit with the retreat group, we switched to WhatsApp. Our messages are inserted here:

Amanda Bailey
Nicely done. You look just like them.

Oliver Menzies
Who?

Amanda Bailey
The spiritual retreat guys. What can you see from there?

Oliver Menzies
Monks, but not many. NINE including the one talking.

Amanda Bailey
Any mid-thirties?

Oliver Menzies
Second from left. And far right, by the lectern. Thoughts?

Amanda Bailey
Can't see a thing beyond where you're sitting.

Oliver Menzies
Must put phone away – unholy glances from spiritual dudes.

[A lot more chanting and singing. Some clanging and footsteps. EC]

UM: For you are my strength and you are my refuge. Rescue me from the hands of the wicked. From the power of the unjust. The lawbreakers. For my enemies have been watching me, they have come together and discussed me. *[Crash! OMG what was that? Are you both OK? Long pause while something happens. I can't quite make it out. EC]*

AB: Are you alright?

OM: Yes!

AB: What happened?

OM: It was the praying bit. The spiritual guys leaned on the chairs in front of them, heads bowed. When I did it, the chair collapsed. Buckled the moment I touched it. Like it knew I shouldn't be there.

AB: The monk who helped you up ... bit too old to be Jonah.

OM: He knew I was an imposter or he wouldn't have ushered me back out here.

DS: *[A disgruntled stranger. EC]* Ssh! We're trying to listen.

OM: It's in *Latin*!

DS: Ssh!

[A bit of scuffling and throat-clearing. Silence. Then the chanting resumes. OMG, Mand, you have nine lives. EC]

File 6

AB: Jonah? *[Didn't you say using his cult name would trigger him? EC]* Jonah?

BJ: *[Not being crude or disrespectful, but if he's Brother Jonah then I have to call him BJ. EC]* Who are you?

AB: Amanda Bailey. I'm writing a book. About the Alperton Angels.

BJ: *[Long pause. EC]* Oh. *[Someone interrupts with what sounds like 'Brother, you are expected in the kitchen', but BJ must wave them away. EC]*

AB: I understand. You want to forget and move on. But a big part of that is being able to talk about it. To understand what happened and why, so it can never happen again. Your knowledge can help others, those at risk of falling under the same spell. The very act of telling your story will help them see through the lies and protect themselves. Your lived experience is valuable to the world.

BJ: How did you know it's me?

AB: Intuition. Something. Do you speak to Holly? Do you know where she is? [*He must shake his head to these questions. I can't hear any answer. EC*]

OM: You must be really embarrassed—

AB: To have us descend on you like this. Especially after … in the chapel.

BJ: Brother Benjamin doesn't usually bring the house down. How did you find me here? [*He has a rich, calming voice. I expected him to sound like a teenager. EC*]

AB: Someone, I can't remember who, gave me a mobile number. I asked for Jonah. They said he's at Quarr Abbey. Who has that phone now?

BJ: An old friend.

OM: I once gave my old mobile to my dad. Big mistake. Suddenly he gets calls from my ex, old uni friends, old workmates, but he's quite a … he was a practical joker and one time, my boss called late at night to tell me there was an early editorial meeting tomorrow. Dad says fine, I'll be there, see you at eight. I forgot to say we have similar voices. Had. So I get to work at nine the next day to find the meeting almost over. They thought I was late. Had to explain it was just Dad playing a joke on them. [*WTF? EC*]

AB: See, anyone can be a victim. All it takes is for someone to pick up on what you lack, need or simply what you want to hear, and give it to you. They create dependence and ultimately shame, in having believed a lie. No one wants to admit they've been tricked. The most vulnerable people are those who think it can't happen to them. That's the key message we're aiming to deliver with this book. Jonah … I'm sorry, I know that isn't your name.

What should we call you?

BJ: Jonah.

AB: But that was the name the angels gave you.

BJ: Yes, I'm Brother Jonah here.

AB: We'd very much appreciate spending some time with you. We could talk about the angels, what happened that night and how you escaped.

BJ: I'm needed in the kitchen for lunch or I'll be very unpopular.

AB: Think about it over lunch. Meet us here, later. Two? Three?

BJ: I'll think about it.

[*He must leave here as you stop the recording at this point. EC*]

File 7

AB: I had to call him Jonah to get his attention, but I didn't think he'd still be using the name the cult gave him. That creeps me out. Ol. Ol. You OK?

OM: Uh-huh.

AB: He's still living in a cult-like environment. Who chooses this unless they want or need to withdraw from the world?

OM: Don't know.

AB: Someone – one of the bods who contact you when you start work on a case like this – they said something like: 'When you're forced into a dark place, you spend the rest of your life on the way back.' Jonah is still on the way back.

OM: Do they vet aspiring monks? Say if a guy's motives were off because he'd been brainwashed before and didn't know how else to live. They must check.

AB: Yet their numbers are low. Just nine monks in the whole monastery. Perhaps they don't ask that many questions.

OM: Hmmm.

AB: He'll need time to think about our proposition. It could mean a return journey.

OM: He's got to talk. I don't want to come back here, no way.

AB: You're on expenses. Let it go.

OM: I don't mean the ferry tickets. I mean this place. It's ... idyllic.

AB: Next time we'll bring a picnic— [*He's not in the mood for jest.*

EC]

OM: Not in a good way. We don't take heroin, not because it's shit, but because it's so amazing we know we'll become addicted. That.

AB: You *like* the idea of this life?

OM: No. I hate the idea. But part of me thinks if I moved in here, I could start again. At least I wouldn't have to deal with the world any more. [*Bit odd. EC*]

AB: You're safe, Ol. You're an atheist. They wouldn't have you.

OM: That's not what I mean. I don't know what I mean.

AB: Hey, the monks brew their own craft beer— [*You stop recording here. EC*]

File 8

[*Unknown Monk is back for this file. EC*]

UM: Brother Jonah has asked me to accompany him. He doesn't wish to answer questions, but he will say a few words on the subject he knows you're interested in. He asks that you respect his intention to speak only of those details he feels ready to disclose.

AB: Please thank Brother Jonah and yes, we will respect his wishes. [*Unknown Monk must leave you alone because you and Oliver whisper together. EC*]

AB: Let me lead the conversation.

OM: I can slip in a question or two at the end. Even if he doesn't answer, we'll see a reaction.

AB: No. Let him speak ... Ssh. [*Movement and a pause as, I take it, BJ and UM enter and settle down. EC*]

UM: Brother Jonah.

BJ: You mentioned a time before I came here. A previous life. It's difficult for me to talk about it. My parents were unable to care for me. I was placed in foster homes, but eventually chose a new family among people who offered a refuge from what had been a disrupted life. Sadly, that choice led to tragedy and the deaths of people I loved. I'm not under any illusions about how the outside world viewed us. But as to the way we viewed ourselves, I think of it as symbolic. Of how we wanted to help people and lead purposeful lives. [*Is there something eerie and other-worldly about his voice? Or is it just what he says? EC*]

AB: I understand. Thank you for explaining.

OM: Do you lead a purposeful life now? Here?

BJ: I believe I do. A life of prayer and contemplation is steeped in purpose.

OM: But you have a kid. Surely your purpose was – is – to be a father.

UM: Brother Jonah is— [*From here on people are speaking over each other, not sure I catch everything. EC*]

UM: That's enough—

AB: It's a— We're very grateful for your—

OM: This monastery is the same twisted world the angels created.

UM: Sir, we agreed—

BJ: We didn't create a world. We tried to save it.

OM: You can leave. You can lead a normal life. You have an eighteen-year-old child, for Christ's sake.

AB: I'm sorry— Oliver, we—

OM: Gabriel is locked up. The other angels are dead. There's nothing to fear. You're safe now.

BJ: Nowhere is safe now. [*Strange thing to say. There's a moment of silence, so you all pick up on something too. EC*]

AB: What do you mean by that?

UM: It's time you both left. Brother Jonah— [*Do I hear a slight scream? Was that a scuffle? Is Oliver fighting monks now? EC*]

BJ: There, oh.

UM: Are you alright?

File 9

[*You're both trudging across gravel. And they're not happy footsteps. EC*]

OM: Are you *pissed*?

AB: No! I had *one* craft beer.

OM: Oh, so you *faked* a fall to stop me making this whole journey worthwhile.

AB: I *slipped* on highly polished flagstones while you were doing your best to kill the *interview* stone dead. Lucky Jonah caught me. [*Angry pause here. Did you fake the fall? EC*] And it's lucky I stopped you making bigger idiots of us than you already had. I *said* leave the talking to me. This is why you get nowhere. You're a blunt instrument.

OM: So fucking angry with him.

AB: Who?

OM: Jonah.

AB: Why?

OM: I don't know. Because he's fallen for it. The angels. This place ... I don't know. Since I walked through the door of the chapel I had a feeling. It was as if my dad was there.

AB: Well, that's nice, isn't it? Perhaps he's watching over you—

OM: You know me, Mand, I'm an atheist. I don't believe this shit so why did I feel so weird? Then I think my dad's dead and he'd love to be alive still and having a pint with me on a Friday night. While Brother Jonah completely ignores his kid. That's why I was angry.

AB: [*You take a deep breath here. EC*] The minute you let your emotions through – or your own opinions, for that matter – you close a door. Allow people to speak. They'll reveal themselves soon enough. [*Long silence. Just footsteps as you trudge back to the car. EC*]

AB: Don Makepeace said he wasn't sure if it had been the right decision to release Holly and Jonah without charge. I think it was the *wrong* decision.

OM: Hmm.

AB: If Jonah had gone through the system, he might have got help. Instead, he's recreated what he had when he was part of a cult. Only this cult is socially acceptable.

OM: Nowhere is safe now. That's what he said. Nowhere is safe now ... now what?

AB: Now the angels are dead?

OM: Is that what *you* thought he meant? I took it to mean nowhere is safe now the Antichrist is at large in the world.

AB: The Antichrist has been 'at large' since 2003. The world is still here.

OM: But it's only just becoming an adult.

AB: Jonah is a vulnerable man. The older monk knew that or he wouldn't have insisted he was there while we spoke to him.

OM: Or he wanted to control what Jonah said.

AB: Either way, we're unlikely to get any more out of him. Thanks to you.

OM: And thanks to *you* all we have to show for our expensive and time-consuming trek is a prepared statement that tells us nothing. [*Ding ding click as the car is unlocked. EC*] We're leaving.

AB: [*Mand, you whisper this next line into the phone. Oliver doesn't hear it. But I do. EC*] I got more out of him than you think.

WhatsApp messages between Oliver Menzies and me, 9 July 2021:

Oliver Menzies
Shit camera strikes again. Get any decent shots of Jonah and the abbey?

> **Amanda Bailey**
> Why?

Oliver Menzies
For my desktop collage. I like to have pictures that inspire me while I'm writing. Shots of the buildings and any of Jonah you managed to sneak.

> **Amanda Bailey**
> Sending through now ... Nice ones of the abbey. One of Jonah but so far away, not even sure it's him. Random blurred monk.

Oliver Menzies
They'll do.

Oliver Menzies' and my visit to the archangel Gabriel

Oliver Menzies and I speak while in a car, driving on a motorway, on 10 July 2021. It is extremely difficult to hear speech under these circumstances. Transcribed as best she can by Ellie Cooper.

OM: Quarter to five. Well, four forty-four. Every day. Even Sundays.

AB: Unplug the phone. You must have enough evidence by now.

OM: Yeah, but I need to prove he's *still* doing it. Without the call records, they'll just say he stopped.

AB: Oh.

OM: Couldn't sleep anyway.

AB: You don't meet the archangel Gabriel every day.

OM: Gabriel Angelis. You couldn't make it up.

AB: He was born Peter Duffy on Christmas Day 1959. Changed it by deed poll in 1991. First comes to the attention of the police in his late teens, couple of acquisitive misdemeanours, including what we now call distraction robberies. Then a more sophisticated chequebook fraud, for which he is sentenced to four years in the 1980s. Don remembers that as he'd just joined the force. Gabriel serves two *then* goes straight for a while. Nothing from 1990 to 2002.

OM: Goes straight or doesn't get caught.

AB: In 2002 he's arrested trying to use a stolen credit card and more are found on him. Police think he's selling or passing them on to an organised crime gang, an OCG. He serves three months in Wandsworth and five in the community. In 2003 he's tracked from the bloodbath at The Assembly and arrested in Ealing.

OM: Didn't get far.

AB: He was on foot. Literally. No shoes.

OM: He's convicted of murdering Harpinder Singh by a single bloody fingerprint on a leaflet in the flat. And although the other angels stab themselves to death, he's accused of mutilating and posing the bodies.

AB: Autopsies and forensics confirm the angels cut their own throats, and mutilation takes place post-mortem. That, plus

Holly and Jonah's testimonies about the way he drew them into the cult, means he's given a whole-life sentence.

OM: He's been inside for eighteen years. Does he *still* believe he's the archangel Gabriel?

AB: Did he ever believe it? He's a con man as well as a murderer.

OM: A con man who believes his own narrative, or a cynical manipulator?

AB: Take me through your interview strategy. [*Silence. I sense a frisson. EC*] Don't be like that. If I don't get in, you need to know what you're doing—

OM: I'm perfectly capable of doing it without your input.

AB: First, chat about random things. How's it going, what's for lunch ... Keep it light. If he says something funny or even a bit sarcastic, laugh like it's the best joke you heard all week.

OM: Mand—

AB: Build a rapport with him. *Don't* let him control the conversation. If he's recounting something, and skips forward, steer him back to the chronology of events. Leave tricky questions till later in the interview.

OM: I know all this.

AB: He's inside for the murder of Singh, which he says he doesn't remember but didn't do. Yet despite appeals, that one fingerprint has kept him inside. His claim of innocence is a weak spot we can exploit. You need to make it clear that you think the murder rap is all part of a big conspiracy. Shit! Yes. We need to talk about eye contact— [*Oliver makes a spluttering, dismissive noise. EC*] I only want you to get the most out of it. For both of us. *If* they let me in, I can speak later on, as if I'm filling in the gaps. And we'll ask about the baby. But he won't know where it went, so ... [*Silence again. Just the drone of the road before you switch off. EC*]

A conversation between Amanda Bailey and an Unknown Woman outside HMP Tynefield, 10 July 2021. Transcribed by Ellie Cooper.

UW: [*Recording starts mid-conversation. EC*] ... drugs and other things. They won't let you in without permission.

AB: I know. I'm supposed to be helping someone who's injured. He can't take notes. [*You sound upset. What's happened? EC*]

UW: Come a long way?

AB: London.

UW: Oh no. Your friend got in OK, though. Aw. He'll be all right. No need to cry.

AB: Not crying. Just ... frustrated.

UW: Least it's not raining.

AB: Thanks for coming over. You should get back in the queue. Don't lose your place.

UW: I won't. The girls'll keep it for me. Who were you gonna visit?

AB: [*You whisper this. EC*] Gabriel Angelis.

UW: The cult leader? [*She gasps. EC*] Are you a follower?

AB: No. My friend and I are interviewing him for a book ... Does he have followers?

UW: See that woman over there, just going through the door? [*She lowers her voice to a whisper. EC*] She's wearing an angel wing necklace.

AB: That's a lot of layers for this weather. The hat seems like overkill.

UW: Yeah, well. Would *you* want to be recognised if you were visiting him?

AB: He still has influence from inside prison.

UW: You'd be surprised, love.

AB: Is she here a lot?

UW: Seen her many a time, but there are others that come and go. You alright now?

AB: Yeah, thanks.

UW: We got to look after each other, don't we? [*Her poor grammar, not mine. Sounds like she's walking away. EC*] Hope your book's a best-seller.

AB: Thanks. [*Gabriel has 'fans' who visit him. A testament to his power and influence, or proof Oliver is right, and people are stupid? I can't decide. EC]*

Conversation between Amanda Bailey and Oliver Menzies. In a stationary car, somewhere near HMP Tynefield, 10 July 2021. You're both chewing. It's gross. Transcribed by Ellie Cooper.

OM: I've got no sympathy, Mand. You knew it was a risk.

AB: Did I ask for sympathy? I hung out by the burger truck, chatted to some girls in the queue. Salts of the earth. Loyal to their men inside. [*He sighs, like it's been hard work. EC*] You recorded the whole thing, right?

OM: Yep. Had to pretend my hand was sore, thanks to you.

AB: Play the file. I want to hear his voice.

OM: I'm fed up with his voice. Let's get home.

AB: Got my AirPods—

OM: NO! Just don't, Mand ... [*Awkward silence. Bit weird. Did he even record it? EC*]

AB: OK. Send me the file. I'll get it transcribed. But tell me what happened, at least.

OM: Argh, let me settle. Pounding headache.

AB: What's he like? [*No answer. EC*] Did you get on with him?

OM: Uh-huh.

AB: What does he say about Singh's murder? Any confession?

OM: You sound like the screws. That's all they wanted to know. Can't remember. No ... it's all spinning.

AB: Mention the baby?

OM: It's all on the file. Let's go. Don't want to hit London in rush hour.

AB: Sure, but let me drive. [*The engine starts. EC*]

OM: Er ...

AB: You've had a long day. Your head's spinning. I'll drive.

OM: Yeah. Thanks, yeah. OK.
    [*Doors slam as you switch places, the engine starts again as the recording stops. EC*]

TO: Paul Cole
DATE: 11 July 2021
SUBJECT: Re: The Alperton Angels
FROM: Oliver Menzies

Paul,

I met Gabriel Angelis today – yesterday now, it's so late. I got in hours ago but can't sleep. Have you ever met him? I need to speak to someone who's met him.

Oliver

TO: Oliver Menzies
DATE: 11 July 2021
SUBJECT: Re: The Alperton Angels
FROM: Paul Cole

Dear Oliver,

I have never met Gabriel personally but I've spoken to people who have. Tell me, did you experience a sudden surge of energy, or burst of involuntary physical activity, like a racing heartbeat, sweating, dizziness, etc., while you were in his presence or, most likely, afterwards?

Paul

TO: Paul Cole
DATE: 11 July 2021
SUBJECT: Re: The Alperton Angels
FROM: Oliver Menzies

Yes! That's it exactly. My assistant had to drive us home. But it wasn't the first time I'd felt like that. You know I'm writing a book about the Alperton Angels. Well, I experienced similar feelings when I met Jonah the day before. Also, when I visited the site of The Assembly as part of my research. My assistant wasn't affected. What could've caused it?

Oliver

Dear Oliver,

I believe Gabriel has a connection to the other side that even he fails to understand. He is a compelling, charismatic man and most people are drawn to him. But someone with particular sensitivities will sense his turbulent psychic energy. It's possible you are more attuned to this than most. I'm sure it is nothing to worry about and hope you feel better soon.

Best wishes,

Paul Cole

An email to me from *White Wings* author Mark Dunning's widow, Judy Teller-Dunning, 12 July 2021:

Dear Amanda Bailey,

I understand you reached out to Duncan Seyfried at Neville Reed about the Alperton Angels case. Several years ago my late husband Mark Dunning wrote *White Wings*, a popular espionage novel partially inspired by it. You'll have heard the very sad news that he recently passed.

I didn't intend to respond to your email while I still felt so raw. But a strange thing happened last night and I have a strong feeling I should get in touch.

We hosted Mark's memorial yesterday, and after everyone had gone home I wandered into his office where everything was exactly as he'd left it the day he died. I sat at his desk and wondered how I'd *ever* sort out the mountain of paperwork he'd accumulated. My husband never filed anything or threw it away. Notes, printouts, research, letters, forty years of it. Now and again he'd sweep a stack or two off his desk and into box files, which he then shoved on to a shelf. I wondered if I should simply burn the lot. I cried at the thought.

Through my tears I reached up and hauled out the nearest box file – literally at random – and opened it. My heart sank at the mess of papers inside. Yet I looked closer and stopped dead. There in front of me were Mark's notes for *White Wings*. I immediately remembered your email and my blood ran cold. My husband wrote thirty-nine books, yet the *first* box file I look in contains exactly what you asked me for. I'm not a strong believer in the supernatural, but I think Mark wants you to have this and handed it to me – knowing I'd never locate the material otherwise. If you give me your home address, I will send it to you.

Please, can you do one thing for me? Keep in touch and let me know if it's useful?

Best,

Judy Teller-Dunning

WhatsApp messages between my editor Pippa Deacon and me, 12 July 2021:

Pippa Deacon

How was your meeting with Gabriel? Been speaking to the OH. Would the governor agree to an interview with G on camera, or audio only? She found the Dennis Nilsen interview on YouTube and would LOVE a splash like that.

> **Amanda Bailey**
>
> Getting the interview transcribed now. Plan to get in with OM failed.

Pippa Deacon

Oh. That's disappointing.

> **Amanda Bailey**
>
> We have an audio file. Will send transcript soon as I have it.

WhatsApp messages between Ellie Cooper and me, 12 July 2021:

Ellie Cooper
Tried to open Oliver's interview, Audio File 444. Not sure if it's a strange format or been corrupted. Can you get him to resend?

> **Amanda Bailey**
> I'll see. He's being weird about it. Either he didn't record it or he did and things went badly, OR it went really well and he doesn't want me to use any of it.

WhatsApp messages between me and Oliver Menzies, 12 July 2021:

> **Amanda Bailey**
> Can you send Ellie the Gabriel file?

Oliver Menzies
Thought I had.

> **Amanda Bailey**
> It was corrupted.

Oliver Menzies
Sounds about right.

Interview with Caroline Brooks, criminal psychologist [*and my tutor. EC*], 12 July 2021. Transcribed by Ellie Cooper.

> [*I cut out some awkward chit-chat and, modestly, some discussion about me. EC*]

CB: ... and she's a star of the department. [*Whoops, forgot that bit. EC*]

AB: Gabriel started out as a petty thief and showed signs of graduating to the fringes of organised crime. But his offending pattern doesn't feel sequential after that. He makes what feels to me a *jump* from acquisitive petty criminal to cult leader and murderer.

CB: Cult leaders thrive on power and power corrupts—

AB: What's *your* definition of a cult?

CB: Well ... [*Slight hesitation. It's not that she doesn't want to commit. She's very careful with her words. EC*] It's when people are drawn away from their lives as individuals to immerse themselves in a separatist organisation under a charismatic leader. Becoming part of a utopian community. Cults start with their own rules and philosophy, even if it seems they are creating an existence without either. This has a counter-culture appeal for those who struggle to find a place in regular society, or who lack a conventional family.

AB: What is it that makes a cult so hard to leave?

CB: If you've given your possessions and money away, you may not have the resources. If you've rejected your family and friends, you have no support outside the cult. But the psychological hold is the strongest factor. Members surrender their sense of self to conform to a new set of standards, routine, behaviours. All to please the leader or leaders. If they break the rules or question the philosophy, they're rejected. It's an invisible stranglehold. By the time a victim suspects the organisation of wrong-doing, they're equally guilty of deceiving others.

AB: We talk a lot about the victims of cults, is it helpful to consider the conditions that create a cult leader?

CB: Perhaps. But, again it's generalisation. A cult is a relationship of coercive control on a grand scale. But it can be a unit of two people: leader and follower. Some mainstream organised religions operate in ways we associate with cults. Society itself ... we tend to say 'cult' when we mean a negative or toxic organisation. As for the leaders, the majority are mentally unstable. As a cult matures and grows, they have to exert more control to maintain their authority over more people. You can make a distinction between leaders who believe their own philosophy and those who do it for sex or money. One definition of a cult is a religion where the spiritual leader is *alive*. They can be seen and heard and spoken to ... guru-led organisations can attract people disillusioned with mainstream religion. We find people raised with a strong religious upbringing are more susceptible to joining a cult.

AB: Do cults target particular types of people? Is there a profile of the victim, I mean?

CB: Many target the wealthy, for obvious reasons. Also young people who are anxious about their futures and the world in general. If someone promises you a new and different way of life, perhaps away from a society you see as flawed … But *anyone* who has experienced something life altering, such as a bereavement, can be vulnerable. In simple terms, as soon as someone knows what you want, they can control you with the promise of getting it for you. But do you know who I think are the *most* vulnerable? People who believe they can *never* be drawn in.

AB: [*You laugh. EC*] My words exactly, but not everyone sees it that way. How do you think the Alperton Angels started, and how did they conduct their activities? Were they even a cult?

CB: In my opinion, they were most certainly a cult. The leaders seem to have believed their own philosophy. They killed themselves rather than live in a world alongside the Antichrist. By the end they would all have been well schooled in ignoring any doubts about what they were doing. It was a small cult, but very typical. Think about Heaven's Gate; they thought they were divine beings who would be collected by a spaceship. Thirty-nine of them died. Then there's Waco: eighty dead. And of course Jonestown. Over nine hundred. Although in those cases the leader – always a man – died with his followers.

AB: Gabriel ran away from the scene.

CB: Yes. That's unusual. Perhaps he'd lost faith in what he had believed in – or never believed it.
[*Aren't we all living in one big cult? From birth we're conditioned to behave a certain way, believe prescribed things and uphold society's norms. Who's to say all those beliefs and values are correct? EC*]

WhatsApp messages between me and Ellie Cooper, 12 July 2021:

> **Amanda Bailey**
> Thanks for putting me in touch with Caroline. She was lovely, articulate – and intimidating.

Ellie Cooper
No problem. Still haven't got the Gabriel file from Oliver.

> **Amanda Bailey**
> Shit. I asked him this morning. OK, will chase.

WhatsApp messages between me and Oliver Menzies, 12 July 2021:

> **Amanda Bailey**
> What's your problem? Just email the Gabriel file to Ellie, FFS!

> **Amanda Bailey**
> Please.

Oliver Menzies
It didn't come out.

> **Amanda Bailey**
> WHAT?

Oliver Menzies
It didn't come out. What Ellie heard is all it is. White noise.

Oliver Menzies
I'll try to remember what he said.

Oliver Menzies
I know you're pissed off but that's that.

WhatsApp messages between me and Ellie Cooper, 12 July 2021:

> **Amanda Bailey**
> Is there really nothing audible on that file?

Ellie Cooper

There are voices under the crackling, but not clear enough.

> **Amanda Bailey**
> Ellie, could you do me a favour and just try to get whatever you
> can. Even if it's one or two words. Noises. Anything.

Ellie Cooper

OK.

Oliver Menzies interviews Gabriel Angelis at HMP Tynefield, 10 July 2021.
Transcribed by Ellie Cooper.

*[Humming, like an electronic device is on, but not functioning properly.
I can't tell if the voices belong to one person or several. I think I hear the
following words. EC]*

Accidents, disease. Chaos always. Predestined ... accept it.

*[Sorry, but that's it. I have a friend who works at a recording studio. I can
ask him if there's anything he can do to reduce the noise? EC]*

Text messages between Mr Blue and me, 12 July 2021:

Mr Blue

We can meet but don't bring anything digital. No recording
devices, phones, cameras.

> **Amanda Bailey**
> When and where?

Mr Blue

I mean it. Not your phone or any phone. They can be traced in
seconds. Don't bring your car.

> **Amanda Bailey**
> Where shall we meet and when?

Mr Blue

Don't use public transport. Even without a travel card, you'll be picked up on CCTV.

> **Amanda Bailey**
> I'll get an Uber.

Mr Blue

Do not get an Uber. Walk.

> **Amanda Bailey**
> Where to?

Mr Blue

Path behind the Ballot Box at the bottom of Horsenden Hill.

> **Amanda Bailey**
> That's pretty isolated.

Mr Blue

One fifteen tomorrow morning.

WhatsApp messages between my editor Pippa Deacon and me, 12 July 2021:

Pippa Deacon

Meant to ask earlier: any news on the baby?

> **Amanda Bailey**
> I'm meeting someone tonight who will give me the details.

Pippa Deacon

Great. That's what we need to get sorted now, Amanda.

WhatsApp messages between me and Ellie Cooper, 12 July 2021:

> **Amanda Bailey**
> Ellie, I want to tell you, in confidence, what I'm doing tonight so you can call the police if anything happens to me. No need to panic. Nothing will.

Ellie Cooper

OK.

Amanda Bailey

I'm collecting Alperton Angels info from someone whose real name I don't know. They want me to meet them in an unlit lane that runs through a dark wood behind a pub. The Ballot Box. It's on the edge of Horsenden Hill in Greenford.

Ellie Cooper

Right.

Amanda Bailey

At 1.15 a.m.

Ellie Cooper

Oh.

Amanda Bailey

I'll call you when I leave, and again when I'm home. It will take me forty minutes to walk there and back, plus however long it takes this person to tell me what I need. Once I've made that second call, you can forget everything – it all went as planned. OK?

Ellie Cooper

Why not drive?

Amanda Bailey

The car stores tracking data. They've told me to leave all my devices at home and walk there.

Ellie Cooper

So they know exactly where you live.

Ellie Cooper

They've picked a place you can walk to. So they must know where you live.

Amanda Bailey

I suppose they must.

Ellie Cooper

They know what you want and they're using that knowledge to control you.

> **Amanda Bailey**
> I'll be OK.

Ellie Cooper

So if I haven't had that second call by 2.15 a.m., call 999?

> **Amanda Bailey**
> No. Give it two hours at least.

Ellie Cooper

Anything could happen in that time.

> **Amanda Bailey**
> It isn't so they can rescue me. It's so they know what I was doing when it happened.

A conversation between Amanda Bailey and Oliver Menzies, in a noisy café, 12 July 2021. Transcribed with a scowl, by Ellie Cooper.

OM: The sound on that file is almost identical to what I hear when the mad squaddie calls me every morning.

AB: We'll see now, won't we? See if *this* file records properly. Right, that's on. That's recording. On, right?

OM: Yes, it's on. What I think is he broke in the night before we drove to Tynefield and tampered with my phone. To sabotage my big interview. He knew how important it was because he'd been listening in on my calls, reading my texts and WhatsApps.

AB: Can he do that? And would he?

OM: Yes. Long background in security comms. Boasted about listening to royal phone calls. You won't believe what he's capable of. The things he did in Iraq. To his fellow squaddies, this is. Long before he even got hold of an enemy soldier. Bullying doesn't come close.

AB: He admitted to it?

OM: Off the record and only to me. I know why, now. If it gets out, he'll know where it comes from. And I'll be next.

AB: What can he do to you, realistically?

OM: Well, he got hold of a porter rumoured to be working for the Taliban, tied him to a tree and set fire to him. From the feet up.

AB: Shit.

OM: No one who worked on that book believes he's given up the mercenary work. He has no emotion except anger, no empathy. He'll kill literally anyone for money. Hounding me is child's play for him.

AB: Hmmm, still says it's recording. Tell me about the visit to Gabriel. As much as you can remember.

OM: So I leave you trying to sweet-talk the officer on the door. I go through security, like at an airport. Then, in the corner of the visiting room ... there he is. [*Silence. EC*]

AB: What's he like?

OM: He looks exactly like all his photos. I swear he hasn't aged a day.

AB: Not gone grey? He's over sixty.

OM: Not a hair. Smooth, well spoken, he's a good-looking man. Wearing a sweat top and jeans. He looks at me with these piercing eyes and smiles. [*He sighs, you both pause for a moment. Clink of cutlery. EC*] So I say ... I say to him ... [*He keeps hesitating. EC*]

AB: What's wrong?

OM: Nothing. I say, 'What were you thinking? Sacrificing a baby, it's madness—'

AB: Ol, he's inside for the murder of Harpinder Singh. The baby was rescued. It's fine.

OM: I know, I know. But you didn't see his eyes, Mand. Anyway, he told me I'm the focus of someone's negative energy. There's someone who wants me dead. And they'll keep on until I am. Not violent, he said, but drip drip. Drip drip. Mand, I didn't say a word about the mad squaddie. How could he possibly know about that?

AB: He's a con man. A narcissistic psychopath. He convinced three men to kill an infant, and they almost did. When that failed, he

145

convinced them to kill themselves, then mutilated their bodies. He's deranged, yet he's spent his entire life fitting in with normal people. He knows how to behave and he knows what makes other people vulnerable. Notice he turned the conversation round to *you* as soon as you asked about his crimes. Absolutely classic behaviour. If only I'd been there.

OM: Maybe, maybe, but it doesn't explain how he knew. *You* know. I've been telling you for weeks. There *is* someone targeting me with negative energy and believe me the mad squaddie *want*s me dead. Not just that. It's word for word how he describes one of his torture techniques. I won't ... it includes dripping petrol into people's eyes. [*You go to speak, but he interrupts. EC*] So I said, 'Yeah, I know someone wants me dead. How can I stop them?' He said, 'You're not responsible for them. They're on a journey and events have to play out. Your journey collides with theirs. Like planets aligning in the sky for a short time, then they move away, each in their own predestined orbit. Nothing you can *do* but accept it.'

AB: It's obvious what his game is. Using up your visit with verbal shit. What did he say about his conviction? Did he make an admission of guilt or mention new evidence?

OM: He said ... something ... he didn't do it. Other stuff. Then he said nowhere is safe. Nowhere's safe now. That's exactly what Jonah said. How did he know that?

AB: We don't know for sure Jonah doesn't correspond with Gabriel. They could be fucking with you.

OM: With us.

AB: Look, our books will dredge up his crime and what he *doesn't* need is anyone reminding the public how dangerous he is. Ol, you can see what he's doing, right? I'm sorry I couldn't get in with you because I've spoken to people like him before. It's all about control.

OM: He has the face of an angel, Mand. I can say this to you, because you know me and that it's an observation, no more. But some people have looks that are just ... Elvis Presley: face of an angel. Jodie Comer. Michaela Coel. Some people just have it.

AB: They have symmetrical faces, clear skin and other things the western eye perceives as genetically attractive. Failing that, a good photographer and Photoshop. It doesn't reflect anything inside. It certainly doesn't mean he's an angel. [*I can't believe you two are having this convo. EC*]

OM: With him, it did. His demeanour matched his looks. As I sat there opposite him, I believed he was an archangel.

AB: He's an arch manipulator. [*There's a pause while you both chew and clink your glasses. EC*]

OM: Is that recording?

AB: Let's see. [*This is what you play back. So, there are two phones recording this convo. And you're recording without him knowing ... again. EC*]

OM: *You won't believe what he's capable of. The things he did in Iraq. To his fellow squaddies, this is. Long before he even got hold of an enemy soldier. Bullying doesn't come close.*

AB: *He admitted to it?*

OM: *Off the record and only to me. I know why, now. If it gets out, he'll know where it comes from. And I'll be next.*

AB: Yep, that's fine. Why would it not work when you were with Gabriel? I have to go. Meeting someone tonight. Late tonight. On a path behind a pub. They say they can help find the baby.

OM: Great. Why so late?

AB: Whoever they are, they're super-paranoid. It may be a great lead, it may be a dead end—

OM: Be careful, Mand.

AB: Like you fucking care, you bullshitter—

OM: I care—

AB: Yeah, about your book!
[*Ends abruptly as you walk away. He did sound kind of concerned, Mand. EC*]

Email exchange between Oliver Menzies and spiritual counsellor Paul Cole, 12 July 2021:

TO: Paul Cole
DATE: 12 July 2021
SUBJECT: Re: The Alperton Angels
FROM: Oliver Menzies

Paul, can I tell you something? My dad died end of last year. He was in hospital but no one knew he would die right then. It took the nurses and doctors by surprise, let alone us. I was at the checkout in Sainsbury's loading my groceries into a bag. I had a sudden feeling. Never had it before, not had it since. Like a wave of darkness descended over me and dropped through me. I didn't know what it was, but it passed and I went home as normal.

When I got the phone call an hour later, I realised I'd had that feeling the very second he passed away.
Oliver

TO: Oliver Menzies
DATE: 12 July 2021
SUBJECT: Re: The Alperton Angels
FROM: Paul Cole

Dear Oliver,

I am so sorry to hear about your father. Yes, that type of experience can occur when someone dies. It is the severance of their earthly connection to you. Birth and death are equally traumatic for the spirit, as it must cross a divide. Each spirit is pushed and pulled equally on either side to facilitate the exchange of energy. In the process our earthly connections may feel that exchange. I believe the feeling is particularly associated with heightened psychic sensibilities.

Your relationship with your father must have been very strong. It is always a difficult time. You have my deepest condolences.
Take care of yourself,
Paul

WhatsApp messages between me and Ellie Cooper in the early hours of 13 July 2021:

> **Amanda Bailey**
> OK, stand down. And thanks for staying up/awake etc.

Ellie Cooper
Did you get what you wanted?

> **Amanda Bailey**
> No. They didn't show. Either got cold feet or – I don't know. I waited around in a pitch-black lane for thirty minutes. Nothing.

Ellie Cooper
Are you home now?

> **Amanda Bailey**
> Yes, just got back.

Ellie Cooper
Mand, they know where you live and they made sure your flat was empty for over an hour. With your devices inside.

> **Amanda Bailey**
> Well, the phone is where I left it on the hall table. Thanks, Ellie. Now to bed!

Ellie Cooper
There could be someone in the flat. Lying in wait for you.

Ellie Cooper
Mand, are you OK?

Ellie Cooper
Mand, please answer so I know you're OK.

Missed call: Ellie Cooper

Missed call: Ellie Cooper

Missed call: Ellie Cooper

**Email from Oliver Menzies to spiritual counsellor Paul Cole,
13 July 2021:**

TO: Paul Cole
DATE: 13 July 2021
SUBJECT: Re: The Alperton Angels
FROM: Oliver Menzies

Paul, I don't believe in these things. Is there a scientific basis for what you've just said? A fact-based, rational explanation for the feeling I had – other than 'pure coincidence'? Please can you explain it? Help me understand.

**WhatsApp messages between Ellie Cooper and me on the morning of
13 July 2021:**

Ellie Cooper
Mand, are you OK? I'm so worried!

> **Amanda Bailey**
> I'm OK. I'm OK. Did you call the police?

Ellie Cooper
No. Shall I?

> **Amanda Bailey**
> No! Absolutely not.

Ellie Cooper
Oh my God, Mand. What happened?

> **Amanda Bailey**
> You were right. There was someone here, waiting for me. But it's not a problem. Well, it is. It's a MASSIVE problem, but not for my personal safety. I'm fine.

Ellie Cooper
Who was it?

Amanda Bailey

I'll explain some day. Thanks, Ellie. For not calling anyone.

Text messages from me to social worker Sonia Brown, 13 July 2021:

Amanda Bailey

Sonia. So I met 'Mr Blue' last night. Why didn't you just say?

Amanda Bailey

OK, ghost me if you like.

WhatsApp messages between me and my editor Pippa Deacon, 13 July 2021:

Amanda Bailey

Hi Pippa. I've traced the baby. But it's not good news. It was a closed, dark adoption. In short, when a child's origins are especially traumatic, they can be placed overseas with no record of where they came from. Canada, New Zealand and Australia are the go-to places.

Pippa Deacon

Can they be traced to those places?

Amanda Bailey

There's literally no paper trail. It's to protect them. Even when they grow up they won't be able to find out. Their only hope is to trace relatives through commercial DNA testing.

Pippa Deacon

Shit. There must be something you can do.

Amanda Bailey

I have an idea for a new angle. It's dark and original. Oliver and I can still work together and spread the story between us, so we'll benefit from Green Street's promo, as before.

Pippa Deacon

I don't know. Can you send a page pitch and first chapter?

> **Amanda Bailey**
>
> Thing is, it'll take some delicate organisation, so I'd rather not say more at this stage. If you give me the go-ahead, for now at least, you'll have to trust me.

Pippa Deacon

OK. Go for it. Meeting Jo for drinks today. Will let her know.

WhatsApp messages between Oliver Menzies and me, 13 July 2021:

Oliver Menzies

I don't believe they are totally untraceable. I just don't. We all have a right to know where we come from. How can anyone say that one particular child has no right to know?

> **Amanda Bailey**
>
> It's not common. Only in exceptional circumstances. This was a high-profile case. Social workers probably thought they were doing the right thing for the kid. Protecting it from people like us.

Oliver Menzies

I'll have to tell Jo at Green Street. She'll pull the whole book. They've never liked me there anyway.

> **Amanda Bailey**
>
> Pippa will tell her. Let's think of other angles. Anything in mind?

Oliver Menzies

No. Mad squaddie taking up too many brain cells right now.

Text messages between me and a council official outside the flat of former news reporter Gray Graham, 14 July 2021:

> **Amanda Bailey**
>
> Outside the flat now. It's boarded up.

Unknown number

I've got keys to the reinforced door. On my way. Delayed.

Unofficial interview with a council representative in the flat of the late Gray Graham, 14 July 2021. Transcribed by Ellie Cooper.

AB: In all these years of being his close friend, I only ever knew him as Gray. Short for Graham, I suppose.

CR: You didn't realise he was *Thomas Andrew* Graham. Yet you were so close. How old was he?

AB: I ... don't know.

CR: How did you meet him?

AB: At work. Years ago. He was a stringer – a roving reporter on the local paper I started on.

CR: What was he like? [*So many questions. She's suspicious ... EC*]

AB: Great at the job. He'd done it for years. I mean, yeah, if something happened in the borough, he'd be first on the scene, guaranteed. Like he had a sixth sense for what was going on. Knew all the right people. Asked the right questions.

CR: What was he like as a person?

AB: Quite lovely. [*OMG, I don't think you knew him at all. EC*] Looking around, I can see he had, er ...

CR: His flat doesn't give much away, does it? [*Awkward pause while the CR and, quite frankly, I silently doubt your claim to being his friend. EC*]

AB: No, I suppose it doesn't.

CR: Nice you stayed in touch, though.

AB: Yes. [*These pauses are excruciating. Make it stop! EC*] He always had a tale to tell.

CR: He obviously lived very ... frugally. If someone came here expecting to snap up Mr Graham's valuables ... jewellery or cash, for example, they'd be sorely disappointed.

AB: They would. Any valuables have been *snapped up* already. Luckily, I'm only interested in documents from the decades he worked for *The Informer*. We diligently maintain our archives. Local news gathering is very different now. Gray was from a bygone era. It would be a shame if that time died with him.

CR: I'll be in the hallway.

[*I heard your sigh of relief she's gone. EC*]

WhatsApp messages between me and Oliver Menzies, 14 July 2021:

> **Amanda Bailey**
> Remember Gray Graham?

Oliver Menzies
Old stringer who only came in to the office for Christmas drinks?
Where he'd bore us all with stories from his early days on the job.

> **Amanda Bailey**
> Yep, him.

Oliver Menzies
Didn't know him 😂

> **Amanda Bailey**
> Died alone in a grotty council flat.

Oliver Menzies
Not surprised. He was paid peanuts, and only when his pic or story made it into print. If it was spiked for any reason, he got nothing. They wouldn't even pay him expenses. Developed his own pics to save money.

> **Amanda Bailey**
> Died before he could tell me who asked him to say Jonathan Childs was first on the scene of Singh's murder. When he wasn't.

Oliver Menzies
Isn't this the second bod who's croaked before you could speak to them? 😂

> **Amanda Bailey**
> The curse of the Alperton Angels.

Oliver Menzies

The curse of Amanda Bailey. With this and the baby you're not
having much luck 😂

> **Amanda Bailey**
>
> Do you know shorthand?

Oliver Menzies

Do you? No. Because we both did a sub-standard training
course.

> **Amanda Bailey**
>
> Hmm. Would've been VERY useful.

**A scan of my handwritten note to Aunty Pat. Undated, but I posted it
through her door after sundown on the evening of 14 July 2021:**

Dear Aunty Pat,
It's been so long since we spoke, let alone met. Hope you're
keeping well. I bumped into Robin's wife (Claire?) a few years
ago. She said Uncle Jack died.
    You and I may not have parted on the best of terms, but life
is too short to hold grudges. Your memories of things that
happened many years ago vary markedly from mine, but my feeling is that we can each maintain our differences of opinion and
still have a relationship. It would be a shame not to, as there are
so few of us left in the family. Shall we meet? Perhaps a coffee
or something informal?
When are you free? I can make any day this week.
Amanda

Note posted through my letterbox before sunrise on 15 July 2021:

Amanda,
It's been 26 years since you decided to leave. This family
never recovered from the lies you told about it. The stress

of it all killed your mother. Robin and Jacquie had to go through school with the stigma of being your sister. Even Mark and Joanna felt it as your cousins.

Nonetheless, what you say about grudges holds some water. Where family is concerned it should never be too late to mend broken bridges – even when there could never be enough water flowing beneath them to wash away the damage.

I don't want you in my house. There's a Costa in Harrow. I'm there today and most Thursdays after 11.
Patricia Bailey

A scan of my handwritten note to Aunty Pat that I posted through her door, also before sunrise, on the morning of 15 July 2021. Welcome to my family:

Dear Aunty Pat,
Thank you. Your willingness to forgive and forget is much appreciated.

Just one thing: you will have retired by now, but I remember you taught secretarial skills to Plymouth Brethren women at a college somewhere in Hertfordshire. You explained that they reject modern technology, but still use typewriters and other old-style office equipment to run their businesses so, unlike other colleges, your department kept its secretarial teachers. I wonder, if I showed you some pages of shorthand, could you translate it?
Amanda

A meeting between Amanda Bailey and her Aunty Pat at Costa Coffee, Harrow, 15 July 2021. Transcribed by Ellie Cooper.

AB: Ellie, I'm in Costa waiting for my Aunty Pat who I haven't spoken to since a traumatic family showdown and slanging match twenty-six years ago. She is the last person I want to see on this entire earth. But I need something and there's no faster way to get it. I found a stack of old spiral notebooks in Gray Graham's flat, full of shorthand, which I can't read. Hopefully she can. Ignore everything she says, and everything I say, except for when she translates these notebooks. [*Sound of a heavy thud on a table. EC*] The things I do for this job.

[*I cut out stuff I can't unhear. OMG, Mand, I'm so sorry. EC*]

AP: Why should I do this for you?

AB: Because I'm family?

AP: You never even admitted it. You're not admitting it now!

AB: Admitted what?

AP: That it was all lies.

AB: Well, because it … [*You take a deep breath here. EC*] Well, OK it was all lies.

AP: I knew. I knew it was.

AB: Every last word. [*Awkward silence. You obviously didn't lie. She must know that. EC*]

AP: [*Huffing sound. EC*] Well, are they Pitman or Gregg?

AB: There's more than one type of shorthand? [*Shuffling of paper and flicking of pages. EC*]

AP: There is, and everyone develops their own style over time. Ah, it's Pitman. [*Mumbles. EC*] I might have known you'd show your face when you wanted something.

AB: It's a cold case, Aunty Pat. You might uncover something that changes the course of history.

AP: This here. She summarises the contents at the top of each page. [*I can hear a page is flicked over between each headline. EC*] 'Seagull flies into old folks' home, stays three weeks, outlives two residents.'
'Woman stabbed to death in flat, boyfriend on run.'
'Runaway barge injures three.'
'Policeman shot in stomach, small bore, will live.'
'Man stabbed in street.'
'Lesbians grow lychees on doomed allotment, council won't comment.'
'Three-car pile-up on A40, firemen cry.'
'Burglar trips, lands on cactus. Might sue.'

'Council meeting delayed by rail protest.'
'Police called out five times in one night by spider building web across sensor alarm.'
'Convicted drug dealer found hanged under canal bridge.'
'Dog avenges brother's death, probably not true.'

AB: Does it say the dates of these stories?

AP: No. But on the inside cover ... it looks like April slash May 2001.

AB: Do any of these say January 2003? [*Shuffling and thudding. EC*]

AP: This one says November 03 slash March 04.

AB: Try that one.

AP: 'Mayor opens Christmas fete at Woodend School.' [*The page flips between each headline. EC*]
'One-man protest over bin schedule blocks dual carriageway.'
'Old Eric is Santa again, thirty-seven years on trot.'
'Drinks six thirty onwards.'

AB: That's a personal note, isn't it? And that double line ... could mean the end of the year. I'm looking for a week or two in early December. [*Pages turning. Stops abruptly. EC*]

AP: The Alperton Angels. Is that what you're looking for?

AB: Yes! Where does it say that?

AP: She's drawn a thick square line around it. As if she added that title in at the top when she realised this all referred to the same thing.

AB: Aunty Pat, please can you read it out, from here on? [*She sighs. I don't think she relishes the idea. EC*]

AP: 'Young girl. Sounds hysterical. Baby. Bus garage. Canal. Old Cow & Gate place at Alperton? Baby born in old baby food warehouse. Going to hospital. Were they OK? Find out. What's these symbols? Could be satanic. Witchcraft. Devil worshippers move in behind bus garage.' Now, after this, there's a space. It's as if she wrote the next bit at a different time. See, the first is neat. Follows the ruled line. But down here the words are scrawled in a *big* hurry. See?

AB: Yeah. You're right.

AP: Doesn't stick to the lines at all. I'd guess it was written in the dark. It says ... [*She pauses here. Struggles to read the words because they are unclear, or distressing? EC*] 'Blood. Three dead. Stabbings. Nasty, nasty.' [*OMG, no wonder you're both quiet for a bit. EC*] That's all.

AB: He was there and never told anyone.

AP: He? A man wrote this? Oh well, he must've done it. Guilty conscience. Else why keep it quiet?

AB: Indeed. Why else, Aunty Pat?
[*Mand, if this means what I think it does, then it was Gray Graham who found the bodies of the Alperton Angels. EC*]

Divine

by

Amanda Bailey

One

Freelance news reporter Thomas Andrew Graham – known to his colleagues as Gray Graham – started his career in the long hot summer of 1976. The first event he reported on was a swarm of ladybirds that blew across London from the Thames Estuary. He described a heaving carpet of red as the creatures settled on roads and pavements.

By 10 December 2003 Gray Graham was a veteran reporter. He'd seen bypasses, tower blocks and housing estates planned, objected to, protested against and built anyway. He'd covered the celebrations across the borough for the Royal Wedding in July 1981. He'd watched from a press box at RAF Northolt as Princess Diana's body was flown back from Paris in September 1997. To say Gray Graham had 'seen it all' would be a cliché, but no less accurate for it.

As this chilly Wednesday drew to a close, only a story of particularly newsworthy proportions would have tempted him out of his warm flat.

'Baby born in old baby food warehouse' is scribbled in Pitman shorthand on his pad, along with a note to find out whether mother and child pulled through. This feel-good story could make tomorrow's deadline for Friday's paper. But then, something else is scrawled across the page: 'Devil worshippers move in behind bus garage.' How Gray knew these stories were unfolding is a mystery. Did he have an informal arrangement with police officers? A quid pro quo whereby he reported stories – or not – in return for regular leads? Where was he when these stories broke? Riding in police friends' patrol cars in return for cash? The newsroom at *The Informer* had long considered his story-gathering skills to border on the psychic, but the simple fact was, no one ever asked.

Gray scrapes open a tumbledown door and squeezes through into the old warehouse. His torch sweeps back and forth, his eyes search the floor for evidence of devil worshipping: occult symbols, candles, pentagrams … an atmospheric picture in this gloomy light could make the front page.

What he sees instead are creeping pools of black liquid. As his footsteps approach, he slows. His torch beam reveals these pools to be not black, but red. There's a carpet of crimson across this entire floor. Gray instinctively takes a step back as the sticky pool reaches his shoes.

Then he sees them. One after the other after the other. Twisted, bloody, shocking. Gray Graham has stumbled upon a scene so horrific, later that night hardened police officers would ask to leave the site. Ritual suicide and post-mortem mutilation. A literal bloodbath that sends Gray hurtling back in the direction he came, tripping and stumbling until he's back under a streetlight, in the normal everyday world, where he can calm himself down and dial 999 [*but did he dial 999? Find out*].

And so began the case of the Alperton Angels.

3

Fishing for my New Angle

WhatsApp messages between me and retired detective chief superintendent Don Makepeace, 16 July 2021:

> **Amanda Bailey**
> Hey Don! How are you? Quick question: who found the bodies of the dead angels?

Don Makepeace
I think the girl disclosed something – enough to trigger a 999 call – once she was at the hospital. No idea who made that call.

> **Amanda Bailey**
> Perhaps the nurse who treated Holly in A&E. Cheers, Don.

Don Makepeace
You heard Gray Graham died?

> **Amanda Bailey**
> I did, yes.

Don Makepeace
Found dead in a housing association bedsit. A sad end for someone who had been quite the local face in his day. Don.

> **Amanda Bailey**
> Yes, he was quite the local face.

Text messages between me and A&E nurse Penny Latke, 16 July 2021:

> **Amanda Bailey**
> When you treated Holly in A&E that night, did she mention the dead angels in the warehouse?

Penny Latke
Eeeeeeeeeeek! So excited to help with your book! 💀

> **Amanda Bailey**
> Trying to get to the bottom of who, exactly, made the 999 call that led police to the basement.

Penny Latke

How cool would that have been? But no, it wasn't us. I didn't even hear about it till I saw it on telly. When is your book out?

WhatsApp messages between me and Oliver Menzies, 16 July 2021:

> **Amanda Bailey**
> Got an interesting discrepancy regarding who exactly found the angels' bodies. Looks like it was Gray Graham, but no formal record of it.

Oliver Menzies
If it had been Gray, he'd have bored everyone with the tale every Christmas party.

> **Amanda Bailey**
> More than that, it was national news. He could've sold his eyewitness account.

Oliver Menzies
First rule of journalism: don't become the story. It never ends well.

> **Amanda Bailey**
> To document and broadcast an experience like that. It's in the public interest.

Oliver Menzies
Why would he even have been there before the police?

> **Amanda Bailey**
> If he couldn't adequately explain why, he might have kept quiet.

> **Amanda Bailey**
> Because he was breaking the law some other way himself. Or feared being implicated. Or simply didn't want to compromise the source of his local leads. His living depended on it.

Oliver Menzies
I say again: why would he have been there? A derelict building on a rundown industrial estate?

Amanda Bailey

Because either he WAS involved in the events or he went to the warehouse that night because

Oliver Menzies

Well? Because what?

Amanda Bailey

Because he sensed something was up and couldn't explain why. Everyone who knew Gray said how instinctive he could be. That he was at crime scenes before any other media. What if he had a sixth sense that led him to the Alperton warehouse that night?

Oliver Menzies

Do you believe in things like that?

Amanda Bailey

There are some perfectly sane and intelligent people who do. Judy Teller-Dunning is a respected American journalist and author. But when she unexpectedly found some notes after her husband's funeral, her first thought was that he had 'shown' her where they were.

Amanda Bailey

Do I believe it? I am not so sure.

Email from Cathy-June Lloyd, Cold & Unsolved Murder Club chair, 17 July 2021:

TO: Amanda Bailey
DATE: 17 July 2021
SUBJECT: Re: A small favour
FROM: Cathy-June Lloyd

Dear Amanda,

Further to your email, Cold & Unsolved have been beavering away to see what we can find out for you about the case of the Alperton Angels. We've been reading news reports in chronological order and can't help but notice there's a body that comes and goes.

Harpinder Singh's body is discovered in Middlesex House on 9 December, having been deceased for several days. His murder is eventually linked forensically to Gabriel Angelis and thus he becomes part of the Alperton Angels mythology.

In the small hours of 11 December 2003 reports emerge of multiple stabbings in an abandoned warehouse. Some early police reports state there are two bodies, some say three, some say four.

Later that day the number of dead is given as three: the 'angels' Michael, Gabriel and Elemiah.

But Peter Duffy, aka Gabriel Angelis, the cult leader, is actually on the run. His mugshot is circulated and he's recognised by a hostel resident in Ealing and caught on 13 December. He's dishevelled but uninjured. The young cult members: Holly, Jonah and their baby are long since whisked away by the authorities.

This is where the body count takes another turn. Reports now name Christopher Shenk, a local petty criminal, as the 'angel' Raphael, and the *third* body found in the warehouse.

While police officers may have been mistaken over the names, Jonah knew very well which was which and his interview stated that the man he believed to be the archangel Gabriel was dead.

While we have no explanation for this anomaly, members of the Guildford Cold & Unsolved Murder Club believe this should be called not The Case of the Alperton Angels, but The *Mystery* of the Alperton Angels.

We'll keep at this case, Amanda; it's too intriguing to stop now!
All the best,
Cathy-June Lloyd

WhatsApp messages between me and Oliver Menzies, 16 July 2021:

Amanda Bailey
Just forwarded an email. What do you think?

Oliver Menzies
Who are these people?

Amanda Bailey

A murder club. Don't pull the face I know you're pulling right
now.

Oliver Menzies

A murder club. Quirky-looking girls and guys with beards.

Amanda Bailey

I'm a quirky-looking girl, you're a guy with a beard

Oliver Menzies

Well, I picked up on the different body numbers straight away.
Hysterical hearsay in the immediate aftermath of a horrible
crime.

Amanda Bailey

'Three bodies' comes from Gray Graham and he was THERE.
We know there were three bodies in the basement of that
warehouse before the police arrived. Singh's body was found
the previous day in Middlesex House. Four bodies. It's very
straightforward. Why the confusion?

Another email from amateur detective David Polneath, 17 July 2021:

TO: Amanda Bailey
DATE: 17 July 2021
SUBJECT: The Alperton Angels
FROM: David Polneath

Dear Amanda,

I haven't received a reply to my last email, so I wonder, did it arrive? I
never know if my account is being hacked or messages intercepted.

This whole case is so emotive. Angels, demons, troubled teenagers
failed by the system, cult members mutilated in a violent bloodbath, a
baby in peril, rescued at the final moment in an heroic showdown ... It's
no wonder writers and filmmakers were inspired by it. But what if they
were all unwittingly colluding with a smokescreen?

I have a theory that somehow the media got hold of this news too
soon after the events, so a planned cover-up couldn't be finalised. They

had to work quickly and off the cuff to keep the truth under wraps.

We have to be careful though, Amanda, you and I.

Yours,

David

Amanda Bailey's guest appearance on the *Fresh Ghost* podcast, hosted by Dave 'Itchy' Kilmore. Recorded at the Soho Studio, 18 July 2021. Transcribed by Ellie Cooper.

AB: Ellie, I'm about to take part in this podcast. They discuss supernatural phenomena and conspiracy theories. Ignore all that. Just transcribe anything about the Alperton Angels. [*As requested, I cut the chat about UFO sightings, ghost stories and serial killers. This is all I have left. EC*]

DIK: [*What can I say? Those are his initials. EC*] So, a genie is trapped in your cupboard and he offers you three wishes, plus the option to free him. What do you say? First wish.

AB: My first wish is that every time I wish for something, I'm granted two more wishes.

DIK: Nice one. That way your wish account will always be in credit. Second wish?

AB: I wish that no one else ever has a wish granted.

DIK: Now, that's a bit mean, Amanda. Why do we have to forgo our wishes?

AB: Because you might wish me dead.

DIK: Not before the end of the podcast. After that do you have a third wish?

AB: No, because I already have an endless supply of wishes and can use them at my leisure.

DIK: Do you free the genie?

AB: Yes. Why not?

DIK: Because ... once he's free he will reveal himself to be, not a genie, but a *demon*. You have freed a demon to walk the earth.

AB: Well, I write about evil events. It can only be good for business.

DIK: So, Amanda, you've written about the murders of Jill Dando, Rachel Nickell and Suzy Lamplugh. What's next for you?

AB: The case of the Alperton Angels.

DIK: Awesome. In my opinion not one that's been properly covered, don't know what you think ...

AB: It's not an easy one to research. There seems to be a mysterious cloak of secrecy around the case. *[Amanda Bailey, are you trying to fan the embers of a conspiracy theory? EC]*

DIK: I was only thirteen at the time, but I remember hearing about it. Do you think the lack of, um, documentary investigation – by that I mean journalism, books, TV, etc. – do you think that points to a conspiracy?

AB: It could. But I don't know what that could be.

DIK: I've got a theory, well two theories. We're looking at, one: a cover-up of professional failings; or two: a cover-up of supernatural phenomena that would create panic if it were to get out.

AB: Well, that's what I hope to find out, Dave. Can your listeners help?

DIK: Fresh Ghosters: if you have any theories, any thoughts ...

AB: Any memories or personal experience that could help me investigate this case ...

DIK: Jump on to our selectively moderated discussion forum. And I understand there's a reward?

AB: There is, but as I don't have a demon granting my wishes, the reward is just glory.

DIK: Just glory, guys!

AB: A name check in the book.

DIK: That is glory worth having!
[I cut out the rest. EC]

TO: Oliver Menzies
DATE: 18 July 2021
SUBJECT: Re: The Alperton Angels
FROM: Paul Cole

Dear Oliver,

Many apologies for my delay in replying to your email. I have been on a spiritual retreat, far away from any internet connection. You ask me to explain what I mean by 'the other side' and Gabriel's potential link to it. I will try.

We visit this earth many times and live many lives, but returning is never guaranteed. It's a privilege and an opportunity. We choose aspects of our life before we are born – our parents, for example – but there are rules. We must counteract light with dark in every life we live. In turn, each of us must endure difficult lives in order to enjoy brighter, happier lives in future.

We are part of a collective consciousness, yet we are each on our own journey. For spiritual evolution to take place, we must be born with no conscious memory of the other side. Dreams are our bridge between the worlds and I believe that is where Gabriel has an unusual gift. However, most of us will experience things that make us wonder. How did that happen? What *was* that? Events that have no logical explanation.

You may think our earthly lives are preordained. That everything happens for a reason. Fate. Destiny. Not necessarily. We have free will. We can enjoy sudden success, joy, riches ... as well as accidents and disaster. Our lives can go horribly wrong at the hands of others.

I believe Gabriel has a psychic power and a connection – as to whether he is the archangel Gabriel, of that I am less convinced.

All the best,

Paul

A page torn from the novel *My Angel Diary* by Jess Adesina:

Wednesday the whirly-third of Glitter-spin

There's a new girl. And she's an angel, too.

Thursday the whirly-fourth of Glitter-spin

So, what *do* you do when another angel arrives in your cosmic orbit? I'll tell you what *I* do. Nothing. I am struck speechless and frozen to the spot. Her name's Ashleigh. She's from a public school, so her parents must have fallen on hard times. Perhaps her mother gambles online, or her father is in prison for illegal dealings on the dark web. She has long brown hair with blunt ends. Miss Crosby asked Daisy to look after her. Huge moment of glitter-pointment. If she'd asked Georgia, I could have, without an attention-grabbing breach of clique boundaries, actually spoken to her. I know at this point you're wondering: how can Tilly be so sure this new girl is an angel too? You can't tell just by looking, and she hasn't even spoken to her yet. Well, I'll tell you the secret of how we recognise each other: angels born on earth must wear their wings in their eyes. Ashleigh has wings in her eyes. And I am in love (again).

A page torn from the novel *White Wings* by Mark Dunning:

Celine smiled coquettishly at the ambassador. Her Givenchy gown was so minimalist in structure and fashioned from a material so sheer, his gaze would never reach her customised Manolos. Dissected and rebuilt not by Mr Blahnik, but by Gabriel. One false step would activate the device, blow her cover and scupper an entire operation with interested parties larger and shadier even than *their* organisation. If the explosion didn't do the job, Gabriel would finish her off with pleasure. The term killer heels had never been so apt.

The ambassador's diplomatic eyes skimmed Celine's gazelle-like body the way a butterfly skims an outcrop of pink pampas at the end of summer. Somewhere inside she acknowledged a faint wave of disgust that this man had known her since childhood and was, in fact, a distant cousin of her father's.

While she would have preferred to believe Gabriel valued her for her whip-smart mind and breath-stopping beauty, she knew that really, it was for this. Her impeccable connections. Because Celine had the poise and the accent. The style and the content. She could glide into these events, through the corridors of power, seven-star hotels, towering office blocks, super yachts and penthouse suites ... right up to the gods of world society without even the lowliest security officer checking her credentials. Once inside, she could do anything.

Celine's eyes flicked left and right. She kissed the ambassador on both cheeks and stalked past. The click-click of her heels broke an admiring silence as men and women alike paused to admire the compelling lines of her shoulders and slink of her hips.

Pages torn from the script *Divine* by Clive Badham:

INT. LIVING ROOM, FLAT — THE NEXT DAY

LOUD SCREAMS from the rocking Moses basket under the coffee table. The clock reads 11.30 a.m. Holly, in cheap pyjamas, stamps into the room, sees the room's empty, stamps out and bangs on a nearby door.

                HOLLY

    Jonah! Jonah!

Thumps and mumbles from behind the door. Jonah, also in pyjamas, squints out, face creased with sleep.

                JONAH

    Uh?

                HOLLY

    It won't stop. Where's Gabriel?

So sleepy he can barely answer …

                JONAH

    Gone.

The Baby's SCREAMS are insistent. Jonah lifts it out of the Moses basket, jogs and pats it.

INT. KITCHEN, FLAT — DAY

Holly, face like thunder, mixes a bottle of formula and shakes it.

INT. LIVING ROOM, FLAT — DAY

Holly hands Jonah the frothing bottle. He finally gets the teat in the Baby's mouth. Blessed silence. They watch the Baby feed.

                         HOLLY
          How can you do it?

                         JONAH
          (shrugs)
          Gabriel says it's safe.

Holly leans in and stares hard at the Baby.

                         HOLLY
          Pure evil. Beyond our worst dreams. So
          evil, not even death can stop it.

                         JONAH
          Gabriel will stop it.

                         HOLLY
          And us.

Holly's gaze lingers first on the Baby, then on Jonah, but
nothing breaks his concentration.

INT. LIVING ROOM, FLAT — DAY — LATER

The Baby sleeps in its Moses basket. Holly watches from a
safe distance. We may hear far-away CHURCH BELLS clang. A
thought occurs to Holly, she jumps up.

INT. HALLWAY, FLAT — DAY

Holly peers into Jonah's room. He is fast asleep on the bed,
HEADPHONES on. She darts away, grabs a coat, slips through
the front door, gone.

EXT. OLD CHURCH — DAY

It's Sunday. Elderly CHURCHGOERS file through the doors
of a crumbling old church. Holly, head down, joins the

line, slips through, last. The doors BANG closed behind her.

INT. CHURCH — DAY — A SHORT TIME LATER

Holly slides on to a back pew. As the service begins, she eyes religious statues, images. Jesus, Mary, a saint, an angel. Her eyes close, she breathes, concentrates. The images swirl into … A CHAOTIC, DREAM-LIKE VISION. Some images heavenly, some hellish, all confused with DEMONIC SCREAMS.

                         PAM (O.S.)
          Welcome.

Holly's eyes snap open. Back to reality. We've jumped forward in time. The service is over. People file out. PAM (60s, sharp, responsible) looms over Holly, her smile friendly, but curious.

                         PAM
          I'm Pam. Haven't seen you here before. New
          to the area?

Holly nods.

                         PAM
          Your mum and dad not here?

Holly studies Pam's bright, open expression.

                         HOLLY
          I don't have a mum or dad.

                         PAM
          I'm sorry. Who looks after you?

                         HOLLY
          The heavenly forces. I'm an angel. My soul
          is divine.

Even Pam can't pretend she's not taken aback.

                    PAM
        Well … where do you sleep?

                    HOLLY
        With an archangel. We live in the flats
        above the shops. There's a group of us.
        Angels.

Pam nods, thoughtful. She looks Holly up and down, evaluates
her state of dress, cleanliness, health.

                    PAM
        We'd love to see you all here. Will you
        bring the others?

Holly locks eyes with a smiling Pam.

EXT. HIGH STREET — DAY

Holly wanders away from the church, switches her phone on.
MISSED CALLS and MESSAGES. It RINGS. She answers.

                    GABRIEL (O.S.)
        (hysterical whisper)
        Where are you? We've had to leave it alone
        to look for you!

                    HOLLY
        I only went to church.

EXT. STREET — DAY

Gabriel edges along the pavement, phone to his ear, worried
eyes on the window of a flat. He paces angrily, grips the
phone, struggles to keep his voice down.

                    GABRIEL
          Get back! Now! Run!

He ends the call, looks desperately to the window, then
along the street. Waits.

EXT. HIGH STREET — DAY

As Holly jogs across a road, she spots Jonah, his expression
dark as thunder.

                    JONAH
          Why did you leave? Who did you speak to?

                    HOLLY
          No one. Only a woman.

Jonah and Holly stamp along. Jonah is quietly irate.

                    JONAH
          She could have been sent to kill us. To stop
          us destroying it. You know what Gabriel
          said. No contact with anyone. Ever again.
          Everything from before is over.

                    HOLLY
          (scowls)
          I know.

                    JONAH
          Other people's reality isn't ours now.
          This is our life. This is what we're here
          for.

EXT. STREET — DAY

Holly and Jonah pant to a halt before Gabriel. He seizes her
arm, whispers harshly …

                    GABRIEL

        You made us leave it alone! Exactly the
        sort of fuck-up the dark forces are waiting
        for.

Jonah and Gabriel glare at Holly.

                    JONAH

        She told someone who we are.

Shocked, Holly glares at him.

                    HOLLY

        (to Gabriel)
        Just a lady at the church. She asked who
        I live with.

Gabriel paces with frustration, barely contains his anger,
hisses in her ear.

                    GABRIEL

        Now we have to go there and put her mind at
        rest. More risk. All because of you.

                    HOLLY

        Sorry.

Gabriel glances to the flat window. His face drops. He freezes.

                    GABRIEL

        There's something up there.

Holly and Jonah glance desperately up at the window. A
slight shadow moves behind it. They start and gasp. At the
window the curtain moves. A FIGURE appears. It fills the
window with the enormity of its presence. Holly and Jonah
squint up at it in horror, but seconds later Gabriel's face
changes to a relieved smile.

                    GABRIEL

        You know who that is … come on!

His mood totally changed, he jogs across the road. Holly and Jonah trot behind.

INT. LIVING ROOM, FLAT — DAY

Gabriel leads Holly and Jonah into the room. ELEMIAH (40s, male, huge) smiles at them all, holds up a door key. He is dressed casually, his manner serene. The Moses basket rocks on the coffee table. Holly and Jonah burst into smiles, run to him.

> HOLLY/JONAH
> Elemiah!

He laughs, hugs them both, then he and Gabriel hug affectionately.

> ELEMIAH
> (seriously, to Gabriel)
> It was alone—

> GABRIEL
> Holly left the flat. Jonah and I had to go
> and look for her.

> HOLLY
> It won't happen again.

> GABRIEL
> Give me the door key.

Holly fishes it from her pocket, hands it to him. She glances at Jonah's hard expression, and to the Baby, before she skulks from the room.

INT. BEDROOM, FLAT — THE NEXT MORNING

Holly wakes. She lies beside a sleeping Gabriel. Jonah is

asleep on his other side. Holly glances at them, slowly swings her feet to the floor. The sun streams through the curtains across her face.

                    GABRIEL (O.S.)
          What are you thinking?

                    HOLLY
          About good and evil.
Gabriel swings his legs over the side of the bed. Sits beside Holly. Sunlight touches them both.

                    GABRIEL
          Can't have one without the other.

                    HOLLY
          Have you ever met a truly evil person?

                    GABRIEL
          (thoughtful)
          Truly evil? I have. Once.

                    HOLLY
          How could you tell?

                    GABRIEL
          It was in their eyes. They were afraid of
          me. Caused as much damage as they could.

                    HOLLY
          What did you do?

Gabriel grins, winks.

                    GABRIEL
          (whispers)
          I got my revenge.

He pads from the room, leaving Holly on the edge of the bed, bathed in sunlight.

Jonah feeds the Baby. Gabriel makes coffee, but Holly seems preoccupied, perched on a kitchen stool. Her toast untouched, she stares hard at a COIN on the counter.

> HOLLY
>
> Why can't I move things with the power of my mind?

Gabriel bustles about the kitchen.

> GABRIEL
>
> Your mind is mortal. Superpowers not included.

> HOLLY
>
> Do you have superpowers?

> GABRIEL
>
> Wish I did.

Holly glares anew at the coin. Jonah holds the Baby, wanders to the sink, chucks its bottle in.

> HOLLY
>
> What can we do, then?

> JONAH
>
> Here.

She takes the Baby. Jonah replaces Holly on the kitchen stool.

> GABRIEL
>
> Our power is in being. Not doing.

Gabriel plonks a CARTON of juice on the counter, spreads jam on more toast, checks the coffee.

                         GABRIEL
     In celestial form our energy guides
     mortals. Helps them. They have free will,
     but in the mortal realm our powers are
     mortal. We're messengers. Usually.

He hands the toast to Jonah, coffee to Holly and sits opposite
them at the counter. They eat, drink and look to him.

                         JONAH
     But not this time?

                         GABRIEL
     This time we have to <u>do</u>, not be.

The Baby cries in Holly's arms. She rocks it.

INT. LIVING ROOM, FLAT — DAY — LATER

Holly and Jonah lounge on the settee, stare at the TV,
bored. The Baby sleeps in its Moses basket. Gabriel appears
from the corridor, groomed, coat on. Holly and Jonah sit
up, suddenly anxious.

                         HOLLY
     Where are you going?

Jonah throws her a look, which she returns with defiance.

                         GABRIEL
     I won't be long. Don't leave. Not for
     anything, OK?

They nod. Gabriel smiles, winks at them and slips out.

INT. LIVING ROOM, FLAT — DAY — LATER

A violent, complex FANTASY GAME plays on a tiny screen. The
MYTHICAL HERO battles an EVIL BEAST. The Hero wins points,

but is suddenly beheaded. GAME OVER.

Holly lies on the settee, bored, casts aside the hand-held electronic game. Jonah studies the view from each window in turn, his eyes peeled for danger. Holly watches him.

> HOLLY
>
> Are you scared?

> JONAH
>
> (too quickly)
> No.
> (beat)
> Gabriel knows what to do.

> HOLLY
>
> Get rid of it?

Jonah looks back to the window. He nods.

> HOLLY
>
> It looks normal. You'd never know what it
> really was.

Jonah slides onto the settee beside her. Both watch the sleeping Baby.

> JONAH
>
> If it weren't for us, it would unleash evil
> like no one's ever known. Destroy mankind.

> HOLLY
>
> Can it control our thoughts?

> JONAH
>
> It can't hurt us. Gabriel said.

Before Holly can reply … KNOCK KNOCK at the door. They jump up, stare wildly. Silent panic.

                              JONAH
                 (whispers)
              Don't answer it!

They creep to the door. Jonah peers through the spyhole.

INT. FISHEYE OF APARTMENT BLOCK CORRIDOR — DAY

A WOMAN (20s, smart) looks up and down the corridor.

INT. HALLWAY, FLAT — DAY

Jonah moves aside. Holly dives in to look herself.

                              HOLLY
              Didn't you see her coming?

                              JONAH
              She must have made herself invisible.

INT. FISHEYE OF APARTMENT BLOCK CORRIDOR — DAY
The Woman takes a last look at the door, turns to go.

INT. HALLWAY, FLAT — DAY

The Baby SCREAMS loudly. Holly and Jonah freeze.

INT. FISHEYE OF APARTMENT BLOCK — DAY

The Woman hears something, turns back.

KNOCK KNOCK.

                              WOMAN
              Hello?

INT. HALLWAY, FLAT — DAY

Jonah jumps to the spyhole, whispers to Holly …

> JONAH
>
> Shut it up!

Holly pads back to the living room. Jonah holds his breath
as the Baby's cries subside.

INT. FISHEYE OF APARTMENT BLOCK CORRIDOR — DAY

The Woman reluctantly turns and leaves.

INT. HALLWAY, FLAT — DAY

Holly rocks the quiet Baby. Jonah turns from the spyhole.
They exchange terrified glances.

> JONAH
>
> The dark forces. They've found us.

EXT. STREET — DAY

The Woman reaches the corner. With an air of knowing, she
turns and looks back. Her eyes dart straight to the window
of the angels' flat. From the glint in her eyes, we know
Jonah is right. Moments later she turns away, rounds the
corner. Gone.

WhatsApp messages between Ellie Cooper and me, 19 July 2021:

Ellie Cooper

You OK, Mand? Haven't heard from you for a couple of days.

> **Amanda Bailey**
>
> Reading and thinking. The baby is a no-go area so need a new angle. Might use the angels' influence in pop culture as a springboard to explore how shocking crimes have the power to change some attitudes and reinforce others.

Ellie Cooper

That's deep. I thought your brief was to rehash the case for a beach read?

> **Amanda Bailey**
>
> You're right.

Ellie Cooper

Heard from my friend with the recording studio. He's got round to Oliver's interview with Gabriel. Said it's a thing called 'bleed'. He can treat it, and it might bring out more words, but says he'll have to stay after hours, use his work's equipment and risk his job. He's angling for money basically.

> **Amanda Bailey**
>
> OK. Let me think. Thanks, Ellie, you're a star.

Text messages between Dave 'Itchy' Kilmore and me, 20 July 2021:

Dave Kilmore

Hey Amanda, have you heard the podcast? Dropped last night. We're already getting responses to your call-out for info. You can see them on the forum yourself. I'll get contact details by DM. OK to forward them? I'll filter out the energy vampires, violent shitheads and downright perverts. After that, believe it or not, there are a few left 😂

Amanda Bailey
Cheers, Dave. Haven't listened yet, sorry. Will tune in when I get a moment. Yep, might as well send them as they've bothered to reply.

Anonymous email sent to the *Fresh Ghost* info@ address, 20 July 2021:

For the lady who appeared on the show. I've got a weird story about the Alperton Angels. I don't tell people often because I feel stupid saying it. But I'm sure I wasn't mistaken. I was in a police station in Wembley the night the bodies were found. At least ten thirty or eleven at night. My wallet was stolen in the pub and I was at the desk reporting it. The station was arranged with a space in the middle where the desk sergeants worked and there were separate areas either side: one for the public and one for police bringing arrested people in from the car park. I could see across the desk to that side. While the sergeant was taking my details, I glanced across the counter and there's Christopher Shenk being brought in. Now, I'd known Chris, or Shenky, at school, but hadn't seen him for years. I'd heard he was dealing drugs, running round the area pretending to be a gangster. He didn't look at me. No one logged him in at the desk, he was led straight through and out the back, I assume to the cells. Thought nothing of it at the time. Days later I caught his name in the paper. He'd died the night of the Alperton massacre. It said he'd joined a cult and believed he was an angel called Raphael, like the Ninja Turtle. Made my blood run cold. Always a shock when you hear someone you've known has died, but this chilled me for another reason. I even dug out the police report about my stolen wallet to check, and I had. I'd seen Shenky that same night, at around the time the angels must've killed themselves. He wasn't being released when I saw him, he was going into the copshop. How could he have been in two places at once? I've thought back to that glimpse I had of him. Was he really being escorted by coppers, or was he walking through alone and I was the only one who saw it? Did I witness his doppelganger at the moment he died? I've never been able to explain it. Never got my wallet back either.

Printed out from the *Fresh Ghost* forum, 20 July 2021:

One of our counsellors tells a story about the Alperton Angels. He says his brother was at school with the Asian man who was killed. He said the newspaper reports about his life up to then weren't true.

Interview with Galen Fletcher, in The Doll's House Café, Harrow on the Hill, 21 July 2021. Transcribed by Ellie Cooper.

> [*I cut out the bit about him explaining his counselling work in a boys' school. EC*]

AB: Thank you for responding to the podcast—

GF: I didn't hear it, one of my students did. He remembered me talking about my brother and the angels, so ...

AB: Sure. What is that connection? If you could explain for the record.

GF: My brother was in the same year as Harpinder Singh at school. They were friends.

AB: So your brother went to school in India?

GF: No, this is the strange thing. Harpinder was, I believe, *born* in Delhi, but his family moved to London when he was a baby. He was schooled here.

AB: Which school?

GF: *Here.* This one. [*You pause in disbelief, as did I. EC*]

AB: *Harrow* school?

GF: Yes. [*Harpinder Singh went to one of the most prestigious boys' public schools in the world? EC*] The reports after his body was found said he'd recently arrived from Delhi. Well, if he had, then he was there on holiday. They spoke as if he was scratching a living in a restaurant, that he'd been burned out of a rented room and was housed in emergency accommodation. It's not impossible – anyone can fall on hard times – but that doesn't sound like the guy I remember. Very sad if he'd ended up in such circumstances. Oh, and they got his age wrong. He wasn't twenty-two. He was twenty-nine.

AB: What do you remember about Harpinder?

GF: I should say he was always Harry Singh to us. He and Clem knew each other at prep school in Ealing. Then they both came here. Harry was outgoing, energetic. Bright, but not as focused as Clem. I remember him in all the school plays. Excellent at chess.

AB: So he was more outdoorsy than academic?

GF: Yes. A people-person. He and Clem did the Duke of Edinburgh Award together. Harry went for gold, but fell behind in maths and English. I think Clem helped him as much as he could. This was years before I arrived. They were eleven years older than me.

AB: Which uni did Harry go to?

GF: I can't recall. It wasn't Oxford or Cambridge. I *think* he read law somewhere, but Clem went to Edinburgh. He was studying medicine and had no time to keep up with friends. They lost touch and so did we ... the rest of the family.

AB: How did you *know* the Harpinder Singh found dead in Alperton in 2003 was the same friend of your brother's from so many years before?

GF: The picture they used. As soon as I saw it ... You know the one?

AB: This?

GF: Yes. He's standing with his head in a towel. It looks like a Sikh turban, but Harry never wore one. His hair was short, all the years we knew him, anyway. The picture is cropped very closely around his face and head. *This* is the photograph it comes from. [*He shows you something. EC*]

AB: Oh. [*You sound surprised. EC*]

GF: It's a group shot of the boys from his house; that's the accommodation where they live in term time. They'd been wild swimming and this was taken just after they'd climbed out of the river. You can see Harry is holding the towel on his head. That's my brother, Clem. They'd be seventeen or eighteen here, not long before they left.

AB: It's definitely the same picture. It seems a strange one to use. If he went to Harrow there'd be formal pictures of him in uniform with his class.

GF: Like *this* one. That's Clem, that's Harry ... taken no more than a year before the other picture. It's always seemed to me they wanted him to appear more ... *Indian* when they reported his death. As if he'd only just arrived in the UK as an economic migrant. He'd lived here all his life. The family were wealthy, with businesses all over the world. He was very ... and I hope this isn't an offensive thing to say: he was very *English*. Very western.

AB: This is a small, grainy picture. How did you recognise your brother's old friend, someone much older than you, who you hadn't seen in a decade?

GF: That's a favourite picture in my family. We've all got one, framed. I know every pixel of it. [*He pauses. EC*] Clem is right in the centre. The summer after this, he taught street kids in Peru on an exchange. He was academic, sporty and good with people. What else is there?

AB: When did Clem die? [*He pauses again. How did you know he was dead? EC*]

GF: In 2000. He was twenty-six. It happened overnight. He had a heart condition we didn't know about ...

AB: I'm sorry. [*Silence. EC*]

AB: Did Harry get in touch then? He'd been so close ...

GF: I understand my parents messaged him through the contact details they had, as did other friends. His family seemed to have moved abroad. If any of those messages reached him, he didn't reply. Which wasn't so unusual. No one knows what to say in a situation like that. Some people just say nothing.

AB: True.

GF: I was actually here, at school myself, when they told me. [*A long pause. EC*] And I'm *still* here.
[*I cut out your goodbyes. EC*]

WhatsApp messages between Oliver Menzies and me, 21 July 2021:

Oliver Menzies

Wrong name, wrong age, wrong biographical details. The only
thing that links penniless immigrant Harpinder Singh to posh
Harry Singh is this blurred picture. It could be that all the details
they released about the dead man are correct – they just used
the wrong photograph.

> **Amanda Bailey**
> You could be right. But Galen went to Posh Harry's funeral.
> And Posh Harry's family were in court for Gabriel's trial and
> sentencing. You can google his sister's statement afterwards.
> Get tissues. Moving stuff.

Oliver Menzies

In that case I'll watch it AFTER my meeting with Jo at Green
Street 😬

**WhatsApp messages between me and retired detective chief superintendent
Don Makepeace, 21 July 2021:**

> **Amanda Bailey**
> Hi, Don. What made you think the baby in the Alperton Angels
> case was adopted by family of Holly's? I've found something out
> recently. Let's just say that if it's true, it's only part of the story.

Don Makepeace

Facts get warped every time someone tells them. I may have
got it wrong or been deliberately misled. Are you sure the
baby's destination is the best place to look, Amanda?

> **Amanda Bailey**
> Did you trace Marie-Claire?

Don Makepeace

I drew a blank. Don.

Email exchange between Oliver Menzies and spiritual counsellor Paul Cole, 21 July 2021:

TO: Paul Cole
DATE: 21 July 2021
SUBJECT: Gabriel
FROM: Oliver Menzies

Gabriel dreamed about me.

First, he said my purpose was to look after my dad while he was ill. That's it. To look after my dad at the end of his life. If that's true then I lived my first thirty-seven years without any purpose, then my purpose kicked in for less than three years, then it was over. He said I'm an angel. He said he'd dreamed about me and that an orchard would be significant.
Oliver

TO: Oliver Menzies
DATE: 21 July 2021
SUBJECT: Re: Gabriel
FROM: Paul Cole

Dear Oliver,

The concept of a purpose was something Gabriel used to manipulate people. It's a strong sense within us. I doubt very much that was your sole purpose. We have many that change throughout our lives. I must also iterate that despite Gabriel's fascinating connection to the other side, I believe he is nonetheless a chaos maker. He has a gift but he uses it for his own gain, not for the benefit of others. I would exercise caution in your dealings with him.
All the best,
Paul

TO: Paul Cole
DATE: 21 July 2021
SUBJECT: Re: Gabriel
FROM: Oliver Menzies

Do you believe in evil, Paul? Not as a religious concept, but as a *force*? I've been reading about places where really bad things happened. Torture. Abuse. Murders. Some people think those places become infused with the negative energy of those 'evil' events. They call it 'stone recording'. It's not a ghost or vampire, but an energy. Listen. I don't believe in religion or spiritual things, but for me this has a scientific basis. Electrical and magnetic energy are invisible but we know they exist, right? They can be stored and released at will. Could the force of evil, of negativity, generate an energy that is similarly controlled?

I'm working on a new angle for my book about the Alperton Angels and think I may have something. Interested in your thoughts.

Ol

WhatsApp messages between Oliver Menzies and me, 21 July 2021:

Oliver Menzies
Jo wants me to submit an updated proposal. Nagging feeling it's a step on the ladder that leads to them pulling it. I submit, they reject. Binned.

> **Amanda Bailey**
> Perfect time to pick up our research trip. Let's find some new angel angles.

Oliver Menzies
Not Alperton again.

> **Amanda Bailey**
> We haven't finished. You keeled over and we had to leave, remember? This time we'll also go to Wembley and Sudbury. Retrace the angels' steps in reverse.

Oliver Menzies
Didn't keel over.

Text messages between former social worker Ruth Charalambos and me, 21 July 2021:

Ruth Charalambos
Heard you're working on the Alperton Angels case. I worked with 'Holly' before she absconded from care to live with the angels.

Amanda Bailey

Thanks for getting in touch, Ruth. Is there anything you'd like to say about the case?

Ruth Charalambos

Yes. Holly was a mature young woman who decided for herself where and with whom she wanted to live.

Amanda Bailey

Children in care can seem mature, when they are MORE vulnerable.

Ruth Charalambos

I know that. Not Holly. She was different. Very different actually. If we failed on any count, and I'm not saying we didn't, it was simply we weren't used to working with girls like her. In the end, even if we had forcibly removed her from the angels, she would only have gone back to them.

Amanda Bailey

That's the hold controlling predators have over their victims.

Ruth Charalambos

Holly wasn't a victim. Not a normal one.

Amanda Bailey

OK. Ruth. This is all off the record. Can you tell me Holly's real name?

NB She didn't reply.

Research trip to Alperton and the surrounding area, made by Amanda Bailey and Oliver Menzies, 22 July 2021. Transcribed by Ellie Cooper.

OM: This whole place is so … nondescript.

AB: That's what's great about it. The traffic intersection is constantly busy. Up there: Middlesex House where Singh's body was found. It's a block of short-term accommodation. These buildings: empty for years. The bus garage, behind which was the warehouse, now those flats. And down here, by the canal, where barges, walkers and joggers pass by. Anything can happen here and no one notices, because they're all going somewhere else.

OM: And it's a crossroads.

AB: More a T-junction—

OM: Not if you count the canal as an arm. [*You both huff and puff down steps. There's a long gap in conversation. EC*] Got my new angle. I've been working on a murder map.

AB: A what? [*Rustling as he unfolds something. EC*] Holy shit, Ol. What is that?

OM: This is the local area with every murder from the seventeen years prior to the angels' massacre marked with a dot. I experimented with connecting them, to see if there's a pattern.

AB: It's the most OCD thing I've ever seen. Must've taken you days. Why seventeen years?

OM: The year Holly was born.

AB: Why that year?

OM: Let me finish. It's a mess of lines, sure, but if you start again on a clean map, take each dot and connect it to just one other, you get this. [*Triumphant rustling. Followed by a tense silence. EC*]

AB: That's incredible. [*I can't tell whether you're lost for words because what he's showing you is revelatory, or not. EC*] What does it mean?

OM: One three, one eight. They're arranged in a spiral, with this dot at the centre.

AB: The central dot is the site of The Assembly. But what's one three, one eight?

OM: Chapter thirteen, verse eighteen of the Book of Revelation. The exact Bible verse that describes the beast, the Antichrist. [*There's a long pause here. EC*]

AB: Wow.

OM: You know me. This is not me, is it? And yet, look. Now, there's a scientific theory called 'stone recording'. It says everything that happens imprints energy, positive or negative, on its location. The accumulation of energy in certain hotspots influences how we feel in those places and, potentially, future events there.

Mand, listen. The Alperton Angels thought they were saving mankind by destroying the Antichrist. But they underestimated the strength and determination of the dark forces. Because from 1986, the year Holly – the Antichrist's earthly *mother* – was born, the darkness began to ring-fence the site of The Assembly. A place that *would have been* holy. Murder after murder, each one intensifies negative energy at the centre of the site, until the positive energy that would have aided the destruction of the beast at the time of the alignment was completely overwhelmed. The angels didn't realise it, but their Assembly had been made a *satanic* site. When they tried to destroy the Antichrist it was, in fact, *protected* in that place, saved and spirited away. The angels are left reeling at their failure and implode. [*You could drive a bus through the silence here. EC*]

AB: I don't know what to say, Ol. [*Tell him Bible verses are ancient, man-made scriptures, mistranslated many times and misinterpreted even more. They have nothing to do with murders in west London. EC*] You could have something here.

OM: I have. My new angle. That the baby born eighteen years ago really *was* the Antichrist. And still is. A book on how the Alperton Angels were right all along. [*He hates this type of thing, doesn't he? EC*]

AB: I mean, it's quirky, and if the kid can't be traced now, there's no danger of anyone finding them and trying to finish the job, or turn them into a figurehead for the occult ... if Craig can impose a link between Dennis Nilsen and HIV, then surely there's mileage in your idea.

OM: There is. I know there is.

       [*This recording ends abruptly. I've messaged you. EC*]

WhatsApp messages between Ellie Cooper and me, 23 July 2021:

Ellie Cooper

I'm worried, Mand. Oliver is usually so sceptical. That murder map ... Is he losing perspective?

Amanda Bailey

Chill 😂 Pippa and me are in touch with Jo at Green Street. We're keeping an eye on him. He's had a tough time lately. It's best to let him work through it. Especially someone as stubborn as Ol 🙄

Ellie Cooper

Phew! I knew you'd be on top of it.

Amanda Bailey

BTW your friend with the recording studio – what's his price for cleaning up the Gabriel interview? Whatever it is, say yes.

WhatsApp messages between my editor Pippa Deacon and me, 23 July 2021:

Pippa Deacon

Your friend Oliver is looking at evidence the angels were right about the baby. That the Antichrist walks among us 💀

Amanda Bailey

How do you know?

Pippa Deacon

Jo and I met up last night. We get along like a house on fire.

Amanda Bailey

His father died last year, he's dealing with a stalker, legal things and his mum's in a home. He'll snap out of it eventually.

Pippa Deacon

What do you mean? It's a fabulous idea! I just hope your new angle is as good. I know it will be. I have every faith. But let's just say I really, really hope it is.

Amanda Bailey

Conversation between Amanda Bailey and Oliver Menzies in St Barnabas Church, Sudbury, 22 July 2021. Transcribed by Ellie Cooper.

OM: Freezing in here.

AB: Stone walls.

OM: Do you sense an atmosphere?

AB: We're two ambitious, competing individuals. It's how we roll.

OM: Not us. I mean this place.

AB: It's an old church, so ...

OM: What is *that*?

AB: Their famous stained-glass window. Very old.

OM: They're cooking someone's head in that pane.

AB: The vicar explained the story. That's the king and that's a mother in the crowd. These people are all starving. They ask the king why the crops failed and he says it's because this woman, here, gave birth to a demon. She says no, my son's a regular kid. The king says, 'Prove it. We'll try to kill him. If he's not a demon, God will save him.' The mother, confident her lad is *not* a beast from hell, says OK. They kill him with a sword, he dies, and is declared a demon. That's his mum, looking very sad. [*You got this story totally wrong, Mand. EC*]

OM: That's the king.

AB: Yeah, it's the king, he's back to square one because there's still no food and the people are still starving ... [*No, the king's son is killed and eaten, then the woman won't give up her son like she promised, that's the story. EC*] The moral is: being proved right is not always the best outcome.

OM: There's something in the air here. I can feel it. [*Rustling of a sweet packet. EC*]

AB: You can smell my aniseed cubes. Here.

OM: Cheers. [*More rustling. EC*]

AB: Come on, let's go. We need to find the angels' original apartment.

AB: Peter Duffy, aka Gabriel Angelis, lived in this block after he was released from prison, courtesy of a housing association. This is where they were when Holly had the baby. Then they moved to a derelict block in Wembley, and finally to the Alperton warehouse, via Middlesex House across the road. They behaved as if they were on the run, but there's no evidence they were actually being pursued.

OM: Not by earthly forces.

AB: If you read between the lines of Holly and Jonah's testimonies, you can see the adult angels created a paranoid environment. The kids were convinced there were dark forces closing in who would protect the Antichrist and destroy *them*.

OM: They needed the alignment to kill it for good.

AB: We've assumed the adult angels believed that too, but ...

OM: What?

AB: Let's say they *didn't* believe it. Would they lie just to maintain control? The psychology of cult leaders is complex. Power, sex, acquisition of wealth, delusions of grandeur. It's all there with Gabriel. The teenagers were vulnerable, but no doubt, in their own ways, the others were too.

OM: Head's spinning, Mand. Need to sit down.

AB: Sure, sure. Over here. [*A pause while you help him. EC*]

OM: Happens every time ... every time I get near to the angels.

Anonymous response printed from the *Fresh Ghost* forum

I don't have any inside information about this case, but it's always intrigued me. The angels. How did such a disparate group of individuals even meet, let alone come to such an out-there belief in their own divinity? Gabriel must be a truly charismatic, influential and dangerous man.

This text reply came out of the blue from former social worker Ruth Charalambos (who I last spoke to on 21 July), 23 July 2021:

Ruth Charalambos
Rowley Wild.

> **Amanda Bailey**
> OK. Thanks.

WhatsApp messages from Ellie Cooper to me, 24 July 2021:

Ellie Cooper
Hi, Mand. My friend says thanks for the bank transfer and has come back with his cleaned-up file from Oliver's visit with Gabriel. I've transcribed it and sent both files to your Dropbox. If you fancy a chat when you've read it, call me or text.

Ellie Cooper
Call me anyway, please 🙊

Improved recording of Oliver's meeting with Gabriel at HMP Tynefield on 10 July 2021. Transcribed by Ellie Cooper, 24 July 2021.

> [*It starts midway into a conversation, as if Oliver forgot to start the recording. EC*]

GA: ... yours is to be a comfort to your father in the final years of his life. Which you've done and you can feel proud of that. Your purpose is complete, Oliver.

OM: What now? Find a new purpose?

GA: Once you've fulfilled the reason you came to earth, that's your moment of completion.

OM: I *die*?

GA: The energy of your purpose that keeps you on the earth releases its hold. It's a triumphant moment, yet it also means you are vulnerable to other forces. Accidents, disease, and the energies driving other people's purposes. I have a strong feeling you are the focus of another's negative energy ...

OM: [*He clears his throat, hesitates. EC*] Yeah ...

GA: There's someone you've worked with. Their energy is inclined to create chaos, perhaps one huge moment of chaos, perhaps a multitude of tiny moments, but chaos always. They appear strong and courageous, yet they are a dangerous person to be the focus of because they are determined to a fault. They won't stop until their own purpose is fulfilled.

OM: Shit! There *is* someone, there is ...

GA: Ssh. Oliver, ssh. I don't see your collision with their energy as ending in violence, so much as in slow increments of pain. Drip drip. Drip drip. Does that make sense to you?

OM: Yes. But I've spoken to the police. I've got lawyers involved. He still stalks me. How can I stop him?

GA: You're not responsible for them. They're on a journey and events will play out. Your journey collides with theirs. Like planets aligning in the sky for a short time, before they move away, each on their own predestined orbit. Enjoy freedom in the knowledge there's nothing you can *do* but accept it. [*A long pause in the convo here. I don't know what to say, Mand. Poor Ol. This guy has really spooked him. And me. EC*]

OM: I've got to do this interview, but I don't ... [*He's sobbing. EC*]

GA: You can tell everyone that even though I have no memory of The Assembly or events leading up to it, I know I'm innocent of the crime I've been convicted of. The Assembly, for me, was a moment of rebirth. My mortal incarnation was torn away and reflected before me. It was a pure white sheet. It's how I *know* I didn't kill that unfortunate young man. If I had, his murder would overshadow me. Weigh me down. [*He pauses here. There's something about his voice. EC*] I also have a specific message for you, Oliver. I've dreamed about you. You're an angel, like me. Your body is mortal but your soul is divine. In my dream you were above an orchard. An orchard will be significant in the events that will finally draw you back to the other side. It's not a warning, but an assurance. Nowhere is safe now.

UV: [*An unknown voice. EC*] Time's up, gents ...
      [*That's where it ends. Mand, I'm really freaked out. EC*]

WhatsApp messages between Ellie Cooper and me, 24 July 2021:

Ellie Cooper
Gabriel has the most compelling, seductive voice I've ever
heard. He talks and his words bypass my critical mind. Literally I
stopped transcribing to listen to him. Had to go back and listen
again. What is that?

> **Amanda Bailey**
> That's a charming, highly intelligent, narcissistic psychopath
> with well-developed people-reading skills. His whole life he's
> used his powers of manipulation to survive. He's not going to
> stop now. His influence over others is akin to hypnosis, a gift, a
> sixth sense.

Ellie Cooper
No wonder you had to drive home after this. In minutes Oliver
was reduced to a sobbing wreck. How did Gabriel know his
father had just died?

> **Amanda Bailey**
> Cold reading?

Ellie Cooper
And the trouble he's having with the mad squaddie? There's no
way he'd know that.

> **Amanda Bailey**
> We all have enemies, right?

Ellie Cooper
I don't – none I'd easily believe would want me dead.

> **Amanda Bailey**
> You should get out more 😜 Don't worry about Ol. I won't let
> anything really bad happen to him.

Ellie Cooper

Please keep him away from pubs and restaurants called The Orchard.

> **Amanda Bailey**
> 😄 Yes, and actual orchards. I'll do that for you

WhatsApp messages between me and true crime author Craig Turner, 24 July 2021:

> **Amanda Bailey**
> Craig, babes, can I use your log-in for national archives? Don't want to use mine 😵

Craig Turner
Will dig out and send 😊

Craig Turner
Remember it's Sunday, babes. Chill please.

A list of names printed from National Archives, under the heading: Notting Hill & Ealing High School, 2002–3. Among them two are highlighted:

Adesina, Jessica A.
Wild, Rowley F.

Meeting with author Jess Adesina at Warrior's Arrow Fantasy Bookshop, 26 July 2021. Transcribed by Ellie Cooper.

AB: Hi, Jess!
JA: Who to?
AB: It's for someone else ...
JA: What's her name?
AB: If you could just write: 'To Rowley Wild, thanks for inspiring *My Angel Diary'*. [*Long pause here. Have you accosted this woman*

as she's signing books? EC]

AB: Only joking. You can just sign it, that's fine. [*You must switch the recording off, then on again for this next bit. EC*]

JA: What do you want?

AB: You were at school with Rowley Wild: 'Holly'. Why didn't you say? [*You don't get an answer to that one. EC*] Do you remember the circumstances that led her to leave and live with the angels?

JA: [*She sighs. EC*]

AB: The character in your series of books meets another girl at school and an adult man and moves away from home to live with them both. The angel thing represents bisexuality as far as I can see.

JA: It's more pansexuality and alternative lifestyles. The angels inspired the series, but it's not Rowley's story.

AB: You and Rowley were in the same year at school. I'm from this area myself and I know there aren't many girls who go from Notting Hill & Ealing High into the care system. It would've been the talk of the school. What happened to her?

JA: She was only at the school for a few weeks at the end of term. Look, her family were eccentric. There was chaos, drugs and neglect. She moved to a foster placement, then back to the family home, but she met a man and … that was it. She didn't come back to school.

AB: That man was Gabriel?

JA: I believe so. The Alperton events happened at the end of that year. I'm sorry. I can't say any more, it's not my story to tell. [*The cheeky mare's been telling Holly's story in book after book for years. Anyway, someone else seems to take Ms Adesina away from you at this point. EC*]

AB: Ellie, Rowley is spelled ROWLEY and pronounced to rhyme with 'holy'.

WhatsApp messages between Oliver Menzies and me, 26 July 2021:

Oliver Menzies

So, when rich folk sink into addiction so hopeless they can't care for their own kids, it's just 'eccentric'.

> **Amanda Bailey**
> Welcome to the world, baby.

Oliver Menzies

Holly/Rowley isn't your average teenage runaway. She comes from a rich home and goes to a private girls' school in Ealing.

> **Amanda Bailey**
> Cult leaders target people with wealth. What better mark than a troubled, isolated teenage girl, whose parents are oblivious, and whose status means the authorities turn a blind eye?

> **Amanda Bailey**
> Social services aren't used to educated, articulate teenagers who appear mature. Nothing to do with her being more intelligent or less vulnerable. It's not even about them being incompetent, but unlike the other kids they work with, she has money to fall back on.

> **Amanda Bailey**
> A social worker I spoke to was defensive. Can we blame them for prioritising those youngsters who have literally nothing?

> **Amanda Bailey**
> You know how convincing Gabriel is. He got to you in under ten minutes.

Oliver Menzies

He did not. I admit he was intimidating, but I held it together. I sent you my Gabriel interview. Send me your social worker interview.

Oliver Menzies

Please.

Amanda Bailey

That's hardly quid pro quo, is it? Your Gabriel interview didn't come out!

Oliver Menzies

Not my fault. His turbulent energy scrambled the airwaves.

Amanda Bailey

You don't need my social worker interview. You need priests and satanists.

Oliver Menzies

Jo says to look at the case from a conventional standpoint, then gradually present evidence that seems to prove the baby really was the Antichrist. I've got to leave it to the reader to decide, while pretending I'm agnostic and on the fence.

Oliver Menzies

I'll only use a couple of quotes. Just so it looks like I did formal research.

Oliver Menzies

Go on.

Oliver Menzies

I said 'please' a few messages back.

Amanda Bailey

I'll redact anything pertinent to my angle – you can't have my key quotes.

Oliver Menzies

What's your new angle?

Amanda Bailey

Chill. It doesn't clash with yours. Totally different.

Oliver Menzies

If you don't tell me, I won't reveal my mystery interviewee. You're still itching to know.

Oliver Menzies

Ah, ghosting me! That means I win!

Amanda Bailey

WhatsApp messages between true crime author Minnie Davis and me, 26 July 2021:

Minnie Davis
Hello, gorgeous girl 🙂 Just submitted final edit. In garden, feet up, mug of coffee. How you?

> **Amanda Bailey**
> Knee deep in angels, demons and social workers. Found the boy, closing in on the girl. Big disaster re the baby.

Minnie Davis
They're DEAD? 😖

> **Amanda Bailey**
> Could be. In fact, they might as well be. We'll never know. Dark adoption. No way to trace it.

Minnie Davis
That's a thing? Sorry, Mand.

> **Amanda Bailey**
> Looking on the bright side, it frees me up.

Minnie Davis
How about treating the case like the kid really was the devil? I'd read that.

> **Amanda Bailey**
> Mr Sceptic-Atheist Oliver M has gone spiritual-for-pay and bagged that option. I've got another angle, but things need to slot into place for it to work. If not 😬

Minnie Davis
You poor thing 😖 shout if I can help. Only waiting for proofs to come back these next couple of weeks.

A scan of my letter to David Polneath, 26 July 2021:

David Polneath

26 July 2021

Dear David,

Apologies for my lack of communication. I've been busy organising interviews, writing preliminary notes and revising plans for my book on the Alperton Angels. Thanks for your emails. I decided to contact you in the hope old-fashioned snail mail is less easily intercepted. There's something I wish to share.

I've had a recent encounter with what I can only describe as the powers-that-be. It was unlike any other in my entire professional life. They arranged to meet me at an isolated spot – a lane behind a pub, close to where I live, in the middle of the night. I went there, but no one showed. When I got back home, there was someone in my flat, waiting. There were no signs of forced entry. I would soon realise that in itself was a warning.

This person, someone I'd never seen before in my life, told me in no uncertain terms to stop looking for the baby. They gave me a cover story that would explain to my editor why it can never be found. Their instructions were to say its new identity is protected by a closed, dark adoption: a process only undertaken in exceptional circumstances. It may be true, it may not, but my only option was to agree and I have, so far, complied with their 'request'. They didn't threaten me overtly, but I was left in no doubt they could dispose of me at a second's notice if I continued my search.

I've not been able to speak about this even with close friends and colleagues. It happened a couple of weeks ago, but I've been in denial and lying to everyone.

You're right, there's a mystery behind the case of the Alperton Angels. But am I prepared to be the one to uncover it?

Yours sincerely,

Amanda

PS You mentioned meeting up to exchange information about potential contacts. Please, can we do so?

Text messages between me and TV producer Debbie Condon, 26 July 2021:

> **Amanda Bailey**
> Hi, Debbie. When you were working on DERELICTION, exposing cracks in the care system, did anyone lean on you to stop?

Debbie Condon
Social services weren't exactly forthcoming, but no one got heavy or legal, if that's what you mean. Strange you should email me today. I've been tidying the office and found a great spec script about the Alperton Angels. The writer must have sent it to us years ago. DIVINE by Clive Badham. Have you read it?

> **Amanda Bailey**
> I've heard of it. Do you have the whole script?

Debbie Condon
Yes. Would you like to see it?

Text messages between me and TV producer Phil Priest, 26 July 2021:

> **Amanda Bailey**
> Hey, Phil. Quick question about your TV series ASSEMBLY. Did anyone try to shut you down?

Phil Priest
No. We got what they call now an intimacy coach to convince the actors to do the more explicit stuff.

WhatsApp messages between Oliver Menzies and me, 27 July 2021:

Oliver Menzies
Are you awake?

> **Amanda Bailey**
> Mad squaddie still on the line?

Oliver Menzies
Yep, so got up early to drag my eyes over these tedious transcripts you sent.

> **Amanda Bailey**
> No need to thank me.

Oliver Menzies
Something weird. Can't believe you didn't spot this.

> **Amanda Bailey**
> Go on.

Oliver Menzies
That social worker Julian Nowak. You talked to him on the fifth. He remembers the case of Holly and Gabriel being in the early 90s. I know people make mistakes about timings, but ten years out? He distinctly says it's not long after he qualified. That's a big life moment to anchor his memory to.

> **Amanda Bailey**
> I picked up on that. Don must've referred me to the wrong social worker. I've a feeling he mixed up the names with an earlier case. He knows so many people and he's no spring chicken.

Oliver Menzies
How about another explanation. Holly, Jonah and Gabriel really are divine, ageless beings. Angels.

> **Amanda Bailey**
> Wow. You're taking this new angle seriously.

Oliver Menzies

They all describe Holly as mature. Don said the same thing to me. She could be hundreds of years old in a teenager's body. Gabriel is the same, but his human incarnation is physically older.

> **Amanda Bailey**
>
> Like in INTERVIEW WITH THE VAMPIRE? Holly is Claudia and Gabriel Lestat? 😄 Fun fact: River Phoenix was cast as Molloy, the interviewer, but died weeks before he could shoot his scenes. Christian Slater took the role. Donated his fee to charity to break the curse.

Oliver Menzies

No one is ten years out on something that happened 'early in their career'.

Text messages between me and Police Chief Inspector Mike Dean, 27 July 2021:

> **Amanda Bailey**
>
> Further to our chat on 24 June, could you clarify something? You say Holly reported being under pressure from Gabriel to steal credit cards when you were 'new to the force and the area'. This was before the Alperton Angels, a missed opportunity to intercept the cult. Exactly how long before the events of 2003 did Holly make the report?

Mike Dean

1990 or 91. No earlier than that, for sure.

> **Amanda Bailey**
>
> That would've made Holly four or five years old.

Mike Dean

She was late teens.

> **Amanda Bailey**
>
> The Holly in the Alperton Angels case was seventeen in 2003.

How can she have been the same age and reported the same crime thirteen years earlier?

My notes on the adult angels and Harpinder Singh, sourced from a variety of online news archives and Wiki:

'Michael' – Born Dominic Jones, in Leicester, England on 18 September 1961
Trains as an electrician, moves into retail sales. Marries in 1981, divorces 1985 citing irreconcilable differences. Marries again 1990, divorces in 1998 after arrest and charge of ABH re his wife. Works for Dixons and latterly PC World. Alan Morgan ('Elemiah', see below) works briefly at PC World in the early 2000s, which is thought to be the first connection between them. Also several short spells in jail for fraud and theft.

'Elemiah' – Born Alan Morgan, in Port Talbot, Wales, on 27 June 1967
Leaves school at fifteen. Long spell of unemployment. Moves to London. Meets Gabriel in prison when it is believed he becomes the first angel follower. Described as friendly, funny and gentle. Artistic and practical, with a tendency to be easily led.

'Gabriel' – Born Peter Duffy, in Lewisham, London, on 25 December 1959
Father absent, mother alcoholic and drug addict. Nomadic childhood moving between relatives and foster homes. Series of short prison sentences for fraud-based acquisitive crime. Described as intelligent and charismatic. Given a whole-life sentence for the murder of Harpinder Singh and the post-mortem mutilation of the other angels.

'Raphael' – Born Christopher Shenk, in Perivale, London, on 13 April 1978
Left Northolt High School at sixteen. Did a bricklaying apprenticeship that led to a short career as a builder. Lost touch with his home crowd as he got in with local gangs. A string of minor raps for drug possession and dangerous driving. His family saw him only occasionally following

his descent into drug crime but had no idea he'd become involved in a cult.

Harpinder Singh – Born in Delhi, India, circa 1981, age given as 22
His death considered a ritual killing by the angels in the days leading up to The Assembly. Reports suggest he was drawn unwittingly into their world. Housed in emergency accommodation after a fire in his rental flat. Worked in a Southall restaurant. His identity disputed by a friend of Harry Singh, who was born circa 1974.

WhatsApp messages between me and Oliver Menzies, 27 July 2021:

> **Amanda Bailey**
> None of the angels' backgrounds appear to be religious, not even Gabriel's. I wonder what triggered his belief he's an angel.

> **Amanda Bailey**
> To our knowledge he hasn't been diagnosed with any condition that would give him delusions. Might have been exposed to religious teachings in prison.

Oliver Menzies
Dreams. Dreams are our link to the other world. He was told in a dream he's the archangel Gabriel born on earth to destroy the Antichrist.

> **Amanda Bailey**
> He changed his name in the early 90s so if he still believes it now … that must've been some dream.

Interview with two Unknown Restaurant workers in Southall, 27 July 2021. Transcribed by Ellie Cooper.

> *[I cut out your order for a takeaway. Tarka daal, veggie bhuna and garlic naan. Good combo. EC]*

AB: Worked here long?

URı: Yes.

AB: What was it called back in the day?

URı: Hmmm?

AB: Punjab Junction?

URı: Yes. [*He sounds reluctant, Mand. EC*]

AB: I used to come here *all* the time. Didn't you have a waiter called Harpinder? Harpinder Singh? [*No answer that I can hear. EC*] Is he still here? [*A burst of clattering and sizzling drowned out his reply. EC*]

UR2: Can I help? [*This is someone new. EC*]

AB: Just chatting to your colleague. I was a regular, eighteen years ago. When Harpinder was around. How is he, alright?

UR2: You can go. I'm tired of police here. [*Well, that escalated quickly. EC*]

AB: I'm not police.

UR2: So why you asking for Harpinder? Who remembers a waiter? You know what happened.

AB: I'm writing a book on the Alperton Angels. Newspaper reports said Harpinder Singh worked here.

UR2: He worked here but ... If I were you, I'd not throw his name about, nor Shenky's right? For dead men they still have enemies.

AB: Why?

UR2: They had a racket out the back. The last owners.

AB: Drugs?

UR2: We're under new management now. All clean. We're making it work, giving young people a chance. See him? Lost his family, so he lives upstairs, works here, goes to college in the day. Boy at the door is on a management training course for the disabled. But we still have to live and work in this community. Do you understand what I'm saying? Your man tried but didn't get them all. Not by a long way.

AB: [*You whisper this. EC*] Was Harpinder Singh undercover here? At Punjab Junction?

UR2: [*So does he. EC*] You didn't hear it from me. Here's your food. On the house. Just go.
[*OMG! Messaging you! EC*]

WhatsApp messages between Ellie Cooper and me, 27 July 2021:

Ellie Cooper

Harry Singh joined the police! 😱

> **Amanda Bailey**
>
> He was undercover at a restaurant where drugs were being traded or moved. Chris Shenk, or Raphael, was very much in the mix.

Ellie Cooper

It explains why Harry didn't get in touch with Galen Fletcher's family when Clem died.

> **Amanda Bailey**
>
> And why his death was reported as if he WAS that penniless waiter, fresh from India. They had to protect the whole undercover operation and all the other players in it.

Ellie Cooper

Wouldn't the Singh family object to their late son being depicted so inaccurately?

> **Amanda Bailey**
>
> Unless it's explained to them other lives are at risk.

Ellie Cooper

So exciting! Let's meet up for coffee. We haven't had one of our long chats in ages 😟

> **Amanda Bailey**
>
> Soon. Still at the intense phase, pulling all-nighters and all-dayers, babysitting Spooky Menzies and worrying about my new angle.

Please pass this message to Amanda Bailey.

I am now a primary school teacher, but in 2004 I worked as a researcher for a television director. My boss wanted to make a documentary about the Alperton Angels so we began pulling contacts together and trying to get broadcasters interested. Almost as soon as we started, my boss took a phone call. She left the office, told me to lock up and that she'd see me the next day. That night she died in a fire at her home. It was ruled an accident. The documentary was never made. I don't know why I'm telling you. It was such a long time ago. I heard you on the podcast – my son had it on – and I felt compelled to let you know what happened to Suzi Korman. Sorry.

Printout of a news story dated April 2004:

DEAD WOMAN NAMED

The woman killed in a house fire on Lordship Lane, Wood Green, has been named as documentary maker Suzi Korman, 41. Ms Korman lived alone at the flat where the fire broke out in the early hours of Tuesday morning. The fire service say initial signs are the fire started at an old electrical point.

WhatsApp messages between Oliver Menzies and me, 27 July 2021:

Oliver Menzies
Did you know repeated numbers are messages from the divine?

Amanda Bailey
Read it somewhere.

Oliver Menzies
Especially 444. If you glimpse a 444 – anywhere – it means angels are communicating with you.

Amanda Bailey

I read that too, but what are they saying? Get your health checked out. Do the lottery this week. Don't get on that plane. As a theory, it's a bit vague. Does it work the other way? If you see 666 the devil is watching you? 😈

Oliver Menzies

Listen. I had a meeting about the mad squaddie. Police say they can't link him to the nuisance calls. It's an old electronic number and the dialling codes make no sense, so they can't track it. I'll forward it to you. I can disconnect the landline so if the calls start coming through on my mobile, they'll know it's a stalker and they'll be easier to trace.

Amanda Bailey

Good news then.

Oliver Menzies

But if it's not him, who is it?

Amanda Bailey

Any number of people, surely? You can't have pissed off just one person your whole life 😂

Amanda Bailey

Or, radical proposition here: it's merely a fault on the line.

Oliver Menzies

There's someone or something there. They're trying to get through, struggling to communicate. Mand, I'm not crazy, you know that, but these calls come at 4.44 a.m. Every single day. What are the angels trying to tell me?

WhatsApp messages between my agent Nita Cawley and me, 28 July 2021:

Nita Cawley

Everything OK?

Amanda Bailey

Yes thanks 😊

Amanda Bailey

Is something wrong?

Nita Cawley

I've had an email saying you're working too hard on the book.
Someone is worried about you.

Amanda Bailey

Oliver! HE'S worried about ME? It's him who's taking phone
calls from angels FFS!

Amanda Bailey

The only thing he's worried about is being dropped by Green
Street. He's trying to get my book cancelled or at the very least
postponed so HE'S in a stronger position with THEM. I know
how his mind works. He's playing you. Don't fall for it, Nita.

Nita Cawley

It's not Oliver Menzies.

Amanda Bailey

Who then?

Nita Cawley

Ellie Cooper. She says you're working round the clock and this
case is dredging up childhood trauma.

Amanda Bailey

So much for confidentiality. Is it any wonder I don't talk about
feelings? This is what happens when I do.

Nita Cawley

She's just concerned, that's all.

Amanda Bailey

Well, it's good of her, but Ellie should look after herself, not
worry about me. You know she was in accounts at Kronos until
I lobbied to have her moved to editorial? She was my protégé,
Nita. And I'm still supporting her NOW!

Nita Cawley

Which is possibly why she doesn't want you under too much pressure.

> **Amanda Bailey**
>
> I could get my interviews transcribed online or do it myself, FFS!

Nita Cawley

Calm down, Mand. She doesn't know you as well as I do. I know you're fine. Pippa knows you're fine. You're fine. The book is well under way.

Nita Cawley

Please don't tell Ellie I told you. If you react badly, she won't say anything the next time when someone might REALLY need an intervention. Please. For me.

> **Amanda Bailey**
>
> OK. I won't say anything.

Text messages between Dave 'Itchy' Kilmore at *Fresh Ghost* podcast and me, 28 July 2021:

Dave Kilmore

Had a message from a guy who says he was one of the first paramedics on the scene of the angels' massacre. Jideofor Sani. Now retired.

> **Amanda Bailey**
>
> Ace! Thanks, Dave, send me his deets.

Dave Kilmore

Bear in mind he 'won't write anything down', wants to 'meet Amanda in person' and only 'somewhere private'. Alarm bells

> **Amanda Bailey**
>
> I'll be careful. Thanks, Dave.

220

WhatsApp messages between Oliver Menzies and me, 28 July 2021:

Oliver Menzies
You've gone quiet.

> **Amanda Bailey**
> I'm fine, thanks for asking. Gone QUIET? It's been sixteen hours since we last messaged.

Oliver Menzies
Shall we meet up this afternoon? Check our new angles don't clash.

> **Amanda Bailey**
> OK.

WhatsApp messages between true crime author Craig Turner and me, 28 July 2021:

Craig Turner
Hi, babes! Keep meaning to ask: did you get an audience with the archangel Gabriel?

> **Amanda Bailey**
> No. Long story.

Craig Turner
So sorry, babes. Gutted I mentioned it.

> **Amanda Bailey**
> 😂 It was worth a try. I sat outside and spoke to ladies in the queue instead.

Craig Turner
All waiting for their banged-up men, love 'em!

Amanda Bailey

Craig, quick question: you visited Dennis Nilsen countless times and corresponded with him for years. How did you stop yourself getting too involved?

Craig Turner

By 'involved' you mean ...?

Amanda Bailey

Liking him. Respecting him. Enjoying his company. Assuming he felt the same about you. Sympathising with him. Making excuses for him. Believing his lies.

Craig Turner

It's a balance, Mand. I needed Denny-boy to trust me enough to open up, and that meant building a relationship. It happened organically. We had a lot in common. Both gay, both grew up in rural Scotland, both middle sons with absent fathers. He was a lonely man who struggled to navigate a hostile world. We clicked. He didn't lie – not to me.

Meeting with Oliver Menzies in Costa Coffee, Westway Cross, Greenford, 28 July 2021. Transcribed by Ellie Cooper.

[*I cut out the bits where you get coffees and find good seats. EC*]

AB: How's it going?

OM: Slowly. Got other things taking up brain space. Mad squaddie's people have set up a mediation meeting.

AB: And the book?

OM: Thinking, googling, scrolling, reading background info. I'll start in earnest soon. You?

AB: Same. Once I've written the right chapter one, the rest falls into place.

OM: And how many have you written?

AB: Two. Neither are *the one*.

OM: What's your new angle?

AB: [*You pause for a long time. Presume you don't want to tell him,*

but can't think of an excuse not to. EC] The Alperton Angels'
influence on popular culture. From the novels and TV series
it's inspired to the discussions online. I'm linking it with cult
theory. How the human mind is susceptible to non-logical
beliefs. A cult can still be influential long after its leaders and
followers have imploded. I'm exploring the fact people still
subscribe to the ethos of the angels today – and believe that
sometime in 2003 the Antichrist was born on earth. For example
... [*I think you show him your phone. EC*]

OM: Graffiti from the flats in Alperton? What *are* those marks?

AB: Angel symbols. Here, these were drawn for me by one of the
police officers who found Holly in the warehouse. That building
was destroyed. These symbols are new.

OM: True.

AB: I've found the symbols online. This one represents Gabriel, that's
Elemiah, and Michael. There are no symbols for Raphael and
nothing for Holly or Jonah. They told the kids they were angels
and gave them new names, but not angel names.

OM: The men are archangels. Holly and Jonah are ordinary angels.

AB: No doubt told they'll eventually become archangels if they do
as they're told. Most cults have a ladder of favour. You rise or fall
according to your devotion to the leader—

OM: No. If you look at this from the standpoint that the men were
archangels in human form, the teenagers were their earthly
assistants and all have a link to the other side that allowed them
to channel energy ... a lot of stuff becomes clearer.

AB: Hmmm. Ol, have you written to Gabriel since your visit?

OM: [*His turn to pause. He doesn't want to say, which means he has.
EC*] Why would I do that?

AB: [*Another long pause while you slurp and probably scowl at each
other. EC*] Remember they got him on the murder of Harpinder
Singh, but he's also responsible for the other angel deaths. He
convinced them to kill themselves, then mutilated their bodies.
He's insane and all the more dangerous because his charisma
makes those delusions seem rational. If someone is vulnerable,
they can be drawn in.

OM: Thanks, but I'm not vulnerable.

AB: What I mean is, we're *all* vulnerable. I've been reading about the language of cult leaders. That's how the brainwashing happens. Through words.

OM: Yeah, I know.

AB: Does Gabriel reply to your letters? [*No verbal reply I can hear. EC*]

OM: Noticed how many witnesses to events in this case have died? Not counting Harpinder Singh and the angels themselves. Jonathan Childs, Gray Graham, Mark Dunning ... but they didn't die immediately after they encountered the angels. They died recently. Since I started work on this book for Green Street. It's as if people who could shed light on the case for me are being systematically removed.

AB: You think they were murdered? Who by?

OM: Dark forces protecting the Antichrist.

AB: Killing *you* would be simpler.

OM: Other writers would take my place. Jonathan Childs found Harpinder Singh. Gray Graham found the dead angels. Kill the guys who found the bodies, and you'll never have a first-hand account of the undisturbed crime scene ever again.

AB: Jonathan Childs's widow disputes the claim he found Singh's body.

OM: Who's to say Childs told his wife the truth?

AB: And Mark Dunning? As far as we know he didn't find any bodies. He just wrote a novel inspired by the case shortly after. He wasn't killed back then. But Suzi Korman, a documentary film maker, was killed in a house fire in 2004, hours after starting work on the case.

OM: I guarantee Mark Dunning and this Suzi each had *something*. A germ of information, useless on its own, that I would have put with all my other research and completed the puzzle, leading to me exposing the truth behind the case.

AB: What truth would be *that* sensitive?

OM: That the angels failed to destroy the Antichrist. The architect of the end of days is walking the earth now, watching, learning, waiting to make their move, and come to power. [*OMG, Mand. Got to admit, it's a strange coincidence. But did those people die because of Oliver's research – or yours? EC*]

OM: Remember when we visited the site? As soon as I got near the portal, my senses were scrambled. I almost fainted. That was them, trying to block my power. It happened again after we met Gabriel. Remember how I wasn't able to drive? Then I had that episode outside the angels' first apartment.

AB: Well ... all this is great for your new angle. Remember Jo's advice, though. Present the mystery, but let your readers join the dots.

OM: Yeah, yeah. [*Another long silence. Drinking and thinking ... EC*]

AB: Gabriel told you he couldn't have murdered Singh, because he saw his own soul in a dream and it was pure. Do you believe he's innocent?

OM: How do you know he said that? [*Did you not tell him we cleaned up his interview file? EC*]

AB: You mentioned it.

OM: When?

AB: In the car on the way back from Tynefield.

OM: I didn't.

AB: How else would I know? It's a strange way to declare innocence. Why not just say 'I didn't do it, it's a mistake,' or 'I was framed'? It sounds as if he genuinely can't remember whether he did it or not.

OM: I have no evidence either way.

AB: If Gabriel didn't kill Singh, then who did?

OM: The dark forces. Was Singh himself a dark force?

AB: Did you read *My Angel Diary* by Jess Adesina? [*He must shake his head. EC*] It's a young adult series of books inspired by the angels. An epic romantic journey. It's funny, crazy, and has a quirky main character called Tilly who quote unquote *knows* she's an angel, i.e. bisexual. There are four books and the character grows up with her readers. It starts when she's at high school and in the last book she marries an older man, while her girlfriend marries another man. They all live polyamorously ever after in adjacent flats. It's basically Jane Austen with avocado on toast.

OM: It sounds [*he must pull a face or something. EC*] but then, I'm not the target market.

AB: In the last few pages of the final book, Tilly admits none of them are angels, they all just share a difference. That's the moment of self-realisation she has been working towards the whole time. The angel thing is a metaphor for something she can't express. Once she learns to express it, she sheds her angel wings, so to speak, and can move forward into her life, which is where we leave her at the end. Quite moving.

OM: Thanks for the spoiler.

AB: I might not even have linked it to the case if I hadn't found an interview Adesina gave to *Grazia* ten years ago. She clearly states she spoke to someone involved. I then found out she and Holly went to the same school ...

OM: Let me guess. Holly was at the school for only a short time. There's no way this Adesina knew her from reception class to sixth form. [*You pause here as if you're surprised he knew that ... EC*]

AB: Right. Yes, that's what she said. Holly came from another school and was only there for a term.

OM: Holly isn't a teenager, Mand. She looks young, she acts young, even down to causing trouble and putting on a façade of naivety ... Holly and Jonah are eternal beings.

AB: That's what you'll hint at in your book, right?

OM: Uh-huh.

[*Messaging you. EC*]

WhatsApp messages between Ellie Cooper and me, 28 July 2021:

Ellie Cooper

There's something about this case. It burrows insidiously into your mind, then sets about changing it.

Amanda Bailey

Hey, Els! You caught me with my feet up, glass of red, scrolling through Netflix 🙇 You may be right there. It's logic versus instinct. Head and heart. Some people see a coincidence and that's all it is to them. Others see it as evidence of supernatural forces at work.

Ellie Cooper

Or earthly criminal forces up to no good 🙇

Amanda Bailey

Oliver thinks he's logical and rational, but this case has brought out the instinctive thinker in him. You remember the two police officers, Rose and Khan?

Ellie Cooper

They responded to Holly's 999 call and saw, or didn't see, angel symbols painted on the ground?

Amanda Bailey

They both saw angel symbols. But weeks later, when Khan was shown a photograph that disproved what he'd seen, he 'knew' he had to have been mistaken. He believed the hard evidence he was presented with. Rose, on the other hand, didn't – because for him, there are forces that defy understanding. In the face of coincidence and unexplained phenomena we are all at the mercy of our own thought processes.

A story printed out from the Sussex section of the BBC News website and dated 28 July 2021:

FIRE DEATH MAN NAMED

The man who died in a house fire in Lewes yesterday (Tuesday 27 July) has been named as David Polneath, 67. Firefighters were called to the house on Bishop's Road at 2 a.m., but were unable to reach Mr Polneath. He was declared dead at the scene this morning. Neighbours paid tribute to the retired accountant who lived alone. 'He was a quiet, friendly man who was interested in the world and always had a project on the go,' said one, who did not wish to be named. Police say it is too early to determine if the fire is suspicious, but that the large amount of paperwork in the flat helped the fire to spread.

WhatsApp messages between me and Oliver Menzies, 28 July 2021:

Amanda Bailey
Did an amateur sleuth called David Polneath contact you?

Oliver Menzies
No.

Amanda Bailey
He was an accountant. Retired. Took up the Alperton Angels as a hobby. He was smart, rational, invested in the case and seemed forensic in his approach. I gave him your details. Thought he might have something.

Oliver Menzies
An amateur sleuth? Have I got to listen to some twat's obsessive ramblings? Kill me now.

Amanda Bailey
He died last night. In a mysterious fire. Just popped up in my feed. See the link.

Oliver Menzies
Shit. Shit, that's not good.

Oliver Menzies
That makes five people dead. Four of them immediately before or after connecting with ME on this case.

A page torn from the novel *My Angel Diary* Book 2 by Jess Adesina:

The misty-magic of glowvember

I'll call him Gabriel. The angel man. He reminds me of Gabriel the cat. Could he be a divine reincarnation? Realistically, no. Gabriel the man was born at least thirty years before Gabriel the cat was born. And Gabriel the cat is still alive and well. Still, cats have nine lives, who's to say it's all in the same body or at the same time?

I'd be flattered if someone likened me to a cat. They may be murderous psychopaths, but when they decide to, they can be the sweetest, gentlest most loving creatures on earth. If a psychopath chooses to be sweet, gentle and loving, it means so much more than when a non-psychopath does the same.

Gabriel the man has wings in his eyes, but it's his voice that sweeps me up and carries me away.

A page torn from the novel *White Wings* by Mark Dunning:

The corridor stretched to a pitch-dark vanishing point ahead of her. A kaleidoscope of scarlet and green, glossy wood and gold brocade. The house was a living relic of a time long since passed. Nothing was younger than a century and a half, except the flickering light bulbs and an unmistakable odour of 4711. Celine twitched her perfect nostrils. *Not the eau de cologne*, she mused, *but spray, polish and wax intended to emulate it.*

There had to be at least fifty doors. She glided past the first few, her BB heels somehow too elegant to dent the vintage Persian silk beneath them. Her body weightless like a dream. Her wings brushed the antique candle holders as she passed. Each delicate fringe of Murano glass rippled, then shivered and shimmered as the teardrops kissed each other in her wake.

Celine studied each door, her senses acute for what might be on the other side. Not here. Not here. Here? A door identical to the others. But a glance left and right, delicate fingers tapered around the handle and she glided swiftly and silently through until the corridor was as still as when she found it. Except for the dying chimes and a single white feather that wafted back and forth on its ever-downward journey.

This was the room. The library. Celine inhaled as if she could read the very ions and particles in the air. Her eyes, as deep and liquid as a fawn's, suddenly narrowed. It was here. Beneath the window. Alone. Unprotected. She floated to it.

It shone as brightly as any treasure. Her heart pounded, her lips parted ... her wings wrapped her in the certain knowledge she had done everything Gabriel asked of her and together they would take this ... thing and make it vanish.

INT. LIVING ROOM, FLAT — EVENING

Gabriel looks dishevelled. He sits at the kitchen counter, stares at Jonah and Holly over his coffee mug.

> GABRIEL
>
> Did she look official? Police, council, social services?

Holly and Jonah shrug. Gabriel sighs non-committally.

> GABRIEL
>
> She must have been sent to rescue the Antichrist … When they send someone it's usually a woman.

> JONAH
>
> Why? When they're weaker.

Holly looks from Jonah to Gabriel.

> GABRIEL
>
> Because in the mortal realm, <u>their</u> powers are mortal too, like us. If they use force we resist, so they use charm. Most of us are men and in the mortal world women distract men from their purpose.

He twinkles at Holly.

> GABRIEL
>
> No offence.

> JONAH
>
> (nods at Holly)
> How come <u>she's</u> a woman?

Holly looks to Gabriel, the same question in her eyes.

                          GABRIEL

          Her purpose is to look after a baby, so she
          chose to be a mortal female (he indicates
          Jonah) with a protector.

                           JONAH

          You said _my_ purpose is to protect the baby.

                          GABRIEL

          We all have that purpose. Our energy forms
          a shield around it.

                           HOLLY

          But protecting something so evil doesn't
          make sense.

Gabriel searches for words to explain the unexplainable.

                          GABRIEL

          Unless we destroy it at the right time, in
          the right way, a century of sacrifice, of
          waiting, of working, will end in disaster.
          It must be protected until that time.

Gabriel pulls Holly and Jonah towards him.

                          GABRIEL

          But we're not alone. We have each other
          and there are more, a network that will
          make this possible. There are forces at
          work on both sides of the divide.

Holly and Jonah listen intently as if to a great teacher.

                          GABRIEL

          But their keenest weapon is authority.
          We're breaking earthly laws, so we're
          vulnerable.

The Baby CRIES. Gabriel drains his cup, stands.

                            GABRIEL
         My turn …

As he leaves, Holly's eyes follow him.

INT. LIVING ROOM, FLAT — NIGHT — LATER

Gabriel lolls on the sofa, Holly and Jonah either side. Arms
and legs intertwine sleepily. A FANTASY FILM ends. Gabriel
clicks a remote control. The screen changes to a MENU PAGE
of a VIDEO GAME. Jonah grabs two HANDSETS from the floor,
throws one to Gabriel.

                            GABRIEL
         Just one. I'm up early, dude.

With boyish enthusiasm Jonah and Gabriel set up their
characters on screen. Holly watches them, their bond … She
drags herself up and exits to the bedroom unnoticed.

INT. CORRIDOR, FLAT — THE NEXT MORNING

Holly sidles along the wall. From the doorway she peers into
the living room across which she can see Gabriel darting
back and forth in the kitchen. The coffee machine GROANS.

INT. KITCHEN/CORRIDOR, FLAT — MORNING

Gabriel, smartly dressed in a cheap suit, grabs door
keys and phone, hurries through to the empty corridor.
He tiptoes along it, past Jonah's door, then Holly's. The
front door CLICKS behind him. Seconds later, Holly's door
opens slightly. She glances behind her at the Baby, asleep
in its Moses basket, then heads for the front door.

INT. LANDING, FLAT — MORNING

Holly slips out of the front door, pads away. Behind her the door appears closed, but the latch is drawn in and it is therefore OPEN.

EXT. STREET — DAY

Gabriel strides along, following a map on his phone. Crosses the road. A face in the crowd. Behind him Holly follows at a safe distance.

EXT. CARE HOME — DAY — A SHORT TIME LATER

Gabriel stops outside a pleasant, modern, municipal building. He looks at his phone, at the building, checks a slip of paper in his hand before striding inside. The sign reads: MEADOW VIEW CARE HOME.

Holly secretes herself behind a hedge, follows it to the window, peers through. Gabriel sits with THREE ELDERLY PEOPLE. We hear nothing, but see him smile, laugh, kiss hands … they are charmed. He sits down beside them and, talking all the time, opens a book, starts to read aloud.

Holly's eyes drop to Gabriel's ankle and the unmistakable shape of his ELECTRONIC TAG. With an air of thoughtful relief, Holly slips away.

The page is torn off. There are four pages missing …

INT. LIVING ROOM, FLAT — NIGHT — LATER

Gabriel and Elemiah burst into the room. Holly and Jonah jump up, but stop in their tracks. MICHAEL (30s, thin, smart with an eerie, ethereal air) slips in behind Elemiah.

> ELEMIAH
>
> Holly. Jonah. (beat) Michael.

Holly and Jonah take in the strange newcomer, then look to Gabriel for guidance. His smile is edgy.

> MICHAEL
>
> Here they are. Our heroes. I've been told all about you …

He glances to Gabriel, paces.

> MICHAEL
>
> … and all the good work you've done. Yet our defences are breached. Now they've found a weakness they'll claw and claw at it. We won't be safe until the alignment. When it's forever out of their grasp.

Michael paces to and fro. All eyes follow him.

> MICHAEL
>
> But there's a pressing problem. The mortal vessel used by the darkness will draw the force of earthly law to us. It must be erased.

Holly and Jonah are blank.

> MICHAEL
>
> The body. Get rid of. We must.

They start with alarm.

> HOLLY
>
> Hasn't it burnt up or dissolved?

MICHAEL

Don't look so worried! We'll sort it out.

(to Gabriel) Won't we?

Gabriel almost nods, serious. Elemiah and Gabriel slip out. Holly and Jonah face Michael.

MICHAEL

Focus on your purpose.

The Baby MEWLS in its Moses basket. Michael freezes, wanders over to it.

HOLLY

It needs feeding.

She moves to the kitchen, retrieves a bottle of formula. Michael pulls the Baby's covers aside. His fingers stroke its cheek. His expression is strange, thoughtful. Gabriel and Elemiah slip back into the room.

ELEMIAH

(to Michael)

We need to speak … alone.

Holly brushes past with a bottle.

GABRIEL

Holly, Jonah …

Holly and Jonah file out. The door closes behind them. Gabriel, Elemiah and Michael wait for silence. Then …

ELEMIAH

Stabbed in the neck, chest, everywhere. Fuckloads of blood. I'll have to take up the floorboards, replaster.

Gabriel shifts, uncomfortable.

                              GABRIEL

        The kids heard a commotion in the corridor.
        They shouldn't have opened the door … he
        staggered in.

Michael stares at Gabriel, must know he's lying.

                              MICHAEL

        Whatever. It can't stay here.

                              ELEMIAH

        There's an empty flat next door. We'll put
        it there.

                              MICHAEL

        For <u>fuck's</u> sake! Who was he?

                              GABRIEL

        Neighbour. Flat down the corridor.

                              ELEMIAH

        Does he live alone?
        (Gabriel nods)
        Take the Baby and get out.

Gabriel explodes in a wordless burst of frustration.

                              GABRIEL

        It's too soon.

                              MICHAEL

        What about <u>them</u>?

                              ELEMIAH

        They've served their purpose. (loaded looks
        fly between Gabriel, Michael and Elemiah)

INT. BEDROOM, FLAT — EVENING

Holly sits on the bed, feeds the Baby. Jonah curls up opposite, watches. Holly frowns, thoughtfully.

> HOLLY
>
> Who's Michael?

Jonah shrugs.

> JONAH
>
> Another archangel.

> HOLLY
>
> He isn't like Gabriel. Or Elemiah.

> JONAH
>
> I think he's higher.

> HOLLY
>
> Will we ever be archangels? When we're older?

> JONAH
>
> (shakes his head)
> We're normal angels and that's that. We need an archangel to guide us.

Beat.

> HOLLY
>
> I wish we could do things. Fly. Blow things up. Or heal people.

> JONAH
>
> That's not our purpose. Our mortal bodies won't let us.

The Baby stops feeding. Holly rubs its back, thoughtful.

INT. LIVING ROOM, FLAT — NIGHT

Elemiah and Michael face an anxious Gabriel.

> GABRIEL
>
> They're a cover. And they're a great cover.
> I can't be seen with it, can I? Nor can
> either of you.

Michael's piercing eyes bore into him.

> MICHAEL
>
> (despair)
>
> Oh Gabriel …
>
> (beat)
>
> We have to do this now. Bring the baby to
> me.

Gabriel takes a breath, obediently leaves the room.

The following exchange between me and aspiring screenwriter Clive Badham is stapled together and paperclipped to the above script:

TO: Clive Badham
DATE: 28 July 2021
SUBJECT: Divine
FROM: Amanda Bailey

Hi Clive,

Hope you're well. Did I mention I'm moving into film as a producer/director? Well, an industry friend absolutely raved to me recently about your award-winning script *Divine* and I simply had to read it. I asked her to send it to me. I hope you don't mind. I'm in the middle of reading it now.

Thanks,

Amanda

Text message to me from Clive Badham, 28 July 2021:

Clive Badham

Hi Amanda. You've made my day! That's awesome news! When you've read it let me know and we can chat. You'll need contacts and info. I've got some good friends in tech and post. I'll be a valuable partner in the venture.

4

Closing in, Despite Everyone's Best Efforts to Piss Me Off. Correspondence, Interviews and Background Reading

WhatsApp messages between my editor Pippa Deacon and me, 29 July 2021:

Pippa Deacon
Seen today's DAILY WATCH? Page 14.

> **Amanda Bailey**
> I was up till three researching this new angle. Still in bed.

Pippa Deacon
Their lead story online. Check it out.

> **Amanda Bailey**
> Phone on 1%. Give me a sec.

> **Amanda Bailey**
> WHAT THE FUCK???? SHIT SHIT FUCKING SHIT.

Pippa Deacon
Did you know he was writing that?

> **Amanda Bailey**
> NO I FUCKING DIDN'T.

> **Amanda Bailey**
> Sorry, Pippa. I had no idea. Need to simmer down enough to
> read it properly, understand the implications and approach the
> matter with calm dignity.

> **Amanda Bailey**
> AND HE'S USED MY PHOTOS. THE LYING CHEATING
> ARROGANT WITLESS FUCKER.

A partial printout from WatchOnline dated 29 July 2021:

ALPERTON ANGELS teen is MONK.

- **Still calls himself JONAH**
- **Found happiness in isolated MONASTERY**
- **Prays SEVEN times a day**

- **Wears ROBES, breeds PIGS, brews ALE**
- **REFUSES to talk about DEATH CULT**

By OLIVER MENZIES for WATCHONLINE

A man rescued from the Alperton Angels death cult as a teenager in 2003 now lives at a secluded monastery surrounded by picturesque countryside on the Isle of Wight. Quarr Abbey (pronounced 'core') is home to a small community of Benedictine monks who pray seven times a day, farm pigs and brew ale. The monks do not have televisions or mobile phones and avoid using the internet.

Despite his connection to the violent death cult that revelled in sacrificing babies and led to the deaths of four men, the man declares he is finally happy and has found his purpose in life. However, he still refers to himself as 'Jonah', the name given to him by cult leader and convicted murderer Gabriel Angelis.

Who were the Alperton Angels?

The Alperton Angels followed cult leader Gabriel Angelis, real name Peter Duffy, and were based in Alperton, north-west London. They believed they were angels whose purpose on earth was to kill the newborn Antichrist during a particular alignment of stars.

Angelis, who changed his name by deed poll in the 1990s, gave his followers biblical names like Michael, Elemiah and Raphael. They targeted runaway teens to help with their supposed divine mission.

The cult came to a bloody conclusion in December 2003 when the mutilated bodies of three followers were discovered in an empty warehouse. The body of a further victim, waiter Harpinder Singh, was linked to the case. Angelis fled the scene but was soon arrested and charged with Singh's murder.

Two teenagers who had absconded from foster homes to join the cult were taken back into care. Police officers at the time praised the girl and boy, both 17, for alerting the authorities. It was thanks to them the girl's newborn baby avoided death at the angels' hands. As minors, their identities were protected.

Where are the surviving Alperton Angels now?

Gabriel Angelis is serving a whole-life sentence at HMP Tynefield.

'Holly' the teenage girl and her baby were given new identities and are said to be thriving.

'Jonah' has recently been found living at Quarr Abbey and describes himself as finally happy with his spartan religious life.

WhatsApp messages between Ellie Cooper and me, 29 July 2021:

Ellie Cooper
I don't read it, but the Daily Watch sidebar popped up in my browser and I couldn't help noticing a story by Oliver M about Brother Jonah. Did you know he was writing it?

> **Amanda Bailey**
> No. And I am royally pissed off.

WhatsApp messages between me and Oliver Menzies, 29 July 2021:

> **Amanda Bailey**
> What the fuck were you thinking?

Oliver Menzies
When? What? Do you mean the Watch thing?

> **Amanda Bailey**
>

Oliver Menzies
Filed it when I thought Green Street might pull my book.

> **Amanda Bailey**
> Why? How could this possibly help?

Oliver Menzies
It links my name to the case and I get to be a published 'expert' on it. More leverage with Jo. But if she cancelled my commission, at least I made some cash out of it. The Watch

never seemed that interested and sat on the story for weeks.
I forgot about it. Guess they were just waiting for a light news
day.

Oliver Menzies

If it's any consolation, they totally rewrote what I sent them.

> **Amanda Bailey**
>
> I can't believe you've been so low and underhand.

Oliver Menzies

It's all in the public domain. Fair game. Anyone could find Jonah,
it's just that I did.

> **Amanda Bailey**
>
> I did. I found him, NOT YOU. I should have a co-writing credit on
> the piece. At least.

Oliver Menzies

Now you're splitting hairs.

> **Amanda Bailey**
>
> AND you procured my photographs under false pretences and
> submitted them in your name!

Oliver Menzies

Only a couple were used. Look, it's a throwaway piece. It's
already been knocked off the lead spot. It's even slipping down
the sidebar.

Oliver Menzies

See, overtaken by Liz Hurley's 'age-defying bikini' and Kylie
Jenner's 'daring sideboob dress'. Chill out about it. I'll treat you
to dinner some time.

> **Amanda Bailey**
>
> And it compromises BOTH our books. We want to generate
> interest in this case just prior to our publication dates. Not so
> early that every hack and rag is suddenly on the case, looking
> for the baby, printing spoiler pieces and stealing our thunder.

Oliver Menzies

Thought you said the baby couldn't be found.

Oliver Menzies

OK, ignore me.

Oliver Menzies

Are you STILL sulking?

> **Amanda Bailey**
>
> What now?

Oliver Menzies

You said the baby couldn't be found. Now you're concerned someone else will find it.

> **Amanda Bailey**
>
> The fact it can't be found is news in itself.

Oliver Menzies

The Watch doesn't seem to think so. I mentioned it in my piece and they took it out.

Email exchange between me and WembleyOnline editor Louisa Sinclair, 29 July 2021:

TO: Louisa Sinclair
DATE: 29 July 2021
SUBJECT: Question
FROM: Amanda Bailey

Hey Louisa,

I've been totally ripped off by Oliver Menzies. The sneaky shit has gone behind my back and published a piece on an Alperton Angels teenager under his sole byline. I organised the interview for both of us, asked the only salient questions of the day and even took the fucking pictures. I'm seething.

Anyway, he gave away a key piece of info in his original submission. He doesn't even realise how pivotal it is. That the baby was placed for adoption in such a way that it could never be traced. The *Watch* glossed over it with a vague platitude, like 'it's settled in its new life'.

Why would they not publish that info? Also, they did no further reporting or photography. I feel that should tell me something, but what? Any ideas?

Amanda x

TO: Amanda Bailey
DATE: 29 July 2021
SUBJECT: Re: Question
FROM: Louisa Sinclair

Hey,

Lol! I'd never have thought Oliver Menzies of all people would get one over on you, Amanda.

Reasons the *Watch* cut out that detail: the simplest explanation is they couldn't verify it. Otherwise, there could be a super-injunction – remember the first rule of super-injunction is that you can't mention super-injunction – but could an eighteen-year-old adoptee afford the hundred-grand legal fee?

There is one other possible reason – they're keeping their powder dry while they plan to feature the story in greater depth at a later date – perhaps they have someone already on the case, trying to trace the baby, or about to write something about it not being traceable. A little article like this is a good barometer of interest. See how many clicks it gets, how many comments, how many shares. Gives them an idea of what resources to divert to it.

Check out the comments section beneath the article. Always surprising how people won't come forward with info but will write it anonymously on a news site.

Louisa

WhatsApp messages between Oliver Menzies and me, 30 July 2021:

Oliver Menzies
I feel like shit.

Amanda Bailey
Good. It was a shitty thing to do.

247

Oliver Menzies

Not the Jonah story. This mediation meeting with the mad squaddie. They tried to paint me as the guilty party. Said I'd hounded a brave war hero and victim of PTSD. Wanted an apology FFS. Gaslighting bastards. And you're still pissed off too. And I'm still woken up at 4.44 a.m. every day.

> **Amanda Bailey**
>
> Don't think I've forgiven you. I NEVER will.

Oliver Menzies

Oh well, that's me feeling a lot better.

> **Amanda Bailey**
>
> There's an interesting comment beneath your Daily Watch piece. Will paste it 👇

> **Amanda Bailey**
>
> 'My uncle was in the police and he said strange things happened when they arrested Gabriel. One minute he was injured, and the next he wasn't. His wounds healed themselves. No one who witnessed it would ever mention it again. He'd also say things the coppers wouldn't understand, then something would happen to make sense of what he said, and they'd all be freaked out.'

Oliver Menzies

Where? I've just looked and can't see it.

> **Amanda Bailey**
>
> You're right, that comment's disappeared 🙀 I copied and pasted it an hour ago. The moderator must've removed it. Wonder why.

Oliver Menzies

I told you. There's something going on. Something about him.

> **Amanda Bailey**
>
> It's a mythology. Similar stories have been told about other notorious murderers. Fred West especially. Many opportunistic killers seem to have an instinct for when they are unobserved.

They'll snatch victims in broad daylight and no one spots them.

Oliver Menzies

Listen. What if a 'sixth sense' is a BIOLOGICAL trait of psychopathy?

>**Amanda Bailey**
>
>Psychopaths lack empathy. If anyone is totally cut off from psychic or any other sort of connection, it should be psychopaths.

Oliver Menzies

True, they don't process emotion the way neuro-typical people do. Yet they have an acute understanding of how those who experience empathy behave. They recognise love, sympathy, guilt and obligation, without feeling any of those complex emotions themselves. They understand what drives others to act and exploit it accordingly. What if 'empathy' in psychopaths is simply replaced by this 'sixth sense' for how others behave? THAT'S a scientific basis for something otherwise unexplainable by logic.

>**Amanda Bailey**
>
>By the time we know someone is a murderous psychopath, they've had years of trial and error dealing with the empathetic world and a lifetime to hone their observational skills.

Oliver Menzies

I know that. But Gabriel is different. This is what I'm wrestling with, Mand. See, meeting Gabriel PROVED to me there's something special about him. That there are people and events that defy rational explanation. I know I'm smart. I'm not easily fooled. So there must be something in it. If you'd met him, you'd understand.

>**Amanda Bailey**
>
>But he refused to meet me.

I emailed the London Fire Service press office to ask about David Polneath. Jayden Hoyle replied with the below, 30 July 2021:

TO: Amanda Bailey
DATE: 30 July 2021
SUBJECT: Re: The late David Polneath
FROM: Jayden Hoyle

Dear Ms Bailey,

Thank you for your email regarding Mr David Polneath who was sadly declared deceased at the scene of a fire at Belgrade Mansions on 27 July. I am very sorry for your loss and understand he was a dear friend and close colleague with whom you were working.

Unfortunately, his flat is still cordoned off and the police haven't yet released it. They await the findings of the Fire Investigation Unit who will ascertain whether the blaze was suspicious. I have attended the residence myself and can confirm that no paperwork and no electronic appliances are extant. The entire apartment has been totally gutted by the conflagration, which began in the lounge and was pulled through the rooms by a series of flashovers and draughts that channelled the fire horizontally from the front window to the rear doorway. Luckily the residences on either side and above were not affected. Whatever Mr Polneath was working on for you, I am afraid it is lost.

I am sorry to have no more positive news for you at this time.

Yours,

Jayden Hoyle
Public Relations
London Fire Service

WhatsApp messages between Ellie Cooper and me, 30 July 2021:

Ellie Cooper
Everything OK, Mand?

Amanda Bailey
All good. Thanks, Ellie.

Ellie Cooper

It's just you've gone quiet on the transcription front. Are all your interviews done?

> **Amanda Bailey**
>
> I haven't written the right chapter one yet. Working on the third now. Once I get that killer opening, I'll be a lot happier.

> **Amanda Bailey**
>
> I mean, I am happy now. Chilled, relaxed. No need to worry about me.

Ellie Cooper

I DO worry about you. I know how hard you work. But you ARE allowed to take it easy.

> **Amanda Bailey**
>
> Someone else is dead. An amateur sleuth who'd been investigating the angels for years. He emailed early on but I was trying to find the baby then and ignored him. When my angle changed, I got back in touch. He had a theory about a cover-up but I didn't get a chance to speak to him. He died in a house fire on Tuesday.

Ellie Cooper

Did he ever speak to Oliver?

> **Amanda Bailey**
>
> No. If there are dark forces at work, they're following me, not him 😱

Ellie Cooper

Be careful, Mand. It's all probably coincidence, but messing with things like that ... Do you even have to write this book? At your age you could do whatever you want. Read. Write. Travel. Find someone and settle down. I hate to sound like an elderly relative, but before it's too late.

> **Amanda Bailey**
>
> Find someone? Not me. I let someone go just before starting this job.

Ellie Cooper

Let them go? It sounds like you fired them 😊

> **Amanda Bailey**
>
> 🔫 I don't trust relationships. Only happy when there's just me to think about. Married to my job – that's what they say 😊

> **Amanda Bailey**
>
> At MY age? You cheeky fucking millennial 😂 How old do you think I am?

Ellie Cooper

Well, you fell out with Aunty Pat 26 years ago. If you were aged 16 to 20 then, you'd be 42 to 46 now.

> **Amanda Bailey**
>
> I'm 38. I was 12 when I put myself into care and fell out with Aunty Pat and the rest of my family.

Ellie Cooper

OMG, Mand. I'm so sorry. That's tragic.

> **Amanda Bailey**
>
> No. It's the best thing I ever did.

Divine

by

Amanda Bailey

One

David Harris Polneath had spent his life adding things up. As a corporate accountant for [*find out where*] he'd balanced ledgers, then spreadsheets, then accounting systems with equal attention to detail. He wasn't about to stop in June 2019 when, at the age of sixty-five, he finally retired. Because David Polneath had a project. More than a hobby. An interest that saw him get up at six each day and go to bed by eleven. The Alperton Angels.

Sixteen years earlier David was glued to one particular news story with a fascination that transcended prurient interest. It started with four dead men, two traumatised teenagers and a baby in a derelict warehouse in north-west London – and ended with the chilling news that a small but intense death cult had been recruiting vulnerable children under the nose of social services.

While he was getting up and going to work day in, day out, David could keep his feelings under wraps. The work ordered his thoughts, the routine was comforting. He could ignore the angels and the memories they triggered. The darkness that threatened to well up and drown him in its wake. Now, he was ready to use his own trauma to help solve a case that ordinary, regular people simply did not compute. Because for David, to understand how the Alperton Angels did what they did, you had to have been a vulnerable teenager yourself. And he had.

I first met David when my own research into this mysterious case began. From the start I was baffled by personal accounts that were equally credible, yet completely at odds with each other. What's more, these accounts often differed on the type of facts no one usually gets wrong, even forty years later, let alone eighteen. One professional remembers a key player pulling a knife and threatening to kill a child. Someone else who was there saw nothing of the sort.

I soon understood why David was fascinated by the Alperton Angels. What began as an exercise to banish his own demons gradually morphed into something quite unexpected. For the first time in his life, David found that things didn't add up. Dates, names, places, times. Facts. His conclusion was as unnerving as it was short: there had been a cover-up, a smokescreen still in place today. And David vowed he'd get to the bottom of it, if it was the last thing he did.

***

The fire service was called to a blazing flat in the early hours of 28 July [*find out exact timings*]. It had started in the lounge and, thanks to a succession of flashovers and backdraughts, was pulled from front to back, incinerating everything in its path. Paperwork, records, computers, notes. Nothing was left of one man's painstaking two-year investigation. What had he discovered that was now lost for ever? I cursed the fact I had put off meeting David until I had completed interviews with people directly involved in the case. I mourned the tragedy that had befallen him, but in the back of my mind was the suspicion this hadn't been an accident.

An investigation into the fire found it had started at an overloaded electrical socket. No one was to blame, and relief was voiced that the fire had not spread to neighbouring flats. David's body was identified by his dental records. One of the few things about his death that did add up.

5

The Closer I Get, the Further Away I Seem

WhatsApp messages between retired detective chief superintendent Don Makepeace and me, 30 July 2021:

Don Makepeace
I'm inviting you for lunch. Quaglino's at one. Don.

> **Amanda Bailey**
> Today? 😳 To what do I owe this honour?

Don Makepeace
Yes?

> **Amanda Bailey**
> You bet!

WhatsApp messages between me and Ellie Cooper, 30 July 2021:

> **Amanda Bailey**
> Don Makepeace has invited me to Quaglino's for lunch.

Ellie Cooper
Yum! Send the file through when you're ready.

> **Amanda Bailey**
> Telling you just in case. So you know where I will be.

Ellie Cooper
OK.

Meeting with retired detective chief superintendent Don Makepeace in Quaglino's, 30 July 2021. Transcribed by Ellie Cooper.

> [*Unusually for a meeting between you and Don, there's no chit-chat or gossip before you get down to business. EC*]

AB: Don, when we met back in June, did you know I had no hope of finding the baby?

DM: I suspected.

AB: Why didn't you say?

DM: I warned you to be careful. I don't know the ins and outs of this case, but I know there *are* ins and outs.

AB: Five people connected to this case died prematurely. [*A long pause. EC*]

DM: Most of us have a story. *That* story. The one that doesn't quite add up. I want to tell you mine.

AB: Go on.

DM: Many moons ago I was a young traffic officer working out of Hillingdon. One night shift my colleague and I were called to an accident on the M40. We arrived to find a distraught couple, their car stopped on the hard shoulder. They were searching for something. We soon discovered they weren't the accident, but rather the witnesses to it. Now, this was a time before there were barriers in the central reservation. The couple had been driving along, when a car from the opposite carriageway veered, out of control, across their path, causing them to brake suddenly. The rogue car flew off the road, down an embankment and plunged into dense undergrowth. You couldn't see into that thicket, even with a police torch. The couple were beside themselves, imagining the occupants trapped in the car, possibly injured, so I called for back-up. We had six patrol cars, an ambulance, twelve coppers and eventually the police helicopter with its floodlight. We turned that stretch of embankment over more than once. No car. The couple insisted on staying to help with the search, and that's what I couldn't forget. Their distress, the detail in their account. The car was a mustard-yellow Mini Clubman with a green strip across the top of the windscreen, a common sun visor at the time. The face of a young man, petrified, behind the wheel. A sticker on the passenger window for Windsor Safari Park. Were there children in the car? But the search was fruitless. At daybreak we had to call it off, tell the couple they'd been mistaken. They were probably tired and full-beam headlights on the opposite carriageway had momentarily blinded them. It appeared a car was crossing their path but it was just an optical illusion. Reluctantly they left the scene. But I couldn't forget them. I was on day shift, a week or so later. It was a quiet day, so I decided to drive past the spot, give it one final check. I trawled the place we had searched and found nothing. But I continued under the bridge and along the road some way ahead of where the couple had said they saw the car. I hadn't gone far when I glimpsed a chrome bumper buried in the undergrowth. To cut a long story short, a mustard-yellow Mini Clubman with a green sun visor and Windsor Safari Park sticker *had* skidded off the road. Its driver was declared deceased at the scene. A young man of twenty-one in his first car. Died on impact with a tree. [*Shit, what a story. No wonder you both take deep breaths after that one. EC*]

AB: Wow. If you hadn't had a hunch and returned to the scene, he would never have been found. That's a moving story, Don.

DM: That's not the story, Amanda. Remember I'd moved a good quarter of a mile *ahead* of where the couple saw a car go off the road. The car I found had been hidden in the undergrowth for six months. The remains inside were skeletal. [*This is creeping me out. EC*] When the accident happened, no one saw it. The young man was driving back from a friend's house, alone, and was reported missing when he didn't arrive home. His parents were distraught. Had he been murdered, taken his own life or simply walked out on them? It wasn't a happy ending. But at least it gave them closure.

AB: What was the explanation for that discrepancy in time?

DM: Certain colleagues joked the young man's ghost re-staged the accident so his remains would be found. But I put it down to mere coincidence. Witnesses are mistaken about what they see and it just happened to be near the site of a previous, similar accident, involving a popular car, in a popular colour, with stickers common at the time. But I never forgot that case and shortly before I left the force, I looked it up again and read through the documents. With the benefit of an entire career's experience, I hoped to see in those few pages an explanation for the time lag. Evidence I was right and that it wasn't supernatural at all. And I did. I found something I missed at the time.

AB: What was it?

DM: It was a transcript of the 999 call that had summoned my colleague and me to the scene. It wasn't made by the couple who witnessed the accident. It came from a phone box just off the next motorway exit. This was long before mobile phones. The caller had seen a yellow Mini Clubman skid across the carriageway and into the bushes. He told us another car had been obliged to brake sharply and stopped on the hard shoulder. Two people in that car had got out to help. This driver did the right thing, pulled off at the next exit, found a phone box, reported the accident, then drove on his way. That call meant the couple *weren't mistaken*, Amanda. Someone else had seen the same accident they witnessed, *six months after* it happened.

AB: Wow. That's …

DM: It's evidence … that some things simply have *no* logical explanation. Perhaps everyone should come across such an experience once in their lives. And when you do, the best course of action is to stay the fuck *away* from it. [*There's something about his tone, Mand. Anyway, I cut out a stilted discussion about the starters. You both have scallops and heritage tomatoes. Here's where it gets interesting again. EC*]

AB: I'm worried a colleague of mine is falling under the spell of Gabriel Angelis.

DM: Oliver Menzies? [*He laughs at the idea. EC*] Well, if he sprouts wings and starts calling himself an archangel, you'll know why.

AB: Have you met with *him* lately? Have you told *him* about the yellow Mini Clubman?

DM: No. No need, Amanda.

AB: Why not?

DM: Because he's not like you [*he lowers his voice. EC*] he's not likely to get anywhere near the people who want this all kept quiet. So *he's* not in any danger. Please take note.
[*I hope I'm not speaking out of turn here, Mand. But do you think you could listen to what he says? I cut out everything else because it didn't seem as important as the above. EC*]

WhatsApp messages between me and true crime author Minnie Davis, 30 July 2021:

> **Amanda Bailey**
> Hey, Mins! How goes it?

Minnie Davis
Hello, gorgeous girl! 🌝 Basking in personal glory. Pippa's feedback: solid treatment of the crimes, plus dark, left-field angle. Just the type of book to launch Eclipse. Phew!

> **Amanda Bailey**
> Brilliant! Well done you. Actually, I've got a favour to ask. Would you approach someone for me? Need to minimise my name in connection to this case. I could create a false ID but with no traceable background it would instantly ping radars.

Minnie Davis
I get it. What is it you want?

> **Amanda Bailey**
> There was a girl who briefly attended an independent school. I need to find out which school she came from.

Minnie Davis
Not on Facebook, Twitter, Instagram?

> **Amanda Bailey**
> Nothing. No social media presence at all. Probably changed her name since then. She was Rowley Wild.

Minnie Davis
Leave it with me, gorgeous! 🌝

WhatsApp messages between me and Oliver Menzies, 30 July 2021:

> **Amanda Bailey**
> STOP WANKING! Hey, how goes it?

Oliver Menzies

Busy.

> **Amanda Bailey**
>
> Fancy meeting up? Chat about the case etc?

Oliver Menzies

No.

> **Amanda Bailey**
>
> Go on! You miss my smiling face and hearty cheer.

Oliver Menzies

Email from spiritual counsellor Paul Cole to Oliver Menzies, 30 July 2021:

TO: Oliver Menzies
DATE: 30 July 2021
SUBJECT: How are you?
FROM: Paul Cole

Dear Oliver,

I haven't heard from you in a while and hope you are well.

Previously, we spoke about dreams and how they connect us to our otherlife. But even if your dreams are elusive, you can still harness that link for peace and healing. Art can transport our consciousness to a higher place. Can you use music to change your mood? A favourite track, descending a rabbit hole of recommended music on your streaming service ... all can help ease anxiety and refresh the psyche.

I often recommend exploring creativity to my counselling clients. Your local adult education college will run art classes. You could write your story down, or if you're musical try composing your own tune. Finally, getting out and about, alone or with friends, can be a transformative tonic. I frequently set myself the challenge to say 'yes' to every invitation I receive!

Many people I've worked with have found the above helpful in overcoming their low mood. Please feel free to contact me at any time.
Paul

AB: Ellie, I'm interviewing Sabrina Emanuel, a retired social worker. She's a wonderful lady and we go back a long, long way. I wanted to speak to her earlier about the baby but she was busy moving abroad. Let's see if she remembers anything. You can cut out whatever isn't relevant to the angels. [*I cut out your conversation about her move to Portugal, the weather, the beach, the balmy nights ... EC*]

AB: I've never properly thanked you for everything back then.

SE: No need. You're a success story I often think back on.

AB: I'm a *success* story?

SE: Yes! Of course you are.

AB: The lovely guy I've just ditched might disagree.

SE: What happened? Tell me.

AB: Oh, I don't know. I don't like them when they're edgy and I don't trust them when they're nice.

SE: You don't trust yourself, darling. Perhaps you don't trust things to go right in your life. But they will. When you meet him, you'll know.

AB: Sabrina, I'm afraid I met him years ago. I had what you might call *feelings* for someone, but then he did something that meant I could never trust him again. As time went on, I realised it had destroyed my trust in everyone else, too. I still can't forgive him. Not until he loses as much as I did. [*I cut out her advice to you about learning to let go and trust others. You seem a bit upset here, Mand. Who are you talking about? You switch off the recording, then start it again later. EC*]

SE: I remember the angels, oh yes. My colleague worked with Holly when she first escaped them. She was like you: a young woman who took control of her own life when no one else would.

AB: To be honest, some of the material is a bit ... [*A long pause here. EC*]

SE: Close to home?

AB: Close to home. Literally! As you know.

SE: Well then, you'll understand what drove Holly away from all the adults that had let her down.

AB: I do. I was lucky. I never met a Gabriel. What happened to Holly? I've been told she was taken in by family.

SE: Family? Well, yes. She hadn't been in care when he'd got his claws into her, so she went back to her mother. A college course was organised. In the end, she was fine, Amanda. My friend heard she was studying to be a social worker. She looked out for her name in professional circles, but never saw it, so perhaps she decided it wasn't for her.

AB: And the baby?

SE: My friend doesn't remember a baby at all.

AB: Would it be conceivable your colleague wouldn't have been told that Holly had had a baby taken away?

SE: They'd *have* to know. It would be too significant for Holly's mental and emotional state.

AB: Exactly. [*A long pause here. EC*] Sabrina, can you remember when this was? When you – your friend, I mean – dealt with Holly.

SE: Yes, I remember exactly. I got married that year. It was 1991. Not so very long after I worked with you.

AB: The Alperton Angels was in 2003.

[*I cut out the rest of your chat. I have a few ideas, though. Going to message you. EC*]

WhatsApp messages between Ellie Cooper and me, 1 August 2021:

Ellie Cooper
There are two Hollys.

> **Amanda Bailey**
> Morning. Only just awake.

Ellie Cooper

Gabriel was with one girl in the early 90s and another in the early 2000s. He called them both 'Holly'.

Ellie Cooper

For the first Holly, things ended much better. She hadn't been under Gabriel's spell as long, didn't have a baby, and was rescued or escaped. The SECOND Holly wasn't as lucky. She had a baby and was caught up in the Alperton Angels bloodbath. That's the Holly we're looking for.

> **Amanda Bailey**
> Good work! Well done 😊

Ellie Cooper

You knew?

> **Amanda Bailey**
> I worked it out when dates and times didn't add up. Only, I don't want Oliver catching on just yet 🤫

Email from Oliver Menzies to spiritual counsellor Paul Cole, 31 July 2021:

TO: Paul Cole
DATE: 31 July 2021
SUBJECT: Listen
FROM: Oliver Menzies

This is big and I'm the only one who can see it. Most people won't understand, but you might, Paul. Listen.

There's a change coming. Art, literature and music have been predicting it for a century or more. Literally messengers have been coming down to earth to warn us, in the form of musicians, artists and writers. And this is the time they were warning us about. Gabriel was our last chance to save ourselves and we failed him. The Antichrist escaped. Now the only person with a connection to the other side is imprisoned. Nothing can stop it now.

Don't you see, Paul? The Alperton Angels were right. The Antichrist is here.

Oliver

WhatsApp messages between true crime author Minnie Davis and me, 1 August 2021:

Minnie Davis
Hello, gorgeous girl! Mission accomplished. Rowley Wild moved to Notting Hill & Ealing High School from Gordonstoun.

> **Amanda Bailey**
> Gordonstoun? That's posher than posh.

Minnie Davis
Princes Charles, Andrew and Edward, Balthazar Getty ... Establishment of choice for the aristocracy and anyone who has the money and the inclination to join them.

> **Amanda Bailey**
> Did you find out why she left and when?

Minnie Davis
She was there from September 2001 to May 2003. It states 'relocation'. I'd say that's a polite term for 'parents can't afford the fees'.

> **Amanda Bailey**
> So Rowley is taken out of her exclusive public school in Scotland and sent to a private day school in London, right at the end of summer term.

Minnie Davis
Parents not penniless. Just down to their last few million.

> **Amanda Bailey**
> She had a traumatic home life and then a new school to navigate. It must've been the final straw.

Minnie Davis
Want to know an interesting thing? Rowley Wild appears in inverted commas throughout the documentation. 'Rowley Wild'. I've got a couple of avenues I can try. Let's see 🤞

An email out of the blue from former prison inmate Ross Tate, 1 August 2021:

TO: Amanda Bailey
DATE: 1 August 2021
SUBJECT: Wandsworth
FROM: Ross Tate

Dear Mrs Bailey,

I been asked to write to you by a fella called David Polneath. Only I can't get an answer off him now, so not sure what else to do. Here goes anyway.

He wants me to tell you about my time inside with Gabriel Angelis, just like I told him when he came round. I was in Wandsworth in 2002. Did eight months for money laundering but I was stitched up by my boss. Us white-collar prisoners stick together inside, so I knew Gabriel pretty well for a good six months of the time I was there.

Have you met him? He's different. There's something I can't describe to you. It's not a bad thing either. It's in his eyes. When he talks to you, the world stops turning. He listens like he *wants* to hear what you got to say. You feel he knows everything about you. And he gives advice like it's from his heart.

I'm not gay. Not even prison bent, but I wanted to spend as much time as I could with Gabriel. I weren't the only one. Soon as our doors opened for association, we'd all troop out of our cells into his. We'd listen to him talk like he was our messiah. I'm not religious either but can't describe it any other way. I admit there could be a bit of competition to be close to him. Only natural, isn't it? When men are together there's always competition, right?

Suddenly Gabriel isn't as available as he was. His cell door is shut and he don't come out much. Later, I find out two new fellas have got right in with him. They're both done for diverting computer supplies from the PC World warehouse into their own lock-up and selling them on. They meet Gabriel and suddenly the rest of us aren't welcome no more. I'm not saying it's wrong, but it is what it is, yeah? The three of them were as thick as thieves. Them two fellas were Dominic Jones and Alan Morgan. The two angels who died in Alperton. I look back and think, that time must've been the start of the whole thing.

Me and the other lads couldn't tell if Gabriel had seen something in them and wanted to cut the rest of us out, or if they'd seen something in him and wanted him for themselves. It's a mystery. David called it a dynamic, between Gabriel and these two guys.

What I can say is that Gabriel only told certain people they were angels. I can hear you laughing now, Mrs Bailey, because there are no angels inside, are there? I never really wondered why some were singled out like that. David says it's the vulnerable ones. Gabriel has an instinct for who's likely to fall under his spell.

All I know is he never told me I was an angel. But if he had, I'd have believed him. I'd believe anything that man said.

If you hear from David, will you do us a favour and let me know? Yours faithfully,
Ross Tate

WhatsApp messages between Oliver Menzies and me, on the morning of 1 August 2021:

Oliver Menzies
OK. This is big.

> **Amanda Bailey**
> What is?

Oliver Menzies
The case of the Alperton Angels. The MYSTERY of the Alperton Angels. No one realised it at the time. People are blind to it. I know – I was blind to it myself once. I've found out some things these last few weeks that explain it all. And I'm more involved than I ever realised.

> **Amanda Bailey**
> You mean the mad squaddie?

Oliver Menzies
No, no. He's nothing. I called him after the mediation ordeal. Apologised. He was fine. Gracious even. We're going for a drink. He's not calling me every morning.

Amanda Bailey

You're finally getting some sleep, that's good.

Oliver Menzies

At 4.44 a.m. every morning THEY call me. It's a sign they're
watching.

Amanda Bailey

Remember what Jo said. Highlight any mysterious anomalies,
but leave the reader to make the other-worldly connection 👻

WhatsApp messages between me and Oliver Menzies, later on
1 August 2021:

Amanda Bailey

I'm looking for references to the Alperton Angels in popular
culture. What was the Ibiza track you mentioned way back?

Oliver Menzies

'Starz' by Widmore & Schmoozy. Ace choon and lyrics.

Amanda Bailey

Cheers. Will check it out now.

Amanda Bailey

You won't know where the moon is till you look up to the sky.
You won't know where your wings are till you fall and have to
fly.

Oliver Menzies

Like I said, great lyrics.

Amanda Bailey

Shame there are no others. They repeat them 400 times in this
remix alone 😱

Oliver Menzies

Philistine. You know songwriters and musicians have a
subconscious link to the other side. Heard it from an expert and
been doing my own research. You just need to listen. Really
listen.

Amanda Bailey

💡

Oliver Menzies

I'm serious. Mozart, Beethoven and Bellini were all child prodigies. John Lennon and Paul McCartney were basically children when they made music that influenced generations to come.

> **Amanda Bailey**
>
> True. They were teenagers when they wrote 'Eleanor Rigby'. A song about end-of-life regret 🪦

Oliver Menzies

I read that each time we're born on earth our connection to our previous life fades only gradually. So, in youth we have an insight and perspective on the entirety of life that we lose with experience. Hence young people write so eloquently about regret.

> **Amanda Bailey**
>
> Wow. Never thought about it like that before.

Oliver Menzies

That's not all. Listen. There's music that literally predicts the future of music. Tago Mago by CAN. That shit is from 1971. It's like seeing a mobile phone in a Monet. Mind-blowing.

Oliver Menzies

But you know who's really interesting? Vangelis – his name literally means 'an angel'. I've had his work on repeat all day. He's a messenger. In the early 70s he was in a band called The Four Horsemen. They had a song called 'Aphrodite's Child'. Just listen to it, Mand. It's about NOW. They put out an album in 1972 called 666 – the number mentioned in the apocalypse of John 13/18. The beast.

> **Amanda Bailey**
>
> Who led you to these conclusions? Gabriel?

Oliver Menzies

💩 My letters were returned, undelivered. Marked inappropriate correspondence. The governor was using me, Mand. Seeing if Gabriel would make a confession or hint about pushing for a retrial. Pointless.

> **Amanda Bailey**
>
> So where are you getting all this info from?

Oliver Menzies

Like I said, I'm in contact with an expert.

> **Amanda Bailey**
>
> Would this be that spiritual counsellor who emailed ME first? Paul Cole?

Oliver Menzies

He's fascinating. I'll show you his emails one day. I'm not some mindless follower, I'm checking out everything he says. See, it's not just music. Before music became a driving artistic force behind our culture, it was literature that pointed us towards the future. H. G. Wells, Jules Verne and George Orwell. All three were prophets.

> **Amanda Bailey**
>
> All men, these visionary artists. Not one woman. So much for the Age of Aquarius.

Oliver Menzies

What's that got to do with it?

> **Amanda Bailey**
>
> The Age of Aquarius is a new era led by female energy. I've been reading about this stuff lately. Anyway, none of your alleged 'prophets' predicted the Antichrist would escape destruction in a warehouse in Alperton in 2003.

Oliver Menzies

Don't be ridiculous. It's symbolic. But you know the most indicative thing? The predictions have stopped. No more music. Music as an art form that grows, changes and influences generations – dead. Writers, artists, no one is predicting the future any more.

Interview with a Mystery Woman in Northala Fields park, 2 August 2021. Transcribed by Ellie Cooper.

AB: Don't cut anything out of this, Ellie. It's 5 a.m. and I don't know who I'm meeting. [*Early-morning birdsong and light traffic. EC*]

MW: Amanda?

AB: Oh. Right. It's you. So we *have* met before.

MW: Yes, who gave you my number?

AB: Jonah. I visited him in the monastery.

MW: How did you know to find him there?

AB: I was given his old phone number. Whoever answered told me. [*The woman sighs. EC*]

AB: While I was there, I stumbled, he pushed a slip of paper into my hand with your number on it. Nothing else.

MW: Then he trusts you.

AB: I have no idea who you are or how you're connected to this case – except that two weeks ago you sent me on a wild goose chase while you broke into my flat and waited for me to return. Great party trick, by the way. [*OMG, Mand, be careful. EC*]

MW: It's not a game. That didn't put you off and I *need* you to know the level of security you're dealing with.

AB: Friends in high places keep warning me. Contacts with potentially key information have died suddenly, and my colleague, who by his own account is never wrong, has almost convinced me the Antichrist is about to end the world. [*You almost make her laugh here. EC*]

MW: There's a lot about this case that's hard to explain.

AB: What role did you play in it?

MW: I can't be specific. My work is security based.

AB: There are no true crime books that conduct anything like an in-depth investigation. I'm beginning to understand now there's a reason for that.

MW: Correct. I will say this. You can write a book about the failure of the care system to protect the children in it. You could examine the power of cults and how difficult it is to break the hold some people have over others. Or you could focus on the religious mystery. Potential supernatural goings-on. Any of those subjects are fine. [*Shit, Mand, so none of those are the truth. Who is this creepy woman? EC*]

AB: OK ... [*You're both quiet for a long time. EC*]

AB: Were you there? In the warehouse? The night of The Assembly?

MW: What makes you ask that?

AB: Call it intuition. One of those things you can't quite explain. Like why Harpinder Singh was depicted as a penniless migrant when he was a former public schoolboy from a wealthy family.

MW: Like I said, I can't be specific.

AB: He was undercover, living in a flat near the angels. Why? I wondered if he was watching them, but they moved around every few days, while Singh was at Middlesex House for weeks. I know he was connected to Chris Shenk via the restaurant. Singh worked there and Shenky sold drugs out the back.

MW: [*She's obviously walking away here. EC*] I'm sorry ...

AB: Marie-Claire! [*Quite a pause here. I think you shocked her. EC*] Why was the baby spirited away? It was taken from Holly before social services could get there.

MW: So people like you never find it. [*So quiet I could barely hear this. EC*]

AB: What's so special about that child?

MW: There won't be any more warnings, Amanda.
[*OMG, Mand, stick to your new angle. The popular culture thing. It'll be great. This book's only a holiday page-turner. It's not worth it. EC*]

A slip of paper, torn from the margins of a Bible. On it, in hurried handwriting, is the name 'Marie-Claire' and a scribbled telephone number.

WhatsApp messages between Ellie Cooper and me, 2 August 2021:

Ellie Cooper

Is the Mystery Woman the police officer Marie-Claire, who was
at the scene of The Assembly?

> **Amanda Bailey**
> Possibly. She's a woman of colour in her forties. She'd have
> been in her late twenties at the time.

Ellie Cooper

Did she also collect the baby from Holly, immediately after Aileen
left? The duty manager of the children's centre, Maggie Keenan,
says it was collected by a black woman and a white man. It
surprised the social workers who expected to collect it the next day.

> **Amanda Bailey**
> Again, possibly. Only Maggie Keenan remembers Marie-Claire
> as Caucasian. 'Marie-Claire' could be an operational name used
> by several undercover officers 🤔

Ellie Cooper

The baby wasn't missing so whoever collected it must've been
legitimate. Social services might have accidentally sent two
teams of social workers 🪦

> **Amanda Bailey**
> Ellie, in 2004 a respected filmmaker, Suzi Korman, tried to
> make a documentary. She was warned off, and when that didn't
> stop her, she died in a house fire. But two TV drama series aired
> a couple of years later. One exposed failures of the care system.
> The other created a fantasy with demons and hellfire. No one
> warned THOSE filmmakers.

Ellie Cooper

What can it be that they're STILL trying to keep quiet?

> **Amanda Bailey**
> The woman I met in the park just now was the one who gained
> access to my flat, without any sign of entry, while I was waiting

behind the Ballot Box pub on 13 July. She told me to stop looking for the baby. What is it about me – and Suzi Korman – that they're afraid of?

Ellie Cooper

A respected documentarian. An experienced journalist with a background in true crime. Either of you might just get to the bottom of it. Shame you had to abandon your search for the baby.

> **Amanda Bailey**
>
>

Ellie Cooper

?

> **Amanda Bailey**
>
> You know me better than that.

Ellie Cooper

???

> **Amanda Bailey**
>
> I've never stopped looking for the baby 🧑

WhatsApp messages between Oliver Menzies and me, 4 August 2021:

Oliver Menzies

Are you awake?

> **Amanda Bailey**
>
> I am now.

Oliver Menzies

I've been reading Gray Graham's transcripts. These pages you had translated from his notebook.

> **Amanda Bailey**
>
> Yeah. He was there, right? He found the angels' bodies. Not something officially recorded at the time.

Oliver Menzies

I know why he was such a good stringer. Always first on the scene.

> **Amanda Bailey**
>
> He had the police in his pocket. Knew the borough like the back of his hand.

Oliver Menzies

He 'saw' crimes before they happened. These notebooks aren't just him writing shit down at the scene. It's automatic writing done when he was half asleep, half awake. It's a dream diary. He had a connection to the other side.

> **Amanda Bailey**
>
> Wow. I'll read it again, but if he had a party trick like that, he'd have told us about it every Christmas.

Oliver Menzies

NO! He HAD to keep it quiet. It was his secret advantage.

WhatsApp messages between true crime author Minnie Davis and me, 4 August 2021:

Minnie Davis

Hello, gorgeous girl! Found out a few things. Might or might not be rel. The daughter of the 7th Marquess of Carlisle left Gordonstoun shortly before 'Rowley Wild' arrived at Notting Hill & Ealing High. She's called Georgina Ogilvy. Her mother was Lady Helen Carlisle and father, Frederick Ogilvy, Lord Carlisle. They met in rehab and by all accounts were well suited, having lots of addictions in common. He was a very distant and very disgraced second cousin to the Queen.

> **Amanda Bailey**
>
> Thanks, Minnie. You're a star. How were they disgraced?

Minnie Davis

Check them out on Wiki. He invested the already-dwindling family millions in cocaine and heroin. Died of an overdose in

2009, the day after being released from prison. He'd just served
a sentence for possession with intent. Helen was also in and out
of rehab and psychiatric care. Died last year.

> **Amanda Bailey**
> What does Wiki say about Georgina?

Minnie Davis

Next to nothing. Their only child. Born 1986. They clearly wanted
to hush up their fall from grace by giving her a new name when
she was forced to 'relocate' to a cheaper school.

> **Amanda Bailey**
> And that would've made it easier for the angels to give her
> ANOTHER name. She was used to adults with chaotic lifestyles
> renaming her.

Minnie Davis

Not thought of it like that, but yeah.

> **Amanda Bailey**
> So Holly's baby has aristocratic lineage, which means a familial
> claim to it may well have been kept out of the news to protect
> its identity, seeing as its adoptive parents would have a high
> profile themselves. This secret adoption wasn't to another
> country, but to a higher level of society.

Minnie Davis

Know anyone who can worm their way in with the toffs? They
may get you further, but I've exhausted my source and about to
start pre-publicity for ROSE & MYRA.

> **Amanda Bailey**
> You're a star, Mins. Thanks. Good luck for pre-pub and if you
> need me to help you out with ANYTHING in future, just shout
>

Minnie Davis

Email exchange between me and Cathy-June Lloyd, Cold & Unsolved
Murder Club chair, 6 August 2021:

TO: Amanda Bailey
DATE: 6 August 2021
SUBJECT: The Mystery of the Alperton Angels
FROM: Cathy-June Lloyd

Dear Amanda,

The amateur detectives of Cold & Unsolved are back with more
intriguing facts! One of our members – and he deserves a big shout-
out for this: Rob Jolley – has been trawling local news archives for the
whole of north-west London on microfiche – and after four weeks he
found this. Hope you can read my scan, it's from the personal ads in the
Hillingdon Times, 3 April 1990:

ANGELS FLY OVER THE MASTER BREWER.
ASSEMBLE IN FESTIVE ARK 01 ▮▮▮▮▮

The same ad appears with identical wording for the following three
weeks. Whoever booked the ad, paid for it to appear during the whole
of April 1990.

Now, this is thirteen years before the Alperton Angels case, no mobile
phones or internet. If you had a clandestine message to communicate,
chances are you placed a coded classified ad in your local newspaper. As
you know, they were pretty untraceable, because they could be dictated
over the phone and paid for in cash. Useful for people having affairs and,
according to our long-standing member Tony Morris, who recalls that
era well, sex workers advertising their services. But we also understand it
was a common method of communication between criminal informants
and their police handlers.

We have no way of knowing what this particular message refers to, but
we've had a decent stab at trying to guess. Here's our most likely conclusion: Angels means the cult of people who would later become the
Alperton Angels.

The Master Brewer was a hotel and function centre situated on a flyover of the M40 motorway at a place now known as Hillingdon Circus.
It's not only a junction on one of London's key arterial motorways, it's also

a transport hub with nationwide coaches and the London Underground nearby.

'In festive ark' has stumped us, but Julie Gormley, one of our newer members, thinks 'festive' may mean Holly and 'ark' may mean the archangel Gabriel.

The telephone number bears an old London dialling code based at the South Harrow telephone exchange, but with its reach far into the surrounding area, we can't pinpoint the location any more accurately than this.

We think the Master Brewer is being indicated as the venue for something clandestine. It was an ideal place for a quick exchange and easy getaway, either into or out of London.

Whatever the Alperton Angels were doing in 2003, they were also doing thirteen years earlier, in 1990. What was it, and why did it go so wrong after flying under the radar so long?

We are dying to know what you think of this, Amanda, and look forward to hearing from you.
Cathy-June Lloyd

TO: Cathy-June Lloyd
DATE: 6 August 2021
SUBJECT: Re: The Mystery of the Alperton Angels
FROM: Amanda Bailey

Dear Cathy-June,
Thank you. Especially to Rob Jolley for finding that classified ad. I can imagine what a task he had locating something so small.

What you've found has chimed with what I've noticed. Some police officers and social workers I know have spoken about 'angel' activity in the early 1990s. Twenty or thirty years later their memories are merging with what happened in 2003.

So, 1990 is the height of acid house music. Illegal raves were held around the outskirts of London and the Home Counties every weekend. This local newspaper was published on a Friday. The message could indicate a meeting point for music fans. If they called that number from a phone box once they arrived, they'd be given the exact location of the rave. The ad appeared week after week – same meeting place each week.

Equally, it could be a transaction point for drug dealers exploiting that scene.

Angels fly over the Master Brewer. I'm originally from the area myself and remember the Master Brewer hotel. It's both a specific place, yet a large area, much of it inaccessible due to the motorway intersection and the railway bridge. There are few meeting places for large numbers of people. The hotel had a car park, but if young music fans gathered there the police would soon be called and the meeting point closed down.

I can't help thinking, though, it's like the warehouse in Alperton. It's like Middlesex House where Harpinder Singh was found. It's an area of transition. Any people there are inevitably on their way somewhere else, and that makes it an ideal place to go unnoticed.

Thanks again, Cathy-June, and thanks to your murder club too. Some things feel clearer now.

All the best,

Amanda Bailey

Email exchange between Oliver Menzies and spiritual counsellor Paul Cole, 6 August 2021:

TO: Paul Cole
DATE: 6 August 2021
SUBJECT: The beast
FROM: Oliver Menzies

OK, so this is my problem with the Antichrist. How could Gabriel be so *sure* the baby would *definitely* grow up to be evil? Because if someone gave it to me and said, 'This kid's the beast, it'll destroy the world', I'd just make sure it never left the farm, if you see what I mean. Keep it down, stop it *doing* anything.

But while I'm at it, some other kid grows up somewhere with rubbish parents and a chip on its shoulder and it *becomes* the 'beast' that destroys the world. How does Gabriel's prophecy take into account factors we know are fundamental to human development, such as upbringing, opportunity, luck, personality, etc.? Interested in your thoughts.

Also: think about this. Our world is on the cusp of the Age of Aquarius. A time when the universe favours female power. The new

Antichrist could be a woman.

TO: Oliver Menzies
DATE: 6 August 2021
SUBJECT: Re: The beast
FROM: Paul Cole

Dear Oliver,

Thank you for your email. These are key questions.

For the Antichrist to realise its powers, it must gravitate towards the upper echelons of society, where it has the opportunity to exert its influence. Otherwise, it will be impotent. The Antichrist is drawn to fame and wealth because they are short cuts to power. However, I believe the beast will also gravitate towards high and powerful positions subconsciously, because there are forces moving obstacles out of its way. As pawns are moved aside in a game of chess, to protect the queen as she makes her way across the board.

I've no idea how Gabriel was so certain. As for whether we have attained the Age of Aquarius, I'm not so sure. The world doesn't seem to be as equal as that just yet! But do continue your research; I believe you have some very pertinent and interesting topics here for your book. Best wishes,

Paul

Text messages between me and Police Chief Inspector Mike Dean, 6 August 2021:

Amanda Bailey
Hi Mike. When we spoke on 27 July you mentioned a female officer interviewed Holly in 1990. Can you remember her name?

Mike Dean
Nikki Sayle. She chairs a group for retired female officers; you might get in touch with her that way.

The first of June at two p.m.

Ashleigh wants a baby. There, I've committed it to my angel diary and that makes it real. She's been casually mentioning it for weeks. I've been changing the subject.

Who will be the father? Gabriel or Joseph? If she has a baby with Gabriel, does that mean I have to get knocked up by Joe? Do *they* decide who gets to be daddy first? If only the non-angel world knew the traumatic decisions we face on a daily basis. Do I even want a baby in the flat? There's only just room for us in this relationship, let alone another angel-being. A new, innocent one with chubby cheeks and tiny wings in its eyes.

She's out now with Gabriel. I'm not jealous. I'm jealous but it's OK. I'm really jealous. At the back of my mind I know one day, and soon, she will wave that positive test before my eyes like a magic baby wand of doom and the deal will be done. I'm fine with it. I'm fine.

The sixth of June at six p.m.

So, the last diary entry I made five days ago feels like a childhood crayon drawing fallen under the fridge and forgotten. It's a long story. Settle in.

Ashleigh came back later that day, having been out with Gabriel for a suspiciously long time. I opened the door. There she stood in the corridor. My eyes fell to what was in her arms: a tiny baby wrapped in a navy-blue garment I would later discover was an Adidas hoodie.

What the actual? Like, come on. 'Whose is it?' I asked. That was back when I thought a rational explanation might be possible. 'I don't know,' she whispered. 'But look! It's perfect.'

Reader, it was cute, but whose was it?

It was outside the library, she said, and I swear the wings shimmered in her eyes. I was frozen to the spot, speechless, as she slid past me into the hall – in a few short steps of hers I was accessory-after-the-fact to a child abduction. I've not been studying law for long, but that rap sheet in my head was getting longer with every step. Failure to report a crime. Aiding and abetting a known criminal ...

Gabriel's footsteps clattered up the stairs. He careered into the corridor, dived through the front door, slammed it shut and threw himself against it panting with relief. I started to say something. He shushed me, waved us both into the kitchen.

'Can someone explain?' I ask. Ashleigh replies, but her eyes stay firmly on the baby, 'It was abandoned in a buggy. No one wants it, Tilly. This is the solution.'

'The solution to what?' I can't think of any problem borrowing someone's baby without telling them solves, but then, I'm just a simple angel trying to get by on earth.

'The usual way is too complicated. This is the answer. Look at her face.' Instead, I look at Gabriel's face as he pulls the curtains firmly closed.

'Stay away from the walls where the neighbours will hear. Tilly, when Joe comes back, you and me, we'll go out and pick up food and equipment. We've got a few hours before word spreads, then we have to batten down and wait for the high-alert phase to pass.'

I'm not silent for long.

'We have to take it *back*, Gabriel. It belongs to someone. Someone *else*.' I have visions of the poor mother or father, forced to leave their child alone for a split second, distracted, tired or overwhelmed, now living a nightmare ...

Ashleigh throws a wounded glance in my direction, then turns her pleading eyes to Gabriel. 'We don't have to, do we?'

'No!' he replies. What is this, mass hysteria? 'It's safer here.' I'm not sure if the police siren is from the outside world or inside my spinning mind.

What I definitely hear is the front door slam as Joseph ambles in, oblivious. He stops dead and with that uncanny way he has, reads the room in an instant.

. 'Whose baby is that?'

'Ashleigh took it from outside the library.' I get my story in first.

'We can't keep it,' Joseph whispers, 'all hell will break loose. Give it to me, Ash.'

Something about the way he says it. The tone of his voice. Ashleigh's eyes. Gabriel's eyes.

Joe takes out his phone, flicks his fingers across the screen, hands it to me. I'm frozen for a moment. Will Ashleigh give him the baby? Or will she put up a fight?

Joe calmly and quietly lifts the child out of her arms.

I glance down at the phone. 666. The number of the beast? But no, Joseph had keyed in 999. I flipped the phone and tapped the red button. As I waited on the line my wings folded together, smaller and smaller, because the outside world was about to come crashing in on us.

A page torn from the novel *White Wings* by Mark Dunning:

Gabriel clutched Celine's hand as they tore through the hot night streets of Madrid. The fact she was barefoot and nude, save for her pure silk gown, held together by gossamer threads over her shoulders, did not stop her keeping pace with him. Her long legs and smooth thighs leapt gutters and kerbs like a gazelle crosses an arid plain before the rainy season makes the journey impossible.

Their wings carried them, unseen, as the sky above burst into light with the orange glow of the fallout. Gabriel and Celine turned, almost stopped to watch. Flames and gases reached high into the sky. Beautiful like a red diamond. The rarest of them all.

Celine breathed, captivated. The sirens began. Wailing banshees. Gabriel stood behind her, casual glances left and right. That need to appear normal. Part of the everyday world. He hugged her. They appeared like two lovers whose romantic evening has been interrupted but not even a catastrophic explosion at the embassy could blight their love. No one who saw them could guess they were behind the blast, nor that their job was still only half done.

First responders swarmed around the dying and wounded. Numerous tiny fires billowed smoke as Gabriel's black Lamborghini Gallardo picked its way to the centre of the chaos and sighed to a halt. Celine leapt like a mayfly to open the trunk, Gabriel close behind. Their wings soared behind them to screen its contents from view. The body was barely recognisable. He was beaten, broken beyond repair. But too human for vapour-disposal. His body, connected to the earth with unbreakable chains, must be destroyed this way.

Celine, wisp-slim but ant-strong, hauled the dead BioBot from the trunk, tossed it into a nearby fire already brimming with bodies consumed beyond recognition. It sunk into the scene like a stone beneath quicksand. Like the truth sinks lower with every telling of a lie. Forever a victim of the fiery atrocity, not the fists and boots of their comrades. Finally, and just as quickly, Gabriel and Celine were gone.

Pages torn from the script *Divine* by Clive Badham:

EXT. DERELICT HOUSE — DAWN

The sun rises on an old shell of a house. It squats behind a hedge, abandoned, forgotten. The VAN in its drive … a face at the upstairs window.

INT. UPSTAIRS ROOM, DERELICT HOUSE — DAWN

Holly feeds the Baby, peers furtively out of the filthy window, down, on to the roof of the Van. She watches as Michael jumps in. The engine starts.

EXT. DERELICT HOUSE — MORNING

The Van reverses out of the drive. It roars on to the road and away in a puff of exhaust fumes.

INT. UPSTAIRS ROOM, DERELICT HOUSE — MORNING

Holly moves away from the window, places the near-empty bottle down and hoists the Baby upright. She looks at it. It holds her gaze for a long moment. Holly's face melts into a smile and she kisses its forehead.

JONAH

It's manipulating you.

HOLLY

Go back to bed.

JONAH

Why are you up anyway?

Holly waves the bottle at him. Beat. Jonah's air softens, he moves towards her.

285

HOLLY

What's The Assembly?

JONAH

Where we hand it over, so others can
destroy it.

HOLLY

Is it here? Today?

JONAH

It's not the alignment yet.

Jonah turns away, slips out. Holly stares at the Baby for a
moment, pads from the room …

EXT. DERELICT HOUSE — MORNING

The house stands desolate as traffic ticks by.

INT. KITCHEN, DERELICT HOUSE — DAY

Holly rinses baby bottles in the old sink. Her tired eyes
gaze through the broken window on to an untidy yard. She
shakes the bottles, crouches to a shelf beneath the sink
and stands them carefully to dry. She rises.

A FACE AT THE WINDOW.

Holly gasps in horror, recoils, slips and scrambles away
across the floor. The Woman who has been following them,
ASHLEIGH (26, angelic) peers in. Around her neck is a simple
PENDANT of ANGEL WINGS. Her eyes meet Holly's as she cowers
on the floor.

ASHLEIGH

Hello. Who are you?

Holly's eyes dart to the stairs and back. She picks herself

up, cautiously nears the window again.

                         HOLLY
          Holly. What do you want?

                        ASHLEIGH
          I need to know you're OK.

Holly hesitates. Perplexed.

                        ASHLEIGH
          That you're not being held against your
          will.

Beat. Holly studies Ashleigh's face.

                         HOLLY
          We can go any time.

Ashleigh barely hides her surprise.

                        ASHLEIGH
          We?

                         HOLLY
          My boyfriend and me.

Ashleigh nods thoughtfully.

                        ASHLEIGH
          What's his name?

                         HOLLY
          Gabriel.

Ashleigh nods, her expression unreadable. O.S. THE BABY
screams in the room above. Ashleigh's expression changes.

                        ASHLEIGH
          Oh my God.

She stares in disbelief at Holly. Holly looks desperately
to the stairs. She turns back to the window but Ashleigh

is gone. She dashes out. The kitchen is empty as Holly's footsteps pound up the stairs.

INT. UPSTAIRS ROOM, DERELICT HOUSE — DAY

Holly darts to the Moses basket …

INT. KITCHEN, DERELICT HOUSE — DAY — LATER

Holly creeps in, the Baby in her arms. Small random NOISES as it settles. She rocks it, gently, peers out of the window, cranes her neck all around. Nothing. No one. Her eyes fall on something. The kitchen door. She turns the handle. LOCKED.

INT. FRONT ROOM, DERELICT HOUSE — DAY — LATER

Holly sits in a pool of sunlight on the bare floorboards, cuddles the Baby. The door falls open. Jonah. He's been there for some time. Holly sees his censorious expression.

                    HOLLY
          I'm getting it to sleep.

Jonah moves to the window, peers out at the hedge. Holly glances to the door, lowers her voice.

                    HOLLY
          Do they take the demon out or destroy the
          whole baby?

                    JONAH
          That's not for us to know.

                    HOLLY
          Do you feel bad?

It's to save mankind.

Holly frowns to herself.

HOLLY

Can we go out? For a walk?

JONAH

No. They'll get it. In here our energy
shield protects it.

Holly's gaze wanders from the Baby to the window.

INT. KITCHEN, DERELICT HOUSE — EVENING

Gabriel searches bare cupboards in fading daylight. Just
tins of baby formula. Holly and Jonah watch.

GABRIEL

If there's no food, we don't eat. Simple.

He stamps away to the living room. Jonah moves off after him.
Holly stares around the kitchen. She takes a tin of baby
formula and turns it over, thoughtfully.

ASHLEIGH (O.S.)

(whisper) Holly!

Holly jumps, nearly drops the tin, quickly pushes the door
almost closed.

ASHLEIGH

Ssh!

HOLLY

Who are you?

ASHLEIGH

Ashleigh. Holly, I need you to do something.

Ashleigh's sincere eyes plead with her.

                    HOLLY
          No. No. Go away.

Holly looks quickly to the living room, places her hands
over her ears in confusion.

                    ASHLEIGH
          You're in terrible—

She sees Holly's distress and stops. Beat. She steels
herself to say it …

                    ASHLEIGH
          I'm just like you. An angel. I was born in
          a mortal body to fulfil a purpose in the
          earthly realm. To watch and protect you
          while you fulfil yours. Do you understand?

Holly nods.

                    ASHLEIGH
          Good. Holly, you're all in terrible danger
          so long as you're together. It's breaking
          you down.

Holly's face flickers …

                    ASHLEIGH
          I can save you all. Just bring the Baby and
          come with me—

                    GABRIEL (O.S.)
          Holly?

Holly jumps. Ashleigh ducks away. When Holly looks back,
she's gone. Gabriel appears in the doorway.

                    GABRIEL
          What are you doing?

                              HOLLY
          Looking for food.

She holds up the tin of formula.

                              HOLLY
          What about this?

Gabriel pulls a face.

                             GABRIEL
          No. Thank. You. Come on.
He ushers her out. When she's gone, his face changes. He
checks the kitchen door. Locked. Takes a final look round,
snaps off the light, closes the door. Firmly.

6

In Search of Ashleigh

Text messages between me and Cathy-June Lloyd, 9 August 2021:

> **Amanda Bailey**
> Did the lovely Mr Jolley find any interesting newspaper ads from the Alperton Angels case in 2003?

Cathy-June Lloyd
Not yet, but he's got a week off and is working on it.

> **Amanda Bailey**
> 👍 Thank you. One more thing: when you were going through the documents did you or anyone else come across a woman called Ashleigh?

Cathy-June Lloyd
Give me a moment, Amanda, I'll ask.

Cathy-June Lloyd
The verdict from the WhatsApp group is that no, we haven't found an Ashleigh in relation to the Alperton Angels case.

WhatsApp messages between me and Oliver Menzies, 9 August 2021:

> **Amanda Bailey**
> Woooo! Your ghastly ghosted friend here … I'm taking you out out.

Oliver Menzies
Busy.

Oliver Menzies
Where to?

> **Amanda Bailey**
> An old passageway under a motorway. I'm working from 30-year-old memories, but back in the 80s it had a distinctive arch and elaborate grilles. My aunt's house is near there. Me and my cousins would dare each other to run through the tunnel and back again. Google Street View shows that both entrances are covered by undergrowth now. Clearing it is a two-person job.

Oliver Menzies

For crying out loud, it's 'my cousins and I' – and I knew there'd
be a reason to invite me. I'm the muscle.

> **Amanda Bailey**
>
> It's for your book. Some of our contacts have mixed up the
> Alperton Angels of 2003 with a man who befriended teenagers
> and told them they were angels in the early 1990s.

Oliver Menzies

How is this spooky passageway relevant?

> **Amanda Bailey**
>
> A hunch. Call it a sixth sense.

Oliver Menzies

OK. I'm in.

Meeting with Oliver Menzies beside what sounds like a motorway, 10 August 2021. Transcribed by Ellie Cooper.

AB: Ellie, please transcribe everything we discuss. I'll have to switch
it on and off in case he spots the phone. Just run the files
together in one transcript. Thanks. [*You got it. But should you be
recording him without his knowledge? EC*]

AB: The Master Brewer, a three-star hotel, was on that patch of
wasteland over there. Very 1960s architecture. I found this
picture online.

OM: They overdid it with three stars.

AB: It was a local landmark for years. This used to be called the
Master Brewer Roundabout.

OM: Now there's no Master Brewer and no roundabout. Shit, I'll get
run over here, Mand. Where's this haunted alley?

AB: Follow me. We can't get there the way I used to, the road's been
rebuilt. But I know another route into the fields.

AB: [*You walk for a bit without talking. EC*] Stop, stop. This is it.

OM: You used to run through *there*?

AB: It's an old pedestrian subway from when a much older pub stood on the Master Brewer site. This underpass was made so people from the houses back there didn't have to cross a busy road on their way to and from it. But the pub became a hotel with a car park, the roundabout became a flyover and an intersection with its own pedestrian subway, so the passageway fell out of use. My cousins brought me here once. I was only about six, but remember so clearly that detail in the cement of the archway. It's still visible.

OM: Holly. Holly leaves and berries. Mistletoe.

AB: A festive arch. If I hook that tree, you snap the branches off with the shears. [*The next bit is just you guys clearing weeds out of the way. EC*]

OM: Lower.

AB: Yep.

OM: Hasn't been cleared in decades. Ow! You thorny bastard!

OM: [*Silence for a bit. EC*] The shit is that? Mand. Mand! MAND!

AB: Keep *still*! I've got it. It's gone.

OM: Phew. If that bit me, I'd have anti-social superpowers and no friends.

AB: I think that's it. See if I can squeeze in.

OM: Yeah, but will I?

AB: [*A little while later. EC*] Here we go.

OM: Wait. Here.

AB: What's that?

OM: Obsidian. Protection in unknown places. Keep it in your pocket.

AB: ...Thanks.

OM: I smell foxes.

AB: This is another of those places. Like Alperton. You can hear the traffic and trains as people whizz past overhead. All going somewhere else.

OM: A crossroads. Neither here nor there. Where there's a weakness in the fabric between worlds, and anything can happen.

AB: Well, nothing grows. No light, no water. It means the walls are preserved. Look. [*You both pause here. EC*] The symbol for Gabriel. Blue paint. Thirty years old.

OM: You remember this from back then?

AB: Not at all. I was here before the angels. Why paint this down here?

OM: This is an assembly. Like the warehouse thirteen years later. A place angels come together to intensify their energy. There has to be some sort of psychic portal here.

AB: Ol, can you check the rest of the wall for angel symbols? My eyesight is worse in this light. [*Footsteps, mumbling and rustling. EC*]

OM: No. Nothing. Not even regular graffiti.

AB: A single angel symbol. Gabriel was on his own, then. With Holly. But what did they plan to do? Destroy an earlier Antichrist?

OM: [*He whispers this bit. EC*] The remaining angels are all in hiding. Jonah in a monastery, Gabriel in prison, and Holly wherever. They all know something. This here was the start of it, Mand. The end of days. First the horsemen: War, Famine, Pestilence and Death. Then the fifth seal: religious persecution. The sixth seal: climate change, and the seventh and final seal ... when the angels assemble for the silence that precedes the second coming of Christ. [*You're both silent for a long time. EC*]

AB: It's a happy ending, then.

OM: Remember I said no one's predicting the future any more? Because it's too late. There's no future. This is it. The end of days. [*You don't seem to question Oliver's ramblings, Mand. Aren't you concerned about him? EC*]

WhatsApp messages between Ellie Cooper and me, 10 August 2021:

Ellie Cooper
Check your inbox for the latest file. Do you think Oliver is becoming obsessed with the spiritual side of the angels case?

Amanda Bailey

😄 Yeah, he is a bit. It keeps him away from my angle 😀

Ellie Cooper

You've found the baby? 😱

Amanda Bailey

When I find out what REALLY happened that night, it'll lead me to the baby. Give me a moment to send some messages and I'll tell you what I've got so far.

Text messages between me and Clive Badham, 11 August 2021:

Amanda Bailey

Hey there! Just reading through Divine again. Love, love, love the character of Ashleigh. OMG she totally pops! I'm thinking Carey Mulligan, Ana de Armas, Chloe Grace Moretz. Just out of interest, is she based on a real-life person from the case?

Clive Badham

Awesome! I LOVE all those actors. They'd each bring something to that role. No, I made Ashleigh up as a plot device to get Holly away from Gabriel and Jonah. She waits and watches, then: BAM! She explodes their whole world. Does it matter she's fictional? Will the actors prefer to play someone real?

Amanda Bailey

No, no. Makes no difference to them. Just want to have all the facts when I speak with them. Great. I'll be back in touch when I've contacted their agents etc.

Clive Badham

TO: Ellie Cooper
DATE: 11 August 2021
SUBJECT: My findings so far
FROM: Amanda Bailey

Thanks for the file. Right, this is where I'm at. All top secret. 🤐

Gabriel had a 'Holly' with him and was up to something in 1990. He placed the same cryptic small ad in a local newspaper for a whole month. The message led to a disused passageway under the M40 motorway in west London, where I found a thirty-year-old angel symbol just like the ones the police officers found on the floor of the warehouse and that Oliver and I found in the stairwell at the luxury flats that stand there now. We don't know any more about early nineties angel activity yet.

Our Holly, from 2003, came from a troubled background and absconded from the care system, but she was different. Her parents were drug-addled aristocracy. She'd been at Gordonstoun School but uprooted to London. That summer she went AWOL from what was no doubt a chaotic life. If the baby was born in early December, then she'd have been three months pregnant at the end of the school term – precisely when she absconds to live with Gabriel. If her baby was adopted by extended family, as I was told way back when I first started this, then it was a 'dark' adoption because they don't want anyone knowing that Lady Georgina and the baby she had at seventeen were involved in such a sordid case. So, my next task is to find Lady G and as much as I can about the Holly from 1990.

Of the three fictional works I've been reading, two have just thrown up a very strange coincidence. *My Angel Diary* by Jess Adesina and *Divine* – an unproduced script by a wannabe screenwriter – both feature a character called Ashleigh. In each case she's a woman associated with Holly who potentially comes between her and Gabriel. The scriptwriter claims he made that name and character up. The ever-slippery Jess Adesina is yet to reply to my message.

Meanwhile, I await some documents from the late Mark Dunning, whose widow has sent me a package by courier. She seems to believe he wants me to have it, and sent her a sign from beyond the grave. I'm happy to get that info any which way it comes to me.

Nowhere in any of these three stories is there an angel called Raphael.

If you think of anything I may have missed, Ellie, let me know. I feel nearer the baby than ever. While Oliver couldn't be further away.

Mand x

Interview with Nikki Sayle, retired police sergeant, at Starbucks, Watford, Friday 13 August 2021 💀. Transcribed by Ellie Cooper.

[I cut out the usuals. She sounds very old. Seems you got this interview just in time. EC]

AB: I've known Don Makepeace for years. Only, it was Mike Dean who gave me your details.

NS: He said you'd be in touch and not to talk to you if I didn't want to. He's one of the good guys, and he doesn't want anyone getting in trouble just for making a wrong decision years ago. Nor do I.

AB: I understand. I'm only interested in this case, nothing else. Nikki – can you please explain what you recall from that interview?

NS: I will. Is your tape running?

AB: Yes. Well, it's not a tape. *[I cut out your brief history of voice-recording technology. EC]*

NS: It was the early 1990s, as you said on the phone. I remember this girl because she had a strange story. She said the archangel Gabriel took her in when she'd had a row with her mum. This fella told her she was an angel and that together their purpose was to rid the world of evil. Something like that.

AB: Did she have a baby with this man?

NS: Not that I knew of. What struck me at the time was this girl had left the man, but still believed she was an angel.

AB: How old was she?

NS: Seventeen, which wasn't as *young* as it is now. Hadn't been so long since girls got married and left home at eighteen or nineteen. She'd gone to live with this chap voluntarily.

AB: What crime was the girl trying to report Gabriel for in 1990?

NS: He'd told her the Antichrist was waiting to be born on earth and

300

when it was, they would look after it to make sure it didn't do any evil. But while they were waiting, seems he wanted her to conduct fraudulent credit card transactions, which she resisted. He was losing interest and to her this change in him meant he'd been warped by supernatural forces and was in danger.

AB: What did the police think of that?

NS: Laughed her out of the door. It was only because she was obviously vulnerable that myself and Mike Dean listened to her.

AB: OK. So there'd be no record of these conversations?

NS: We didn't record the complaint. It was all statistics back then. If we came across a case we had no chance of closing, we didn't open it. But I could see what this was and soon took it away from Mike. It was a woman thing. Best all round if the girl was taken back to her mum.

AB: Go on.

NS: Classic lover-boy technique. This Gabriel made her believe she was in a relationship with him. He'd bought her all the clothes she wanted, shoes, bags, CDs, jewellery. She had the most beautiful necklace of angel wings. Not a cheap one, either. It was no wonder the poor girl was swept off her feet. Luckily her mother had got her the contraceptive jab or she'd have ended up like the Alperton Holly. All Gabriel wanted was for her to go thieving for him, but he kept her under control with the angel story. He was a lifelong fraudster but needed someone young, pliable and with no police record to take all the risks. When she proved herself smarter than that, she was out on her ear and he was on to the next one. But his hold over her was so strong, the girl was still living the fantasy he'd created. We call it coercive control these days. I was proved right years later when the Alperton Angels were uncovered. That poor girl hadn't been so lucky. Ended up having a kid by him. [*There's a pause here. EC*]

AB: It's a strange MO.

NS: You see it all. I warned the girl he was a con man who only wanted her for what he could get, and to take this as a lesson learned. Told her to get back home to her mum, find a boyfriend her own age. I even dropped her home and that's another thing sticks in my memory. She asked me to drop her off at the gates of a huge estate down in Surrey.

AB: She was from an upper-class family?

NS: Far from it. Her mum worked there as a groundskeeper. Lived in a little cottage on the outskirts of the land. You'd have to be an impetuous teenager to leave somewhere like that for a grotty flat in Staines. [*You both laugh, but I know what you're thinking here, Mand: part of Gabriel's MO is to target girls who have links to high society. Money is the root of all evil. EC*]

AB: Nikki, this girl's name was Holly?

NS: She introduced herself as Holly at the nick, but as I dropped her off, she admitted her real name was Ashleigh. With an i, g, h.

AB: When the Alperton Angels case happened, did you report this earlier incident?

NS: Mike and I talked about it, but only to check we hadn't recorded the girl's report back then. Gabriel was going down for murder anyway so we decided to keep quiet. The girl, wherever she was by then, wouldn't have thanked us for dredging it up and dragging her into it.

AB: Mike mixed up the two Hollys when I first spoke to him.

NS: Well, we're both getting on a bit now!

AB: Nikki, is there any possibility at all that in 2003 it was the *same* girl as in 1990?

NS: No. I met her mum and chatted across the doorstep. The girl in 2003 was a care absconder. You've spoken to Farrah Parekh?

AB: I've not even heard that name before.

NS: She was a PC in 2003, interviewed the girl from the Alperton Angels. You're in contact with Don Makepeace? Well, he would know that.

AB: He probably forgot to say. Thanks, Nikki.
[*I left out your pleasantries. The Ashleigh thing is really strange. Mand, does it occur to you that Don Makepeace doesn't want you to find either Holly? EC*]

WhatsApp messages between Ellie Cooper and me, 14 August 2021:

Ellie Cooper

Sorry to message in the middle of the night but something just occurred. Telling Holly and Jonah the baby can't be killed 'until the alignment' ensures they DON'T kill it. Because that's not what Gabriel has in mind.

Ellie Cooper

He hoped the first Holly would have a baby. When she didn't, he started using her to commit petty fraud until she left him and went home. He tells these girls the baby is the Antichrist so they won't bond with it, or feel bad when it 'disappears'.

Ellie Cooper

Mand, I think Gabriel intended to SELL Holly's baby. It fits with his criminal MO. He's a convicted fraudster. He pulls the other angels in with the promise of cash ...

Ellie Cooper

The Assembly is when Gabriel passes the kid to its adoptive parents who've paid him for it 👀

> **Amanda Bailey**
> Morning! Thanks for this. Good thinking 😘

Interview with Police Sergeant Farrah Parekh in Amanda's car after visiting the Starbucks at Greenford Quay, 16 August 2021. Transcribed by Ellie Cooper.

> *[As ever, in the absence of instructions to the contrary, I'll cut out any pleasantries. EC]*

AB: Can you explain when and how you interviewed Holly from the Alperton Angels in 2003?

FP: It was the day after the massacre in the warehouse. She'd spent the night in a children's centre. We interviewed her at Alperton nick. I led the interview, but we had to tread carefully, she was young and had been through a trauma. There was an appropriate adult in attendance. All by the book.

AB: Of course.

FP: We wanted to know what had happened the previous night, first and foremost—

AB: Had you been told how many bodies there were?

FP: [*She pauses here for a quite a long time. Interesting. EC*] They said four, I think, er … It was a long time ago. From what I recall, Holly was still under the influence of the cult. She talked as if she was an other-worldly creature inside a human body. It was strange. But she was brainwashed to believe it. She described the baby as the Antichrist.

AB: Where was the baby at this point?

FP: It had been taken away. [*She lowers her voice. EC*] I don't think she got it back. That was it. Social services took over. Best thing.

AB: It was eventually adopted?

FP: I don't know.

AB: Was Holly distressed the baby had gone?

FP: She'd been through so much it was hard to tell. I'd have to say, no. [*Pause. She's lost her train of thought. EC*]

AB: Sorry. Sorry to interrupt. What did Holly say had happened the previous night?

FP: She said the angels had organised an assembly to destroy the Antichrist. An alignment of stars meant its death would rid mankind of evil. If it survived the alignment, mankind was doomed.

AB: Right … What had gone wrong with that plan?

FP: She said the archangels were stopped from fulfilling their mission by the dark forces and they all had to die because they'd failed.

AB: All of them?

FP: The angels were all dead except her and Jonah. That's what she told us.

AB: Gabriel escaped, though. He was arrested days later. He went on the run.

FP: Perhaps she was protecting him. Hoped we wouldn't go looking for him. She was under his spell. They all were.

AB: Yep. I understand he's a charismatic individual.

FP: I wasn't there so can't say. I know Gabriel had already killed a man by then. The young Indian boy—

AB: Harpinder Singh.

FP: Yep.

AB: Farrah, I'm going to show you something I haven't shown anyone else. Here.

FP: [*There's quite a pause. EC*] What am I looking at?

AB: The scene of the angels' massacre.

FP: That's a grisly one.

AB: I know. It was taken by Gray Graham, a local reporter. Old-school newshound. He was first on the scene. When this photograph was taken, Holly had been escorted from an upper-floor room by two heel-kicking beat coppers who thought she was a psychiatric case. She'd left this scene earlier, climbed the stairs and called an ambulance for her and the baby.

FP: I've never seen that picture before.

AB: No one has. It was among Gray Graham's things when he died last month. Along with his notebooks. [*Shit, Mand, you never mentioned this picture. EC*] Can I show you something?

FP: Sure.

AB: See that body. Alan Morgan or Elemiah. There, Michael, real name Dominic Jones. Nowhere in any of these shots is Christopher Shenk, or Raphael. Police statements say his body was found on a half-landing, a flight of stairs away from the basement. However, I've received anecdotal evidence he was somewhere else entirely that night. This arm is that of the teenage boy Jonah, he's alive and uninjured, but clinging to a third body. The archangel Gabriel.

FP: Really? How can you tell?

AB: I scanned the print and enlarged it. Here, compare it to the mugshot of Peter Duffy, aka Gabriel Angelis.

FP: He can't have been dead. He must've got up and run off after this was taken. [*Long pause while she no doubt studies this picture again. EC*] Well, whatever. He was caught and put away, that's what matters.

AB: Yep. Although Holly told you hours later that *all* the adult angels were dead, and here's a picture that backs that up. Something terrible happened to cause this bloodbath. But something else happened after that. I don't think even Holly knows what that was. Do you? [*She pauses again. This woman either knows more than she's letting on or doesn't want to know. EC*]

FP: Do I agree that *something* happened, or do I *know* what it was?

AB: You tell me.

FP: [*Does she shake her head here? There's some kind of non-verbal communication. Only you know what it is. EC*] And that's all I can say.

WhatsApp messages between Ellie Cooper and me, 16 August 2021:

Ellie Cooper
Can I see the photo, Mand? 💀

> **Amanda Bailey**
> You don't want to. It's what Gray Graham stumbled on when he was after mood shots for a fluff piece about a baby born in an old factory.

Ellie Cooper
Did he ever sell it?

> **Amanda Bailey**
> No, and it would've been an earner too. It was in a blank envelope, buried in a box of fetes, fairs and fun run pics he developed but discarded.

Ellie Cooper
Why not just tear it up?

> **Amanda Bailey**
> Exactly. I think he was afraid of it. Too scared even to throw it away.

Ellie Cooper
Please can I see it?

Amanda Bailey

[?] Print Error [?]

Ellie Cooper

I see what you mean. Gabriel looks dead here. So who was tried
for Singh's murder? Who did Oliver visit at Tynefield prison?

Amanda Bailey

Whoever it was, they looked exactly like that dead body on the
ground. Like Peter Duffy's police mugshot It's a mystery.
Although … the pragmatist in me agrees with Farrah. Gabriel
can't have been as dead as this picture suggests.

Ellie Cooper

Jonah is clinging to the body. According to Aileen he was
'wishing' him back to life. But was Gabriel just playing dead? Is
that possible? What if Jonah is clinging to him here, not because
he was overcome with grief and emotion – but because they
heard Gray Graham enter the room and wanted to ensure no
one examined the 'body' too closely …

Amanda Bailey

You should be writing this book, Els 😊

WhatsApp messages between Ellie Cooper and me, in the early hours of 17 August 2021:

Ellie Cooper

I had a thought and now it won't go away. What if Gabriel WAS
dead … and Jonah healed him? Brought him back to life 😳

Amanda Bailey

😊

Ellie Cooper

Ignore me. It's late. I'm going to bed.

WhatsApp messages between my editor Pippa Deacon and me,

20 August 2021:

Pippa Deacon

Hey! How's it going, Amanda?

> **Amanda Bailey**
> Great. Why?

Pippa Deacon

Nothing. Just that Jo says Oliver's gone AWOL. I know you're busy, but I said if you heard anything, you'd let me know and I'd reassure her.

> **Amanda Bailey**
> He's fine. Tell Jo he's at exactly the same stage I am: gathering research together and getting a good start on his new angle. We're in touch and I'm supporting him at every step. His spiritual angle will be awesome. And mine even more so 😜

Pippa Deacon

You're a star! 😊

WhatsApp messages between me and Oliver Menzies, 20 August 2021:

> **Amanda Bailey**
> Whaaa! How goes it? You avoiding Jo?

Oliver Menzies

It won't matter if I am. We're at the end of days.

> **Amanda Bailey**
> Ol, many cults have predicted the end of time. And that includes some mainstream religions. On the one hand, it focuses everyone's attention. On the other ... when that date comes and goes, it's a bit embarrassing 😳

Oliver Menzies

I'm well aware of that. This is different. Listen. The Alperton Angels weren't only right about the Antichrist, they were our last chance. I've done the reading, spoken to experts. But I know too much. I'm staring into the abyss. Not for me, personally. For the whole of civilisation. The only thing, now, that can save us from the end of days is a new messiah. And I don't see one.

Oliver Menzies
Ghost me if you like. Makes no difference.

> **Amanda Bailey**
> Thinking. Not ghosting.

Communications between me and social worker Sonia Brown, 21 August 2021:

TO: Sonia Brown
DATE: 21 August 2021
SUBJECT: Holly
FROM: Amanda Bailey

Hi Sonia,

Holly was the daughter of a duke. *That's* why it was a dark adoption. Privacy. Shame. Whatever else having a daughter who absconds with a cult leader and has his baby would bestow on a family with wealth and influence.

I know that much, so it won't be a big leap for you to tell me where she is now. Because Lady Georgina Ogilvy has no online presence. A Google search simply says she was born. Rowley Wild, the first pseudonym that hid her parents' disgrace, is equally elusive. Has she kept her angel name, 'Holly'? Jonah has. Do they both still believe themselves to be angels? I need to speak to 'Holly', Sonia. Either one will do.
Amanda

Sonia Brown
Amanda, drop it. This goes all the way up, and no one will break ranks for you.

> **Amanda Bailey**
> 'Break ranks'? What is this?

Sonia Brown

Why focus on Holly, the baby? Why not Gabriel?

> **Amanda Bailey**
>
> I suppose because he's bang to rights, safely inside

Sonia Brown

He's maintained his innocence from day one. If his conviction for Singh's murder is overturned, then that life sentence will be re-examined too. He's done more than enough time for the other charges.

> **Amanda Bailey**
>
> True. If the murder conviction evaporates, Gabriel will be free.

Sonia Brown

If that man gets out, no one is safe. He'll melt away, find people to manipulate and control. Even people who know EXACTLY what he's like are as vulnerable as the unsuspecting – knowledge ISN'T power, and that's terrifying.

Sonia Brown

You can put him in a cage for fifty years, the second he's released he'll go back to his old ways. It's all he knows. He's a spider. The only thing he can do is spin a web.

WhatsApp messages between Ellie Cooper and me, 23 August 2021:

Ellie Cooper

Mand, can I show you something? Link below:

A ROYAL COMING OF AGE

The eldest child of Prince Edward and Sophie, Countess of Wessex, Lady Louise Windsor prepares to turn 18 at the end of this year. Often described as the Queen's favourite grandchild, Lady Louise has grown up out of the spotlight and attends a private school in Ascot.

Ellie Cooper

The Alperton Angels baby is Lady Louise Mountbatten-Windsor, the Queen's seventh grandchild, sixteenth in line to the throne

Ellie Cooper

What you were told at the very start was correct. Holly's baby was taken in by family. The Wessexes. Her father was a distant cousin to the Queen. It's a royal cover-up 👁

> **Amanda Bailey**
>
> Thanks, Ellie, you're doing a fantastic job. Keep it between us, though. Please?

Ellie Cooper

Cross my heart 😊

WhatsApp message from Ellie Cooper to me, later on 23 August 2021:

Ellie Cooper

The police officers were led to believe symbols in the warehouse were significant. The symbols were erased so their testimonies would be discredited. Social workers were told they were to blame. People from the local church still think they played a part in the cult deaths. All this draws the attention of everyone involved AWAY from who the baby really was.

IntCourier delivery card:

Sender: Judy Teller-Dunning
Message: You were out so we left your package in the blue bin

---

A neatly handwritten diary, US letter size. Loose pages stapled together:

10 December 2003, London

Excited and apprehensive. Heard a lot about the British police force, but got to clear my mind and experience this fresh. Hope the ne'er-do-wells and miscreants of London town aren't planning a vacation. Remember Boston? The curse of Mark Dunning struck. It was the quietest night the department had ever known. Only two calls. A mis-dial and a shoplifter at a kiosk. Does that make me a lucky talisman or a hex?

If my next novel is set in London and Paris, I've got to see those cities. Not the tourist trail, but the underbelly. Is that even possible? So fucking false and strained. They'll be on their best behaviour. I'll be super polite and ever so grateful, guv'nor.

No one tells you how lonely research trips are. Me and my thoughts jus' rollin' along. Wish Judy was here. But with her writing commitments and Harrison's new school ...

Jonathan called. He'll be at Alperton tube station, 8 p.m. checked I had the dough. Bet no one knows he's getting five hundred pounds sterling (yep, seven hundred bucks) for taking me out in his patrol car. Is it usual here that writers pay for a ride in a 'panda' car? One thing he was clear about: no cameras or recording equipment. I am to observe and absorb, only.

Been planning the tube journey. Buy a ticket in the ticket hall at South Kensington. Get on a Piccadilly Line train going west to Rayners Lane and get off at Alperton. The line splits in two and loops round at the end, so who knows? I could be back here at South Kensington by 8 p.m. I'll allow two hours for the journey.

Sitting in my room, watching the clock tick its way to 6 p.m. It's dark outside. It's dark inside because light bulbs seem to be rationed in London hotel rooms. It's cold because the radiator is off. It's winter. I want a roaring fire, heat, rage, passion, excitement. I just want something to happen tonight.

On a new page, in the same hand, yet less neat, spidery, changed somehow...

Thank God, we've taken off. Switching flights was easy. Told them my mother's sick, I've got to get back before it's too late. It's way too late. She died in 1977. Turns out I play an anxious, terrified, guilty man all too well. They got me on this plane. Never heard of the airline. It stops at Reykjavik and I have to change at JFK but, whatever.

I won't forget last night <u>ever</u> - but feel I should document it. Who for? Me? Someone in the future who might <u>need</u> to know what happened? Why am I so uncool? This is what I hoped to find. Careful what you wish for, huh?

PC Jonathan Childs was waiting outside the station. Said to call him JC. Younger than he sounds on the phone. Sweaty, twitchy. If he hadn't been in uniform, in a patrol car, I'd wonder if he really was a bobby. He drives me round the corner, parks in an unlit street and counts the bills from my envelope. Drops it in his lap, drives another few blocks without even fastening his seat belt. Leaves me on the back seat, locked in, while he dives through a doorway, cash in hand. He's gone seven minutes. The place is dark, urban and depressed. It's soon deserted. Word a police patrol is around travels fast.

Jonathan reappears, much calmer. We drive off. I ask my stock questions. How busy will it be? Which crimes are common in this area? What's your worst call to date? Ever met the Queen?

We stop a car with a missing tail light. The driver promises he'll get it fixed and is sent off with no charge. I help JC move a damaged hoarding off the sidewalk. A radio call sends us to a small house where neighbours heard raised voices. The couple inside swear they had the TV too loud. The man has a bruise on his face. Back in the car Jonathan says domestics are 'the pits' because 'you can't do anything'.

Around 11 p.m. we meet another patrol car, this one with two male officers in it. Jonathan smokes and laughs with them outside the car. I try to get out and join them. I'm locked in. They glance through the windscreen at me. Don't ask who I am. They must already know as I hear them rib JC about driving 'the most expensive taxi in London'. The guys get a call, rush off, blue lights and sirens.

JC drives me to a gas station and buys us coffee and what I assume is a stick-shaped cruller, like my grand-mother would make. I take a bite, hungry for the sugar rush. It's heavy goddamn pork meat in pastry! Not for the first time tonight I adjust my expectations.

Around midnight, we're called to a street disturbance. Two gangs of men. A face-off. No weapons, just shouting in a foreign language. JC sighs, weary, describes them as 'rival families' who are 'always kicking off' but 'usually pipe down before it gets nasty'. A few men on the fringes melt away at the sight of the patrol car, and more disappear when JC gets out. Still, there's an air of tension. He heads straight for the leading men, talks to them. Without a figure to get behind, the remaining crowd disperses. Only a few left now. The lead guys calm down. For the first time I'm impressed by this young guy. I want to hear what he says.

I try the car door. It's open. Another first. I get out. His back is towards me. Something instinctive moves my hand to my wallet, inside pocket, check it's safe from light fin-gers. I spot the guy as he spots me, but his reaction is way over the top. He hollers, his face terrified. The other guy follows suit. It occurs to me, too late, they think I'm reaching for a gun.

JC spins round, waves me back to the car, but whoosh. The biggest guy sweeps him off his feet to the floor. The other uses his foot to keep him down, like JC is their ransom against getting shot by me!

So, these rivals are suddenly on the same side. JC almost gets up, is slammed down by a boot. He shouts into his radio

314

'officer down'. Yells at me to get back in the car. I put my hands up to show the guys I'm unarmed. Distant sirens close in from every direction.

We were in that moment for an eternity. The rivals, now comrades in arms, shout, panicked, clueless how to resolve the stand-off they started. As police patrol cars scream into the street, they throw their hands in the air, back away from JC, who jumps up. Officers of all shapes and sizes leap to his aid, including the two guys JC smoked with earlier.

Forgotten, I creep back to the car, shut myself in. JC is fine. The rival guys are fine. They amble away together. Everyone laughs it off. Patrol cars roar away as quickly as they arrived. JC and I are alone again in the car. The look he gives me in that rear-view mirror makes me pee a little. Finally, he says he'll drop me back at the station. He means the tube station.

So, my grand excursion in a British police car might have been brought to an inglorious end if JC were not 'dying for a fag'. On the way to the tube he drives up to a car-park barrier at the edge of a field, bordered by woodland. Not just closed for the night. This place has been closed years, but JC knows the code. He opens the barrier and there we are, parked alone at a lookout point that gives us a view across the London night skyline. I ask where we are. Horsenden Hill.

As JC smokes out of the car window, I sense he was more shaken by being held hostage back there than he let on to his colleagues.

I apologise. He tells me, 'Don't worry about it, mate.' Then he gets a call, not on his police phone, but on another, deep in his pocket. He throws his cigarette away, leaps from the car, slams the door, shouts back at me to 'stay put this time' and walks a good distance away before he finally answers the call, too far for me to hear. He talks on the phone for a while and when he returns, looks worried.

'Something's come up. I can't take you back yet. You'll have to get down on the floor.'

I must have looked as blank as I felt, because he snaps, 'Mark! Get down on the floor and keep your head down.'

I stammer out a 'why?'

'Someone's gonna come and give me something. Be here any minute. Don't move, don't sit up, just ... stay there.'

He rolls the window up and locks the door. I'm pressed against the filthy floor. My mind winds back to the envelope of cash he took through a dark doorway. He wouldn't be the first cop in bed with a drugs gang.

In no time I hear another car. Its engine runs as voices, low and firm, give instructions with no room for questions. Footsteps round the car. If they look down, they'll see me— JC jumps to bring those footsteps back with a needy question. The trunk opens. This is it. The drop. THUD. Something heavy lands in the trunk. A drugs haul? If so, then it's the size and weight of a grown man.

Slam, slam, slam of doors, one of them the trunk. I eye that back seat and wonder if there's a chance what's on the other side isn't a body.

'Stay down,' JC hisses as he jumps into the driver's seat. 'I'll tell you when to sit up.'

We drive in silence. JC nervous at the wheel. Me jammed behind the seats.

'What's back there?' I figure there's no harm in asking.

'Something they want rid of,' JC says. 'We'll take it somewhere and lose it.' I try to speak again, but JC shushes me.

Finally, we pull in and stop. I glance up. It's dark, but there are people around. I hear footsteps, shouts, slamming doors. More grim than urgent. A larger vehicle pulls in nearby, but manoeuvres away. Someone shouts to keep the exit clear.

Voices again. I hear the trunk open. The car's suspension is relieved when whatever's in there gets hauled out. I chance my arm, peer through the window. JC is deep in conversation with a guy. The grey kind. Could stand up in your stew and you wouldn't know his height, weight, age ... couldn't tell you then or now.

I duck down as two figures carry something past me. They wear police uniforms, or at least I think they do. The trunk slams behind them. That's it, there. Whatever JC picked up in the car park. An unmistakable body-shaped mass.

I try the car door. Locked. But the driver's door may not be. Slowly I crawl between the seats, my bag gets hooked on a gear lever, I lose a shoe and have to fish for it. Finally, I'm there. Click. The door opens. I slide out, try to look grey too, like I have a job to do, like I belong there. I shadow those grey guys and the unwieldy package they carry between them.

As soon as I slip through the doors, I think I know what this place is. A meat-packing plant. It's cold, stark and smells of blood and flesh. Further in, I'm not so sure. The cops have rigged up lights so they can work through the night. Soon as I'm in I hear raised voices. 'You don't move anything,' says one.

'We thought he breathed. We saw him breathe,' says one of the grey guys.

'He could have been alive. We sat him up and tried to revive him, then carried him where it was lighter and we could see,' the other one adds. This 'grey guy' is female ... a young black woman. Pretty.

'Well, WAS he breathing?' snaps the officer, and glares from one to the other.

'No.'

'Where'd you find him?'

'Through there, up the stairs, on a half-landing.' She points beyond, nowhere near the patrol car that body had just come out of, nowhere near the car park or wherever it'd been before then.

'I'm really sorry. I'm NEW and he's just a PCSO.' This girl blinks around at the disdainful looks, winces, simpers like she got shit for brains. But her and the guy stood cringing at her side ... I _SAW_ them. They were waiting like fucking hawks for JC to arrive with the body. The way they carried it ... wasn't the first time. They were a team.

Officer in charge sighs, stares at the girl's badge. 'Well, Marie-claire, fucking take it back and put it where you found it.' They mutter apologies, shuffle away, towards an old doorway, not the one they'd manoeuvred through from outside. The mood in the room sends an air of utter disgust after them.

No one spots me as I press myself into a corner. I hear muttered vows to report the officers. Did anyone know them? Kids sent out without proper training. That's when I see what's on the floor right here in this room and something happens to me.

There must be a thing. A primeval reflex when you see blood, innards. I remember when a colleague on the New York Times recounted watching a kidney transplant. Big story he was super interested in. Soon as the surgeon made the first cut, he saw the red flesh, smelled the burning cauterisation and passed out cold. Medical team were diverted to help the stricken journalist on the floor of the operating theatre. He told the story for years. I laughed so hard. What a dork. It was routine surgery. How could he have been so squeamish?

Makes sense now. If you see a body torn apart then you're in danger too. That wild animal could get you next. I suddenly understood the tangle of red on the floor, the bodies. Three men, mutilated guts, throats cut ... I lost my legs, sank down ... and that's the last I remember for, I don't know how long.

'Wake up, Mark.' JC slaps me on the cheek, hisses in my ear. 'Get the fuck up, mate.'

I come to, shaking. Almost pass out again when I realise I'm still in the room.

'Ssh. Get up. Come on.'

He hauls me up by my arm, bundles me outside. 'You nearly

318

gave me a fucking heart attack,' he says, outside, where we weave through a jumble of parked police vehicles. JC lights up a cigarette, offers me one.

'What is this place?' I whisper.

'Old baby food warehouse.'

'Who were those people and what did they take out your trunk?'

He blows smoke from the corner of his mouth. 'Best you don't know, Mark. Forget you saw it.'

'Forget I saw a dead human being in the trunk of a patrol car, dragged into the scene of ... of ....'

JC scoffs between puffs. He gets in close, whispers, 'Human being? He just killed the nicest guy you could hope to meet. In cold blood. Great guy and a great officer. Friend of mine, young Sikh fella. We trained together in Hendon.' JC shakes his head. I see real emotion, tears in his eyes. 'So don't be losing any sleep over that piece. The guys who kicked his head in won't.'

My hands shake as adrenalin disperses through my blood-stream. Delayed shock. Finally ...

'Did you know this was going to happen tonight?'

'D'ya think I'd have let you in the car if I had?' He laughs. 'Look, you got to visit a multiple-murder scene. You got some exciting stuff for your book, eh?'

'I can't write about it or I'll be the next one in the trunk of the car.'

He laughed. 'Yeah. Them, they don't give a shit about you.'

'They don't give a shit about anyone.' I nod towards the building.

'Oh, the others,' JC scoffs. 'Just some cult, offed 'emselves.'

Got back to the hotel at gone 2 a.m. Packed my case, took a taxi to Heathrow. A few hours later, here I am. As far away as possible from four dead men whose lives just crossed with mine.

WhatsApp messages between me and Oliver Menzies, 25 August 2021:

Amanda Bailey

Christopher Shenk or Shenky. There are links between the other angels: prison links, work links. But not him. Said to be a petty criminal and drug dealer, although he'd never been sent down.

Oliver Menzies

Raphael. The angel of healing for Jews and Christians. Angel of the resurrection in Islam.

Amanda Bailey

He doesn't appear in any of the fictional accounts from the time – not as himself or as Raphael.

Oliver Menzies

Fiction. FICTIONAL ACCOUNTS. Do you know what 'fiction' means?

Amanda Bailey

These fictional accounts – two novels and a script – are contemporary to the events. Fictional as they are, they still have historical value. Each of these writers picked up on something subtle, a nuance of the case, lost to us now, that even they didn't realise.

Oliver Menzies

Listen. Gabriel is the messenger. Michael is the angel of war who will preside over the end of days. Elemiah the angel of protection, Raphael of rebirth. The four corners. Four horsemen. Four four four.

Amanda Bailey

Are you sleeping OK, Ol? Still being woken up every morning?

Oliver Menzies

I wait for it now. It's proof. Evidence I'm right.

Amanda Bailey

Well, if it's the end of days, can you finally tell me who your mystery interviewee is?

Oliver Menzies

😄 No, Mand. I enjoy winding you up too much.

WhatsApp messages between me and my editor Pippa Deacon, 25 August 2021:

> **Amanda Bailey**
> Just a heads-up: it might be an idea for Jo to check in with Oliver after all. I've no idea how someone as fiercely rational as he is could ever be obsessed with the esoteric side of a case, but ... 🪦

Pippa Deacon

When did you last hear from Minnie?

> **Amanda Bailey**
> Minnie? Few days ago. Maybe weeks. Why?

Pippa Deacon

Hmmm. She was in the middle of clearing her quotes and suddenly stopped replying.

WhatsApp messages from me to true crime author Minnie Davis, 25 August 2021:

> **Amanda Bailey**
> Hey, Mins! You avoiding Pippa?

> **Amanda Bailey**
> So, I've left a couple of messages ... You OK?

> **Amanda Bailey**
> Getting worried now. Reply asap please, Minnie.

WhatsApp messages between me and true crime author Craig Turner, 26 August 2021:

Amanda Bailey

Babes, you heard from Minnie in the last couple of days?

Craig Turner

Not for ages. Her book's out soon so probably busy.

Amanda Bailey

Pippa can't find her. She's gone AWOL.

Craig Turner

Spooky. But we know Minnie. She'll surface sooner or later.

WhatsApp messages between me and true crime author Minnie Davis, 27 August 2021:

Amanda Bailey

Mins, please reply. Craig and I are worried about you. I won't tell Pippa you've been in touch.

Minnie Davis

Oh, Mand, I've got a situation with my feminist writer.

Amanda Bailey

Ah, that's what it is. 🙄 I thought you'd have a problem there. People don't just give away their work. What exactly have you got in writing from her?

Minnie Davis

Nothing. It was an unspoken thing. But a proof-reader put question marks over some of her content. When I asked for confirmation, she suddenly went quiet.

Amanda Bailey

Is that all? 😔 Bods don't understand how quickly you have to work. She'll be fine. You've credited her in the back, right?

Minnie Davis

Yeah, but 😠

> **Amanda Bailey**
>
> It's only a few quotes and passages. What can she possibly object to?
>
> **Amanda Bailey**
>
> Even if she wants you to pull something – it's no big deal. Reword the quote and find a friendly bod whose name you can attribute it to. I could help 😬

Minnie Davis

I used the whole thing, Mand. Right at the start I said, 'Can I use all of it?' She said, 'Fine, women should help each other.' So I did.

> **Amanda Bailey**
>
> What do you mean by ALL of it? Surely you rewrote it at least.

Minnie Davis

It was too good to change. It was fresh, different, exciting. She'd found documents and records I could never hope to get my hands on. Her analysis was spot on. It had atmospheric, spine-tingling photographs and gorgeous illustrations. Just perfect.

> **Amanda Bailey**
>
> Shit, M. You need to speak to Pippa about changing the credit or something. Joint credits? Not the end of the world. I don't know, but give her a call. Please?

Minnie Davis

That's not it, Mand. Turns out this wonderful feminist thesis isn't really for Women's Studies, Criminology & Media.

> **Amanda Bailey**
>
> What's it for, then?

Minnie Davis

Practical Art in Society. That's a degree course, who knew? Her brief was to create a work that appears academic but is entirely fictional. To show that facts can be created and anyone can be taken in, all they need is the right deceiver.

Minnie Davis

Mand, she MADE UP those exciting new facts. Forged the documents. Faked the photographs. She's been awarded a First because it was so good it fooled a professional.

> **Amanda Bailey**
> Who did she fool?

> **Amanda Bailey**
> Oh. I see.

Minnie Davis

Every fact in that essay is utter bullshit. From the very first page. No, from the first LINE! It says: 'Myra and Rose both had sisters called Avis and went to schools situated on roads called "Hertz Lane".'

> **Amanda Bailey**
> Avis and Hertz are car hire companies.

Minnie Davis

I KNOW THAT NOW!

> **Amanda Bailey**
> Pippa didn't spot it? No one else?

Minnie Davis

Haven't you heard? Pippa's left her girlfriend for Jo Li Sun at Green Street. She's been distracted for weeks. The others are turning these books around so fast. Anyway, it's not their job. It's mine.

> **Amanda Bailey**
> Shit. Really sorry, Mins. But you need to tell Pippa. She can start doing what they do in this situation. Damage limitation?

Minnie Davis

How could I have been so stupid?

WhatsApp messages between Ellie Cooper and me, 27 August 2021:

Ellie Cooper
If the father of the sixteenth in line to the throne is a convicted murderer and cult leader who believes he is the archangel Gabriel, it's no wonder they want it kept secret.

Ellie Cooper
Holly must have been absorbed back into the aristocracy one way or another. She probably married a viscount and lives in an ancient country house. Does she know her baby is being raised as the Queen's grandchild?

Ellie Cooper
You OK, Mand? Haven't heard from you in a while.

> **Amanda Bailey**
> Sorry. Lots going on. Ellie, I've been messaging this guy who wrote the unproduced film script. Leading him to believe I'm a budding film producer. Only, there's something off about him. The way he refuses to talk properly about the inspiration behind the film. He fobs me off with 'I made it up', 'I read everything around the case' – when I know he must've had inside info to have used the name 'Ashleigh'. Not just that, other details too. There's only one way to find out for sure.

Ellie Cooper
You're meeting him?

> **Amanda Bailey**
> I'm going to call his bluff and suggest it. But it's my guess he won't meet me. He'll suggest a phone call or cancel at the last minute. Because he's not who he says he is.

Ellie Cooper

Text messages between me and Clive Badham, 27 August 2021:

> **Amanda Bailey**
> Clive, we should meet. Put this relationship on a professional footing before your script gathers so much heat it sweeps us both into a rolling fireball 🔥

Clive Badham
Absolutely. When and where?

> **Amanda Bailey**
> Near you. Where did you say you're based again?

Clive Badham
Stoke Newington. There's a great little coffee place called Café Z on Stokie High Street.

> **Amanda Bailey**
> This afternoon?

Clive Badham
2 p.m.? This is fabulous, Amanda. I can't wait! 😱

> **Amanda Bailey**
> Nor can I 😊

WhatsApp messages between me and Ellie Cooper, 27 August 2021:

> **Amanda Bailey**
> Well, I'm here. So far, Mr Badham has neither arrived nor cancelled.

Ellie Cooper
How long do I wait before reporting you missing this time?

> **Amanda Bailey**
> Call me in an hour. But you won't have to wait that long. No one will meet me here. Least of all a Mr Clive Badham. But she's watching me. Right now.

Ellie Cooper

She? Who?

> **Amanda Bailey**
>
> Holly.

Ellie Cooper

The second Holly? The Alperton Angels Holly? Lady Georgina?

> **Amanda Bailey**
>
> Yes. Well, if my hunch is correct. I hope so. I hope it's her and that she can see me.

> **Amanda Bailey**
>
> Wait, who's this?

Ellie Cooper

OK, so she's arrived? I'll give you an hour from now and call you.

> **Amanda Bailey**
>
> Shit shit shit! It's Clive Badham. Wannabe script writer. Hasn't stopped talking about Divine since he arrived. He has mood boards and lists. Lists of special effects, locations, props. Nutritionally balanced menus for the crew. A statement on the diversity he wants to see 'in front of and behind the camera'. Don't even start on the list of actors. Tom Cruise is on it and he's not even at the top!

Ellie Cooper

No! OMG, Mand, that's so funny! 😂

> **Amanda Bailey**
>
> I'm in the toilet but there's no window or other means of escape. I can't talk any more about 'Jay Horror'. I've no idea who she is. How can I get away from this excruciating little man?

Ellie Cooper

Go back to the table, I'll call and say there's an emergency in the office. Put me on speaker. I'll sound tearful, the works.

Amanda Bailey

Thanks, Els. Call in five. Fuck my false hunches. Never listening to them again, they are liars!

Ellie Cooper

And J-horror is a particular style of Japanese horror film

🕐 🕐 🕐 🕐 🕐

Meeting with Clive Badham in Café Z in Stoke Newington, 27 August 2021. Transcribed by Ellie Cooper.

[OMG, Mand! I see what you mean. I'll cut out everything he says apart from the bits about how and why he wrote what he wrote in the script. That's most of it. For the record, I agree with him about the original versions of The Ring, The Grudge *and* Dark Water *being much better than the remakes. EC]*

AB: But what made you choose that name in particular? Ashleigh.

CB: It's a nice name.

AB: It is, but it's unusual.

CB: If you don't like it, we can change it.

AB: Another work inspired by the angels features a character with the same name. Same spelling.

CB: Which one?

AB: *My Angel Diary* by Jess Adesina.

CB: Don't know it. Coincidence. Let's just change it. I'm not married to the name. What would you rather call her? *[How does he look when he says this? Do you believe him? I also cut out a lot more chatter about his musician friend who can 'drop tracks' and his other friend who 'works in post' and can do the 'overlays' for mates rates. EC]*

AB: I'll think about it. Clive, the supernatural is hinted at throughout this story, but I've read your script a few times now, and it's about much more than its special effects—

CB: Not a problem, Amanda. I'll make it super gory. If we give the baby a snake's tongue and horns, make it impervious to flame—

328

AB: One thing you leave out—

CB: Go on.

AB: Holly giving birth to the baby. A demon being born on earth. Seems like a very dramatic moment, but you don't include it in your script ...

CB: No problem. We can include that scene. You're right, it would be super horrific and dramatic. [*Sorry, pretty much everything else is just rambling about his vision for the film. Then you go to the loo, and when you return, I call like a hero and get you out of the meeting. EC*]

AB: Phew. Thanks, Ellie. I've escaped. I'm running down the road like the office is ablaze. I've just discussed that script with Clive Badham and I felt he was talking about something different. The more I spoke to him about what he thought the story was, the more I could see the script he wrote, that I've been reading, isn't a horror film at all. [*Interesting. So what is it? EC*]

WhatsApp messages between me and Ellie Cooper, 27 August 2021:

Amanda Bailey
Oliver said artists pick up more than they realise because their subconscious is in touch with the other side. So do I have to believe that, while writing his script, Clive B coincidentally picked up on things he has no way of knowing, just because he was tuned into the psychic wavelengths? Because I don't believe that.

Ellie Cooper
Mr B wrote his story shortly after the Alperton Angels case hit the news. Could he have stumbled upon documents then, never realising how sensitive or secret they were?

Ellie Cooper
Also, the case is 18 years old. He could have found those details in news items that have since been taken down.

Amanda Bailey

He claims to have done little or no research. Just made it up in line with what he enjoys about demons and horror films. Yet his script is more interesting than that. It feels as if it has subtle clues in it. But then, I feel the same about Jess Adesina and her edgy coming-of-age novels. I'm at a loss how either of those writers knew what they knew. But that's me FEELING and not researching. I sound like Oliver.

Video-call interview with Jideofor Sani, retired paramedic, 28 August 2021. Transcribed by Ellie Cooper.

AB: Ellie, I'm about to interview a guy who got in touch after the *Fresh Ghost* podcast but wouldn't write his story down. He might be a paranoid fantasist, and he might be interesting. Story of my life. Cut out the pleasantries as usual. [*You got it. I cut out the bit where you ask how to pronounce his name and he says just call him Jidi. EC*]

AB: Jidi, you were a paramedic at the time of the Alperton Angels.

JS: Yes. I'm retired now.

AB: You said you attended the scene of the murders, but weren't happy writing anything down, or talking on the record.

JS: Are you recording?

AB: No. We're off the record. [*Mand! EC*]

JS: It's always been ... [*A pause here. Is he emotional, or ... nervous? EC*] touchy for me.

AB: Would you like to take me through what happened that night?

JS: Well ... we were called to a place by the canal in Alperton. Police were already there. We'd been warned there were bodies and a young man injured.

AB: OK, so that would be a normal thing to be told?

JS: Yes. It's useful so we pay attention to details. If we're called on by the coroner or police at a later date. That was how I thought of it.

AB: What did you see when you arrived?

JS: There was a young man clinging to one of the bodies. Police were talking him into letting go. But we had to examine him, so we administered a mild sedative. He came away and we checked him. He was uninjured and a police officer arrived ... he was taken away.

AB: Did you see the rest of the—

JS: It was very, very bad. [*Lots of pauses and hesitation. EC*] My first thought was a gang killing. Later I heard it was a mass suicide and they were all members of a cult.

AB: Can you describe that scene a bit more for me? How had the angels been killed?

JS: Gunshot wounds to the head. [*Wait ... hello? EC*]

AB: Sorry?

JS: They'd each been shot once in the head. And mutilated. Throats cut and chest wounds. Entrails extracted and spread around. [*OMG, Mand, is this guy for real? EC*]

AB: They'd been *shot*? Are you *sure*?

JS: Yes.

AB: Were those wounds visible? On all three angels? I've seen photographs from the scene—

JS: Tiny entry wounds, behind the ear. Execution-style. I checked each of them, looked for pulse and respiration, so I saw closer than anyone. I doubt it would be visible on a photograph.

AB: But it was a crime scene—

JS: Yes. But everyone should have the dignity of being declared deceased. Especially when they've passed away on the street.

AB: For sure.

JS: I am from a small village in Nigeria. We believe death is not the end of life, but unless certain traditions are observed, the person will not pass on to the ancestors. They will remain in limbo. It is merely superstition, but for me, I would always make that declaration in my head for a deceased person. Whoever they were or how they died. It is respect.

AB: How many did you declare deceased that night? [*He doesn't answer. EC*] Jidi?

331

JS: Three. There were three people dead. [*There's such a silence here, Mand. There's something he doesn't like about that number. EC*]

AB: Only there were four bodies that night, weren't there. [*No question mark, because this isn't a question. EC*]

JS: You know?

AB: Yes, it's a bit clearer now. I think a scene that appeared to be a bloody and chaotic mass suicide presented certain people with an opportunity.

JS: I read later there was another body elsewhere in the building. I'd left by then, so that man was not declared dead …

AB: What is it that plays on your mind about this case, Jidi?

JS: I declared three dead at the scene. Another was found later. Four. Also, a young man was found in a flat. Five. But I read about the case and it says: three at the scene, one at the flat. Four.

AB: Four. So somewhere along the line we *do* lose a body.

JS: This will sound crazy to you, Ms Bailey. I have lived here *many* years and it sounds crazy to me. But for a while afterwards I would think of that man who was not declared dead. I'd think that perhaps he couldn't pass through to the ancestors. And so he came back. [*OMG. You're both silent for a while. EC*]

AB: It's a yellow Mini Clubman.

JS: I'm sorry?

AB: Someone once told me about a yellow Mini Clubman. They said everyone should have one. A story that plays out in a way you can't explain.
        [*You stop the recording here, Mand. OMG, I'm going to message you. EC*]

WhatsApp messages between Ellie Cooper and me, 28 August 2021:

Ellie Cooper

The angels were assassinated. By whom? And why the discrepancy between body counts?

Ellie Cooper

Are firearms mentioned in relation to the angels at any time?

> **Amanda Bailey**
>
> Not by the bods I've spoken to, and not in the three works of
> fiction I'm reading. Not even in Mark Dunning's spy novel.

Ellie Cooper

Are you keeping an eye on Oliver, Mand? I worry about him.
When I messaged to ask how he was, he replied with a calendar
marked with a date for 'The End of Days'.

> **Amanda Bailey**
>
> He'll be fine. I'll snap him out of it. Soon. When I'm ready

Divine
by
Amanda Bailey

One

Oliver Menzies thought he wanted to be a journalist. He'd scraped his way through a history degree, had a passing interest in politics and always read the front of the newspaper before he turned to the back [*is it obvious I mean the sports pages?*]. But when his mother's friend organised a place on a newspaper apprenticeship scheme, he didn't count on his fellow trainees being better, brighter and hungrier than he could ever be.

Menzies dressed his feelings of inadequacy in practical jokes of the variety we would consider bullying and abusive today. On one occasion he deliberately told a young, female colleague the wrong venue for after-work drinks. It meant she was waiting, alone and vulnerable, at night, in a rough suburban pub.

What might have started as a harmless prank turned into anything but. When she finally realised what he'd done and left the venue, some-one followed her. She was attacked and robbed, not just of her posses-sions, but of everything she'd been working towards. Her coursework gone, she was alone, injured and confused. She abandoned the appren-ticeship rather than admit what had happened. Most distressing of all, she was robbed of the sight in her left eye. She was never the same again.

This young colleague wasn't as fortunate or privileged as Menzies or the other trainees. She'd barely read a book in her life, never been to uni-versity or lived in anything like a functioning family. She didn't realise then how vulnerable she was, but something in Oliver did. She was just learning what trust was – and with one thoughtless practical joke, he destroyed it in her. For ever.

He may have forgotten the incident, or chose not to remember it when the two met again years later. But she hadn't, and she soon realised he'd learned nothing in the intervening years. He regarded others who fell for tricks, scams, lies and fraud as stupid, 'pig-shit thick' and unworthy of his regard. Well, when Oliver Menzies was commissioned to write a true crime page-turner on the Alperton Angels, he would discover just how easy it is to be influenced, deluded, controlled and ultimately betrayed by someone you trust.

You don't need to be a charismatic individual to influence others. You just need to use the right words, at the right time, to show them certain things and hide others. They'll do the rest all by themselves.

THIS IS IT! My new angle!

7

The End of Days?

My third meeting with the Mystery Woman from 2 August (and that first meeting on 13 July). I now know her to be 'Marie-Claire'. Transcribed by me this time. I don't want Ellie tangled up in anything that might backfire. Backfire. Lol. 30 August 2021:

AB: Thanks for meeting me again. What should I call you?

MC: Marie-Claire. If you like.

AB: Your operational name? [*she doesn't answer*] Mark Dunning immortalised you in *White Wings*. Celine is an angel with powers of invisibility who does the bureau's dirty work.

MC: I don't read fiction.

AB: Don Makepeace tells a story about a yellow Mini Clubman that skids off the motorway. A couple stop to try to rescue the driver. But it's disappeared. Days later, Don searches a wider area and discovers it, tangled in undergrowth, the driver dead. Only, it didn't crash days ago, it's been hidden from view for six months, its driver a missing person.

MC: Every police officer in the Met has heard that story. Most of them tell it too, and claim *they* found the crashed car.

AB: Don explains it as a vision from the other side. The driver wanted his body found.

MC: Bizarrely, that's considered a happy ending.

AB: I have an alternative ending. A small car skids off the road, hurtles down the bank, comes to a halt on a dirt track beside a field. The unharmed driver simply changes gear and drives away, rejoins the road further along. That's why the couple fail to find the vehicle. When Don returns to the scene he searches a completely different area and finds the remains of a yellow Mini Clubman. The coincidence is enough that he tells the story. Over time, both cars become the same make and colour with the same stickers and the same sun visor. Eventually: the same car. The story becomes a popular myth.

MC: No one wants the alternative ending.

AB: Christopher Shenk wasn't an Alperton Angel. He was a small-time drug dealer who discovered Harpinder Singh wasn't a shy Indian waiter, but a police detective, undercover and about to blow open an OCG. Did Shenky intend to kill Singh, or just warn him? It didn't matter to the police officers who kicked Shenky to death. His body was dumped at the scene of the Alperton Angels massacre and his story lost in theirs. Passing him off as Raphael, a secret cult member, avoids questions about how he came to die.

MC: You don't know everything—

AB: I know the angels were fatally shot in that basement. You're right, I don't know why. Not just to hide a body. I get the feeling it was all very convenient for someone, until Gabriel got up and walked away. How did he do it? He's framed for Singh's murder to put him inside. Someone somewhere is determined he'll never get out. [*She's silent for a long while.*]

MC: Give me your phone.

[*She takes it and turns it off before she speaks again. I can't prove anything of her subsequent conversation, but she told me what happened to Gabriel and it explains a lot.*]

WhatsApp messages between my agent Nita Cawley and me, 30 August 2021:

Nita Cawley
Have you heard about Minnie Davis? She copied a student's entire thesis and was only found out when a proof-reader did some basic fact-checking. It was all an arty hoax. Pippa is livid.

> **Amanda Bailey**
> It could only happen to Minnie.

Nita Cawley
It's not so much the yawning errors and jokes – anyone can fall for that. It's the fact she copied someone else's work. That's what Pippa can't forgive. The book's cancelled and she is too, so heads up, Mandy: distance yourself from her. No bargepole would be too long, if you know what I mean.

WhatsApp messages between true crime author Craig Turner and me, 30 August 2021:

Craig Turner
Have you heard?

> **Amanda Bailey**
> Yep.

Craig Turner
What part of 'don't become the story' did she not understand? Stupid cow. How she didn't notice some of those howlers, I'll never know.

> **Amanda Bailey**
> She trusted the woman.

Craig Turner
Come on! Those two primary school essays supposedly written by Myra and Rose a decade apart, with their 'chilling similarities'. They both mention Google, FFS!

> **Amanda Bailey**
> You've read it? I dunno: laziness? Complacency? Still trust at the end of the day.

Craig Turner
At the end of the day it gets dark! Someone's leaked the whole thing. Twitter's on 🔥

> **Amanda Bailey**
> Shit, poor Mins. Hope she's OK.

Craig Turner
The student was on Jeremy Vine this morning, laughing like Muttley about it. All I can say is, if that's feminism, I'm glad to be a gay man. We look out for each other.

> **Amanda Bailey**
> Like your friend Dennis, who gained the trust of vulnerable gay men, murdered them, chopped them up and boiled the bits?

Craig Turner

Totally different. Denny was a product of his time and place. No homophobia, no Dennis Nilsen. His response was extreme, I'm not condoning it, but it was totally in context.

WhatsApp messages between me and Oliver Menzies, 30 August 2021:

> **Amanda Bailey**
> Hey! How goes it? Let's meet for a chat. We can compare notes, talk about where we are with our new angles.

Oliver Menzies
Busy.

> **Amanda Bailey**
> I need to set the record straight on a couple of things 😳

WhatsApp messages from true crime author Minnie Davis, 1 September 2021:

Minnie Davis
So everything went to shit, hit the fan then that shitty fan hit another fan 💩

Minnie Davis
Pippa says Craig's book will launch Eclipse. She's throwing a party at The White Swan.

Minnie Davis
Should be good. They've invited RuPaul.

Minnie Davis
Fancy popping along? We can meet for a drink beforehand. I've been thinking … we could work on something together when you're done with the angels. Got a few ideas to run past you.

Minnie Davis
Thing is, I've got to pay back my advance, but no one will touch me.

Minnie Davis

Mand?

Minnie Davis

OK. So it turns out the fearless Amanda Bailey is just as scared
as everyone else.

**Text messages between Cold & Unsolved member Rob Jolley and me,
1 September 2021:**

Rob Jolley

This is Rob from Cold & Unsolved.

> **Amanda Bailey**
> Hi, Rob. Got any news?

Rob Jolley

First, who are you and how do you know me?

> **Amanda Bailey**
> Amanda Bailey. I've been speaking to Cathy-June Lloyd about
> the case of the Alperton Angels.

Rob Jolley

Just checking. You can't be too careful. Anyway, I've found it:
a new message relevant to the events of 2003. But it didn't
appear in any of the regular local newspapers, just a limited
circulation advertising paper called the Free Herald. It was
distributed door to door, free of charge, to a very small area that
spanned Ealing and Brent.

> **Amanda Bailey**
> Can you send a picture or scan?

Rob Jolley

Best not. I've committed it to memory. For four weeks from
28 November to 19 December 2003, the Free Herald carried
a personal ad that read: ANGELS FLY INSIDE ERMINTRUDE
FENCING.

Amanda Bailey

That's it? No phone number? Is it an anagram?

Rob Jolley

You must be very young, Amanda. Ermintrude was the cow in The Magic Roundabout. Fencing = gate. Cow & Gate.

Amanda Bailey

Angels fly inside the Cow & Gate warehouse. The previous newspaper ad directed someone to an underpass, where angel symbols were painted. Angel symbols were painted inside the Cow & Gate warehouse. It's directions for someone. A location.

Rob Jolley

The Assembly where they intended to sacrifice the baby. Seems there were lots of people who thought they were angels, and this was how they met up before mobile phones. Shocking.

Amanda Bailey

No, Rob. There were only ever three angels. Gabriel, Michael and Elemiah. But thank you, that's a vital piece of the puzzle.

Text message from a mystery number, 2 September 2021:

07█████████████

Can we meet? We trust you not to record the conversation. Call for the location.

WhatsApp messages between me and Ellie Cooper, 2 September 2021:

Amanda Bailey

Els, I'm meeting someone in Richmond. The woman who answered Jonah's old phone. Just so you know where I will be.

Ellie Cooper

OK.

AB: Els, I'm waiting by the café in Richmond Park. The woman who has Jonah's old phone asked to meet me here. He described her as an 'old friend'. It's her, Els. The Alperton Holly [*A pause while you wait for her to arrive. I can hear someone approach, but there's a moment, you're taken aback. EC*]

AB: Oh! Jess. I wasn't expecting *you*.

JA: So now *I've* surprised *you*.

AB: But ... you're not who I spoke to on the phone. You're not who told me where Jonah lives.

JA: No. She's waiting in the woods. It's more private there.

AB: Who am I meeting?

JA: You'll see. [*You walk in silence for a bit. Then the footsteps stop. EC*] So, this is Amanda. Amanda, this is ...

GA: Georgie Adesina. Pleased to meet you. [*OMG, Mand! Lady Georgina. She sounds very calm and well spoken. EC*]

JA: As you might guess: we're married.

GA: I hadn't guessed. But ... I ... so you met at school.

JA: We did, didn't we?

GA: Briefly, before ... it all happened.

AB: This is ... thank you for meeting me. I have so many questions—

JA: Before you go on, this meeting is to say ... well, Georgie can tell you.

GA: I know your background, Amanda. You'll understand that, like you, I've put that part of my life away. I've moved on. Jessie and I have two children together. I'm not Holly. The person I was then is dead. I have no interest in keeping her alive by telling the story.

AB: I understand, but Jess has been telling your story for years in *My Angel Diary*—

GA: We both have.

JA: We started it to help Georgie explore the experience, didn't we?

GA: Therapist after therapist suggested I write it down. I did, I wrote exactly what happened, but it didn't help. If anything, it gave the experience *more* significance. So we changed the narrative, to a positive, vibrant story ...

JA: The first book, when Tilly discovers she's an angel ...

GA: It was a revelation, that I could control what happened. Make it my own. Do you remember that, Jess? It helped *so* much.

JA: It was cathartic.

GA: It was, and readers picked up on that. They loved it.

JA: They love it still. We're hoping to revisit those characters, when the girls are both at school full time; we'll go back to it, won't we?

GA: Tilly, Ashleigh, Joe and ... Gabriel have to navigate their thirties, after all.

JA: Like our readers. [*Aw, I can see what they mean. They obviously love the books. EC*]

AB: Ashleigh. Is Ashleigh a real person?

GA: I owe my life to Ashleigh. [*Is that Jess shushing her here? EC*] She's Tilly's soulmate in *My Angel Diary* for a good reason. She doesn't have that name any more ...

JA: And before you jump to any conclusions, it's not me.

GA: She gave us her blessing to use it.

AB: What role did Raphael – Christopher Shenk – play in the Alperton Angels case?

GA: I don't know. He wasn't part of our ... family. I only saw his picture in the paper afterwards. Maybe he was a friend of ...

AB: Gabriel? You struggle to say his name even now. How did he convince you and Jonah to believe you were angels and a baby was the Antichrist? It's such an incredible lie. Did he prove it in some way, say with magic tricks, or—

GA: Nothing like that. If you don't understand how we could have believed lies like that, it's because you haven't met a predator who saw your vulnerabilities. Who gave you what you wanted and manipulated you, all while making you feel as if *you* were the one in charge. You just haven't met them.

JA: Yet.

AB: I understand how rewriting the story has helped you. But the *actual* story. There's something about the truth of this that needs to be told. To help others in similar situations now, or in danger of falling for coercive individuals in the future—

JA: We disagree.

GA: We won't be telling our children what happened to me.

AB: Really?

JA: They don't need the weight of that history on them.

GA: Nor do I want the story told. Ever again.

AB: I understand, but it won't go away—

GA: It will.

JA: Two hundred thousand pounds. More than you'd ever make from the book. We'll sign the documents here and I'll transfer the funds immediately. Take yourself on holiday. Buy whatever you want. Think about it for a few minutes if you like. [*Wow, Mand. They must really want this to go away. You're quiet for ages. Just think of what you can do with all that money! EC*]

AB: I wondered why there were no true crime books about the Alperton Angels. You pay off anyone who gets this far. I guess Mum and Dad didn't squander the entire family fortune after all.

GA: I don't like doing it, but it's for us and our children.

AB: What happened to the baby?

GA: The baby?

AB: The baby you rescued from the Alperton Angels. They're almost eighteen. Where are they?

GA: I've no idea ... taken away.

AB: I was told it was adopted by your family. Where are they now?

JA: Two hundred and fifty thousand.

AB: I don't believe Gabriel Angelis killed Harpinder Singh.

GA: The right person is in prison.

AB: The Alperton Angels. Who were they really? Who was Marie-Claire?

JA: Three hundred thousand. That's my final offer. [*There's a long silence here. I can't tell what's happening. EC*] OK. Well, that's up to you. [*It sounds as if you're walking away. You're turning down so much money, Mand. EC*]

AB: Wait.

JA: Changed your mind?

AB: You said you'd done it already. You'd already written down exactly what happened and it didn't help.

GA: A creative writing class at college. I wrote a film script and used my school name, Rowley Wild. I hoped it would help create some distance for me, but no ... I threw it away. No one else but us even read it.

AB: [*As you walk away, you whisper ...*] Except the tutor. [*The recording ends here. Oh my God, Mand. That isn't Clive Badham's script. Lady Georgina wrote it. Divine isn't inspired by the Alperton Angels case, it's what ACTUALLY happened. EC*]

WhatsApp messages between Ellie Cooper and me, 2 September 2021:

Ellie Cooper

OMG, Mand, I've just transcribed your meeting with Jess and Georgie.

> **Amanda Bailey**
>
> Clive Badham told me in one of his first emails: he works in a call centre and teaches creative writing to young people. He STOLE Holly's script years ago. He won an award for it and is STILL trying to get it made. He doesn't even realise what it is.

Ellie Cooper

Mand, you have a first-hand account of what happened the night of the Alperton Angels murders, and no one knows it but you!

> **Amanda Bailey**
>
> It's only part of the story, Els. It's just what Holly experienced. I need to piece it together with everything else. With what I've got from people who were also there – Gray Graham, who took the first photograph of the crime scene, and Mark Dunning, who was riding in a patrol car with a dodgy copper.

Ellie Cooper

Does it say how Harpinder Singh died?

> **Amanda Bailey**
>
> Yes. But it's the end – The Assembly. There's no Raphael in the script. There may have been an alignment of stars that night – but there was also an alignment of cover-ups. The characters of Holly and Jonah are antagonistic, distant and frosty with each other. They aren't a couple. She was genuinely clueless about where the baby went. What Don told me about her family adopting it can't be true.

Ellie Cooper

It still fits with the baby being Lady Louise Windsor Will you tell Oliver these new developments?

> **Amanda Bailey**
>
> Now why would I do that? 😜

Ellie Cooper

Because you've been deceiving him for long enough?

> **Amanda Bailey**
>
> 🤫

Pages torn from the script *Divine* by Clive Badham:

EXT. WAREHOUSE — NIGHT

A derelict monolith, black against the dark night. Once a factory or warehouse, it is neither now. Blind windows, doorways linked by the skeleton steel of old fire escapes that wrap their steps and platforms round the floors. The concrete car park, cracked by weeds, is almost deserted. A VAN, stationary. Through the windscreen, Michael and Gabriel watch, nervous.

INT. VAN — NIGHT

Holly and Jonah huddle on the floor. Holly rocks the Baby in its tatty Moses basket, tries to catch Jonah's eye, but he deliberately avoids her gaze. On the pretext of resettling the Baby, Holly hauls herself up, peers through the windscreen. Her desperate eyes search the darkness …

>   MICHAEL
>   (harsh whisper)
>   Get down!

No sign of Ashleigh. She ducks back down.

>   HOLLY
>   What are we waiting for?

>   JONAH
>   Ssh! All the other angels.

Michael and Gabriel, both tense and brooding, share an unreadable glance.

EXT. WAREHOUSE — NIGHT

Finally, a movement. A door opens, two floors up. A FIGURE on the platform. Elemiah.

INT. VAN — NIGHT

Gabriel and Michael jump, hiss …

GABRIEL

Now!

MICHAEL

Move!

GABRIEL

Quiet!

EXT. VAN — NIGHT

Four figures exit the van, file quickly towards the building, leap a broken step, climb the fire escape and disappear one by one into the shadows of a second-floor doorway. The building is as dark and silent as it ever was.

INT. SECOND FLOOR, WAREHOUSE — NIGHT

The open-plan floor was once an office. The angels, even Elemiah, seem tiny in this cavernous space. Holly, her eyes everywhere, gathers the Baby in her arms and pushes the Moses basket away with her foot.

GABRIEL

What are you doing?

HOLLY

It won't settle.

JONAH

Leave it. It'll be dead soon anyway. (to Gabriel) When does the alignment start?

GABRIEL

Soon. We must protect it until then. Don't hurt it.

Holly and Jonah micro-react …

                         JONAH
          But we are going to kill it?

                         HOLLY
          It's the Antichrist, isn't it?

Before Gabriel and Michael can reply …

                    ELEMIAH (O.S.)
          How 'bout this?

A CAN of SPRAY PAINT in hand, Elemiah indicates something
on the floor, a way off. Gabriel scowls at Holly and Jonah …

                       GABRIEL
          Stay there.

He jogs to Elemiah. Gabriel takes the can, SPRAYS the floor,
as if making good Elemiah's attempts, whispers advice about
… What? Holly watches, puzzled.

Finally, Elemiah takes the can, jogs towards the fire escape,
disappears down it.

                    MICHAEL (O.S.)
          Give it to me.

Holly rips her gaze from Elemiah's retreating back, snaps
round to see Michael, arms outstretched to take the Baby.

                       MICHAEL
          Your job's done. You've served your
          purpose. Give it to me.

Holly's terrified eyes flick round the vast space. No sign of
Ashleigh. No salvation. Nothing.

                        JONAH
          Give it to him.

My purpose is to protect it until the
alignment. You can have it once we're at
The Assembly.

Michael hesitates, no answer. He can't think as quickly as
Gabriel. Jonah glances around.

JONAH

(to Michael)
Where is The Assembly? Here?

MICHAEL

Downstairs. Come.

Michael stalks away towards the fire escape. Jonah throws a
glowering look at Holly, then follows. Holly eyes the Moses
basket, her BAGS of baby things … but leaves them, keeps
the Baby in her arms as she follows at a safe distance, her
senses alert for any sign of Ashleigh.

INT. THE ASSEMBLY — NIGHT
This is the BASEMENT floor of the derelict warehouse. Eerie
CANDELIGHT illuminates the scene. A DOOR is propped open to
reveal a pedestrian entrance/exit. Elemiah, hood up, face
obscured, keeps watch. His eyes scour the outside world. From
the door, a route to the centre of the floor is painted with
STRANGE MARKS in blue SPRAY PAINT. It ends in a CIRCLE of
SYMBOLS. Fresh paint glistens. Holly and Jonah are captivated.
Gabriel puts his arms around them both. Holly freezes.

JONAH

What does it mean?

GABRIEL

That's us. Gabriel, Michael, Elemiah. So the
dark forces know who they're dealing with.

JONAH

Where are the other angels?

MICHAEL

What other angels?

Michael paces the floor, his eyes flick from Gabriel to his watch and back again. He paces away, as …

JONAH

All of us. The angels here on earth who'll make up The Assembly.

HOLLY

You said we'd all gather to destroy the Antichrist. Angels assemble at the alignment to arrest for ever the forces of darkness. You said that was prophesied.

Holly and Jonah look to Gabriel. Michael mutters.

MICHAEL

Tell them.

GABRIEL

That we're archangels …

MICHAEL

(to Gabriel)
For fuck's sake!

JONAH

Tell us what?

HOLLY

That once we've served our purpose … we die.

Jonah runs to Gabriel, throws his arms around him.

JONAH

She's turned. She doesn't believe in you and wants me to doubt you too.

Holly locks eyes with Gabriel, hers plead with him.

                        HOLLY
          Prove it. Show us you're divine. Then I'll
          believe in you.

Gabriel shakes his head.

                        JONAH
          I believe in you.

                        GABRIEL
          Don't. Believe in you.

                        HOLLY
          Who is Elemiah waiting for?

                        GABRIEL
          A man will arrive and leave a case. He'll
          take the Baby and that's it.

                        ELEMIAH (O.S.)
          (shouts) Here!

Elemiah jogs back to the others. Gabriel grabs Jonah and
Holly, Michael tears the Baby out of Holly's arms. She
SCREAMS. As Gabriel, Elemiah, Holly and Jonah retreat,
Michael and the Baby sink into shadow on the opposite side.
Gabriel keeps his hand over Holly's mouth.

SILENCE FALLS. An overhead clip-light shines down on the
centre of the painted circle. It's an eerie, satanic scene.
FOOTSTEPS as a MAN in a dark suit paces his way into
the warehouse. He carries a large SUITCASE. A momentary
hesitation as he sees the painted symbols. Gingerly, he
follows them to the pool of light …

                        MICHAEL (O.S.)
          Stop.

The Man stops dead in the centre of the circle.

MICHAEL (O.S.)

Your name.

MAN

Don Makepeace. I have everything as we
discussed.

MICHAEL (O.S.)

Leave it there, put your hands on your
head, turn around, walk slowly towards the
door.

DON

The Baby …

MICHAEL (O.S.)

At the door you stop. You wait and you do
not turn round.

DON

Is the Baby here?

MICHAEL (O.S.)

If everything is as we agreed, you'll get
the Baby.

DON

How can I be sure you'll keep your side of
the bargain?

MICHAEL (O.S.)

Trust me.

Don places the case in the centre of the circle, links his
hands on his head, turns, steps towards the door. Michael
leaves the Baby on the floor, alone, approaches the case. He
kneels, undoes the clasps, takes a breath, flips it open.
His eyes widen with what he sees.

DON *BOUGHT*
THE BABY?

BUNDLES of bank notes. He takes one out, flicks through, but wait … He freezes, gripped by horrified realisation. Behind the first few genuine notes is BLANK PAPER. SUDDENLY the Baby SQUEALS. Don jumps. A spell is broken, because that very second …

HELL — SLOW, QUIET AND DEADLY — BREAKS LOOSE.

Pfffft. Michael sits up, as if startled by the noise. Holly eyes the Baby, wriggling in the shadows, but Gabriel renews his grip on her. Gabriel, Jonah and Elemiah barely dare breathe as they watch Michael exhale slowly, seemingly transfixed by the money. Only … Michael sinks forward until his head rests in the open case. Blood seeps on to the FAKE NOTES. DEAD.

AS SOON AS THEY KNOW THE BABY IS THERE AND OK, THEY SHOOT

Gabriel, Elemiah, Holly and Jonah START in sudden, horrified realisation. Their eyes search the darkness. Nothing. Gabriel's grip on Holly momentarily lapses. She takes the chance to burst free, scrambles across the floor, through the blood, to the Baby, scoops it up, heads for the fire escape.

Elemiah runs to stop her, but: pfffft. He drops to the floor. DEAD. Holly is showered with BLOOD. She stops, stares at Elemiah, whose lifeless eyes seem to plead with her. She clutches the Baby, turns back to the fire escape, but stops again. She is face to face with a DARK FORCE.

It's dressed entirely in BLACK. No eyes are visible through black goggles. It holds a black gun with a long, narrow barrel, a silencer. It sees the Baby, recoils, sinks back into shadow.

Gabriel scrambles up, the light catches him … Pfffft. He drops to the floor. Jonah SCREAMS, leaps on top of him.

> JONAH
>
> You can't kill him! He won't die! He's divine!

The DARK FORCE re-emerges, looks for Holly, but she's GONE.

THEY DON'T KILL HOLLY OR JONAH. WHY NOT?

EXT. WAREHOUSE — NIGHT

A shadow — Holly, the Baby in her arms — leaps up the spidery staircase, up and up, disappears into a second-floor doorway. Just as several DARK FORCES tear out of the building, look all around, split up, desperately search the car park.

INT. SECOND FLOOR, WAREHOUSE — NIGHT

Holly slips in, hurries to the BAGS she left earlier. She kneels, carefully lowers the Baby into a BAG, wraps and conceals it. Finally, her shaking hands fumble to retrieve the PHONE from the pocket where Ashleigh hid it for her. Trembling fingers stab 999.

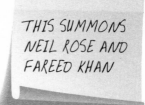

THIS SUMMONS NEIL ROSE AND FAREED KHAN

EXT. WAREHOUSE — NIGHT

During the following V.O. Holly creeps to another exterior fire escape, edges slowly down it, until she finds a broken window where she can see into the basement.

> OPERATOR (V.O.)
> What's your emergency, caller?

> HOLLY (V.O.)
> I've got a baby.

> OPERATOR (V.O.)
> You've had a baby? Is it breathing?

> HOLLY (V.O.)
> Yes.

> OPERATOR (V.O.)
> Are you on your own?

> HOLLY (V.O.)
> No. Dark forces are after it. The other angels are dead. It's just me and the Baby.

> OPERATOR (V.O.)
> Where are you, caller?

> HOLLY (V.O.)
> The Assembly.

As Holly peers into the basement, she sees:

INT. BASEMENT, WAREHOUSE — NIGHT

Don Makepeace and the case of money are GONE. DARK FORCES work quickly in eerie silence. Michael's body is now lain out, Christ-like, in the centre of the circle. A DARK FORCE straddles it, takes its dead hand, places a KNIFE in it and makes the corpse SLICE ITS OWN THROAT. Then, with studied precision rather than passion, the DARK FORCE slices the body's torso time and again, picks up ENTRAILS, arranges them carefully over the body. Another DARK FORCE drags ELEMIAH from the shadows. He too is made to CUT HIS OWN THROAT and is arranged precisely outside the circle as if by a deranged satanic serial killer.

Three DARK FORCES surround Gabriel's body. JONAH, his face buried in Gabriel's chest, clings with super-human force to the dead man. DARK FORCES try to prise him away. A DARK FORCE with a KNIFE waits, ready …

BANG! A door is slammed open.

The Dark Forces start in surprise, SCATTER to the shadows, watch and wait as … A TORCH BEAM cuts through the dark. A MAN (50s, SHORT, SHARP) strides in behind it, a large CAMERA round his neck. His torch beam sweeps the floor, searches.

EXT. WAREHOUSE — NIGHT
Holly watches from her vantage point through the window.

GRAY GRAHAM ARRIVES.

INT. BASEMENT, WAREHOUSE — NIGHT
The Man slows as he sees the mutilated bodies of Michael and Elemiah. He gasps, wavers on his feet. Can barely take it all in. Unseen by everyone except Holly, his shaking hand snaps a photograph of the awful scene, before he drops to his knees, collapses in a DEAD FAINT. In the shadows, the Dark Forces watch and wait. Earpieces barely make a sound …

EXT. WAREHOUSE — NIGHT

Holly spots something outside … A POLICE PATROL CAR switches off its blue lights, trundles into the car park. Holly starts, leaps silently back up to the second floor, slips in at the doorway, fumbles for a TORCH, shakily shines it out of the broken window. Below, TWO POLICE OFFICERS spot the light, casually head up the nearest fire escape. One DARK FORCE signals to another 'hold position' …

THE ARRIVAL OF ROSE AND KHAN PREVENTS THE DARK FORCES KILLING GRAY. ARE THEY POLICE? ONLY THEY SEEM TO BE _HIDING_ FROM THE POLICE.

An exhausted Holly sinks down among her bags, checks on the sleeping Baby as the POLICE OFFICERS arrive.

INT. SECOND FLOOR, WAREHOUSE — NIGHT — A SHORT TIME LATER
Holly gathers her bags as the two OFFICERS smoke cigarettes out of a broken window. They burst out laughing, barely look at her. We just catch …

> OFFICER ONE
> What d'yer reckon? Witches?

> OFFICER TWO
> You don't know what these signs mean, do
> you? Here?

Holly realises he is addressing her, shakes her head.

> OFFICER ONE
> Let's get you checked out.

Holly arranges her bags so the Baby is invisible. She sticks closely to the Police Officers as they lead her down the steps towards their police car. From the basement window the DARK FORCES watch as Holly and the Police Officers approach the patrol car. The Photographer, who doesn't see Holly or the two Officers, crawls to a seated position, mops his brow, fumbles a phone from his pocket.

> PHOTOGRAPHER (O.S.)
> Police. Police … I just … you gotta come here.

SO GRAY GRAHAM DIALS 999. DOESN'T LEAVE HIS NAME.

INT. POLICE CAR — NIGHT

The car stop-starts in light, late-night traffic. Holly sits in dark silence on the back seat. The Baby carefully placed on her lap, hidden in its bag. Finally, the car pulls up at the EMERGENCY DEPARTMENT of a hospital. Suddenly, the radios blast to life …

> POLICE RADIO (O.S.)
> Code Blue. 444 down.

The Officers jump into action.

THAT'S JONATHAN CHILDS AND MARK DUNNING GETTING IN A FIGHT WITH LOCAL BRAWLERS

> OFFICER TWO
> Jonny's in the shit if that civvy gets hurt.

> OFFICER ONE
> (to Holly)
> We're off, love. You can see the entrance, yeah?

TIME JUMP. HOLLY IS AT THE HOSPITAL FOR LONGER THAN THIS SCRIPT IMPLIES. LONG ENOUGH FOR JONATHAN

CHILDS AND MARK DUNNING TO COLLECT A BODY AND DELIVER IT TO THE ASSEMBLY. THE MOMENT TWO SEPARATE COVER-UPS COLLIDE.

EXT. HOSPITAL A&E — NIGHT

Holly scrambles from the car, bags in hand. It SCREECHES
AWAY, sirens blare, blue lights flash. Holly checks the
Baby is asleep in the bag, steels herself, walks up to the
hospital entrance.

INT. HOSPITAL A&E RECEPTION — NIGHT

It's busy. Holly, dirty, blood-stained and dishevelled,
glazed with shock, walks through the bustle to a Reception
Desk. The RECEPTIONIST (30s, female) looks up. Her expression
changes … this is scene one, where we first met Holly.

INT. CUBICLE, A&E, HOSPITAL — NIGHT — LATER

Holly perches on a plastic chair. A NURSE (20s, female)
examines the Baby, who kicks happily on a nearby bed.

> NURSE
>
> He's fine. How 'bout you? Kept your post-
> nate appointments?

Holly almost shakes her head.

> NURSE
>
> Should look after yourself. Baby depends
> on you. What's his name?

> HOLLY
>
> Where's the toilet, please?

Whoosh … the curtain is whisked open. A POLICE OFFICER (20s,
female, black) peers in. Bright, friendly, efficient, we
will later know her as MARIE-CLAIRE.

MARIE-CLAIRE
FOLLOWS FROM THE
ASSEMBLY. SHE'S
DRESSED AS A POLICE

OFFICER, WHICH
HELPS HER DEPOSIT
THE BODY AT THE
SCENE OF THE ANGELS
MASSACRE.

MARIE-CLAIRE

Hi! Here to collect 'Holly and baby' when
they're ready to go.

The Nurse is alone in the cubicle. She smiles, hands Marie-
Claire an envelope.

NURSE

Yep, here's her referral. She's in the
loo, two doors down on the left.

Marie-Claire's face drops. She snatches the letter, jogs
away.

INT. CORRIDOR, HOSPITAL — NIGHT
Head down, Holly clutches the Baby, hurries along, searches
for a way out. Suddenly, she's face to face with a POLICE
OFFICER (30s, female, white).

AILEEN

Holly? Found you! I'm Aileen.

Aileen is so chatty and friendly, Holly is swept along.

EXT/INT. CAR PARK/POLICE PATROL CAR — NIGHT
Aileen chats gently, leads Holly to a waiting Police Patrol
Car, settles her inside. Despite the breezy conversation,
Aileen notices everything about Holly's handling of the
Baby.

AILEEN

Your partner Jonah is waiting and I'm
taking you both to an overnight unit for
some sleep. How's the little one?

HOLLY

OK.

                          AILEEN
        What's its name?

                          HOLLY
        Doesn't need one.

Aileen's eyes in the rear-view mirror narrow and flicker.
Marie-Claire jogs to the Car Park Entrance just in time to
see the car pull away.

EXT. CAR PARK, WAREHOUSE — NIGHT
The Police Patrol Car with Holly and the Baby in the back
turns into the car park, navigates marked and unmarked
Police vehicles, Official People mill about. We may notice
an unmarked CAR turn in behind it. With a determined Marie-
Claire at the wheel.

EXT. CAR PARK, WAREHOUSE — NIGHT
The car rumbles to a halt under a covered section of car
park. We pull away to see from above …

                    AILEEN (ON RADIO O.S.)
            Sir, I'll need a female officer to watch
            the, er …

Marie-Claire leaps from her car, pulls her police hat on,
straightens her uniform …

                    AILEEN (ON RADIO O.S.)
            Strike that, there's one here. Hi.

                          MARIE-CLAIRE
        Marie-Claire …

EXT. CAR PARK, WAREHOUSE — NIGHT
Holly exits the police car and is face to face with

                            364

Marie-Claire. It's a moment.

FLASHBACK to the DARK FORCE SHE WAS FACE TO FACE WITH JUST A FEW HOURS AGO. IS THIS WHO SHOT THE ANGELS? She backs away, clutches the Baby, SCREAMS.

> AILEEN
>
> Holly, Holly. Hey, this is Marie-Claire; she'll look after you while I collect Jonah …

> HOLLY
>
> No! She's a dark force.

> AILEEN
>
> Oi! You, shut it. (to Marie-Claire) Sorry, Officer.

Aileen and Marie-Claire share a look.

> AILEEN
>
> Sit in the car while I'm gone, Marie-Claire will keep an eye on you from out here.

Marie-Claire nods her assent, as Aileen hurries into the warehouse.

SO WHILE AILEEN IS IN THE BASEMENT TRYING TO GET JONAH AWAY FROM GABRIEL'S BODY, THIS IS HAPPENING.

INT. POLICE PATROL CAR — NIGHT — A SHORT TIME LATER
The Baby searches Holly's eyes. She smiles, rocks it. Outside, Marie-Claire paces, speaks into a phone. Her voice a low murmur, barely audible.

> MARIE-CLAIRE
>
> … in the car with the girl … Gone to shit

... coppers <u>everywhere</u>.

Holly shushes the Baby, holds her breath to listen.

> MARIE-CLAIRE
> (barely audible)
> Let their protocol play out. We'll get it
> back when there's no one to see us.

Holly's eyes widen in horror. She looks at the Baby ... TAP TAP TAP! Holly jumps, followed by relief at ... ASHLEIGH'S FACE AT THE WINDOW. She whispers, anxious ...

> ASHLEIGH
> Holly. Well done. Are you OK?

... as Marie-Claire hurriedly ends her call.

> MARIE-CLAIRE
> (to Ashleigh)
> You shouldn't be here. Get back to the van ...

> ASHLEIGH
> What will happen to them?

Marie-Claire pulls Ashleigh aside. They whisper together urgently. We just catch ...

> ASHLEIGH
> (to Marie-Claire)
> <u>Please</u>. Please!

Marie-Claire gives her a look, hands her a car key. Ashleigh jumps in at the driver's side.

> HOLLY
> It must be the energy shield. There are so
> many humans here, they can't do anything.

> ASHLEIGH
> Who?

                         HOLLY

     The forces of darkness. She's one, like
     the one who tried to take it from the flat.

                        ASHLEIGH

Holly—

                         HOLLY

     We're the only angels left.

Ashleigh takes a moment to swallow her tears. She turns to
Holly. They hold each other's gaze.

                        ASHLEIGH

     Holly, I'm not an angel.

Holly freezes, but not with surprise.

                        ASHLEIGH

     Nor are you.

Holly stares at her.

                        ASHLEIGH

     We're human. Like everyone.

Holly holds Ashleigh's gaze, shakes her head.

                         HOLLY

     No. Gabriel wouldn't make a mistake like
     that. (beat) He's an archangel.

Ashleigh takes a deep breath.

                        ASHLEIGH

     He's not an archangel. He's not even
     Gabriel. His name's Peter Duffy.

Every doubt Holly's had passes across her face.

                        ASHLEIGH

     Listen, Holly, thirteen years ago he told
     me I had a celestial soul, that we'd save

                          367

the world together. He called me Holly.
Just like you.

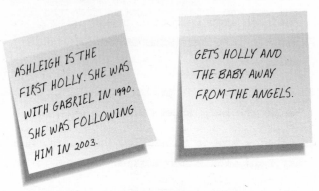

ASHLEIGH IS THE FIRST HOLLY. SHE WAS WITH GABRIEL IN 1990. SHE WAS FOLLOWING HIM IN 2003.

GETS HOLLY AND THE BABY AWAY FROM THE ANGELS.

Holly tries to shake growing horror from her mind. Her hand
flies to the door handle. Locked.

> ASHLEIGH
>
> He's an insidious, predatory man, a spider.
> The only thing he can do is spin a web.

Holly is tearful, as if <u>this</u> is her greatest fear.

> ASHLEIGH
>
> He made you feel special.

Holly stops. Her stillness and silence speak volumes.

> ASHLEIGH
>
> He made <u>me</u> feel special too. (beat) He
> builds a life for you, a family, you fall
> in love with him and you'll do anything.
> (beat) It's just a baby. <u>Your</u> baby. A part
> of you. And she's beautiful.

Holly locks eyes with Ashleigh, shakes her head. This look
is different.

> HOLLY
>
> He's not my baby.

Ashleigh sits back, suddenly uneasy, confused …

TAP TAP TAP. Marie-Claire's face at the window.

> MARIE-CLAIRE
>
> Ashleigh. You've done a great job, but you
> shouldn't be here and you have to go.

CLICK. The central locking clicks open as Marie-Claire's phone RINGS. She turns away to answer it. Ashleigh jogs round to Holly's side, opens her door.

> ASHLEIGH
>
> Jump out. Give me a hug, quick.

Holly climbs out. The Baby makes their farewell hug awkward, but we can see the empathy there.

> ASHLEIGH
>
> What's your real name?

> HOLLY
>
> Georgie.

> ASHLEIGH
>
> Georgie, don't believe what you're told
> just because you trust the person telling
> you. You saved this baby. Don't ever make
> your life about someone else again. (beat)
> Especially not Gabriel. OK?

Holly goes to reply, but—

> MARIE-CLAIRE
>
> Fucking WHAT? Is this a JOKE? (whispers)
> Of course I did …

Marie-Claire's legs almost give way, she drops her phone, struggles to retrieve it. Finally, she hauls herself into the back seat of the car, closes the door, lays her head on her shaking hands.

IS THIS IT? THE MOMENT GABRIEL … COMES BACK TO LIFE?

Across the car park, a brisk Aileen and broken Jonah turn into view. Ashleigh whispers in Holly's ear …

                    ASHLEIGH
          Promise.

She pads away as quietly as she arrived. Behind Aileen and Jonah, unseen by them, a POLICE OFFICER staggers from the warehouse and vomits. He is followed by another OFFICER who paces in distress. As Aileen glances briefly to Marie-Claire, still sitting in the car, Holly rocks the Baby, considers Ashleigh's words.

                    AILEEN
          Right, let's get you three somewhere safe
          for the night.

CLICK, FOOTSTEPS as Marie-Claire jumps from the car and hurries away. Aileen opens the door for Holly …

                    AILEEN
          (into the radio)
          Can I confirm the address …?

Her voice fades as we focus on Holly and Jonah, their eyes locked in mutual defiance.

                    HOLLY
          They're all dead.

                    JONAH
          It'll rise to power. The destruction of
          mankind will be your fault. You were never
          a being of love.

                    HOLLY
          I am a being of love. A human.

Her eyes fill with tears as she fights to accept the unthinkable.

                                HOLLY
        So are you. So were they.

Jonah wavers slightly in his resolve. Has he had doubts too?

                                JONAH
        Why? Why save it?

He edges closer.

                                HOLLY
        Hurting it didn't feel right.

                                JONAH
        The dark forces turned you. If you won't
        kill it, I will.

Aileen, still on the phone, glances to Holly and Jonah, sees
something Holly can't — a KNIFE in Jonah's hand. She drops
the phone, leaps into action …

                                AILEEN
        Hey!

The spell broken, Holly jumps away … Aileen treads firmly,
but carefully.

                                AILEEN
        Jonah. Give the knife to me.

                                JONAH
        I like being an angel.

                                AILEEN
        Put the knife down. Kick it to me. Now.

                            GABRIEL (O.S.)
        Give her the knife, Jonah.

Jonah spins round. Nothing. No one there, just distant
Police Officers, distracted, distressed by something … Aileen
pounces on the knife. With expert timing, she holds it at

arm's length, quickly searches Jonah for further weapons. The knife drops THUD into a safety container.

INT. POLICE PATROL CAR — NIGHT — A SHORT TIME LATER

BANG. The driver's door slams shut. Aileen starts the engine. Holly holds the Baby, sits as far away as possible from a handcuffed Jonah on the back seat.

> HOLLY
>
> Will you arrest him?

Aileen looks back, fixes them with a stern stare.

> AILEEN
>
> You two want some sleep tonight, right?
> So do I.

They nod. Aileen starts the engine, turns away.

> AILEEN
>
> I'll put it down to trauma, if you both
> behave yourselves. Promise? (they nod) And
> if the unit asks my name, say Marie-Claire.

Aileen chuckles to herself.

> HOLLY
>
> If someone asks you about tonight, not now
> but years in the future, what will you
> tell them?

Aileen locks eyes with her in the rear-view mirror.

> AILEEN
>
> I'll think of something.

Holly settles back into the seat as the car pulls out of the car park and away from The Assembly.

MAGGIE KEENAN
WAS RIGHT, AILEEN
FORGOT THE LIE
SHE TOLD.

> **Amanda Bailey**
> I've found out who the baby is, Don. Sorry.

> **Amanda Bailey**
> What I mean is, sorry you had to lie. But nothing stays a secret for ever.

Correspondence between me and Oliver Menzies, 6 September 2021:

> **Amanda Bailey**
> I know who Christopher Shenk was.

Oliver Menzies
Raphael.

> **Amanda Bailey**
> There was no Raphael in the Alperton Angels. Only in the Ninja Turtles.

Oliver Menzies
The fact you can't see something doesn't mean it isn't there. All it means is YOU can't see it.

> **Amanda Bailey**
> Heard about Minnie Davis? She based her book on a project about fake news by an art student. She had no idea until a proof-reader flagged up a trail of anomalies.

Oliver Menzies
She should've checked the facts.

> **Amanda Bailey**
> Thing is, she did. She checked them by clicking on urls provided by the student, who'd linked them to doctored web pages that seemed to confirm the 'facts' in her thesis.

Oliver Menzies

I don't even know the woman. Why are you telling me this?

> **Amanda Bailey**
>
> Got a confession 😳 I found something out about the Alperton
> Angels. A few things. Actually, a lot of things and didn't let you
> know.

Oliver Menzies

So? I do my own research, have my own contacts.

> **Amanda Bailey**
>
> Sure. But there's one thing that's pretty fundamental.

Oliver Menzies

Surely several things. That Holly was Lady Georgina Ogilvy,
distant cousin to the Queen. That the Alperton Angels baby was
adopted by Prince Edward and Sophie, Countess of Wessex.
That Lady Louise Mountbatten Windsor is about to turn
eighteen while the world remains unaware of what she really is.

> **Amanda Bailey**
>
> Who told you that? You're supposed to be writing about the
> supernatural.

Oliver Menzies

Not any more. There's something more important to do.

> **Amanda Bailey**
>
> Like what?

Oliver Menzies

Destroying the Antichrist. Saving mankind.

> **Amanda Bailey**
>
> Oliver, stop playing games. I'm being serious.

Oliver Menzies

So am I. The Alperton Angels were right. But they were betrayed
by Holly. She wasn't an angel, just the baby's mother. She was
lured in by the dark forces.

Amanda Bailey

She wasn't the baby's mother. Olly, I need to tell you a few things. Let's meet up.

Oliver Menzies

Too late.

Amanda Bailey

OK, I'll rattle through the stuff you should know. Here goes:

Amanda Bailey

Gabriel, Michael and Elemiah were lifelong criminals. They met in jail.

Amanda Bailey

We know Gabriel was planning something in 1990. He befriended a troubled young girl, set a lot of things up, but it failed in its early stages. The first Holly went to the police and was taken back home. Who knows how many other attempts he made? Each failure simply honed his MO.

Amanda Bailey

Gabriel has few material resources. Just an ability to pull others into his orbit and make them believe him. His 'thing' is to convince vulnerable people they are angels with a divine purpose. When, in 2003, he found Georgina Ogilvy, a troubled child of fallen aristocracy, he hit the big time.

Amanda Bailey

Unlike in 1990, he's now got Jonah, too – and a much grander plan, steeped in revenge.

Amanda Bailey

No one will look twice at a young couple with a baby. Holly and Jonah can move around, hidden in plain sight. Remember the men all have criminal records and no money.

Oliver Menzies

Amanda, listen. You believe you've found a great conspiracy but these events have been foretold for decades. Holly, Jonah, Michael, Elemiah ... pawns. Players in the ultimate elevation of the beast. The real manipulation has happened on a psychic level – to ensure that as soon as the Antichrist comes into its power, it can use it.

> **Amanda Bailey**
> Give me an example.

Oliver Menzies

Gray Graham. How did he know to go to that obscure, derelict location that night? His psychic ability. He was drawn to the warehouse by dark forces. His arrival saved the Antichrist from destruction by the angels.

> **Amanda Bailey**
> Gray Graham had no sixth sense whatsoever. He had a nose for a story, long-standing police contacts and specialist receiving equipment. He LISTENED IN on police radio transmissions.

> **Amanda Bailey**
> I went to his flat after he died, saw the old radio, read his notebooks. You saw them yourself. They're a mix of what he heard on the airwaves and quotes from scenes of crimes – where he would frequently arrive BEFORE the police!

> **Amanda Bailey**
> He was listening that night. He heard chatter about a baby born in an old baby food warehouse and set off to photograph it. His deadline was the following day. He was low on copy and scrabbling for whatever he could get. An atmospheric night-time shot and feel-good story might just make it.

> **Amanda Bailey**
> Blue paint found on the second floor was where Elemiah rehearsed the symbols used to mark the spot the angels would meet their contact. Later, those practice marks would be erased, causing doubt in the mind of one officer and a discrepancy between their accounts that reinforced the mythology and continues muddying the waters even now.

Amanda Bailey

Dark forces were at the warehouse alright, but they were very real, and they were there because Ashleigh, the girl Gabriel had first called 'Holly' and tried to enlist for his failed plan in 1990, was following the angels and alerted the police. She knew how he operated and wanted to save the new Holly from him.

Oliver Menzies

Holly is just the vessel through which the Antichrist came to earth.

Amanda Bailey

Who do you believe is the father of the baby?

Oliver Menzies

Gabriel or Jonah. Doesn't matter. Biological determination is irrelevant. Simply building blocks that give the Antichrist physical form on earth.

Amanda Bailey

The baby's father is Don Makepeace, the chief inspector who sent Gabriel to prison in the late 1980s. The baby's mother is his wife, Julia. It was a simple case of kidnap and ransom. Emailing you something now.

Meeting with Connor Makepeace, the Alperton Angels 'Baby', 5 September 2021. Transcribed by Amanda Bailey.

AB: And you had no idea until yesterday?

CM: No. Dad said someone had found out so he had to tell me before they did. Do you know who that would be?

AB: No.

CM: He's, like, really angry. They were waiting for the right time to tell me. Not when I'm just about to start uni, right? Never seen him like that before.

AB: Is there ever a good time to discover something so ... traumatic?

CM: True. I mean, it's cool. But a shock.

AB: What did your mum and dad tell you?

CM: That when I was just a few months old, Mum took me to the library. She had another appointment and was in a hurry but I was crying. A young woman approached her and offered to keep me occupied while Mum popped in to return her books. The girl mentioned helping her mother with her sister so was experienced with babies. She wore a uniform from a local private school Mum knew from her teaching work. She was plausible, Mum was desperate and even though she didn't like leaving me with a stranger, she reasoned it wouldn't be for long and, like, what's the worst that can happen? Funny, right?

AB: Yep.

CM: Dad said the girl was with a gang. He'd put one of them away years before when he was a beat copper, so they targeted him, planned it for months. He said they must've followed Mum from the house, but because this girl was so well dressed and spoken, she didn't suspect a thing. Until she came out and saw I was gone.

AB: That must've been terrible.

CM: They said it was, yeah. You know this whole story, right? That's why you were asking me about it.

AB: I know bits and pieces.

CM: For days Dad got calls from the kidnappers and had to look in the local paper for where to drop the ransom. Dad told them he'd pay the money. When he went to drop it off he found all the gang had killed themselves and me safe and well with the girl. She rescued me, along with her boyfriend, so ... I guess they let her off.

AB: How do you feel about it now?

CM: Fine. You know. I don't remember it. It's cool.

AB: Have you read about it, or seen anything on TV? They call it the case of the Alperton Angels.

CM: Like, I think so. But Dad said it's not really what happened. People say they thought I was the devil, but it's just what the gang told the teenagers. They were crims after cash, that's all.

AB: You know the angels, the crims, all died except one?

CM: Yeah. Dad said that was a mistake.

Amanda Bailey

Holly steals the baby. She and Jonah care for it while the angels conduct their communications with Don and organise the exchange of ransom money. But Gabriel didn't count on Don's network of friends.

Oliver Menzies

Believe whatever spin Don throws you, Mand. The Antichrist is here and I know where they are.

Amanda Bailey

Don remembers catastrophic police handling of kidnap cases in the past. Muriel McKay, Lesley Whittle. He knows the protocols and doesn't trust them to get his son back safely. He turns to his old ties with special forces.

Amanda Bailey

When the baby was kidnapped, ads indicating where the exchange would take place had already appeared in the local paper for weeks. Set up in advance to make the whole operation smoother.

Oliver Menzies

You're forgetting something. I was called at 4.44 a.m. every morning. Until yesterday. I waited, but the call never came. That's my sign.

Amanda Bailey

About those calls 😳 I know who made them. I was intrigued, so I traced the electronic number weeks ago. Thought it would be funny if you carried on believing that angels were on the line. Will forward the email. You'll laugh too, I promise. I know I did 😂

TO: Amanda Bailey
DATE: 30 July 2021
SUBJECT: Re: Mystery calls
FROM: BioCleanse Solutions Ltd

Dear Mrs Bailey,

Thank you for your email dated 27 July 2021. I am pleased to inform you that, following an investigation by our outreach team, I can confirm the persistent calls to your landline are being made by one of our decommissioned chemical toilets. Manufactured in the late nineties, this portable unit was fitted with electronics that dialled head office automatically in the event of a fault. In layman's terms, over the past few months it has repeatedly, and at consistent intervals, attempted to call an engineer and request a service. While our systems were updated many years ago anyway, it seems this particular unit was programmed with the wrong telephone number on the production line.

We always strive to remove battery packs before sending our units to landfill. However, it seems this one was scrapped with its battery in situ. Perhaps something happened to charge it and kickstart the auto-dial system. I understand a lightning strike can do just that. Let me assure you, the battery will eventually drain and the calls stop of their own accord.

As a goodwill gesture, BioCleanse Solutions Ltd are pleased to offer you a 10% discount on the purchase or hire of any chemical toilet in our standard range, and 5% off our luxury range.

Yours sincerely,
BioCleanse Solutions Ltd

Oliver Menzies

You knew all this time and didn't tell me?

> **Amanda Bailey**
>

Oliver Menzies

Makes no difference. It's still my sign.

> **Amanda Bailey**
> It's a portable toilet.

Oliver Menzies

My number was programmed into that toilet in the 1990s. Now, just as the baby is about to come into its power, a lightning strike restarts the battery and I get the calls. Me, Mand. It wasn't programmed with the wrong number. It was programmed with the right number, that of the only being capable of saving humanity from evil: an angel in human form.

> **Amanda Bailey**
>
> You're not an angel.

Oliver Menzies

I was born on earth as insurance against the Alperton Angels failing in their mission. They failed. It's now my purpose to destroy the Antichrist.

> **Amanda Bailey**
>
> There's no Antichrist. Just a secret special forces operation to rescue the kidnapped baby of a senior police officer and, unlawfully, assassinate the unarmed perpetrators – an op that collided with a police bid to cover up the murder in custody of Chris Shenk.

> **Amanda Bailey**
>
> Singh was deep undercover at a local restaurant. When he was found murdered, it was clear to police he'd been rumbled by the gang and executed. Local drug dealer and aspiring underworld bigshot Chris Shenk is their only suspect. That night, Shenky dies in custody, never having been OFFICIALLY in custody.

> **Amanda Bailey**
>
> Former special forces sniper and serving police officer Marie-Claire is organising the disposal of Shenk's body. As Don's trusted associate, she's also coordinating the unofficial retrieval of Connor Makepeace and the murder of his kidnappers. Thanks to Ashleigh, who has been following the angels and reporting to her, she knows what Gabriel plans to do.

> **Amanda Bailey**
>
> Ashleigh escaped Gabriel's clutches in 1990. Years later, she spots him with two teenagers, discovers they are as vulnerable as she was and totally under Gabriel's control – but worse, they have a baby. She befriends Holly, who reveals the location of The Assembly.

Amanda Bailey

Ashleigh, believing the angels will harm the baby, informs the police, at which point Marie-Claire realises the location is the same as that given for the exchange of the ransom for Don's son.

Amanda Bailey

Symbols painted on the floor, candles, witnesses who can attest to the satanic nature of the angels' ethos. It was the perfect opportunity to rescue the baby and dispose of both the kidnappers and Shenk.

Amanda Bailey

It didn't all go to plan. Holly escaped with the baby. She called 999 from the second floor, which also alerted Gray Graham, who was listening in on police radio comms. This meant the dark forces – Marie-Claire, Don and their trusted team – had just enough time to arrange the bodies into a satanic tableau before Gray and the police arrived. They had to shrink into the background while official protocols played out.

Amanda Bailey

Marie-Claire and Don followed the police car that took Holly and Jonah to the children's centre, and presented themselves soon after to collect the baby. Connor is soon reunited with his parents. They could have no idea how this case would capture the public's imagination. I'm sure they didn't think they'd still be dealing with the fallout eighteen years later.

Amanda Bailey

No one involved in either operation wants the truth to come out and while both ops were successful, the cover-up remains dependent on everyone believing their own version of events to be true, and the myths about the case enduring.

Amanda Bailey

Since our Informer days we each considered Don a useful contact to stay friendly with. But the truth is, he stayed in touch with US. He probably does the same with other writers and journalists, people who might get too close. There are at least seven people dead thanks to him and Marie-Claire.

Amanda Bailey

He told me to be careful. It was them I had to be careful of.

Oliver Menzies

This isn't about you or Don. It's bigger than that. When I was near the site of The Assembly I sensed a powerful psychic portal. It's happened whenever I've been close to angel energy.

Amanda Bailey

Ol, did you not wonder why I kept giving you stuff? All those drinks and sweets? They all had caffeine in them. I remembered the effect it has on you from when we were at The Informer together 😊 At the massacre site, Quarr Abbey, when we visited the angels' apartment. I even worked out exactly how long it takes for the shakes to start. Eighteen minutes.

Oliver Menzies

Nonsense. You're trying to divert me from my purpose.

Amanda Bailey

That comment beneath your story, about Gabriel's wounds magically healing. You couldn't find it, because I made it up.

Oliver Menzies

Why would you even bother to do all that?

Amanda Bailey

Remember that night before our appraisals at The Informer? Drinks at a place in town. You told me the wrong venue.

Oliver Menzies

Vaguely. What about it?

Amanda Bailey

I ended up on the other side of London. Alone.

Oliver Menzies

So? It was a joke.

Amanda Bailey

I was eighteen. It was dark. I was in a pub on an estate in North London. When I left, someone followed me and punched me in the head. It detached my retina. When I came to, I realised they'd stolen my bag. I had no money, no phone, no travel pass and a two-hour walk home.

Oliver Menzies

It was 20 years ago, get over it.

Amanda Bailey

You damaged my sight FFS!

Oliver Menzies

No way! I didn't mug you, did I?

Amanda Bailey

The following day we had to submit a portfolio of work and a feature about our year on the scheme. The disk I had all those documents on had been in my bag. It was gone.

Oliver Menzies

You were the golden girl. You could've handed in a shopping list and passed the course.

Amanda Bailey

I was traumatised. I knew something was wrong with my eye, but didn't want to admit I'd been mugged. Didn't tell anyone. Didn't report it. I was so used to hiding my emotions I didn't know how to feel. That's why I never went back to The Informer. Didn't graduate from the course. Everything I'd worked so hard to achieve was lost.

Amanda Bailey

All these years later you have no idea what you did to me that night. You're not even listening now.

Oliver Menzies

I'm listening.

Amanda Bailey

You're not. You've just sent an email to Paul Cole, asking him to clarify how a soul crosses the divide in the event of a sudden death.

Oliver Menzies

How do you know that?

Amanda Bailey

There is no Paul Cole. It's me.

Oliver Menzies

Bollocks. You know nothing about metaphysical science.

Amanda Bailey

I know how to google. All the theorys and advice I gave you is online, quite interesting – some of it.

Amanda Bailey

I've been your spiritual counsellor these last few weeks. Suggesting things to you, helping you believe them. I sent you in the wrong direction and left you there.

Amanda Bailey

I only did to you what you did to me.

Oliver Menzies

And I told you I had an interview you'd never get. Well, I didn't. All bullshit and you fell for it. So quid pro quo to you.

Amanda Bailey

🙂 I prefer an eye for an eye 👁

Oliver Menzies

The Alperton warehouse was the site of the resurrection. I sensed it – with or without caffeine. I'd be here right now with or without Paul Cole. It's written in the stars.

Amanda Bailey

There was no resurrection. Gabriel was shot in the head, declared dead, then got up and walked away – how? Well, the bullet HIT his skull, but didn't penetrate it. He suffered a skull fracture, severe

385

concussion and was rendered unconscious. While his body was in deep shock, his pulse and respiration were at such low levels that even a paramedic saw no vital signs on cursory examination.

Oliver Menzies

And what are the chances of that happening? Did you even ask that?

> **Amanda Bailey**
>
> I didn't have to. The sniper told me herself. One in a thousand.

Oliver Menzies

There you have it. Gabriel was saved by forces on the other side.

> **Amanda Bailey**
>
> But those odds shorten considerably when a firearm is fitted with a silencer and fired several times in quick succession. Each shot increases the probability of glitches in the mechanism that can impede bullet velocity and reduce its capacity to penetrate the skull. Gabriel lucked out because there was only one sniper to kill three people and he was the last to be shot, that's all.

> **Amanda Bailey**
>
> He may not be the archangel Gabriel, but Peter Duffy is a lucky man on several counts. Once the angels were dead, the special forces staged a scene that looked like a satanic sacrifice. Gabriel only escaped having his throat cut and being mutilated because Jonah was clinging to him.

Oliver Menzies

I knew who Gabriel was the moment I saw him in that prison visiting room. When my eyes met his. He's the Messiah, but his power is rendered impotent by man. I'm the last angel, Mand. Sent to earth to save humanity.

> **Amanda Bailey**
>
> Gabriel had a traumatic near-death experience and a concussion that seems to have genuinely wiped his memory. He's the same narcissistic psychopath. Still a dangerous, controlling con man. The one thing he isn't is a murderer.

Oliver Menzies

Come up with whatever theory you like, makes no difference to me. I'm doing this.

> **Amanda Bailey**
> Doing what?

Oliver Menzies

Thought you read my email to Paul Cole? 😂 🔫

TO: Paul Cole
DATE: 6 September 2021
SUBJECT: The end
FROM: Oliver Menzies

Paul, when a soul experiences sudden death, can you clarify how that energy is transmuted to the other side? Is there anything I should or shouldn't do to ensure the process happens quickly and smoothly?

See, I've found the Antichrist. It's sixteenth in line to the throne. It can go anywhere, do anything. Its rise to power will be catastrophic. But thanks to me, it won't rise to power. I'm here now. I'll destroy it 🔫 but I know they'll destroy me.

WhatsApp messages between me and Ellie Cooper, 6 September 2021:

> **Amanda Bailey**
> Shit. Oliver told Paul Cole he's going to kill Lady Louise Windsor. He'd lie to me in a heartbeat, but not to his spiritual counsellor. Why does he even think she's the baby?

Ellie Cooper

I told him. I told him Holly's baby was adopted by Prince Edward and Sophie.

> **Amanda Bailey**
> 🙍 But it wasn't, Ellie. The baby was a boy.

Ellie Cooper

A boy? Oh. Shit.

Amanda Bailey

It was Don Makepeace's son, Connor. Gabriel used the angels to kidnap the baby. He wanted cash, of course, but revenge too – Don put Gabriel away years before.

Ellie Cooper

Oops. Sorry. Thought Oliver deserved a break 😳

Amanda Bailey

What did he say when you told him?

Ellie Cooper

Something about wherever it's born in society it'll gravitate to the upper echelons. Obstacles will be moved out of its path to get it to the top.

Amanda Bailey

Fuck. I told him that and a lot more. He gave an angel therapist my details as a joke. I got him back by pretending I'd given his email to a spiritual counsellor. Only it was me 😐

Amanda Bailey

I convinced him Gray Graham was psychic and the angels were calling him every morning. Gave him caffeine sweets and energy drinks so he'd think he was being dragged into psychic portals. Made it seem as if bods who were about to contact him were dying mysteriously. Only had to mention something, like music or art, to send him down a rabbit hole that confirmed his delusions. The power was exhilarating. And it was pretty funny watching him fall for it.

Ellie Cooper

So, everything Gabriel did, you did to Oliver? Some revenge for a wacky email.

Amanda Bailey

That wasn't the reason. It's a long story. I'll fill you in some day.

Ellie Cooper

Is it over? Have you told him the truth yet?

Amanda Bailey

Yes and he doesn't believe me. Says he's going to destroy the Antichrist. Where would Lady Louise be now? Should we call the police? Shit. If I thought he'd take it THIS seriously I'd never have done it.

Ellie Cooper

Let's not panic. What will he do? She goes to a school in Ascot. If he gets there, at worst he'll rant and rave and get dragged away by security.

Amanda Bailey

True. True. You're right. It's nonsense. How will he even get hold of a gun? Thanks, Ellie.

Ellie Cooper

WhatsApp messages between me and Oliver Menzies, 6 September 2021:

Amanda Bailey

Fuck off, shit merchant! Where will you get a gun from?

Oliver Menzies

The mad squaddie. Fate brought us together. Right at the time I need weapons and insight into how close-protection officers operate. He's here with me now 😄 We'll wait as long as it takes. Sending you some pics for the inquest.

WhatsApp messages between me and Ellie Cooper, 6 September 2021:

Amanda Bailey

Ellie, he's on the roof of Lady Louise's school. Here are the pics. He says he's with a troubled ex-soldier who has a gun. No pics to prove that but 😬

Ellie Cooper

You can see schoolgirls walking across the quad. It must be their first day back after summer break.

Ellie Cooper

Mand! I've looked up a map of the school. The roof where Oliver is hiding ... it's called The Orchard Building 😬

> **Amanda Bailey**
>
> I shouldn't have let it get this far. I have to stop him doing anything truly stupid. Driving to Ascot now. This is so you know. Just in case.

Ellie Cooper

In case what?

> **Amanda Bailey**
>
> Oliver says I live in 2001. He's wrong. I live in 1991. I print out my research and archive it as I go. In case it's disputed or queried. Mark Dunning did the same.

> **Amanda Bailey**
>
> Ellie, I'm going to the school and will post something to you on the way. Whatever happens, you'll get it in the next few days. It explains how and why Harpinder Singh died. In case anything happens to me.

Ellie Cooper

Don't go anywhere, Mand. I'm speaking to the police now. They'll get there before you. It'll be fine.

Later messages from me to Amanda Bailey, 6 September 2021:

Ellie Cooper

Everything OK, Mand? I haven't heard from either you or the police. I hope that means you're alright, but can you let me know?

Ellie Cooper

Hi, Mand. Did you go there? Is everything OK now?

Ellie Cooper

Just had a thought: at the start of all this you and Oliver were racing each other to the baby, and in a funny sort of way, you still are!

Of course, I never received an answer.

8

I Take Over from the Late Amanda Bailey on 8 September 2021

I received Amanda's letter as she predicted. Inside was a key, a printout of that final message exchange between her and Oliver, and this handwritten note:

Ellie,
This key opens a safe deposit box. The address is on the label. Inside you'll find my Alperton Angels research. In addition to cuttings and notes, I've printed out every interview, WhatsApp conversation and text message. These are the only versions that exist now - anything electronic has been deleted in such a way that it can never be retrieved.

It's a precaution in case something bad should happen. But it won't. Everything will be fine. As you'll see, Gabriel is innocent of Harpinder Singh's murder.

If anything happens to me, I'll leave it up to you what you do with the enclosed.
Amanda

These are the pages torn out of the third extract from *Divine* by Georgie Adesina (see page 234). Holly slipped out to follow Gabriel and discovers him reading to elderly people in a care home. She returns to the flat:

INT. LANDING, FLAT — DAY

Holly arrives at the front door of the flat. Stops dead. It CREAKS back and forth. Open. Beyond it the light, gentle tones of a YOUNG MAN'S VOICE. Holly, face blank with terrified realisation, pushes the door, tiptoes in. She follows the voice to her bedroom. Through a chink she sees him: a YOUNG MAN (20s, Asian) holds the Baby, whispers gently in its ear. It makes random noises in response. Holly's face blanches, she pads quickly to Jonah's room, opens the door, slips inside.

INT. HOLLY'S BEDROOM, FLAT — DAY — A SHORT TIME LATER

The Young Man paces, jogs the Baby, checks his watch, concerned.

> YOUNG MAN (ENGLISH ACCENT)
> Left you alone, didn't they …?

He turns, starts in surprise. Holly and Jonah stand in the doorway, hands behind their backs, faces fixed with terror and determination.

> JONAH
> Put it down.

The Young Man instinctively hugs the Baby tighter.

> YOUNG MAN
> What are you, fourteen?

> JONAH
> (slight indignance)
> Seventeen.

> HOLLY
> You won't save it. We won't let you.

> JONAH
> Put the baby down.

> YOUNG MAN
> It was crying for forty minutes.

The Young Man holds the Baby firmly. Holly and Jonah look desperately to each other.

> YOUNG MAN
> It needs feeding, it needs changing—

> HOLLY
> (to Jonah)
> He's one of them. He's been sent to save the Antichrist.

                             JONAH
              (to the Young Man)
          We won't let you.
The Young Man shakes his head, mind made up. He marches to
the door, to Holly and Jonah, as if to take the Baby away.
His determined eyes meet equal determination in Jonah's.

                           YOUNG MAN
          Out of the way.

With one fast move Jonah stabs a LARGE KITCHEN KNIFE into
the Young Man's neck. A FATAL wound. Holly smashes him in
the head with a CRICKET BAT. Holly grabs the Baby as the
Young Man falls to the floor. Blood pumps from his neck
wound. Jonah leaps on the Young Man, raises the knife above
his head. His face set rigid, his eyes dead.

As if possessed by a malevolent, unseen force, Jonah plunges
the blade into the Young Man's chest, neck, face. Holly
watches in horror, ducks back out of the doorway to avoid
blood spatter, but she can't take her eyes from the scene.
Finally, Jonah staggers back, stares at the body in shock.
He looks to Holly. Something tacit passes between them.
They scramble from the room with the Baby.

INT. CORRIDOR, FLAT — DAY — CONTINUOUS
Holly and Jonah slam the door shut behind them, check the
Baby … it's calm and unharmed. They stare at the silent
door, weapons ready.

INT. CORRIDOR, FLAT — DAY — MUCH LATER
Holly and Jonah sit in vigil, weapons to hand. A SKIPPING
ROPE secures the door handle to the one beside it. A key
RATTLES in the front door. They jump up. Gabriel slips
in, bags of takeaway Chinese swing from his wrists. He

                              396

sees Jonah and Holly and in an instant his eyes lose their twinkle.

> HOLLY

> They got in and tried to take it.

> JONAH

> We got rid of them.

Gabriel's face darkens with growing alarm.

> HOLLY

> The Antichrist is safe.

Gabriel spots the rope around the door handle. In a single move he unravels it, disappears into the room. Holly and Jonah glance at each other. Seconds later, Gabriel re-emerges, pale and shocked.

> JONAH

> We were asleep. It got in and grabbed the
> Baby.

> GABRIEL

> I closed the door. I know I did.

Beat. Holly shifts.

> HOLLY

> It must've made itself invisible and walked
> through the wall.

> JONAH

> It was watching, waiting.

> GABRIEL

> He's a fucking neighbour!

Gabriel takes a deep breath, pulls the bedroom door closed, ushers Holly and Jonah to the living room.

INT. LIVING ROOM, FLAT — DAY — CONTINUOUS

The Baby sleeps in its Moses basket. Gabriel shoves Holly
and Jonah on to the sofa, paces, thinks.

> GABRIEL
>
> I never said kill anyone, I never said
> that.

> JONAH
>
> It might rise up again.

> HOLLY
>
> They'll send others.

Gabriel looks at their faces, open and innocent.

> GABRIEL
>
> I need to call someone. Wait here.

Gabriel makes as if to leave the room …

> JONAH
>
> We did the right thing, didn't we?

Gabriel's look is unreadable.

When I opened the safe deposit box on 8 September 2021, I discovered the documents you've just read up to 6 September 2021. The only other item was one of Amanda's business cards. It appeared ordinary at first, but on the reverse were two white feathers, taped firmly to the paper. Under one, she'd written: 'Found behind the Ballot Box pub on 13 July, while waiting for Mr Blue. It glowed luminous on the path in front of me.'

Under the other feather, she'd written: 'Found on the shoulder of Ol's jacket as we queued to see Gabriel in HMP Tynefield.'

Things added by me, Ellie Cooper, from 9 September 2021

BBC News alerts on 6 September 2021:

SHOOTING AT ASCOT SCHOOL. ONE DEAD

TWO CONFIRMED DEAD AT SCHOOL

SCHOOL SHOOTING: GUNMAN SHOT DEAD BY POLICE

POLICE: SCHOOL SHOOTING NOT TERROR RELATED

Links to news stories dated from 7 September to 9 December 2021:

ROYAL SCHOOL SHOOTING: DEAD WOMAN NAMED
AS AUTHOR AMANDA BAILEY

ROYAL SCHOOL GUNMAN BELIEVED HE WAS RIDDING WORLD OF EVIL

PROFILE OF ROYAL SCHOOL KILLER: MENZIES AND A FATAL OBSESSION WITH
ANGELS CULT

POLICE: SLAIN JOURNALIST'S FLAT BURGLARY 'AN INSULT'

PROUD LEGACY OF SLAIN JOURNALIST AMANDA BAILEY, BY DON MAKEPEACE,
THE RETIRED POLICE CHIEF WHO KNEW HER

Text messages between myself and Don Makepeace, 9 September 2021:

Ellie Cooper
I'm struggling to find details about the recent burglary at
Amanda Bailey's flat. Has anyone been arrested yet?

Don Makepeace
Unfortunately, after any high-profile killing or atrocity, there are
people who will take advantage. Don.

Ellie Cooper
I went to the flat. Her laptop and hard drives had been taken. Her

400

phone wasn't listed among her personal effects. It's disappeared.

Don Makepeace

There are people in this world who have no scruples when others stand in their way, and no guilt or shame for what they do. If you knew Amanda, you will appreciate that in some ways she was one of those people. Don.

> **Ellie Cooper**
>
> I disagree. But I know the laptop and hard drives were wiped. What happened to her research into the Alperton Angels? It's a mystery.

Don Makepeace

Like so much about this case. I don't know all the ins and outs. Just that there ARE ins and outs. Don.

> **Ellie Cooper**
>
> Like the fact this number is the one Sonia gave Amanda for an anonymous intermediary called Mr Blue. I didn't realise it would be you on the end of it, Don. But it explains why, from the moment she started looking in to this case, Amanda was in danger.

I received no further response from this number.

TO: Judy Teller-Dunning
DATE: 9 December 2021
SUBJECT: Amanda Bailey
FROM: Ellie Cooper

Dear Ms Teller-Dunning,

I regret to inform you of the tragic death of Amanda Bailey. I am sorry to make your acquaintance on such sad terms.

However, I would like to thank you for sending Amanda the file belonging to your late husband, Mark Dunning. I know she read it and that it was interesting background for the book she was working on. I am dealing with her personal effects and will return the file to you in due course. I don't think it had anything directly relevant in it, but thank you nonetheless.

Yours sincerely,

Ellie Cooper

Hi Louisa,

I'm sorting out Amanda Bailey's research and personal effects and have come across some interesting accounts regarding a former special services soldier. He was cleared of some terrible charges a few years ago, but recordings of conversations between Amanda Bailey and Oliver Menzies indicate he is actually guilty of those and many other far worse crimes. I am sure it's a matter of public interest that these are made available and any accusations thoroughly investigated.

I'll forward them and leave it with you.

Best wishes,

Ellie Cooper

Dear Mr Badham,

Via the late journalist Amanda Bailey I am in receipt of a script, entitled *Divine*, which has been distributed and promoted as your own work. I was Ms Bailey's assistant and am continuing her work in so far as I am tying up the ends of her active projects.

I have reason to believe Ms Rowley Wild is the true author of *Divine*. I understand you acted as her tutor for the creative writing course on which she wrote the script. You subsequently submitted it to competitions and producers under your name.

The film festival that placed *Divine* first in the category of Best Unproduced Screenplay of 2005 has been informed and your name removed from their list of 'previous winners'.

If you wish to avoid costly and embarrassing legal action, you are advised to do the following:

1. Shred or burn every physical version of the script you own.
2. Open each digital version, select all text, delete, save and close.
3. Delete each empty document from your hard drive.

I suggest you also take steps to retrieve and delete any full-length versions of *Divine* you may have sent to film production professionals. Even those extracts that feature just the first ten pages.

Please inform me when the above steps have been completed.

Your sincerely,

Ellie Cooper

TO: Ellie Cooper
DATE: 13 December 2021
SUBJECT: Re: Divine
FROM: Clive Badham

Dear Ms Cooper,

I knew Amanda wasn't a proper film producer. Rowley was just a posh girl who took a college course for the hell of it. She was never interested in getting the script made so I don't know what the problem is, but anyway, I've done all you said so you can wind your neck in.

Clive

TO: Ellie Cooper
DATE: 13 December 2021
SUBJECT: Re: CCTV images
FROM: Security Office – Waterview

Dear Miss Cooper,

These are the only images we have of the graffiti vandal who tagged the access room of our Waterview apartment block in Alperton. If you can give us her name, I'm sure the police will treat that information in the strictest confidence.

Sincerely,

Security office, Waterview

I wrote this email to Sonia after I spoke to her, but didn't send it:

TO: Sonia Brown
DATE: 14 December 2021
SUBJECT: Amanda Bailey
FROM: Ellie Cooper

Dear Sonia,

Thank you for our video meeting today. So many people have positive memories of Amanda now she's dead. It was lovely hearing yours. I couldn't help but notice your beautiful pendant. A very simple pair of angel wings, spread as if in flight. Very apt considering our topic of conversation!

As I mentioned, I've been trawling through her archives, in particular those for her unfinished book on the Alperton Angels. It's been tricky putting all the pieces together, but everything adds up in the end.

I hear Gabriel Angelis has launched a bid to overturn his conviction. Without any new evidence to prove someone else killed Singh, it's bound to fail. His 'fan club' were pictured in a news article, standing outside the prison with placards. All women.

I recognised you immediately, despite the hat, scarf and glasses. Only one of Gabriel's followers has a pendant like that. She never realised it, but Amanda saw you at Tynefield, in the queue of prison visitors. You were scheduled to see Gabriel after Oliver. I used some of Amanda's contacts to look you up. You're Ashleigh Sonia Brown. I suppose your brush with the system meant that when you started work, you used your middle name.

You're a hero, Ashleigh. You saved Connor. You rescued Holly and Jonah from Gabriel by playing along with the angel story you knew so well from your time in his clutches. You're determined to keep him behind bars and innocent people safe from his particular brand of coercive control. You do it by playing him at his own game – you've convinced him you're still under his spell.

You drew angel symbols at the site of The Assembly. He tells you to do it, and you do. You prove your loyalty, he confides in you. But you hate him more than anything in this world so you pass every single thing that man says to Don Makepeace.

Don isn't someone who leaves witnesses. He has no intention of releasing his son's kidnapper, the man who would have died if the sniper's gun hadn't misfired and Gray Graham hadn't arrived at a key moment. You conspired together to ensure Amanda couldn't reveal what she knew about that night. Between you, you'll keep Gabriel in prison for the rest of his life, whatever the cost.

You both have willing helpers in the form of Holly and Jonah. Neither you nor Don, nor Marie-Claire, realise it, but they too have a vested interest in Gabriel remaining guilty of Singh's murder. Holly's money comes in very handy. I don't know yet how Jonah helps, but his isolation in a remote monastery doesn't interfere with the plan.

I could hear how delighted you were that the book I'm planning plays right into the conspiracy to cover up what really happened that night. I'm not Amanda Bailey. I won't risk my own life to expose the truth. Thanks again and best wishes,
Ellie Cooper

Instead, I sent this email …

TO: Sonia Brown
DATE: 14 December 2021
SUBJECT: Amanda Bailey
FROM: Ellie Cooper

Dear Sonia,
Thank you for our video meeting today. As agreed, I didn't record the conversation. So many people have positive memories of Amanda. It was lovely hearing yours.

As we discussed, I'm planning to write about how the Alperton Angels cult still has the potential to ensnare people – even all these years later and with the leader firmly in prison. I'll use the story of Oliver and Amanda to drive my narrative. Two truth-seekers who destroyed each other in their race to the light. I may hint that supernatural elements were at play. Or at least fate, coincidence, destiny and other factors beyond understanding. People love that sort of thing. My book will introduce the case to new readers but give those familiar with it a fresh new angle. Should

be a great beach read!
Thanks again for the chat and best wishes for the future,
Ellie Cooper

Interview between Ellie Cooper and Brother Jonah at Quarr Abbey, 17 December 2021. I transcribed it myself and cut out all the pleasantries.

EC: Don and Marie-Claire don't realise you and Holly killed Harpinder Singh. They still believe Shenky did it. [*He doesn't speak, but continues feeding the pigs*] Don almost gave the game away to Amanda when she first mentioned the case. He described Singh as heroic, an undercover officer who died in the line of duty. Quickly corrected himself. He wasn't wrong. Singh never knew it, but he died trying to rescue a baby from what he thought was a life of neglect. [*He stops what he's doing, trudges through the mud to where I stand, on the other side of the fence. His eyes are sad. He lowers his voice*]

BJ: I pray for him every day. Harpinder.

EC: And Christopher Shenk? Do you pray for him?

BJ: I'm afraid I don't know that name.

EC: He was no angel, but he was no murderer either. Just like Gabriel.
      [*We're silent for a while*]

BJ: Have you told anyone? [*I shake my head*] I heard those two journalists passed away.

EC: They didn't pass away. They say Oliver shot Amanda. Then one of Lady Louise's protection team shot Oliver.

BJ: How tragic. I'll pray for them both.

EC: Holly told Amanda where you were, and you passed a number to her when she visited. It got her straight through to Marie-Claire.

BJ: I think we sensed she'd understand.

EC: Or knew Marie-Claire could deal with the problem. In 2003 Marie-Claire was a police officer, but she'd been a special forces sniper. Don enlisted her for a secret, off-the-record operation.

She killed the angels. As the only woman on the team she built a rapport with Ashleigh, who led them to The Assembly.

BJ: We were protected from the—

EC: Marie-Claire was also in the process of covering up another unofficial police operation: the revenge murder of Christopher Shenk. In the years since, she's been responsible for maintaining both cover-ups. Everything Amanda told Sonia and Don went straight to Marie-Claire, who soon realised Amanda was closer to the truth than anyone else had ever been. Closer than Don, Holly, you and Marie-Claire herself were comfortable with.

BJ: I don't know—

EC: The four of you each has a different reason for wanting the myth to remain the story. And Gabriel to stay in prison. So you all pitch in to maintain the cover-up. [*He stops sweeping and stands, ankle deep in mud, surrounded by pigs and for the first time looks me straight in the eye*]

BJ: Will you write Amanda's book?

EC: Not quite. My book is *about* Amanda ... and Oliver. How the Alperton Angels story has the power to influence and twist a rational person's whole perspective.

BJ: What will you say about her death?

EC: That's what I want to speak to you about. Jonah, did a former special forces soldier accompany Oliver to the school, encourage him to lure Amanda there and once they were together and alone, kill them both?

BJ: I wouldn't know—

EC: Don's friend, the mad squaddie. No one knows his real name – not even Oliver and he wrote his autobiography. He's a ruthless mercenary who generated fear in everyone who knew him. He was the only one there. The only one who can reveal what really happened to Amanda and Oliver. [*That's when Jonah gives me a look. Makes a subtle gesture with his hands that draws my eyes to where he stands, ankle deep in mud, shovel in hand, a sea of snuffling pigs rooting happily in their feed. They seem to grunt and squeal extra loudly*]

BJ: I don't suppose we'll ever know. [*It's a while before either of us speaks*]

EC: If Gabriel hadn't convinced you and Holly there were dark
       forces looking for the baby, Singh would be alive today. The
       person most guilty is behind bars. Ironically, if I told the truth,
       he could be released and he's still a dangerous man. He may not
       be guilty of murder, but no one deserves to fall under his spell.
       [*I cut out our stilted, awkward goodbyes and left him in his own
       personal prison, surrounded by mud, straw, shit and snuffling pigs*]

TO: Ellie Cooper
DATE: 3 January 2023
SUBJECT: Amanda Bailey
FROM: Cathy-June Lloyd

Dear Ellie,

I am writing to offer our best wishes for the publication of your book next week. Also, I'd like to say how much all of us at Cold & Unsolved enjoyed the recent television documentary in which you spoke about the Alperton Angels. It was so sensitively done – Naga Munchetty is the perfect presenter. We never had the privilege of meeting Amanda, but we are all great admirers of her work and even helped her with some research.

Watching the documentary, I realise we've discussed Amanda at every meeting since she died. There was something strange about the events at Ascot. They said Oliver shot Amanda, then a police marksman shot him. But if you boil this case down to its bare bones: two journalists, both working on the same controversial case, are shot dead and no independent witnesses saw what happened.

The police and security forces know that school very well because Lady Louise Windsor was still a pupil when the incident happened. Luckily, she was away from school that day – which made us wonder why armed police were on the scene so quickly ...

Both Amanda and Oliver drove to the school, and both were allowed through the gates, apparently without being challenged. The roof of The Orchard Building is the only area in the whole complex not covered by security cameras.

You knew Amanda. Was there anything she and Oliver found that could have led to their deaths? I wonder if there's a way to access her research. It could hold vital clues to why she (and perhaps Oliver, too) was there that day. Could they have been lured?

If you need any help looking into what happened, just let us know. In the meantime, may I extend heartfelt condolences from each and every member of Cold & Unsolved.

Best regards,

Cathy-June Lloyd

On the day my book was published I received an ornate, printed card, delivered by hand with a bunch of flowers:

MANY CONGRATULATIONS ON THE
PUBLICATION OF YOUR BOOK.
WE HEAR IT'S A FABULOUS TRIBUTE
TO AMANDA.
JESS AND GEORGIE ADESINA

Divine

by
ELLIE COOPER

The inside story, by Amanda Bailey's former assistant

How eighteen years after their bloody suicide the Alperton Angels cult claimed two more innocent lives. As told by the woman who had to watch it happen.

ECLIPSE
True crime with a twist

*Eclipse will make a donation to The Amanda Bailey Foundation
to support care leavers with training and employment*

CHAPTER ONE

At the age of twelve Amanda Bailey walked up to a female police officer in a crowded shopping centre and disclosed the abuse she was suffering at the hands of a family member. She requested that she be placed in council care and from that moment on she had to look after herself. She grew up to be a fearless, free-thinking individual who was prepared to take any route to expose the truth, whatever the cost.

At eighteen, and finally in a supportive foster home, she was awarded a coveted place on a local newspaper training scheme. Seemingly unfazed that everyone else was at least two years older, came from stable families and could boast good degrees from established universities, Amanda impressed the interview panel immediately. They liked to back one wild card every year.

I first met her a decade later, when job cuts in local newspapers had forced a move to the editorial department of a true crime publisher. I'd taken a position in accounts there, hoping to find an editorial role as soon as an opportunity arose. Two years on I was still waiting. Amanda lobbied hard for me to be her assistant. When I decided to study for a PhD in Criminal Psychology, no one was more supportive than Amanda.

***

Despite having gained many of her professional skills on that training scheme, Amanda never spoke positively about her time on it. I would discover why only after her death. Oliver Menzies, a history graduate whose mother's friend owned the newspaper, was being out-performed by everyone around him and none more so than the young woman with the wrong accent who had failed to scrape a single A level.

He made digs and comments whenever the opportunity arose. But it was a trick he played one evening that would change the course of both their lives. A childish prank that led to her losing the sight in one eye. Amanda would never be able to forget how that experience destroyed her trust in others. And she certainly never forgot who was responsible.

When they met again years later, Oliver expressed his disdain for the vulnerable teenagers who had fallen for an outlandish story. Amanda realised he had learned nothing in the intervening years. In that moment she decided to show him what it meant to be vulnerable. She could have no idea how successful her plan for revenge would be. Because twenty years after the Alperton Angels were found mutilated in a derelict warehouse, this is no longer a story about people who thought they were divine. It's about a man who believed he couldn't be fooled, and the woman who wanted to teach him a lesson but underestimated the power of the mythology. It's about two people who looked for the truth with dogged determination, but too late – in places that were no longer there, and with names that were constantly changing. They searched until it destroyed them. Their story attests to the power of an intriguing cult that remains a cautionary tale to this day.

That is the simple truth behind the mysterious case of the Alperton Angels.

This message is for you.

What you've just read is research material for a book that should be about a wrongful conviction. Gabriel Angelis didn't kill Harpinder Singh, nor was he responsible for the deaths or post-mortem mutilation of Dominic Jones, Alan Morgan or Christopher Shenk.

He's innocent, while the two people who killed Singh are free.

You could take all this evidence and start a process that might ultimately rectify that miscarriage of justice and expose a wider series of even more deadly cover-ups. But if you do, please bear something in mind.

Gabriel is a dangerous, narcissistic psychopath who has sought coercive control over others his entire life. If you free him, he will only return to the same behaviour. It's all he knows. *You* will be responsible for releasing him back into the community to target a new generation of innocent, trusting people with his compelling lies and instinct for identifying vulnerability in others.

But there's a danger far greater than that posed by Gabriel. Should you make these documents public, you will expose the fact that people in positions of power were responsible for the deaths of three unarmed criminals and an untold number of innocent people who came too close to the truth. I've just read through these documents again and I'm astounded by what they can and are prepared to do to survive. Nowhere is safe from them. If you or I seek to expose their crimes, we will be in danger.

My twins, a boy and a girl, are due in six weeks. I am not in a position to take such risks myself. But depending on how far into the future you're reading this, *you* may be.

So, I am placing these documents back in their safety deposit box. If they are found long after the players in this story are dead then the truth can safely be revealed. If you're reading this any sooner than that, you have a choice.

Go ahead and expose the miscarriage of justice or simply slide everything back into its folders, envelopes and files, and walk away. As I will now.

The decision is yours.

Ellie Cooper
Criminal psychologist and author

For Jill Dando, Michelle McNamara and Lyra McKee
who all, tragically, became the story

Acknowledgements

This book's gestation began when I read Michelle McNamara's incredible work *I'll Be Gone in the Dark* and watched the HBO docuseries of the same name. As a lifelong reader of true crime, it struck me how, in the process of writing about a baffling case, McNamara became obsessed with solving it. As a former journalist myself I could appreciate the tricky balance. A necessary immersion in the subject versus a healthy, subjective distance.

My editor Miranda Jewess, the queen of subjective distance, was as fiercely supportive as ever during the creation of *The Mysterious Case of the Alperton Angels*, although for some of it she was engaged in a gestation of her own. Thanks also to her maternity cover, Therese Keating, who held the fort with equal good sense, expertise and creativity. Together they were a dream team.

Speaking of dream teams, the Viper posse of managing editor Graeme Hall, copy editor Alison Tulett, text designer Lucie Worboys and cover designer Steve Panton devised a visual and textual package that perfectly reflects and enhances this story. Meanwhile Flora Willis, Drew Jerrison, Alia McKellar, Claire Beaumont, Niamh Murray, Lisa Finch and Sarah Ward are, as you read this, probably engaged with marketing, publicity, sales and promotion. Finally, Nathaniel McKenzie and Louisa Dunnigan will work their magic to create a thrilling audiobook. Huge thanks to them all.

My lovely agents Gaia Banks and Lucy Fawcett at Sheil Land Associates are my guardian angels in London, assisted by Maddie Thornham and David Taylor. Meanwhile, foreign rights are wrangled by Alba Arnau. My US agents Markus Hoffmann at Regal Hoffmann & Associates in New York and Will Watkins at ICM Partners in LA keep watch over affairs across the Atlantic.

I am indebted to David Collins, northern editor of the *Sunday Times* and author of *The Hunt for the Silver Killer*, whose exploits during his time as a crime reporter inspired some of those depicted here. Likewise, James Brockett, who shared his recollections of working in local journalism in north-west London in the early 2000s. My police informer Laura Flowers provided some useful intel, while online communities of amateur ballistics enthusiasts shared anecdotes about firearms malfunction and ballistics failure probabilities that proved invaluable.

Thanks to Kathy Buchanan who spoke to me about child protection and safeguarding in the north-west of London in the eras covered here. Then there are those who either spoke to me, or put me in touch with others, but didn't wish to be named, either because they still work in the police, social care and child protection, or because they spoke to me about personal details and events not everyone in their life knows about.

With no experience of the care system myself, I was careful to research this aspect of Amanda's backstory and looked for women who had had comparable childhood experiences, around the same time and place the character did. Hearing memories like these, both traumatic and heart-warming, as well as their adult perspective on that experience, convinced me how difficult it is to do justice to the subject in this book. There were times when I felt it was not even my place to try.

While reading around the subject, I focused on personal accounts of the UK system, as told by adults who were children in care, and some foster carers. There are many, and most will, of course, focus on the very worst experiences. I found the following interesting: *Damaged* and *The State of It*, both by Chris Wild, *A Terrible Secret* by Cathy Glass and *My Name is Why* by Lemn Sissay.

There are as many unheard stories as there are people who grew up in the care system. Not all are as brutal and shocking as the high-profile ones, but they are all valid and valuable.

The list of books about cults and mind-control featured in the early chapters of this book are recommended reading. *Cultish* by Amanda Montell is especially interesting for its study of the language of influence. *Brainwashed: A New History of Thought Control* by Daniel Pick, and *Terror, Love and Brainwashing: Attachment in Cults and Totalitarian Systems* by Alexandra Stein are also fascinating books on this subject.

A number of notorious true murder cases are referred to in this story. I appreciate that reading victim names will evoke painful memories for those who knew and loved them. My apologies to anyone affected.

My friends are endlessly supportive of my writing career, even when it takes me far away either physically or figuratively. They are: Sharon Exelby, Carol Livingstone and Wendy Mulhall, Keith Baker, Felicity Cox, Terry and Rose Russell, Alison Horn and Samantha Thomson. Finally, the wonderful Ann Saffery and my gorgeous, long-suffering and supportive partner Gary Stringer.